Ghosts Rising is a compelling story of redemption and second chances. Retired from the priesthood, disillusioned, fearing he has lived a purposeless life, eking out a lonely existence in a church-owned cabin in Powell River, British Columbia, Rupert receives a letter from his only family, a sister he hasn't seen in fifty-one years. Emotions he hasn't felt in as many decades come flooding back. She's dying of cancer and she wants a reunion, and this is their last chance. She's led a successful business life in San Francisco, but she is as alone as he is. This is a story about finding out it's never too late to embrace life. Rupert can't save his sister from the beast of cancer, but through an embrace, they find a way back to love, and through love back to the life each had run away from those many years ago. This novel celebrates the life that is saved and leaves us with hope. It's never too late.

— *Scott Driscoll, University of Washington*

The author explores with great depth and empathy the life-long impact of love's absence in the lives of a brother and sister. Following their shallow adult lives lived with anger and denial, they discover love's terms of endearment in their later years as the sister is dying of cancer.

— *Robert D. Guthrie, MD, Professor of Medicine, Drexel University; retired System Chair, Pediatrics, Allegheny Health Network*

Ghosts Rising

KENNETH SMITH

bookhouse
PUBLISHING

bookhouse
PUBLISHING

2950 Newmarket St., Suite 101-358 | Bellingham, WA 98226
Ph: 206.226.3588 | www.bookhouserules.com

10 9 8 7 6 5 4 3 2 1

Printed in the United States of America

Library of Congress Control Number: 2022900367

ISBN: 978-1-952483-40-0 (Paperback)
ISBN: 978-1-952483-41-7 (eBook)

Editor: Julie Scandora
Cover design: Scott Book
Book design: Melissa Vail Coffman

To Marion C. Smith, my mother,
in recognition of all she was and could have been.

CHAPTER 1

We are not human beings having a spiritual experience.
We are spiritual beings having a human experience.
– Pierre Teilhard de Chardin

THE OLD MAN STOOD ON THE SEAWALL, staring straight ahead, oblivious to the rising tide. Waves crashed against the wall, splashing his black sandals, but he didn't notice or care. The last rays of sun shone orange on Rupert Calloway's wrinkled face. The islands of the Strait of Georgia looked like black dots floating on an emerald sea. He was in heaven, or as close as he could imagine he'd ever get. Sunsets are not common in the Northwest, but when one came, he would be at this spot until the sky turned from maroon to black. If a rogue wave swept him away, so be it. On some evenings Rupert even yearned for that. Life had not turned out the way he had hoped.

Tonight, though, he was preoccupied. He'd been told someone would be coming by to deliver a document. No one ever came to see Rupert, much less to deliver something important. It had to be a ruse. Yet he was curious to find out who would show up and what this envelope might hold. Jumping down off the wall, he headed up the hill to his little bungalow.

He'd first heard about this last week. A priest he knew from the parish in Whitehall, a small town about twenty-five miles from his home, had called to tell Rupert someone had been inquiring as to his whereabouts. This mystery person wanted to give the old man a "very important message," so the parish priests had deemed it okay to give out his address. After screaming about how that was an invasion of his privacy and making it abundantly clear that, from now on, they were to contact him before giving out his address, he slammed down the phone. Not surprisingly, the priest didn't call back, and the old man got no other information. Then he'd received a certified letter telling him a woman would be coming tonight to deliver an envelope. He hated surprises. When confronted by one, it always put him on edge and made him irritable, although he lived on edge most of the time now, apprehensive and scared. Anger had become a way of life.

Rupert had retired from the priesthood five years ago. He hadn't had to retire at sixty-three, but he'd grown tired of the rituals and daily routine of the parish priest. He'd long ago begun to question the meaning of it all, though he'd had a hard time admitting this to himself. After so many years—fifty-one to be exact—and he felt dried up, desert dry, his body wrinkled by time and a life of unrealized effort. He had come to Powell River to be alone and finally away from the church that had once held his hopes for a future filled with happiness and contentment. Besides, Powell River had become the only town left for him to go. He had no home, no family (he'd had a younger sister once but assumed she was dead), no one he would call a friend, and certainly no priest—all dead or gone and forgotten. The church had been his refuge, even before he left for seminary all those years ago. How could it have failed him so miserably? Who knew and who cared? He didn't, that's for sure.

Now as Rupert walked up to his house on the hill, he was startled by the thought that he hadn't really left the church. It still provided him with this house and a small stipend he used primarily for food. His needs were small, but he had to eat, and he had no other income. Sometimes, though, Rupert thought he wouldn't mind not having food, that maybe he'd rather his life just come to an early end. He had given up what dreams he'd had, seeing them now as only delusions, probably brought on by his unhappiness

As he turned his back on the sun and waves to climb the steep hill, which made up his front yard, sweat dripped into his shirt. Rupert couldn't imagine who in the world had enough interest in him to send a mysterious package. He thought, *What trouble is coming? No good has come my way since . . . who knows, when?* Maybe someone from his old parish had thought to charge him with some sexual abuse. It was happening a lot before he'd left, and even though nothing seemed to ever come of it, Rupert knew he wouldn't be able to live with himself if charged, even if not true.

The house was dark. He always waited until the last moment to flick on a light. Darkness comforted him, maybe a holdover from his childhood. He was born in a small, northern Canadian village where the nights were long most of the year.

The little bungalow Rupert had now was owned by the Catholic diocese of Vancouver, British Columbia. Retirement had given him a legitimate reason to run away. Now he lived near water and a long way from his last parish placement. Most of those he'd met and associated with through the years still served parishes or had retired and gone to live with relatives. No one ever told him where they went, nor did he ask. Although Rupert had few neighbors and a good road to get into Powell River to shop, mostly he stayed home. He'd never felt close to people, even fellow priests or his parishioners. He didn't even like most people. Too many seemed pompous, pretentious, and self-centered, or at least that's what he told himself. He did, however, like looking at the women in his parish. In them he saw beauty, sensuality, happiness, and reasonableness. They were different, not like his fellow priests who always seemed so infatuated with self-importance. This attraction to women, however, was a big problem. It was wrong, a temptation he had to avoid. Even though Rupert had no idea how to avoid them, he came to fear sexual fantasies. If caught looking at a pretty woman's breasts or long legs, his face reddened, and he'd quickly turn and walk away. He didn't want to say or do something inappropriate. But then he did. While alone in his room, he would secretly masturbate while replaying his fantasies. Rupert had hoped the shame he felt after doing this would help him stop, but it didn't. Another failure as a priest. His only solution had been to hide and isolate himself from others, and retirement made that easier than ever. Thinking of himself as a failure and feeling remorse for never finding

God in his life lingered on into his retirement. Rupert lived like a hermit and told people that he liked his quiet time to read his Bible and to pray.

The woman coming to give him the envelope represented a large business consortium out of California. She was coming from the Vancouver airport, one hundred miles to the south of Powell River. He was told she'd identify herself by presenting him with a letter from someone he knew.

Rupert opened his front door and entered the dark house, almost tripping over the throw rug that must have caught in the door and curled up when he'd gone out. He cursed but still did not turn on any lights. The light of dusk still made it possible to see. Walking to his chair, Rupert sat down. He had more than one chair in the room, as well as a coffee table, bookcase, and TV, but this chair was his special spot, well used (brought here from his room in the parish) and comfortable. Removing his wet sandals, he settled down to wait in the darkening room. Oh, the peace Rupert felt at that moment, sitting alone and surrounded by darkness.

It didn't last long, however. His mind clouded, and despair took over. The fear he had felt as he had returned to the house had subsided, but now it returned. His mind started to fall into a darkness he knew well. "No, not now." Rupert reached up and turned on the switch, and a bright light filled the room, but the thoughts of failure that fed the darkness filling his mind did not go away. "No, no, no. Stop it, stop it. Go away. Leave me alone. Go away."

Rupert got up and walked into the kitchen for a glass of water. Without thinking, he grabbed at a glass but didn't hang on, and it smashed on the granite countertop. "Oh my God, now look what I've done. Damn it. Where are you, God? Why abandon me here after I've tried so hard to serve you?" He slumped over, leaning into the glass. He felt nothing.

Then the doorbell rang, shaking Rupert out of his despair and back to the real world. He stood up, saw the mess around him, and then noticed he'd cut his hand. The bell rang again. Grabbing his handkerchief to cover the blood oozing from the wound, he headed to the front door. Opening it, he saw a woman holding a manila envelope. Dressed professionally, she stood there like a soldier at attention about to deliver a lecture.

She looked directly at him and asked, "Are you Reverend Rupert Callaway?"

"Yes, please come in."

As she crossed the threshold, he remembered his bleeding hand. He told her to have a seat and then went back to the kitchen to see if the bleeding had stopped. It had not. He quickly washed it in cold water and tightened the handkerchief more securely.

He then returned to the living room where he saw his guest had sat in *his* chair. Alarmed, he said, "Oh that's where I sit. Please make yourself comfortable over there." He pointed to the couch directly across from his chair. "You'll find the cushions are less worn there."

She did as he said but sat on the front edge of the seat with the envelope securely placed on her lap. She obviously did not want to get too comfortable. He sensed she wouldn't stay long.

"My name is Theresa Gallagher, and I represent the International Asian Pacific Shipping Company with offices in Singapore and San Francisco. The CEO for the American half of the company is Ms. Maggie Callaway, your sister, whom I understand you have basically not seen or heard from for more than fifty years."

"Maggie," Rupert blurted, his voice cracking as he spoke. "Yes, when I decided to go away to seminary to become a Catholic priest, my parents, being good Irish Catholics, had fully supported me. Maggie had not."

"Well, regardless of your family history, I have been charged with delivering this envelope to you directly."

"Are you a lawyer?"

"Yes, I serve as chief counsel on the American side of the company." She handed him the envelope and asked him to sign the affidavit he'd find just inside. He hesitated but then opened the envelope, found the affidavit, and signed it. She abruptly stood to leave. "Well, I must be off. It's getting late, and I have a long drive."

"You're not going all the way back to San Francisco, are you?"

"No, but to Vancouver where I can catch a plane tomorrow morning."

She headed for the door. Rupert jumped to open it while trying to think of something to ask. He knew he would have questions, but nothing came to him. He didn't want her to leave—yet. Besides, he also thought she was nice to look at, even if a little too professional. Rupert called it "too tightly packed," hair pulled back in a tight ponytail, heavy red lipstick that certainly drew your attention, a skirt just short enough to display long glamorous legs, and a blouse left unbuttoned down to the third button, just enough to put her well-formed body on display. *Questions*, Rupert, *think, think*. . . . Nothing. His mystery guest had piqued his curiosity, but his mind had shut down.

Her business completed, Theresa just kept moving toward the door. She didn't try to shake his hand but did say as she left, "Goodbye."

"Goodbye," Rupert said, "and thanks for coming." He watched as she walked toward her car, marveling at how she could keep such a stiff and erect posture.

His teachers in the seminary often criticized him for his posture. "Always walking with your head down, Reverend. Look up toward heaven." *I never was a good enough priest,* he thought to himself.

Rupert looked out again and saw the lawyer getting into her car. He quietly closed the door, leaned against it, and then, remembering his hand, checked to see if the bleeding had started again. It had not. Dried blood was visible through the handkerchief. He wondered how the lawyer had not noticed but then recalled her professional and distant manner. She wouldn't have said anything, even if she'd seen it. He didn't linger long on this thought, however, as he then again noticed the broken glass and mess he'd made in the kitchen. He started to walk toward it, but he couldn't. He just stood there, frozen, in the entryway.

"Maggie!" he screamed.

CHAPTER 2

MAGGIE WAS RUPERT'S YOUNGER SISTER, five years his junior. She was seven when he left for the seminary. The family lived in a remote part of northern British Columbia in a town called Hazelton, about 190 miles northeast of Prince Rupert (a three-hour-plus drive). It was, as he remembered well, a lonely spot where the winters tended to be long and the weather wet and cool.

Precocious, Maggie was also always lonely and isolated, primarily because she was so smart. A few girls had wanted to be her friend, but she mostly denied them access. Excuses like "I'm too busy," "I have to study," and "I'm too tired tonight" soon caused them to give up. Maggie wanted family to provide her with emotional support and thoughtful conversation, even though she knew from about the age of five that getting it from them was hopeless.

She looked up to Rupert, but he paid her little attention. She didn't know it, but he felt intimidated by her smartness, and besides, she was so much younger. He didn't have any friends of his own, but he found time spent alone in his room preferable to being with her. Maggie did all she could to tempt him to play games or just talk to her. She knocked on his door until he let her inside. She asked questions she hoped he'd answer. He was her older brother after all. But her questions just made him want to get away from her pestering questions: "Why does time

never stop?" "Why do we need political parties or a government?" "Why
don't Mom and Dad talk to each other?" or "Why don't we do things as
a family?" He didn't know and told himself he didn't care. Her questions
felt like harassment, just like at school where he was bombarded by them
from teachers and other kids. He longed for someone or something he
could trust, depend on, be supported by, and above all, be understood
by. Rupert didn't talk about his loneliness or how his mother and father
didn't seem able or willing to see the pain he thought must be visible
to them. *They're adults*, he thought. He blamed himself and ultimately
turned to himself for answers, not his sister or his parents.

Rupert had to find something and he did—the priesthood. When he
turned twelve, he left—for good—to begin the process.

A bomb falling on the house could not have hurt Maggie more. She
wondered at first if he was mad at her. After all, getting mad was one
thing she'd seen in him and her parents for all her few years. She cried
and cried, and then, her anger took over, and she stopped talking to
him. What else could she do? She also had no one to confide in. She
too trusted no one . . . but Rupert. Now she truly had no one. From
this point, she told people, "I don't have a brother." The severity of his
betrayal demanded an extreme response.

Though they told her to "grow up" and "be a good girl and be happy
for your brother," she held to her decision.

"Stubborn girl," they said.

Maggie got no support, only shaming. All the attention went to
Rupert and his move to become a priest, a blessing for him and the
family, they thought. No one paid any attention to her or her fragile emotional state. Maggie was abandoned and ignored. Rupert's
response was to think of her as a selfish kid. Everyone else labeled her
an ungrateful child.

After Rupert left, Maggie lost herself in her studies. It was a lonely life
and one she always resented, but academically it paid off. She received a
full scholarship to University of California, Berkeley, choosing to study
business administration. She graduated with honors and was offered
high-level positions at IBM and Johnson & Johnson in New Jersey. She
wanted to stay in California and so turned down those early offers.

Just when it looked like nothing would come, one of her professors approached her about going on to graduate school for her MBA. He was sure she'd be accepted just about anywhere, including at Berkeley. Maggie, however, had grown tired of school, a good place for her to hide, but lonely. While in school, she had stayed in her room or the library most of the time, only having contact with roommates. Generally, they all thought she was peculiar and self-absorbed.

Any men who had asked her for a date, which happened fairly often because Maggie was quite attractive, found her distant, too intellectual, or too much in her head, and rarely asked her out for a second date. Maggie, herself, wondered about the state of her libido. She heard other women talking about sex, but she found that strange and unappetizing.

She had gone home to see her folks only for Christmases and then to attend each of their funerals where she saw Rupert. But by that time, she had fully accepted that she didn't have a brother. He was just one of the many uninteresting Hazelton country folks she ignored.

Maggie decided not to pursue the MBA, at least not at this time, and told her professor.

He wished her luck but no comfort, encouragement, or good cheer.

Gee, thanks, she thought. *Now what do I do?*

Maggie moved out of the dorm after graduation and into an apartment she couldn't afford. She rented her new place with money left over from living expenses given to her as part of her scholarship. She figured she had enough to last about six months. After that, "I guess it's prostitution," she said louder than she'd intended.

Her door had been left open earlier, and an elderly woman passing by overheard her and stopped to say, "Oh no, dearie, don't do that."

"Fuck off."

Though this obviously shocked her self-appointed guardian, Maggie was mad. She slammed her apartment door shut and yelled out, "Don't try to mother me. It's too late for that. So don't even try, you meddling, nosy bitch."

Three months after moving to her apartment, Maggie was sitting at the kitchen table reading *The Old Man and the Sea* for the second time. She liked reading Hemingway primarily because she admired the life he lived.

She considered him brave, courageous, and not afraid to express his opinions, no matter how revolutionary. Even killing himself with that shotgun excited her. *Now there's a man I could go to bed with*, she thought.

Maggie put the book down to allow herself time to just enjoy her sexual fantasy of this strong, hard man. She liked having sexual feelings when they came and worked to keep them going, even sometimes rubbing herself between her legs to enhance the experience.

The phone ringing shook Maggie from her fantasies. "Shit." She answered, trying not to show her exasperation, "Hello, who's this?"

"Hi, Maggie. Good to know you haven't mellowed since getting out of school! It's Professor Mallory from your business law class."

"Oh hi, Professor. Sorry about the abruptness, but you caught me while reading a good book."

"I see. You always did prefer books over people, Maggie."

Maggie didn't know how to take this but decided to stay calm this time, indeed the road less traveled for her. "How can I help you, Professor?"

"Well, a friend of mine, who happens to be the board president of a major shipping company here in town, called me recently. He wanted to know if I could recommend any recent graduates for a top position in his company. It seems the CEO wants to retire in a year or so and, even though they plan to look at people already in the company to fill the role, they also want to look outside for possible new blood. I thought of you as a candidate."

"Me? Why me? I don't have the faintest idea about CEOing anything."

"I know. I remember you never went on to get your MBA, but Maggie, you have the kind of determination, creative business head, and excuse my bluntness, stubbornness that just may make them look at you anyway. For my money, you are more talented than most company leaders. CEOs do usually come from a pool of CEOs circulating from one company to the next, but I, for one, would like to see some new blood in the pool. My guess is you probably won't be liked that much. Sorry, but I had to add that. But you may just be smart enough and ornery enough to win them over. I think it's worth a try."

Maggie didn't know how to respond, but she was glad she had stayed calm and not erupted earlier. "I don't know what to say. What's the name of this company?"

"The International Asian Pacific Shipping Company. It has offices in both Singapore and San Francisco, but I understand the position is in San Francisco.

"Never heard of it, but the name sounds sexy!" She couldn't resist taunting him. "What do I have to do?"

"Well, first, you have to stop the silly joking around and then call my contact. I already gave him your name."

Maggie wrote down the name and number and set it aside on the table. She thanked him, hung up, and went back to her book, trying to revive the old feelings. It didn't work, so she got up, made dinner, and turned on the TV. She'd call this board president tomorrow.

CHAPTER 3

MAGGIE AWOKE TO THE SUN SHINING through her bedroom window. She was wide awake and thinking about the call she wanted to make. Most of her classmates already had jobs, and they had not performed nearly as well as she had in school. Then she remembered she'd turned down two lucrative positions to stay in California. She hoped this shipping company would be her opportunity. She got up, dressed, and headed for the kitchen to make coffee. When she felt fully awake, she made the call.

"Hello, Tim Oberhauser's office."

"Hello, I'm Maggie Callaway, and I was told to call regarding a job."

"Oh, please hold and I'll see if Mr. Oberhauser can talk to you."

Maggie had to smile. *Like me, I guess he didn't go on for a higher degree either.*

"Hello, can I help you?"

"I hope so. My name is Maggie Callaway, and Professor Mallory asked me to call you about a job opportunity."

"Yes, I remember. Is there a time you could come in to see me?"

Maggie didn't want to appear needy but had a hard time hiding her enthusiasm, even though she knew nothing about this company. "Sure, how about this afternoon?"

"That'll work for me. Let's say three o'clock." He gave her the address.

"See you then. Thanks." Maggie set the phone down and, surprising herself, yelled out, "Yes, yes, yes!" while vigorously pumping her fist. She thought to herself, *That's so un-Maggie-like and so unladylike, Maggie.* She couldn't help but laugh as she went back into the kitchen to pour herself another cup of coffee.

CHAPTER 4

WORLD WAR II ENDED IN 1945, the same year Tim Callaway, Rupert and Maggie's dad, took his wife, Mae, to Canada. Ireland had remained neutral during the war, but before war began in Europe, Irish people had already suffered both economically and socially from the war between the Irish Republican Army and the provisional government. After WWII ended, Ireland was less devastated than much of Europe, but some, worried the internal struggle would continue, left their country. Rupert and Maggie's parents were among the Irish immigrants who came to Hazelton in northern British Columbia, looking for work opportunities in the timber mills. Tim felt lucky he could do the hard work and make pretty good money. Cutting timber paid more than most other work in Hazelton but demanded enormous physical strength and stamina.

Mae took care of the kids and spent her days completing household chores. Although she generally appeared to adapt well to this life, she often lost her temper, frustrated by the tedium. Like Maggie, Mae had been an excellent student, but in deciding to marry and move to Canada, she traded any chance of a scholarly life for that of a housewife in a remote foreign land. It turned out to be a bad choice. To her, living in northern Canada and taking care of a family was tantamount to being in prison or, at least, self-imposed exile. She told no one of her feelings, however, holding it all inside, she believed, for the sake of her family.

Tim lived his life among men, and what intimacy and enjoyment he had was with them, not with his wife or children. No one knew much of anything about Tim, except that he worked hard and needed care and feeding when at home. He did have a sexual life with Mae, but as she would attest, that amounted only to masturbating inside her. She found sex with Tim cold, unloving, and devoid of sensitivity to her feelings and needs.

In this distant and passionless environment, Rupert longed for something he couldn't name, and Maggie longed for attention she wouldn't name. Because he found a justifiable escape from this morass of family, Rupert became for his parents the good kid. Maggie, on the other hand, who just rebelled and complained, became the ungrateful child.

Feeling unhappy, unnoticed, and angry, Rupert had turned to the Catholic Church. He didn't go to seminary because of any strong religious feelings. Although he viewed the sermons as fantastical thinking, performing the sacraments and following the liturgy every week inspired in him a certainty, an assurance, even a sense of security in their regularity and consistency. He wanted that security, and when combined with the many promises for a better life or for salvation, he started to see the church as a way out of his unhappiness and despair. No more hardship, no more pain, and no more family to endure. Rupert became so detached from his life at home that Maggie's reaction to his deciding to join the seminary hardly registered in his consciousness.

Now, as Rupert stood alone in his living room, thinking about her and the choice he had made, a low-grade anger began to surge.

Entering seminary, Rupert had been encouraged to disregard his past, his future, and his private life, including hopes, desires, likes, and dislikes. Any feelings could only cloud the "clarity of your thinking," he was told.

He stared at the TV. "I can see it now. I was ripe for manipulation, ripe to do their bidding. My job was to study the Word of God, preach that Word, and minister to the needs of my parishioners. All a big bunch of baloney, hooey, malarkey."

Rupert waited, but the TV didn't talk back. He knew what the TV would say if it could. "That's heresy, Rupert."

He fell back into his chair and started to cry, his anger blossoming into a full-blown rage. He did nothing to control it. All fear of any retribution fell away. He grabbed at the table in front of him, forgetting that it was nailed to the floor. When he couldn't wrench it loose, he went to the fireplace to find something he could lift. Seeing the iron fireplace tools made him smile. "Those will do just fine." Indeed, the poker fit perfectly in his hand. He lifted it over his head and heaved it at the TV. The screen exploded. Glass flew everywhere. Rupert fell on his knees and laughed hysterically. He rolled around on the floor, not caring if he cut himself or not. He was out of control—in a frenzy.

Slowly his laughter turned to sobs. He thought he might be going crazy, which scared him enough to draw him back to reality. After a while, he quieted down and recalled his visitor and that letter she'd delivered. "No, I don't have a sister." But he knew that wasn't true. He sat up, now more in shock than sad. "My God, she's been resurrected. No, that's stupid. She's re-appeared to me after years away. But who's been away—Maggie or me? Am I going crazy?"

The nearby foghorn blared and broke Rupert from the disorienting mist that had covered his normally ordered and well-controlled life. He remembered again where he was and that letter. He stood up, and his head cleared enough to allow him to think again. What could cause Maggie to contact him now and in this way? The method of delivery reflected a formality and legality that alarmed him.

He retrieved the envelope, took it to his chair and sat down. It felt heavy on his lap. He dimmed the lights and, for a while, just watched the fog roll by outside. His usual view of the lights of Vancouver Island was blocked, and everything was eerily quiet. The foghorn continued to sound its warning to ships and maybe for him too. He thought, *I may not be at sea, but I'm surely at risk of hitting a shoal.*

Rupert reached for the unopened envelope in his lap. He had not thought about Maggie for years. His own sister forgotten. Both parents had died. He thought he'd seen Maggie at the funerals, but she'd come and gone so quickly he couldn't be sure. The siblings certainly had not spoken.

"What a family we were—are, each of us living alone, apart, as though we don't exist to each other. Even when together, the parts never made a whole. We lived as if in space without gravity. Each part floated away from the whole and was lost forever."

He hesitated before continuing.

"But maybe it wasn't forever. It seems like a ghost has risen." Rupert shivered at the thought.

Chapter 5

Tim Oberhauser interviewed Maggie and told her to come back the next Monday to meet with a hiring committee of board members. He thanked her for coming and hoped he'd see her next time.

"So, I'm a candidate?"

"Yes. You are most impressive, Maggie, but you lack experience. As a CEO, you have to demonstrate you can manage a company of our size, and at this point, Maggie, you have no track record running anything. A reputation with previous companies is evaluated by investors, and they, as you already know, determine a company's stock price. You'd have to prove you have the mettle to manage us successfully, which means, make money. Now, I know we could survive a big downturn in our stock price, but if the investors would dismiss you outright, that could affect us in the long run—badly I'm afraid. But come back and talk with the committee."

"I'll be here, and thanks for your time."

After she left, Tim started writing his notes for the committee: "Wow, what a lady. I know that is probably the most unorthodox thing I've ever said, but it best describes my impression of Maggie Callaway. Her manner inspires directness and frankness that encourages people (me, for sure) to express themselves honestly. She says what she thinks needs to be said to achieve her goals. She's almost scary, but I do think she could lead us to new levels of growth and prosperity. In our short interview, she showed leadership skills needed for the job and an inherent ability to develop and implement a strategic vision. Maggie could easily command a moment, which I suspect you'll see when you meet her. The big downside is she's young and lacks experience."

The next week, Maggie met with the committee, who offered her a job as a senior administrative analyst. As such, she would make recommendations on problems in the organization and the budget and analyze reports on operating procedures. This would give her needed experience, help her gain a reputation, and prepare for a possible jump to CEO.

Maggie said she'd take the job and see if it worked for her. What she didn't say out loud was, *It's a good enough way to pass the time, and God, I sure could use the money.*

Surprised, but elated to have finally found a job, she returned to her apartment, poured herself a glass of cheap red wine, turned on the song, "We Are the Champions," sat down at the kitchen table, and then let out a yell people heard several apartments away. That night she fell asleep wondering if what she felt was what other people called *happiness.*

The new job started the following Monday, so Maggie had several days to bask in the feeling she had decided after much thought to call *well-being. Happiness* just seemed too strange a concept, while *well-being* seemed more like *good* but with a shade more excitement.

It took three years, but Maggie was finally made the CEO. In that time, she showed the board and organization she learned quickly and performed at a level they might have expected from someone who had already worked as a CEO. Some of the staff reported they feared her but also admired her courage, stamina, and ability to motivate others. "She could get things done," they said.

After becoming CEO, Maggie noticed right away—her employees treated her with a new deference, and she loved it. She knew she had found her place. Maggie quickly began running the company efficiently and successfully. Her employees remained wary of her, though, and called her "iron fisted" behind her back. Feared but respected, she intimidated everyone, even those in the company who outranked her, but she did her job well, so people generally just avoided her whenever they could.

"Good morning, Ms. Callaway" greeted her, but not much followed unless Maggie encouraged it, which was rare. People didn't stop to chat with her voluntarily. They fearfully walked on, looking down. Most never came to like Maggie, but they found themselves still performing at a high level, trying to earn her respect, hoping for a few moments of her admiration.

This worked for Maggie. She had no interest in making friends but appreciated hard work and success. She met with people as needed and hobnobbed with other CEOs around the country, finding them also not terribly interested in the personal side of things unless motivated by some business connection.

She drew the line at having what she came to call *business sex*. She noticed the men around her seemed to not have any compunctions about bedding an ally or opponent. She wondered sometimes what more she might accomplish if she opened her legs to some of these guys, but she saw how these sexual liaisons complicated the business relationship.

The company stock did decline somewhat when she became CEO but soon rebounded and then took off. *I've made it*, she thought to herself. *Or have I?* This question would linger in her mind for years to come.

CHAPTER 6

RUPERT OPENED THE ENVELOPE AND PULLED OUT several sheets of paper with International Asian Pacific Shipping, America, emblazoned across the top of a letter.

Rupert,

By now you have figured out or at least guessed something about me I'm sure you did not know before. The lawyer who gave you the envelope works for me. I had her get your signature, so I'd know you and only you had received it. I had some trouble locating you but found you in Powell River, living alone in retirement.

It pains me to write this after so many years. The wounds I opened and you nurtured have not healed for either of us. I thought I'd never forgive you, my older brother, for not being clever enough to notice my distress and do something about it. Of course, as I reflected on this, I thought the only way you could have helped me would have been to surrender your decision to leave me for your God. Let me see, God vs. sister? I guess I'd always lose that battle.

Did you find him, Rupert? You should know I've never even looked. Mom and Dad worked hard to direct my attention that way. I HAD to attend church until old enough to get away with saying no, which was during my freshman year of high school. Guess they died fearing I was destined for hell, but you, brother, had seen the light. Oh, what a disappointment I was compared to you. They always focused on my salvation, or lack of it I should say, but your decision to become a priest opened a sure path to heaven for you AND them. But because you left me, Rupert, I cast you out of my life, and then you cast me out of yours—forever. How bizarre does that sound? Rumor and innuendo say the Irish can be stubborn. I guess we've proven that without a doubt, eh? (I'm trying to be a little sarcastic, Rupert, but really the die we cast as a family has to have some kind of psychological diagnosis and, who knows, maybe some kind of treatment.)

I've mostly lived my life alone. I married, but even in marriage I was alone. My husband quickly figured out I had little need for him—financially, personally, or intimately. He pulled the plug before I could throw him out. Story of my life—being left. Guess he felt something you felt at age seven, Rupert. Rather than try to hug the bitch, find a more willing squeeze. Sounds like a good idea to me too.

Though very successful, the demanding, controlling woman I became makes me hard to be around. My life became a project with goals and aspirations but was also cold: no hugs. Now at sixty-three and facing death, I reach out to you. Strange? Yeah, to me too. Life has a way of becoming strange, particularly as we age and approach death. I have lung cancer. Too many cigarettes (survival sticks). My cure for stress will end up killing me. I still hold my position at work, though in absentia, and have accumulated plenty of wealth, while also digging a deep reservoir of emptiness and fear inside.

Consider this letter a first foray into opening some kind of a dialogue with you, written or face-to-face. My doctors say I have a year or less left to live. People with this kind of cancer tend not to live long after diagnosis, and I'm almost five years into it.

Theresa, my lawyer whom you just met, will contact you again by phone, to hear your response to my request for contact. You should hear from her within a week from the time of her visit.

I cannot imagine how you must feel right now with this unexpected blast from your past. A sister rises from the dead, so to speak, and appears before you. You probably had hoped for someone or something better to come into your life like this, but no, it's just your little sister. Please, Rupert, feel free to say you're not interested when Theresa calls if that's what you truly want. I can easily reclose the door on my side and would prefer it to having you see me out of sympathy or just plain, old curiosity. I don't know any priests, but word on the street is they can be insincere and do stupid things. Is that you too?

With much fear and trepidation, I'm cracking open the door I closed long ago—but know it's just a crack.

Maggie

Rupert finished reading around eleven o'clock but never left his chair. He couldn't. His mind was reeling. Maggie, Canada, Hazelton, Mae, and Tim whirled in his head but went nowhere. It made him so dizzy he felt sure he'd fall over if he tried to get up. He wondered if this was what it felt like to be on drugs. If so, it sure wasn't enjoyable, but surprising to him, it also wasn't scary.

The menagerie of thoughts spinning around seemed to have taken away his ability to move, but he found he didn't want to move anyway. Had he lost his will to run? *Can I survive this unplanned, unwilled, unexpected and accidental encounter?* he wondered.

The spinning suddenly stopped, but his head and body ached. Rupert forced himself up to see if he could find an aspirin but couldn't focus enough to pick it out from the vitamin D or the Sudafed he took when he had a cold. He did, however, notice the broken glass and the fireplace poker protruding from the TV. In the past, he'd have had to clean it all up before anyone could see what a mess he'd made, but now he did nothing. Instead, he returned to his chair, where his head soon began to droop and his body sank into the cushions. After a short time, he fell into a deep and dreamless sleep.

At sunrise, Rupert woke with the lights still burning bright. He thought, *What a waste of electricity.* As he reconnected with what had happened the night before, he tried to get up, swearing at the pain he felt in his neck and lower back. "I'm too old to sleep like that all night," he said aloud. "Damn aging!" The shock of the night before rushed back, and immediately his back pain worsened.

Numbness would come next if he followed the Callaway pattern. It didn't. His past, long put far away, now shattered the quiet. The attic in his brain exploded, exposing the horrors of his lonely, empty, and miserable life to the light. "Oh, numbness, where are you when I need you?"

Rupert, now drenched in sweat, sat in his chair staring off into space, his mind racing but seeing nothing. He was at a loss about what to do next. Over the years, he had developed habits and rituals for all times of the day, but now he felt unable to even remember his comfortable morning rituals, much less follow them.

Not hungry, he felt a little sick to his stomach. He started to wonder about his sanity. *What's it like to go crazy? Am I having a nervous breakdown?* He remembered hearing that phrase while in seminary when one of the other students had disappeared from school and everyone was told he'd had a "nervous breakdown." He hadn't had the courage to ask about it but did overhear something about too much stress when someone else asked his teacher. Then it hit him. Rupert yelled out, "I'm having a fucking breakdown!" Tears flowed down his cheeks, and his body began to vibrate uncontrollably. He fought to stop both the tears and the shaking, but that only made it worse. "I can't stop it." Rupert grabbed the sides of his chair and tried, unsuccessfully, to stand up. A scream rose from somewhere deep inside him, his head flew back, and then it flew forward, almost throwing himself on the floor.

Then, as suddenly as everything had started, everything stopped. Rupert didn't move. His body froze in place, the shaking stopped, and the tears dried on his cheeks. He knew immediately he had not made himself stop all this any more than he had started it all. Feeling too out of control, he had the instinct was to run, but where would he go? He couldn't run to neighbor for fear they'd see him like this, and that he couldn't tolerate.

At that moment, though, Rupert saw where he could go. He got up and moved to a small table in the living room where he kept his crucifix, prayer beads, pictures of Jesus on the cross, and Mary on her knees before the crucified Christ. Out of habit, he fell on his knees . . . but nothing happened. He expected he would pray, but no prayer came. He always had trouble with prayer, so he'd memorized different supplications to the Lord, but now nothing came to him.

"Jesus," he yelled out loud, scaring himself even more because it had not come as a prayer but in anger, "what's happening to me?"

Rupert Callaway was having a crisis unlike anything he'd had before. As bad as things had ever been, he'd always kept some control. In childhood, he'd held on to the promise of the church; while a priest he'd held on to the hope things would get better if he just could stay out of trouble and follow the rules; and in retirement he mostly had kept to himself, secluded and alone. He managed his life to minimize any disruptions, but he never experienced the relief or satisfaction he wanted.

Through the news about priests abusing children, the resignation of a pope, and the instillation of a new pope, he managed it all. Once he decided something, like becoming a priest, he was able to shut out all distractions—until now. Maggie had initiated a disruption he didn't seem capable of containing.

Rupert looked around and saw a chaotic scene. Shards of glass, sharp and dangerous, were still spread around the kitchen, and an iron poker stuck out of the TV. He began to shake again, first his legs quivered, and then he felt this cold tremor go up his spine, causing him to shiver uncontrollably. He felt cold but noticed he was sweating again too.

This was too much. Rupert felt panic rising and called out for help, but no one heard him. He called out several times, but no one came. How could they? He lived deliberately alone with no friends, hidden from neighbors, hidden from everyone, and it occurred to him, hidden from family. Then everything in his world went black. All he would remember later was hitting the floor hard, knocking over his prayer table, and scattering his ceremonial objects into many corners.

CHAPTER 7

MAGGIE HAD NOT SLEPT, thinking about how Theresa had given Rupert her letter. Alone in her bed, she tossed and turned, her mind vacillating between a kind of satisfaction with what she'd done and a heart-piercing fear of the monster she'd awakened. She'd put in years and years of study and hard work to gain a high level of success, and now the emotional pain and personal longing she'd repressed in the pursuit of all that was unleashed.

"Damn, damn, damn," she shouted out loud, but no one heard the explosion. No one ever heard her. How could anyone? She had always filtered what she said and did through her well-developed intellect. Very little of her true feelings or thoughts ever seeped out. Now, however, painful and sad thoughts about her past filled her mind. Surprisingly, she was not confused by them, nor was she comforted.

Maggie had looked for a partner in life, not because of any particular longing for men or family. She thought relationships were for the emotionally or professionally needy, but she was, at the same time, curious about one. Sex, though she had tried it, did not particularly appeal to her—fun, but messy and too male dominated. (She wondered if that was all her parents had, knowing her father had had a need for sex, which she assumed her mother had accommodated.) Professionally, she didn't need marriage. In fact, she worried a man might become jealous or competitive or feel threatened by a success-ful woman. But marriage was one of those mysteries that intrigued her. So she tried it.

Marriage was probably Maggie's worst failure. Everything she had feared happened. The sex wasn't even fun after the first few times. Promises made before they married disappeared, and her husband soon felt only like arm candy. After she left him, Maggie told her housekeeper that he "lost his masculinity," or sometimes she said it more cruelly, "His dick fell off!" The whole thing had lasted six months.

Now here she was at sixty-three, sick and with no one, feeling much like she'd felt as a child growing up in a family with no interest in her. Sure, they'd seen her as a family member, but how impersonal is that? She was the daughter they took care of, but unless she was sick, needed to be fed, or needed for work at church, she remained unseen.

Rupert had rejected her but not because she'd done anything to him. To him, she was only the sister who lived in the same house, ate the same food, and went to the same school. No one seemed to have given her a thought. Did she have a boyfriend? What did she think about the polit-ical sex scandal called the Munsinger Affair? What kind of music did she like? What did she think about the Vietnam War, death, or religion? What did she want to be when she grew up? It never occurred to anyone in her family to ask.

Maybe if I'd attacked one of them with one of Dad's axes, they'd have reacted to me as someone real with a beating heart and restless mind. That thought had actually crossed her mind. In fact, she had thought about attacking Rupert just before he left. But that wasn't her style. *Even if no one else knows it, I know I'm no killer,* Maggie thought, *though I would have liked to be one sometimes.*

"Oh dear, I am leaking emotion," she said. She slapped her face a couple of times and managed to crawl out of bed. Dressing had become a chore over the course of her illness, and so she thought, *Maybe I just won't get dressed today.* She'd never done that before, but she thought anyone seeing her would probably just excuse it as a consequence of her sickness, although still maybe think she was losing her usual good judg-ment and self-control.

"Well maybe I am. And to scare everyone more, I might just smack someone, the one who irritates me the most today! Lock me up, throw away the key, my life is over anyway!"

Maggie Callaway was having a crisis.

CHAPTER 8

RUPERT WOKE ON THE KITCHEN FLOOR, flat on his back. He had no idea how he ended up in the kitchen or how long he'd been there, but he felt terrible. He didn't want to get up yet, so he sat there with his back against the cabinet door, feeling surprisingly relieved. *At least I'm alive*, he thought but then said out loud, "Do I really want to be?"

He didn't try to answer his question. Maybe he was just too exhausted. Instead, he thought about a hot shower, and this got him up and moving, but not fast. He'd never felt so stiff. Moving was hard, but soon he managed to get himself up and heading to the bathroom.

Rupert reached back to scratch an itch on the back of his head. "What the . . .?" He drew his hand back to find blood and yelled, "Shit, shit, shit." He felt pieces of glass in the blood and remembered he'd been lying in broken glass. Fear took over, and he ran to the shower, jumping in without removing his clothes. *Why take off my clothes when I might be bleeding to death here?*

Blood and glass fell to the floor of the shower but soon stopped. It seemed the wounds had mostly clotted during the night, but he still washed his head multiple times. Then he slowly removed his clothes, checking every part of himself for other bleeding. Finding no broken skin, he finished cleaning up and got out. Rupert felt some relief but was still breathing hard and feeling a little faint, so he sat down on the edge of the tub. His heartbeat and breathing slowed. The towel he'd wrapped around his head showed no new signs of blood, but his body still felt like he'd been twirling around in a dryer. Exhausted, he just sat on the tub until he lost all feeling in his butt. Then he jumped up, smacking himself on the butt several times in an attempt to wake everything up.

After changing into some fresh clothes, he went out and sat in his chair. "Hello, old friend." He leaned back, took several deep breaths, and allowed himself to sink into the folds he knew so well.

It was raining outside. Rupert liked hearing raindrops hit the roof. In Kamloops, they'd get snow in the winter months, but plenty of rain fell too. Now here in Powell River, he saw little snow but lots of rain. Today it felt especially ominous as he looked out into the darkness that matched his mood. He feared staying home in this state, so he decided to go for a drive. To where he did not know but wanted to move to ease the torment of his battered psyche.

Rupert was in the car and out of the house in less than half an hour. The ride into Powell River didn't take long. Downtown had only three main streets. He took Marine Avenue because it passed along the water's edge. As he drove, he decided he'd take a drive on the Sunshine Coast Highway.

First, though, he wanted something to eat and pulled into the parking lot of the Thaidal Zone, called The Zone, one of the few restaurants in this part of town where he found the food fairly tasty. The priest at the Catholic Church and several local ministers in town informally gathered here on Tuesday mornings every six weeks. They had invited him to attend, and he'd gone one or two times. It interested him that they never discussed work, religion, or God. Instead, they occupied their time chatting about the weather (a favorite topic in this part of the world), how the fish were running, and maybe the most interesting topic of all, town gossip.

Today, as he entered, he saw them sitting at a corner table. Rupert moved quickly in the opposite direction and found a seat where he could look out at the water and have his back to others in the restaurant. The place was crowded. The ferry to Blubber Bay would be leaving soon, and those wanting to load up on good food before facing the traditional bland fare on board filled the place. A good curry could even be taken on board and eaten during the crossing. It was still the breakfast hour, but Rupert didn't care. He ordered a bowl of their delicious tom yum goong (spicy shrimp soup), ate it slowly, then left, and climbed in his car.

Rupert looked forward to his ride, even in the rain. If he went as far as Saltery Bay, he could catch the ferry to Earls Cove. Who knew where he would end up? If he drove too long, there'd be a ferry into Horseshoe Bay, and then he could drive on into Vancouver. As he started out, he already felt more relaxed with the events of the last twelve hours fading in his mind. He turned his radio up high, blasting out country tunes he mostly hated, but the sad songs and bluesy music seemed appropriate for the moment.

Willie Nelson came on singing "Crazy." The song caught his attention, not because he'd known love or lost love but because of the resentment that rose up in him whenever he heard the word *love*. He hated it and even those who used it, especially in such a heartfelt way. He'd even grown to hate himself for how he'd had to use it—preach it, praise it, and proclaim it from the pulpit. But he didn't explode in anger. Instead, he said, "Willie, I'm jealous. You know something I don't. Maybe I should have been a musician."

The rain fell hard, making it difficult to see the road. Maybe that numbness he'd longed for earlier was finally hitting him. Rupert drove on with abandon but without incident. At dusk, he was in Halfmoon Bay and decided to stop for the night. Halfmoon Bay was tiny, as were most places along the coast route. The population here probably numbered around 2,500, but it seemed larger because of all the tourists.

Lots of hotels, both large and small, peppered the town. He knew he'd find a place to spend the night because, at this time of year, some would not yet have filled up. Restaurants would be plentiful too. He drove in on Main Street, passing a mélange of restaurants like Sushi Main, Chez Shea, and It's Italia. Tourists ate in these places. Natives liked the local fish places, and of course, the McDonald's was always popular. He'd find something to his taste later. Prices in a tourist town like this ran on the high side. Hotel BLU asked $378 per night. That was way out of his range. The Comfort Inn at $160 would do just fine, so he turned the car up the Carrillo Highway.

Rupert had not known his destination when he had left Powell River. He'd just wanted to drive and think, even if he didn't know at the time what to think about. His mood and state of mind could best be described as scattered, uprooted. Thinking just stirred up more turmoil and pushed his desire to escape, a feeling he had felt often in his life, but could never act out. He couldn't even settle on what the word *escape* meant for him.

Now Maggie had written, and it opened a long-closed, locked, and sealed door to his past. In his desperation to get away from Hazelton, Rupert had forgotten about her and his family. He had hoped to find a better, happier life in the church. He'd not had an abusive past; his mother and father had worked hard to establish a place in Canada. But from early in his life, he had felt unwanted, unliked especially at school where other children distanced themselves from him, calling him to his face "dirty immigrant" and shouting, "Why don't you go back where you came from?" The other thing they called him hurt even worse: "Hey, fatso." Yes, he was chunky, and his peers didn't let him forget it.

His parents, always too busy, never visited the school or offered any comfort. "We Irish are tough," they'd say. To them, a few nasty comments were "nothing compared to surviving the Great Famine of the 1840s or the Crisis of 1914 where we lived on the brink of civil war between the Nationalists and Unionist Volunteers."

At church, though, he felt welcomed and comforted. The sermons, scripture readings, and even the prayers never did much for him, but the personal contact with Fathers Sean O'Connor and Kelsey Quinn deeply affected him. They made him feel like a real part of a community/family. When offered the chance to attend seminary, Rupert had jumped at it.

Now, though, as he drove around Halfmoon Bay, looking for his evening lodging, he was feeling just as confused, alone, and lost as he had felt as a kid living at home. What had happened? Rupert didn't allow these feelings into his life anymore. How'd they get in now?

"Family again," he yelled out in the car. "Damn you, Maggie. You've returned to haunt me, resurrect all my feelings of the failed life I've had."

His anxiety rose. His mind ran loose, untethered to anything or anyone. The loud music and some beautiful views on the trip down had helped distract him from thinking. Now, as he continued to search for the Comfort Inn, he flipped on the radio again. Rupert feared the quiet of the night that lay ahead of him.

He finally saw the inn, pulled into the breezeway, went in, and registered for one night. Rupert had no bags, so moving in amounted to unlocking the room, turning on a light, and relieving himself. Locking the door again before leaving, he went out for food, though he didn't feel particularly hungry. He was going out mostly to avoid having to sit alone in the motel room, which right now seemed like a much worse option.

Stopping at the first fish-and-chips place he saw, he entered. Greeted by smoke and the smell of grease, he sat down, deciding to stay, even though the smell reminded him of all he'd read and heard about the dangers of cholesterol and heartburn. Tonight, Rupert didn't care, feeling like someone who'd fallen into a well and abandoned all hope of escape. If already defeated, why worry about fat and cholesterol? He said, "Too bad for me, I guess."

Surprising himself, though, Rupert ate heartily, smothering his greasy French fries in ketchup. As he finished, he could feel a slight heartburn coming on, but this time, unlike his normal pattern, he did not immediately punish himself for having done what he'd known was bad for him. He just swallowed an antacid and headed out to his home for the night.

His room at the motel had a TV with plenty of channels. Lying in bed, he switched from one show to the next, unable to find anything interesting. Finally, probably somewhere around eleven, he happened upon a channel showing old movies. He started to watch *The Shootist* in what he thought he remembered was John Wayne's last role. It also starred the leggy and beautiful Lauren Bacall. *Oh, great*, Rupert thought, *aging gunfighter dying of cancer!* He watched until he fell restlessly asleep. Awaking before dawn with the TV still on, he switched it off. Then, knowing he'd not go back to sleep, he got himself up, showered, dressed in the only clothes he had, and left his room to find coffee and maybe a Danish.

It was six in the morning but still dark as he drove out. He got himself a large cup of Starbucks strong black coffee and one of those croissant things, got back in the car, but then went nowhere. Rupert sat back and let himself sink into his seat. With the croissant in the bag by his side, he held the cup with two hands close to his heart. It felt warm and surprisingly comforting.

The rain of the night before had stopped, at least for now. The sky was cloudless but still as black as a starless sky. It made him think about how long he'd stayed in the Northwest. Maybe I just like it dark, he said. "Dark days, dark nights, dark Rupert." This made him think how God had abandoned him, left him in the dark. Jesus, according to John, was "The Light that came into the world" of men who lived in darkness. *Then why did you leave me in the dark?* he thought.

Rupert bolted upright as hot coffee flowed into his crotch. "Shit," he said. "Ouch, that's hot. What a dunce you are, Rupert." He quickly grabbed his spilt coffee cup and placed it on the car dash. Next, he grabbed the towel he always had handy for messes. He slowly cleaned up and waited for his pants to cool.

Then, feeling decidedly more awake and ready to go, he started the car and began his drive home—or at least to the place where he currently lived. He never felt like he had a home of his own. Even now, the house where he lived belonged to the local parish. They lent it to him for a small fee with the condition he'd leave if the parish needed it for something in the future. He had taken the house but understandably never felt secure. *That's a feeling I know well*, Rupert realized. He turned the car toward Powell River, his town, driving through the morning darkness with the music again turned up high, the windows open, and his shirt collar turned up against the cold.

CHAPTER 9

After another restless night, Maggie again awoke in pain. She imagined her cancer cells chomping away at her lungs and probably other organs by now. *Consumed from the inside out*, she thought, and it made her shudder, thinking back to five years ago.

On a visit to the doctor for a persistent cough, Maggie was told she might have cancer. She was referred to an oncologist, who confirmed that diagnosis. Though alarmed by the word *cancer*, Maggie really was not surprised. She had started smoking in high school and had known for years about the dangers of smoking. As rational as she was, those headlines did not make her stop. She knew she was addicted but didn't care. Over the years, doctors had told Maggie to quit, but she had said only she would *try* to stop just to make them stop bringing it up.

Like a rebellious teenager, Maggie told one doctor she preferred the tough-woman image she had as a smoker, like Katherine Hepburn sparring with Spencer Tracy or Bonnie Parker, the shameless bank robber/killer. They were brave and sassy women who knew who they were and went for what they wanted. The doctor just gawked at her in disbelief that he was listening to a successful executive, not a juvenile delinquent. She smiled at him but her expression hid her knowledge that she was about to go through a big loss—the loss of her life.

At first, Maggie told no one. She continued to work, put in her normal long hours, and travel as before. Staying so busy, she often forgot about the cancer. Then her pain would come back, and she would have to make another trip to the doctor. During each visit, he urged her to begin treatments, reminding Maggie she was risking her life by delaying. She thought, *So what?* She wondered why they were so concerned about her death. She knew she would die. Everyone did. So why the push to stay alive? Sure, the idea of death scared her, but she had to face it sooner or later.

Someone had once told her that life provided her with opportunities to make a success of herself or achieve recognition.

"What, become famous?" she had asked.

"No, you don't have to become famous, Maggie, but your life is a gift. You have the job of making something of it while you have it."

Maggie had walked away, frustrated but not wanting to get angry. Now, though, she had begun to question her bravado. She liked her job, though the people who worked for her were less important. She liked the money she made but realized she did little with it. She travelled for work, not for pleasure. And she didn't go out to eat much, unless it was for business. Maggie did like to buy CDs and tapes so she could listen to music, and she paid out big bucks for a nice place to live. After that, she had plenty of money to put in the bank. *Do I live for anything else?* she wondered.

Probably because she was now coming closer to a face-to-face meeting with the Grim Reaper, Maggie did come up with what she lived for, things she would have otherwise dismissed as trivial or unimportant.

In college, Maggie loved learning everything from the equations, like Euler's identity, which shows the connection between fundamental numbers, to poetry, like Emily Dickinson's, "Because I could not stop for Death." Maggie had come to know and appreciate beauty while at Berkeley and could pick out beauty from the forest of her life, as she did as a child among the trees back home.

Though she hated her childhood, Maggie had really fond memories of her walks in the woods—the smells; birds, singing and sometimes landing on a branch near her, seemingly waiting for something, or just preening their colorful feathers; the soft earth under her feet with beautiful mushrooms sprouting all around; and the sky, looking so blue above the dark green and browns of the forest.

She wandered the banks of the two rivers that flowed by Hazelton, and she'd sometimes stop to watch the flow, going somewhere she imagined distant and exotic, a place she'd go someday.

Fishermen would talk to her as she passed. "Hi, Maggie. Pray tell, did you go to school today?"

"Of course, I did, Jack. I wasn't out here fishing, was I?"

"Not that I saw. Fishing's pretty good today, though. Look at what I'm taking home tonight." He held up his creel filled with trout.

"Hope you counted 'em, Jack. Wouldn't want the game warden to cart you off to jail."

They would both laugh at this before Jack would wave her off.

"Ain't you got some place to be, Maggie?"

"No, not really. I'm not expected home till five for dinner, and they won't miss me before that. Never do."

That would usually stop the talking, but Maggie always sat there watching Jack fish and sometimes catching one.

One time he gave her a fish to take home. "Here, Maggie, take this home to your ma. I think I caught my limit, and we wouldn't want me to be hauled off to jail, now, would we?"

Maggie laughed, took the fish, and turned toward home.

"Bye, Jack, I'll probably see you tomorrow if you're here. I'll be, I know that. Nothing else to do but homework when I get home."

Thinking about those times along the river and the few people she met during her lonely walks now made Maggie sad. "That I'll miss, even if not much else."

Increasing pain did make her finally begin the recommended chemotherapy treatments. These reduced the size of her tumor, but she started to lose her hair, still had chest pain, and now suffered from nausea and diarrhea. Maggie started to miss a lot of work. People were beginning to wonder what was going on when she finally told the board at their annual meeting and took a leave of absence.

After her chemo and radiation treatments, Maggie waited to see what the cancer would do next. She expected the worst but surprisingly did better than she or her doctors had thought she would. It wasn't easy. She suffered, often unable to sleep because of increasing pain.

Her pain was a good part of why Maggie hadn't slept, but she knew much of her restlessness also came from thinking about Rupert. Now that she'd invited him back into her life, she could hardly not think of him and the life she'd had with or, more accurately, without him. There had been times in her life when she had thought to reach out to him but had pulled back. One such time, had happened about a year after she'd been accepted for her job at the shipping company. She had begun a letter to Rupert with a quote from Maya Angelou she thought would impress him:

> "You alone are enough. You have nothing to prove to anybody."
> I've learned to live without you, Rupert and, I must admit, learned
> to live well. Wealthy and without peer at my work, I have plenty
> of recognition, people everywhere clamoring for my attention. I
> have nothing to prove anymore. I feel strong and impenetrable,
> finally immune to the whims of, let's say, a big brother.

Maggie never mailed it knowing it was all a lie. She had enough awareness, even then, to know she didn't really have any idea what Maya Angelou was talking about. Maggie had wanted Rupert to think he didn't matter and never had, that she'd made it on her own without him.

Now Maggie felt thankful that letter had never reached him. But she wondered if she was ready, even at this point in her life, to have an honest face-off with him.

Growing up in Hazelton, Rupert and Maggie lived as strangers in the same house. They were three grades apart in school, Maggie having skipped two grades because of her precociousness, so they rarely saw each other there. After school, Rupert mostly stayed in his room with the door shut. They didn't talk except on rare occasions, and then he would tell her, in a very animated way, about all the friends he had at school and brag about how he and his friends had stopped at Timmy's for a box of

Timbits on the way home. None of these so-called friends ever showed up at their house. As smart as Maggie was, she couldn't make sense of her brother's behavior, but then her whole family seemed strange. Was she? Probably, she thought. Once you're put into a painting, you never get out. That's where people will find you forever—no escape.

When Rupert left home at twelve, Maggie was really alone, her books, her only companions. Favorites from that time were *A Wrinkle in Time*, the *Nancy Drew* mysteries, and books by Hemingway, whom she'd encountered in high school. She loved his simple, direct, blunt, and as some called it, macho style. He wrote with authority and command, modeling for her how she wanted to live.

NOW WITH THE CANCER, Maggie thought she had to act as she had growing up when longing for friends and having none—tough and not show any weakness, just like any good Irishman and like the Hemingway characters she admired so much. Yet a question haunted her as she faced the end of her life: *Why, after all the success and fame I've had, do I still feel so alone?* Famous and yet alone, why? All the attention, yet never recognized or understood, not so much because no one ever tried to get to know her but because of the depth of her isolation, rigidly enforced. Maggie didn't know if she'd done this to protect herself from a fear of receiving what she wanted, but whatever the reason, she knew her terrible aloneness had driven her to the irrational act of writing to her brother.

"Oh dear, what have I done!" The suspense of not knowing drove Maggie to call Theresa again. "Have you heard anything yet?"

"No, I told you I would call as soon as I hear something, Maggie."

Maggie could hear the frustration in Theresa's voice but didn't care. She was near to panic and had to call just to have something to do.

"Okay, I'll try to wait, but you know waiting has never been one of my strong points."

"Okay, Maggie, hang in there." To herself, Theresa thought, *I hope to God this guy does call and agrees to talk to her. I hate to think what might happen to her, and me, if he doesn't.*

CHAPTER 10

RUPERT DID NOT THINK ABOUT MAGGIE on the trip home. Instead, he reflected on his years in the seminary and the priesthood, the priests from that childhood church who had noticed and paid attention to him at a time when he felt mostly like a piece of shit. He'd never seen those two priests again after leaving Hazelton. They had left the area before his parents died, so other priests had performed the Requiem Mass. Since then, of course, he'd met many priests, but now living away from his family experience, he saw nothing special in them—just ordinary professionals, some trying to work their way up to become cardinals but most finishing their time in the church as priests. Rupert was one of these.

He'd become a priest, but he never found the comfort or meaning of belonging he so wanted. All the sermons and all the scripture he read never came alive for him. He struggled to find some passion in his own sermons, but he never escaped the feeling that they were all just scripted talks. Parishioners treated him with respect, but he noticed he seldom got invited to their homes. He just did his job, and they called him Father. Now retired, neighbors would still call him that, but it held no genuine meaning for him. He remembered seeing the gathering of ministers and local priests at Thaidal Zone before driving out of town and how he'd avoided them. Now he thought, *I have the title of priest, but I don't belong. Where do I belong?* Rupert felt his chest tighten up; tears formed involuntarily and fell down his cheeks. He wiped them away with his sleeve. Then he saw the lights of Powell River looming ahead.

The despair that had grabbed him had not disappeared completely, and he noticed, much to his chagrin, a rising sexual tension, a feeling he'd had before that he hid and unsuccessfully tried to pray his way through. Though the sexual arousal would diminish after a while, usually after he masturbated, it always returned—most often during some time of distress like this.

"Not now," he said out loud. "I have no place to go for prayer here, and I'm hungry."

But the urge was too strong. The stress he was under had sapped his energy, his feeling of value. He knew if he masturbated, he'd feel powerful, strong, and above all, like a man—not emasculated as he felt most of the time. If he masturbated, he'd feel, at least momentarily, fierce and passionate, even a little savage, though thinking that scared him, so he quickly blocked it. He wanted to feel strong like a man, and playing with himself would do the trick. Rupert started looking for an abandoned parking lot and soon found one. He parked well off the road, pulled down his pants, imagined a pretty woman undressing in front of him, and relieved himself. Afterwards, he had a mess to clean up but didn't care. He zipped up, cleaned himself and the car seat, and drove on toward town. The temporary relief he always got after masturbation had settled in.

Guilt would soon follow. By the time he pulled into the Thaidal Zone parking lot, he was consumed by shame. Rupert sat in the car and cried. "What a life I have. Something has to change, and now. What has happened to me?"

Of course, there was no answer. Rupert just sat there and cried, but he knew he would soon get angry. Anger always followed shame for him, though shame wasn't necessary for him to get mad. Then it happened. He grabbed the steering wheel and yanked, just hard enough not to break it but to overly stress unused muscles in his upper back and arms. "Ouch," he yelled, "fuck, fuck, fuck." Rupert banged on the dashboard and then the seat next to him until he was spent and slumped back on the seat. After a while, as he knew he would, he felt relieved, appeased, and satisfied.

This all came to an abrupt halt when he saw cars pulling in the lot near him and people getting out, looking his way, and then hurrying into the restaurant. He hoped no one recognized him. He didn't think they would since, even though he lived in town, he wasn't known by many.

He wiped his eyes, straightened his shirt, and combed his hair. His body ached, so as he got out of the car, he stretched out his arms and twisted his body, like he was trying to get everything back where it belonged before he headed toward the restaurant.

About halfway there he stopped and returned to his car. "Time for a change!" He removed his collar and black jacket. "I think I'll go naked before the masses this time!" Turning a deep red, Rupert headed toward the door.

CHAPTER 11

T HE ZONE WAS PACKED. Between people escaping the spring rains and the ferry crowd, Rupert didn't find one open seat. He decided to wait. Standing off in a corner, he didn't think anyone would notice him since he'd left his collar in the car. The collar liberated Catholics to break into his private space. It always made him feel invaded at the least, assaulted at the worst, but it also made him feel momentarily important.

As he stood waiting, he started to get dizzy and to shake as if he was walking in a cold winter wind. His skin buzzed; his teeth chattered. Rupert wondered if he was getting sick or maybe something worse like having a heart attack. Though tempted by the idea of dying, he knew this wasn't the time for him to die. As that thought took over, his self-control returned. At least he stopped shaking. He still felt sweat running from his armpits. Then a strong urge to escape—he was an expert at leaving things, events, people—swelled up.

He turned back toward the front entrance, but before he could move, someone grabbed him by the arm and said, "Sir, we have a stool at the front counter if you want that."

His face turned a bright red, but he was able to say, "Okay." Rupert didn't have the courage to walk out then. Though still feeling a little unstable, he followed the young man toward his seat. Now he had a menu and a glass of water to help him recover his composure. He drank his water, checked to see if the menu had the dish he wanted, and then waited.

But no one came. The place was so busy he wondered why they didn't hire more staff. Fucking peasants." He noticed a few people from the kitchen look his way. "Oops, sorry." Then he put his head down and shut up.

He pretty much knew what he wanted, but again looked at the menu. Wine was a must. *After the day I've had I should get a bottle, a hearty red*, he thought. That seemed more important than food. When the waiter finally came over, he ordered a bowl of Thai tom yum soup.

"That's it?"

"Yes, and a big glass of Cabernet, please."

"We have only one size glass, sir."

"Just bring me what you have."

"Okay. That should come up pretty quick. You can see how smacked we are tonight. Kitchen has gotten real backed up." He took the menu and left.

Then, just as he started to sink back into the familiar self-loathing, Rupert heard, "Hi!" from the seat adjacent to his. He pointed to himself and said, "You talking to me?"

The woman smiled and said, "Yes, you."

Rupert could feel his face again getting hot, so he assumed he had turned some shade of red.

But she said nothing about that. Instead, she went on, "Dreary night up here in the north woods, eh?"

"Yeah, guess so, but here 'in the north woods' as you call them, we're used to dreary nights. You must be visiting."

"Yes, I just came up from Vancouver where it also rains a lot. I drove up to get away from the city for a while, not the rain. I knew I couldn't get that far away in one evening's drive. I have a room over at the Seabreeze Resort on 101. Lots of small, not very fancy motels up this way. Trip Advisor reported they had a midweek deal, so I took it. People at the front desk recommended this as a local hangout that had decent food. I assume you're one of those so-called locals?"

"You could say that. I moved over here from Kamloops to retire."

"Retired, eh? I'm close to that myself. I turn sixty-five in about six months, and shortly after that, I plan to be out the door, traveling, maybe doing something I've never considered or thought possible before."

Rupert didn't know what to say to that. He'd never had an adventurous spirit, not that he knew about anyway. His retirement had become just as uneventful and routine as his life before retirement.

"What are you retired from?"

"The priesthood."

"Oh, that's not what I'd expected or hoped for in my first meeting up here!"

Her forthrightness stunned him.

"Why?"

"Priests, where I come from, generally live among us common folk like they have a stick up their butts. Sorry for my bluntness. Here I am saying things as though I already know you when we actually just met. Maybe you're different." Her food arrived and she turned to eat.

The waiter then placed Rupert's wine on the counter in front of him. He grabbed it and swallowed a big gulp. *Awkward* wouldn't be a strong enough word to describe what he felt at this moment. *Unstable* was better. Unfortunately, leaving didn't feel like a viable option, but he wished he could. His soup arrived before this stranger could say anything else. Then he shocked himself by saying, "Shall we pray?" Before she could say or do something, though, he said, "Or shall we just eat?" He followed that up with, "Let's eat. I'm hungry." He dropped his head and started to spoon soup in his mouth. "Oh, this is hot and spicy, just the way I like it."

The woman looked at him with some confusion, a cross between intrigued by what she was hearing and perplexed, but decided not to pursue it.

They ate quietly until Rupert couldn't stand it and said, "What's your name?"

Mischievously she answered, "Saint Ann."

He laughed, despite making an effort not to. "Another saint. Do I have to pray to you too? Sorry. That's so disrespectful, and I don't even know you—yet." He tried not to laugh, but it burst out of his mouth, along with the soup he'd just tried to swallow. "I just can't believe I ran into another saint today of all days. But please forgive me. I think I'm out of control. This is not the me I'm most familiar with."

What is this? she wondered. She had hoped to have something exciting happen on this trip north. Her teaching had grown tedious and her writing stilted. She needed a break. Now this surprise. A priest sitting next to her was turning out to be quite a curiosity. She decided not to say anything for now. While glancing his way and smiling, she kept eating. Then something Frances McDormand, the actress, once said came to her: "That's another great thing about getting older. Your life is written on your face." This guy's face had peaks and valleys, the kind of face that could well have been forged in a life of formidable anxiety and stress. Finally, she just couldn't sit quietly. She was intrigued, wanting to see where this was going to go. "I'm Sylvia Plath. My mother was an aspiring writer and named me after the writer Sylvia Plath."

"Rupert here," he replied. "Oh, and please don't call me Father."

CHAPTER 12

SAN FRANCISCO SPARKLED IN THE AFTERNOON SUN outside Maggie's spacious and well-appointed condo, fifteen floors above the street. She was standing at the window, looking out at the gleaming city. She'd never explored it. No time. Other than the daily trips to her office, she had mostly gone to restaurants and meeting rooms where she had work to do. Looking out now, she had to shield her eyes from the bright sun to see better.

She was tempted to pull the curtains and retreat into a book her doctor had recommended, *When Breath Becomes Air* by Paul Kalanithi, a memoir by a doctor facing imminent death from cancer. *No*, she thought, *too depressing a subject for this moment.* Nor did she retreat into any of the lighter fare she had on her nightstand. Instead, she stayed put and looked out at the city, *my city*, she thought to herself. She saw people sunning themselves on roof decks below her. One building even had a pool on its roof, something she thought was pretty bizarre.

But it was the sky that really got her attention. Its intense blue was mostly hidden from view by the bright sun, its depth shrouded by the brilliant light and a fine white mist. As she stared at it, she could pick out particles of color, especially beautiful reds and greens. Maggie felt calmed and at ease with herself. Her body relaxed so much she leaned too far into the window and hit her head on the pane.

"Ow, that hurt, damn it." Her calm feelings quickly transformed into irritation, which propelled her to head to the bedroom, change clothes, and decide to leave the condo. She found her jeans (fashionable blues, not Levi's) and pulled them on under her nightshirt. Then off that came. Now she had to find a shirt. Usually, she spent time considering outfits but not this time. She grabbed a long-sleeved one, something she knew was comfortable, put it on, and buttoned it. Out of habit more than anything, she went to look at herself in the mirror. "Oh piffle, I don't need to do this," she shouted at herself. It didn't change her, though; she still checked out the appropriateness of her choices and the coordination of colors.

Finally, she slipped on some sandals and left. In the hallway outside her door, she ran into one of her neighbors, a middle-aged woman, well dressed, holding one of those shrunken dogs, a poodle she thought, and in the other hand a Victoria's Secret bag. She lived in the second condo from hers as you walked away from the elevator, quite close, but Maggie didn't really know her. They never talked beyond a greeting or a "How are you?" kind of thing. This time, though, Maggie felt a little feisty, a cross between the calm and irritation she'd felt before, and decided to stop and chat. "How are you Ms., oh, I'm sorry, I can't recall your name right now. Memory, you know how it is when we get old."

"Hello. It's Dorothy, Dorothy Washburn. I used to be Dorothy LaSalle. Got divorced some years ago and took back my maiden name."

"That's right, I remember now. Your husband worked in finance as I recall, and you didn't work. Looks like you're still able to go out shopping, Dorothy. Never got any fancy underwear myself, never had a real need. No men to impress!"

Dorothy blushed and tried to change the subject. "Where you off too? As I recall, you worked for some big shipping company. I heard that from one of the other owners since I don't think we've ever shared stories."

"You heard right, but I'm not working right now. On leave." Maggie didn't want to get into her health issues and really didn't think there was any serious topic she'd want to pursue with this woman. Dorothy already struck her as fatuous and not very interesting, so Maggie just ended the conversation. "Nice to have seen you, Dorothy. Got to go. Have a good day."

The elevator was her next stop.

Outside, Maggie headed west where she knew she'd run into shops, restaurants, and tourists mixed among local shoppers. She'd gone many times to restaurants on Chestnut Street for meetings but never just walked into one like someone who was attracted to the decor, food, or reputation. That sounded like fun, but she knew she couldn't walk that far, so she hailed a cab.

The driver turned to her and asked, "Where on Chestnut do you want to go?"

"Just drop me anywhere you like."

He stopped the car at a corner; she got out and started walking, passing people who seemed to have destinations and others just wandering, like her, but browsing the windows and storefronts. Maggie looked in store windows but had no interest in shopping. She did go into a few restaurants she didn't know, but to just look around. After entering, she'd scan the place and try to leave before anyone approached her to talk. She thought of it as a fun game and laughed as she eluded maître d's and dodged tables while running out, imagining herself to be breaking the law and avoiding capture by evil authorities.

In one bar Maggie entered, she saw waitresses dressed in short black dresses and white aprons milling among the patrons who were mostly men. *Big surprise*, she thought. *Men gawking at scantily clad women.* That time she didn't wait to be pursued by anyone; she just walked out shaking her head but also kind of proud of herself for having risked going in a place like that.

After a while she began to feel tired and decided to look for a place that served beer and small plates where she might want to stay. Then she had an idea and stuck out her hand to hail another cab.

"Fillmore Street, please." She knew this street had places that didn't attract the business and social crowd. "You can drop me anywhere."

He did, in the middle of a block.

Getting out, Maggie just walked. Around four o'clock, she passed a pub with a sign above the door—Jaxson. Inside she saw a lively retro saloon with an apparent country motif that drew her attention. It seemed so different for San Francisco. She entered, found a seat at the bar, not too difficult at this early hour, and ordered a pint of Laughing Monk Ale. Maggie couldn't resist something with a name like that. It made her think of her brother. She wondered if he ever laughed or even drank. *A Catholic priest who doesn't drink*, she thought. *Unheard of.* She smiled.

Four o'clock must be a popular time for this place, she thought as it quickly began to fill up, mostly with young patrons, but a few older-looking folks about Maggie's age came in too.

One of those older-looking men sat down next to her. He ordered a glass of Merlot and then turned toward her. "Hello," he said nonchalantly while holding up his glass as if to toast her. He saw she was drinking beer and asked if he could buy her the next one.

"Sure," she said, "but beware. I'm dying and probably not a good catch. You may not want to waste your time here!"

"What's a fella supposed to say after a line like that?"

Maggie thought he sounded a little like a cowboy. *Fitting*, she thought, *cowboy bar, cowboy.* She really wasn't sure she wanted company but decided what the hell. "I'm living on borrowed time, and I already broke my 'good girl' image back on Chestnut." She'd never been brave enough or even interested in a pickup before. Nor had she ever met a cowboy before. "You'll have to figure out your own lines, mister. If you can't figure out your part, best not to start things in the first place."

"Okay, it's a deal. Where I come from and at my age, I learned to be polite to others. How to do that was mostly up to us. So we guess about what to say, or we just do what I did, ask if I can buy you a drink. You look to be about the same generation as me, but maybe you just wanted to scare me off. I've never had someone I just met tell me she was dying."

"Well, I am, and I didn't say that to scare you. I said it because it's true, and you may not want to start talking to someone who only has a limited amount of time left to live."

"Well, you got my attention. If I was bored before I came in tonight, I'm not now. Let's talk. You know, you might want to get to know me too. Or maybe not. Sorry, that was presumptuous of me." He blushed and turned away for a minute, which Maggie found oddly charming. "Let me get that drink for you first."

"Thanks, but I'm okay with this one for now. I said yes before to be polite, which really means to avoid revealing too much too quickly and maybe getting into trouble. I didn't really learn all the 'polite woman' stuff from my parents. Though you don't have to because just hanging around other women in life teaches you. If you want to be a good girl, you do it one way; if you don't mind being seen as a bad girl, you had, in my view, a lot more options of how to act or what to say. Maybe you got some of my bad girl, cowboy. You are a cowboy, aren't you?"

"No, but I consider you thinking that a compliment. I come here often because I like the atmosphere and the music, so maybe in some small way I fit into the cowboy theme."

They both felt more relaxed and settled into quiet conversation. He slowly continued to drink his wine, and Maggie, surprising herself, surrendered to what she thought of as small talk, usually too trivial for her, but now in this moment glorious. *Just what the doctor ordered*, she thought.

CHAPTER 13

RUPERT WAS PERSPIRING. The heat generated in the crowded restaurant, the heat off the spicy soup he'd ordered, and certainly all the wine he'd consumed contributed to his sweating, but it was the anxiety bubbling up inside him that really made him sweat. He could hardly sit still. *I hope she doesn't think I suffer from hemorrhoids or something like that*, he thought.

He kind of liked Sylvia. In fact, though it embarrassed him to admit it, she sexually excited him. Her light-brown hair tied back in a ponytail accented a very pleasant face. He never had liked makeup on a woman, and Sylvia had on only a light shade of lipstick. She wore a tight-fitting shirt that showed off her nice figure and tight jeans. Although she had said she was close to sixty-five, she looked no older than fifty, if that. Under more normal circumstances, Rupert would have gracefully and quickly walked away, but tonight he stayed put—not still. His nerves tingled in places he didn't even know he had nerves, his heart beat wildly, and his knees shook so much he feared she might feel the vibration coming up through her stool. He dropped his head and looked away, wondering what she must think of this nervous wreck next to her.

What Rupert didn't know was that Sylvia actually liked nervous men, feeling more secure and safe around them. She started to tell him about her work and life in Vancouver. At twenty-two, she had married and then divorced at twenty-seven after they both had ventured into sexual affairs. Her affair had not been romantic, nor did it last long. She just did it for "the good sex. My marriage was over by that time. My husband had lost interest in me sexually, probably the result of all the sex he was having with his newfound girlfriend. I thought I was pretty experimental and fun in bed, but I think he wanted a younger version of me."

Rupert thought her sharing this with a stranger was a little inappropriate and dangerous, but he liked it. He doubted she went to church, at least not the kind of church he'd come from. He thought, *probably a Protestant!* He chuckled at his own joke, which made Sylvia uneasy.

"Are you laughing at me?"

"No, no I'm not. Please forgive me. I just had a funny thought."

"Are you going to share this funny thought?"

Rupert blushed. "It was a Catholic joke—archaic but it still bounces around in some circles that Protestants are morally looser than we Catholics."

"And . . .?"

"So, I was thinking you must be a Protestant, which tickled my fancy."

"Well, morally I'm a feminist. I have come to believe, like Virginia Woolf, that 'the eyes of others our prisons; their thoughts our cages.'"

Rupert thought, *How bold, how different.* Though he knew his face was still bright red, he was not about to back out. Something had changed for him in the last twenty-four hours. He'd lost much of the authority he always had over his feelings. Now he found his long-nurtured discipline and self-restraint were wavering and Sylvia a challenge he wanted to accept. But could he?

Sylvia could hardly believe what she'd fallen into when she innocently entered this restaurant. As she talked with Rupert, she could see how conflicted he felt. He was fighting something, and this ignited her enthusiasm to keep talking.

She was an English literature professor at the University of British Columbia with a fascination for all things literary. Over the years, though, she had grown tired of all the political shenanigans that went on among well-educated people competing for attention and recognition. Sylvia told Rupert about all the plotting and intrigue that went on to gain status or just to get more money, but then she stopped mid-sentence when Rupert got up as if to leave, making her wonder what she'd said to make him flee now. She watched him, her fascination with his contradictions growing.

Rupert struggled to stay put, but as Sylvia talked about the politics at her school, memories of all the scheming, even sleaze, he'd encountered in church administration flooded back. Almost involuntarily he tried to stand, but as he did, he felt dizzy and sat back down. What was happening to him? This had never happened before. He'd always felt in control during uncomfortable situations like this, but now nothing felt the same. Then, out of the blue, he remembered that he had left his priest's collar, his protection, in the car. That was it. *Well*, he thought, *too late now*.

Sylvia thought he looked pale and tired, his wrinkles deepened. "What's happening?"

"Wish I knew," he responded.

She reached out to help him either get up or sit down, and that made him jump.

Her hand on him in this vulnerable state startled him. "Don't touch me!"

His command startled Sylvia, and she quickly let go but didn't move far away. He didn't scare her. She knew Rupert was no threat to anyone. In fact, she thought, maybe Rupert should give out a few more orders.

Rupert's fear was still rising faster than the tide back home, but he said nothing. He was glad Sylvia stayed close. If he did faint, maybe she was close enough to keep him from hitting his head on the floor. If he didn't faint, he would just try to enjoy the closeness, the warmth, the bouquet of odors, and the intimacy he had started to feel. Women had gotten close to him before, but those were different. He never felt threatened or close to them. He knew they were really only snuggling up to his collar and what it represented, not him, the person. Then five more words popped unbidden in his head: the one who needed it.

Sylvia looked around the crowded restaurant. No one except her seemed aware of Rupert's apparent distress. *Funny*, she thought. *Isn't he from this area? Doesn't anyone recognize him?* As he struggled like this, she began to see him as a man, not a priest. Sylvia decided to risk touching him again and reached over to steady him.

Rupert said nothing, and she held him at the waist. He didn't even want to say anything. All he wanted to do was to put his hand on her arm and squeeze. He didn't. Actually he couldn't do it. Not yet, but something familiar and strangely different did swell up in him. He detected faith rising up, not faith in a higher being, but faith as in trust, a growing confidence that maybe, just maybe, he wasn't alone in this moment.

They stayed together like this, her holding him and him allowing it all to unfold. They didn't speak with words but with a new language to him—touch—sharing their feelings of safety, concern, and appreciation.

Finally, Sylvia said, "Let me drive you home."

Shocked by her quick return to the world of words, Rupert said, "No thanks," and started to get up. She helped him as he wobbled toward the door but then realized they hadn't paid for dinner. Turning back with Sylvia still at his side, he pulled his wallet out, sat back down, and called the waitress over. "What do we owe you?"

"The bill's right there in front of you," she said, frustrated. It had been a busy night. The waitress took both of their Visa cards and then returned for their signatures. They signed and again started for the exit, Rupert moving better without Sylvia's help now.

He noticed how quickly he'd reverted to his old ways, hiding and lying about himself. It was where he had always been most comfortable, but tonight, he was anything but that. Rupert had never even considered bringing a woman home, and he was now headed out to do just that. His dizziness returned, a result mostly of his confusion about what to do.

Sylvia was excited and wondering what would come next. What happened surprised her.

"Is that offer to drive me home still an option?"

"Sure, let's go."

Sylvia took his arm and almost led him out the door. He felt her touch, but rather than feeling it as a burn that hurt, he continued to feel it as warmth and comfort coming from her. They walked together to his car and got in. (He hoped he'd cleaned the car enough after masturbating.)

Details about how she might get back to her car later didn't even enter his mind, nor, evidently hers since it was not mentioned.

Making small talk as she drove helped Sylvia keep her emotions in check and she hoped his too. "What a beautiful and rugged landscape you have in this area. I've never spent time here, but it has been on my list of trips to take for at least five years. A lot of my travel now comes around work and departmental responsibilities. Recently I've been trying to write a biography and have had to travel some to do research. Not much time remains for me to visit northern BC. When I retire, maybe, but I'll have to wait till that time comes before knowing for sure what I'll do. Probably like you did, just settle down in some remote outpost and hide away."

That woke Rupert from his emotional stupor. "No, my retirement to this beautiful area was determined by the Church, just like my whole life. The local diocese owns the house where I live. I pay a small monthly stipend to make it a rental for tax purposes." Why was he telling her this? He'd just met Sylvia, and yet he wanted to tell her more. He wanted her to know how lonely he'd been for so long, how he'd never found the God of his dreams, and how his sister had just broken down the wall surrounding his heart. Rupert couldn't focus on where to go. Unfamiliar feelings coursed through him. Fear mixed with sadness, disorientation mixed with a surprising sense of inner calm, affection mixed with a desire to run, escape. In addition, though he didn't want to think about it, he was feeling sexually excited. *No, it can't be*, he thought. *Priests are celibate— or are supposed to be anyway.* There'd been plenty of sex in the church, and he knew it was not always consensual, but it was always a secret. He'd never had sex with anyone. But now . . .

Usually good at insignificant and meaningless small talk with church people and always in control, now Rupert felt out of control, jumpy, and overwhelmed. He could not say which word fit him best. He tried reminding himself how people had always seen him as stable, solid, "someone I can lean on" they'd say. He started to tear up but turned away so Sylvia couldn't see him. Then he laughed. "Guess I fooled them," just came out, loud and clear.

Sylvia, who'd continued talking while he was trying to figure out what was happening, stopped when he spoke.

"Oh, sorry, I was just thinking about something else."

She waited for more—nothing came. *Here we go again*, she thought, *just like when he laughed at a private joke.*

They sat in silence for the remaining short drive.

CHAPTER 14

PULLING INTO THE DRIVE, Sylvia saw a small, one-story bungalow. The entrance was lit by a modest porch light, but the darkness of the hour made it almost impossible to see much. "God, it's dark out here," she said. "Guess the stars just don't do the job of a couple of good street-lights, do they?

They both laughed at that. Then she got out, went around the car, opened Rupert's door, much as a chauffeur might have, and waited for him to get out.

Is she going to stay? he wondered to himself. *How weird is this? A woman comes home with a strange man at night, out in the wilder-ness, without protection. Any normal woman,* he thought, *probably wouldn't come in the first place. But if she did, she'd leave right away, heading back to her motel, or she'd be on high alert, ready to run at any moment.*

Sylvia looked at ease, comfortable, almost as if she were right at home. In his current state of mental and emotional turmoil, Rupert questioned himself more than her. What were his motives? Was he a threat to her? He didn't know. *Someone, please tell me, can she trust me?* he thought. His anxiety, which couldn't get much higher, swelled again. He heard Sylvia talking and then made out that she was asking him if he was going to get out. "Oh, sorry," he said and exited.

He must have looked a little unsteady because she gently put her hand behind him.

Rupert took the car handle to steady himself. "I'm okay," he lied. In the side mirror, he caught a glimpse of himself. "Oh my God," he said out loud, "I've lost my collar," forgetting he had removed it before entering the restaurant.

"What collar?"

"The collar I wear, my identity, my uniform." Rupert ran to the house. No key. He fumbled in his pockets and saw Sylvia coming up the porch behind him. It took him about three minutes to locate his keys and open the door, but to Rupert, all his fumbling and struggle to open the door took an eternity. Scared and insecure, he felt split between driving Sylvia back to the restaurant or inviting her in for tea. He entered without saying anything.

Sylvia followed.

Rupert turned on a light, turned toward her, and asked, "Would you like a cup of tea before heading back?"

"Yes."

Rupert laughed again.

"What's so funny, Rupert?"

"This is so bizarre. I just had the thought that I must have fallen down the rabbit hole. I'm in Kansas!"

Now Sylvia laughed with him. "You're nuts!"

"Maybe." He then thought, *Only God knows, and maybe even He doesn't have a clue!*

Rupert directed Sylvia to the living room, and he headed for the kitchen. But before he got far, he saw Sylvia sit down in *his* chair. He said nothing. He couldn't. His brain yelled, Mayday, mayday!" but his mouth remained still.

CHAPTER 15

MAGGIE HAD STOPPED DRINKING, but her new friend ordered a Ballast Point. *Well, at least he has a good taste in beer*, she thought. "Good choice," she said.

"Thanks. I used to live in San Diego where this company started, but now, since it was bought out by a larger company, you can easily get a can up and down the West Coast, maybe farther. It's expensive but has great flavor. Nectar of the gods."

"Not my brother's God, I'm sure," Maggie said. "His God comes before beer, family, or friends, especially family. He serves God, not family."

"Do I hear a little resentment there? Wait—before saying more, let me introduce myself. I'm Jake, Jake Newman." He held out his hand.

Grabbing it with a firmness Jake had not expected, she said, "Maggie Callaway here. Nice to meet you . . . I think."

Jake went on, "Did I hear resentment?"

"No, you think? What was your first clue?"

"Well, from what clues I've heard so far, your brother's about to get cut out of the will."

What's with this guy? Maggie wondered. *Is this what people do who meet in a bar?* She was on foreign soil. She'd traveled to many places, China, Australia, South Africa, but never to a local pub. It was all so new, so different for her, but she had to admit it felt damned exciting. A little chill ran up her spine. "Good idea, but oh, wait, he wasn't even in my will in the first place. A brother who abandons family for his God is not one worth recognizing in life, much less death. Abandoned for God is the worst. How does one compete with that? You can't, even if you want to, and oh, dumb me, I tried. Abandoned by someone for another lover, you can fight like hell and make that person's life quite miserable. With him, I couldn't fight. I'd lost before I started. I cried, internally, of course, when Rupert left, walking out of my life for his Church, the monastery, and a life with his God, not me. Shit, this upsets me so much. Guess I'm still stewing, aren't I?"

Jake felt her ferocity growing. *Maybe she really is almost out of time and needs to get this off her chest*, he thought. He knew many strange things happened in bars, but never to him. That seemed to be changing, and he liked it. "Guess you came in second to God. Hard to beat those odds."

"Damn straight. He fell hook, line, and sinker for an illusion, for an easy way out. Sure, our life at home was hard. Immigrants in a new world, parents trying to survive while hanging on to the old ways. Kids always pay a price for that. You've no doubt heard about all the horrible and goofy things that go on in families, not just immigrant families. But in ours, the kids got neglected. Rupert and I by ourselves had to deal with life's shit side, and there wasn't another side. Did we help each other? No. He followed his chance at salvation, and I was left to figure things out in the real world. Sure, I was smart, but give me a break. Being smart doesn't equal knowing anything, but in the end, my smarts helped me survive, got me wealth and fame but not happiness, satisfaction, or contentment. I've been so mad at Rupert for my whole life. Now I can say that underneath all my vicious and sometimes murderous rage I-I-I so missed him." Maggie turned away from Jake.

He knew she had started to cry. Jake said nothing. She had touched him, his sympathy, his compassion. What could he say? He sat there staring at his beer.

Maggie appreciated the silence. She felt his sympathy, and in that she felt his concern. Maybe for the first time, Maggie felt heard, but she also knew that maybe—no, not maybe, truly the first time—she'd shared her story in this way. She thought, *It takes a stranger . . .* but couldn't finish. She really had no idea where this would all go.

After a while Jake said, "I never had a brother. There were two sisters, one older and one younger—yeah, I'm the middle kid, but no brother."

"Well, Rupert was a brother and all I had. Selfishly I didn't want him to leave me. Right now, though, I want you to know I cared about him. I may never have showed that to him or anyone. What do you expect from a younger sister?"

"Life can be such a bitch," he said.

She agreed wholeheartedly.

Jaxson was filling up. The music had not yet started as the band was still setting up. Maggie had hardly noticed all the activity around them but did notice, as did Jake, the noise level increasing. They became quiet. Their drinks sat in front of them still half full.

Maggie pulled her phone from her back pocket. She needed to call Theresa. Talking so much about Rupert made her want to know if she'd heard from him yet. She dialed.

Theresa answered after the first ring. "No, nothing yet. I thought I'd wait a few days before checking back with him. As I told you before, I will let you know as soon as I hear something."

"Thanks, I'll try to wait." Waiting was all she did now. She waited to die, and more immediately, she had to wait for a response from her brother. *Maybe I'll die first*, she thought. She turned to Jake. "You still here? Waiting for me to die?"

Jake heard the tenseness in her voice, though she tried to mask it with humor. "No, nowhere else to be except with you right now. If you die, I guess I'll have to think of something else to do, but so far, you look alive but preoccupied."

"Well, I don't feel like entertaining tonight."

Jake did not respond to her biting sarcasm, knowing she was baiting him, readying him for the attack to come.

Without his response, Maggie became quiet too. Not for long, however. She quickly became more impatient and angrier. She wanted a fight, and Jake wasn't doing his part to help her get one. This confused her since most men she knew were easy targets for intimidation. They had such fragile egos. Women could easily frighten them with their words or even their dress. Their need to dominate made them vulnerable to manipulation and control.

Probably Rupert too. *Being a good Catholic*, she thought, *he probably lives with such guilt and shame that, rather than outright aggressiveness, he'd offer himself up as the helpful servant, wanting to help this obviously upset woman with her problem.* The priest's defense against vulnerability: show no weakness, control, dominate.

Jake wasn't following pattern. Why? She did not try to answer that but, instead, turned toward him, as if to say something, but did not. The words filling her head were all jumbled up, a disorganized mess. Maggie opened her mouth as if to say or yell something, but instead her head fell forward, and her body slumped over toward the counter as if defeated, a feeling she had struggled against her whole life. Suddenly she'd turned into a child, not the woman who had led hundreds of people every day, directed them in their work, fired them when they didn't perform to standards, and hired more to replace those she let go. The thought of defeat was almost too much to endure. Maggie had never felt more like destroying something than she did right at this moment.

A glass, she assumed must be hers, sat in front of her. It was short and thick at the bottom and felt heavy when she picked it up. She twirled it between her hands and then turned it over, spilling the remains of her drink all over the counter and down on to her clothes. Normally that would have horrified her, but now she hardly took notice. She just kept twisting and turning the glass between her hands. Then she yelled at the bartender. "I want another drink."

When he didn't immediately respond, Maggie started to pound her glass on the bar while yelling—BOOM—BOOM—ba-ba—BOOM—BOOM—BOOM—ba-ba—BOOM. Her head dropped down to her chest on each BOOM and flew back on each ba-ba. A few other patrons near her picked up the beat.

Someone yelled, "Go lady."

The bartender was not happy. He yelled so he could be heard above all the racquet. "Hey, lady, stop that."

"I want another one, now."

The bartender could see she had spilled almost a full glass on the bar. "Okay, Okay, I'll get you one." He went off and returned quickly, placing it on the bar in front of her.

Maggie didn't feel like thanking him or saying anything remotely polite. She took the glass and put it down hard on the counter, sneering at him the whole time.

He just stared at her and said, "If you continue to cause a disturbance, I will need to ask you to leave." Then he walked away to serve others.

Maggie had stared right back at him but remained quiet until he'd walked away. Then she said in a quieter voice than before, "Fatuous fool!"

Jake hadn't spoken a word but now said, "The glasses in this place don't break easily. You really have to bang them a lot harder on the counter. Even then, you may just put a mark in the wood versus breaking one."

His sarcasm annoyed her more. "Oh, just shut up, will you? I'm trying to decide whether to aim this at the head of that barman or at that pretty glass hanging over the bar. Let me think—draw blood or just make a big mess—what?"

Jake didn't want to walk out before he got thoroughly embarrassed or maybe even arrested along with her, but it was tempting. He thought, *This is beyond my pay grade, WAY over my head, beyond reason, for sure.* Since he had no idea what the right thing to say was, he just blurted out a response he might have used with his commanding officer while serving in the military. "Okay, ma'am. Shutting up now."

"Don't call me ma'am. It makes me feel old."

Jake waited to see what would happen next, expecting the worst. But nothing happened. He thought he heard Maggie whimper but didn't dare look. She had slumped over again, so it would have been difficult to see her face anyway. He looked straight ahead, thinking that if he had been a religious man he'd be praying. Jake had run out of resources on the physical and mental planes and felt totally unfamiliar with stuff on the spiritual plane. He thought to himself, *If only I hadn't slept through all those sermons when I was a kid.* This thought tickled his fancy, but he didn't dare laugh. He was trying to not even breathe.

Jake then heard the glass slam down on the table. He looked Maggie's way and saw her take about four napkins, wad them up, douse them in her new drink, and heave it at the waiter. It sailed about halfway there but never made it. Instead, it landed in someone's soup—vegetable beef—just as the patron was about to eat, splashing broth on the bar and all over the patron's face.

Maggie had watched it happen. "Missed."

Jake said, "Uh-oh."

Other people at the bar who saw this just stared at Maggie, not sure how to respond. The man splashed with soup was busy wiping his face. Then he too looked Maggie's way. What happened next shocked everyone.

"Maggie, was that you?" He got up and walked over for a better look. "Well, I'll be damned, it is you, which I must admit, Maggie, is more of a surprise than it was to be doused with soup. What in the world is going on with you? Last I knew you were convalescing after surgery."

Maggie finally looked up at him. "Oh hi, Darryl."

The bartender came over accompanied by several big burly men Jake had not seen before. "I'm sorry ma'am. You are going to have to leave."

When Maggie didn't move right away, he said, "Now."

Jake got up and helped Maggie off her stool. He put forty dollars on the counter for the drinks they'd had and then guided Maggie toward the door.

Darryl, still standing nearby said, "Bye. See you at the office."

Maggie said nothing more, though by now everyone in the bar could have heard her since the once noisy pub had become eerily quiet. She and Jake walked out into the late afternoon sun of San Francisco.

It took a moment for Maggie's eyes to adjust to the blur of the sun outside, but she seemed to wake up from whatever delusion or illusion she'd fallen into inside.

Jake asked if she needed to sit down.

She quickly said, "Yes, but someplace on the street, maybe a bench near a bus stop. I have no desire to enter another restaurant or store right now."

Maggie remembered everything she'd done in the pub, especially how what she'd thrown hit Darryl's soup. The feelings and thoughts that had motivated all that had gone, though she didn't know why. Now she felt ashamed, humiliated, and embarrassed by it all but not remorseful. In fact, even with all her feelings, she started to laugh at how she managed to hit Darryl, a man who prided himself a lady's man. She could still see him strutting around the office in his too-tight jeans, flirting and putting the moves on any of the women he wanted to date (or, more likely, bed). Maggie thought, *If he had not also been so good at his job, I would have fired him. He deserved hot soup in the face.*

Jake was busy looking for a bench, but he also kept his eye on Maggie. Frankly, he didn't trust what she might do next. He saw her laugh, and though curious, he didn't ask what was so funny for fear it might trigger her anger. Finally, he said, "Well, Maggie, it seems we are in a part of San Francisco without bus service. So far, I've seen no bus stops and no benches."

Maggie had never spent much time with men outside of work. She had what she called her "love of learning" to entertain her, and after that, she had the challenges of her job. So now, she wondered, *What in the world am I doing walking the streets of San Francisco, looking for a bench with a man I just met in a bar?* An old voice in her head told her to just walk away. He wouldn't try to stop her, after all, as they walked down a busy street in San Francisco. *Just walk to the street and hail a taxi.* This was tempting and would be easy to do. Maggie knew this voice well. It was her goddess, her higher power, and it had kept her safe over all her years until it hadn't! Though she knew it was crazy, she now thought to herself, *until you got cancer. She failed you, Maggie. You smoked a lot. She never directed you away from the cancer sticks.*

Maggie stopped dead in her tracks. Jake kept walking but then noticed she'd stopped, and he turned to go back. People who'd been walking behind her had to make a quick turn to avoid hitting her from behind. Jake's instincts told him not to touch her, so he just stood next to her, quietly directing other pedestrians around.

The powerlessness Maggie felt overwhelmed her, but now, without any warning, all her questions about what she was doing with this strange man went away. She looked in Jake's direction and said, "Shall we go?"

They then walked on together, Jake still looking for a bench, but Maggie didn't care anymore. She had surrendered to him. The fight she'd always felt before had gone, for how long she didn't know, but for now it was gone.

Though Maggie was beginning to feel tired, she also felt like walking. She imagined she wasn't walking down the street with Jake but was walking either away from something that was or toward something that would be. That caused her to wonder just how a dying old lady like her could still suffer from so much unknowing, so much ignorance about herself. *How can someone be so blind after living with so much self-discipline and knowledge?* she wondered.

"I think I'd like to walk till I drop. I know I said I wanted to find a place to sit, but now I just want to go—and to go with you."

Jake thought to himself, *Wow, this is one weird, fascinating woman.*

"Are you just one stupid, naïve man or . . .?" At first Maggie couldn't continue the thought. "Or are you some avatar? You look like a man, talk like a man, but you sure don't act like a man. Beginning with my father until now, the men I've known have avoided situations where they aren't in charge, avoided complexity, and sought out simplicity."

"An avatar? Boy, my kids would cringe if they heard that. No, I'm no avatar, but yes, I am a man. I always thought of myself as a pretty simple man, Maggie. Between the two of us, your star has shown brighter than mine in this world. Who else could throw a wad filled with snot and spit into the soup of someone she knows in a tavern she's never entered before? Go figure."

Maggie kept walking but slower. She felt more and more weary and wondered how much further she could go. Was she supposed to go until she dropped or until she found something new in her life? "Unrealistic," she said out loud but to no one in particular.

Jake could see that Maggie was tiring fast. "I finally see a bench ahead. How about we sit down? I, for one, am feeling a little fatigued by our walking and all that's happened."

They went to the bench and sat down.

Neither of them spoke. Jake thought about how he'd gone to Jaxson for a drink, a little relaxation, and maybe some good country music but then ended up with this strange and bewitching woman. She was older (he had no idea how old, but he was sure she was older than him), she was dying (or at least said she was), and she evidently lived among the rich and famous of San Francisco, though she certainly didn't act like it. *What a drama*, he thought. *Does facing imminent death change us? Does my fear of death somehow limit me? Has Maggie changed as she has accepted that she soon will be dead?* Jake was torn from his reflections by Maggie asking him to tell her something more about his life.

"Here, I've monopolized all the time we've had so far, and I'm curious about you, Jake. What makes you tick? Needless to say, you confuse me."

"I have no idea what that means, Maggie. What makes me tick? First of all, I don't tick. Clocks tick, I breathe. But on a more mundane level, I love my kids, life in the city with easy access to movies, theater, and the ballet, Italian food, and of course, country music. I live alone in a condo not far from here, so I often stop in at Jaxson, where we just were, in the late afternoon or early evening for beer and music. Nice, friendly place most of the time, and it seems to attract interesting people—like you. When I got there this afternoon, I saw an empty stool AND I saw you on the adjacent stool. From the back you looked relaxed and, because you looked older, no offense, maybe sophisticated enough to carry on a good conversation. I'm beyond looking for the young and innocent who want to impress me or want me to impress them. So I chose the stool next to you."

"Maybe that's something good about getting older," Maggie interjected. "We can talk before seducing each other." She laughed. "Just joking, Jake. For me, getting older meant only more of the same, surviving until I die. I had hoped there was more, just as my brother, Rupert, did. I, however, found hope to be empty. It exists for the ignorant among us who have no idea how to live or for those who get stuck along the way. I count myself among those who got stuck early in life and became cocky in her abilities to go it alone.

"I kept people away by design. I felt safer. I tried to figure life out by myself, and I did pretty damn good, at least if money and status mean anything. Except they don't, Jake. Money and status give the illusion of control and power, but just a few minutes ago, while walking down the street with you, I was struck by the reality of my powerlessness in life. Life conquered me. I have not conquered life. Death is my reward, my final statement. Greatness and smallness both end the same. From pent-house to grave, planted like someone's backyard roses."

Jake had no idea if Maggie was talking to him or to herself. He could hardly hear her she spoke so softly. Though she seemed to be looking out at the street, she acted like she saw nothing. Her body was completely still, so different than she'd been in the tavern. For him, the city street had come alive. He noticed more people coming to the bus stop, more buses stopping, and more people pacing around, some, he knew, hoping they could soon sit down on the bench currently occupied by Maggie and himself. He began to feel self-conscious and started to look for a way out. He found one when his stomach growled.

Across the street from where he and Maggie sat was Mama Leone's, a little Italian bistro he liked. "How about we grab a bite over there, Maggie?"

As usual, Maggie didn't have much of an appetite but liked the idea of going someplace with him. "Okay, but I have no idea if this restaurant is any good."

"I do," he said and led her across the street toward the entrance.

They were directed to a table, sat down, and started to scan the menu. Jake knew he wanted the spaghetti and meatballs. This place had a good spicy sauce and well-seasoned meatballs, the kind even a non-Italian would die for. Maggie spent more time deciding. When the waiter arrived, she ordered a plate of plain pasta. Her stomach couldn't tolerate lots of sauce and spice. Jake gave his order and asked the waiter to bring a nice bottle of Erath Winery Pinot Noir from Oregon. He knew ordering Oregon wine in California was frowned upon by some, but he didn't care.

After the waiter left, Maggie told Jake she didn't plan to drink any more tonight.

"Don't worry about it. I'll just drink the whole bottle."

"Wow. Guess I'm with a budding or seasoned alcoholic."

Jake laughed. "No, Maggie, I was just joking. I'll take what we don't drink home. That's allowed here in California, you know."

Maggie said nothing, but he could see she had a slight smile on her face. She was feeling less irritated and even feeling okay about letting

Jake lead her here. An unsettling sort of "what the hell" attitude had settled over her. Maybe she was tired, but for whatever reason, she didn't or couldn't fight. Their food and wine came. Jake dug in, hungrier than he'd realized.

Maggie took a forkful of her pasta and stopped. "Tasteless."

"Does that mean kind of blah?"

"You got it." Maggie took a sip of the wine and found it very good, but she had no more. She didn't eat much. Then as she sat back in her chair, a question popped into her head, *Is this what people call being happy?* Maggie had just done what she had to do and survived, the good and the bad. But now, she wondered if she was ever happy.

Jake wanted to know more about Maggie. "What do you hope will happen with your brother, Rupert?"

"I wish I knew," she said. "When I wrote my letter, I fantasized that Rupert and I would have this grand reunion, but since writing it, I've mostly regretted putting myself out like that. I don't know what he'll do or say, and it makes me nervous. If he's willing to meet me, maybe we'll find a neutral location to rendezvous, say Seattle, and I'll fly up there with Theresa in tow.

"If I don't hear anything or he refuses to talk, then my path is clear. They say I have maybe a year, maybe less, to live, but as we both know, doctors play a guessing game with patients like me. Of course, they base what they say on the general experience of others who've had lung cancer, but individuals differ. Right? Whatever time I have left I'll let it play out around here in San Francisco. I'll make it to the end as I always have, though this time I am performing the final act. Finis, no more of me on this earth. But then, how much of me have I really lived in my time?"

"Have you ever talked about your life in therapy?"

"Therapy? That's for other people. I face my demons straight on, face-to-face, demon to demon."

"Sounds like you've survived life, Maggie, just like the rest of us. I've stumbled through life, sometimes surprised by it all, sometimes overwhelmed, and even sometimes satisfied with outcomes. Tonight, for example, trying to avoid some bookwork I had to do, I decided to go out looking for entertainment and dinner. Then I stumbled into you. How does this stuff happen? Fiction mimicking real life or real life mimicking fiction?"

Silence.

"Don't answer that. Forget my questions, Maggie. Who cares? Let's get back to you, you the suffering survivor!"

"Well, I'll think about your survivor label, but right or wrong, I've lived life as a bitch, pushing myself and everyone around me to accomplish something. Like the captain on *Star Trek: Enterprise*, my mantra was, 'make it so!' And we did. That company grew tenfold over my career, but now, facing the end, I feel so empty with no family, no real friends, just a few people I've hired to help me, and no hope. Interesting. I wonder, did I ever really have any hope?

"You asked me before what I thought might happen when I see Rupert, and I said I don't know, which is true. But now I think there might have been more truth in that response than I knew. For maybe the first time in my life, I'm taking a step into the void, and though I may sound strong and together, I'm feeling really scared. Literally scared shitless! I've been constipated for the last four days!"

Maggie felt shocked by her own candor in front of someone she hardly knew but she noticed that Jake was just softly smiling—obviously not offended. She looked down at her still-full plate of pasta. She forked some noodles and twirled them right into her mouth. While she chewed, she said, "These noodles are cold, tasteless, and bland." She spit them out. Staring at her plate she said, "I didn't think I could still do that. That was five-year-old Maggie, not refined and polished sixty-three-year-old Maggie." She stopped a moment and then said, "I guess throwing that wad into Darryl's soup qualified as a five-year-old act too, didn't it?" She laughed, but not a shallow laugh like usual. This was a belly laugh, and it rolled out of her.

Jake watched her laugh. Then he started to laugh. "Did they put marijuana in our drinks, Maggie? I feel high."

"I don't think that's what's going on, Jake. I don't know what it is, but I'm loving it."

"Me too."

Finally, they both were able to stop laughing. Looking around, Maggie noticed people staring at them. Jake had seen this too but tried to ignore it. Maggie, however, stood up, removed her napkin, held out her arms, and proceeded to quote from Shakespeare.

All the world's a stage,
And all the men and women merely players;
They have their exits and their entrances;
And one man in his time plays many parts,
His acts being seven ages.

Maggie gave an exaggerated bow, took an erect posture, and sat down.

Within seconds, someone began to clap, and a few others followed. Most in the restaurant looked away, as they might if a homeless person had entered a place like this and caused a disruption.

Feelings of embarrassment rose to the surface, and Maggie looked away.

Jake, feeling somewhat embarrassed himself (some of the wait staff knew him from previous visits), still had to smile at what just happened. He bent low, mimicking Maggie, and said, "These people aren't used to that kind of thing here. They usually have to pay for their entertainment."

Maggie looked over at him and saw he still had a smile on his face. "Believe me, I'm not used to it either, Jake, and I haven't ever paid for it. So unusual, so unlike me," and then she added, "and so much fun." That made her laugh again. This time, however, she worked hard to quell it, hoping only Jake would hear. He did, but no one else even looked over. Maggie straightened up. "Wow. That was different, and, you know what?" She leaned across the table and put her hands around her mouth. "I don't even feel humiliated, like I did. Can you believe it?" She smiled, not because she thought it was funny but because of how proud she felt of herself. "Let's order dessert."

"Okay. I know I'm repeating myself, but you're one strange, no, odd, woman." He then quickly added, "But, I have to admit, pretty unique . . .

to me, anyway. I think something sweet to finish off our evening would work just fine."

Maggie didn't know what to say, but really, she didn't want to say anything. She was savoring the moment. Somehow, she knew if she tried to talk now, she might just try to analyze what happened and THAT, above all, was what she didn't want to do.

She raised her hand for the waiter. He came right over, probably thinking they were going to leave, but when he arrived, she said, "Do you have a dessert menu?" When he looked at her with surprise, she just continued in a normal tone of voice, "We're ready to see what sweets you have tonight."

"Sure, I'll be right back."

Jake added, "Oh, and please bring me a nice glass of sherry, will you?"

"Any particular one?"

"No. Just something not too expensive."

"Okay, I'll be right back."

Maggie and Jake looked at each other. To Maggie, Jake looked happy but also like he was expecting something to happen. To Jake, she had a look of satisfaction but also a look of wonderment. Both were in unknown territory.

CHAPTER 16

RUPERT STOOD IN HIS KITCHEN staring at the tea boxes in the second tier of three in the middle cupboard over his stove and workspace. The first shelf held spices from cinnamon to thyme, in alphabetical order. On the third shelf, he'd laid out items he seldom used, like a bottle of molasses, some honey a parishioner had given him long ago, seasonings for chicken and fish, and some spices he now couldn't recall why he'd bought, such as coriander and allspice.

Tonight, though, Rupert wanted tea. He usually had no trouble deciding which tea, like a chamomile before bed, but now, he just stared at his many varieties. After what seemed a long time, he pulled down a box of peppermint and turned to boil the water. He thought about how many times he'd done this ritual before. Mostly it had become an aimless habit, but he also made tea to try to calm an anxious moment.

Never had he made tea, or anything else, to entertain a woman, and certainly not a woman alone, unaccompanied, unattended, and attractive. Rupert tried desperately to think of it as a normal thing, no big deal, and yet he couldn't. The thought of sex popped in his head, unbidden, despite all his best efforts to stop it. He forgot about the tea and everything else. Dread took over, filling what felt to him like every pore of his body. He stood still, unable to move, momentarily hypnotized.

The teapot began to screech. Rupert did nothing.

Sylvia came in and saw him immobilized in time. Reaching around him, she removed the teakettle from the heat to stop that infernal noise. She then went over and sat at the kitchen table.

Rupert stared into space. He looked old and still a little unstable on his feet.

"Too many tea choices, eh? Complicates decision-making for me too. I always think better to have a few you drink all the time than to just fill the shelf with lots of options." She laughed, which broke the spell.

Rupert looked at her—her delicate smiling face staring back at him. His face reddened. He reached for the teapot forgetting to grab an oven mitt first. "Yeow!" And the pot full of water fell back on the stove, just missing falling off entirely. "Damn, damn . . . you fool, Rupert."

"Maybe I'll have a Scotch if you have some."

"Straight up, no ice, okay?" He didn't wait for her response. Rupert put two Scotches on the table.

He chugged his, she sipped hers.

"Fuck it. If you aren't going to leave, which you probably should, I have a lot to say about how fucked things have recently become in my nice ordered life."

This sudden outburst of profane language from a priest didn't frighten Sylvia but did pique her curiosity.

"I just heard from my sister, through her lawyer, that she has cancer, is dying, and wants to make contact with me. Now mind you, this comes after almost sixty years of no—and I mean that literally—no contact. No verbal or written contact. I can't even recall having had thoughts about her in all that time. Until yesterday, I didn't even know if she was alive or dead, nor did I think I cared. However, now my thoughts and feelings have been thrown into turmoil, jumbled up, unrecognizable. How can this happen? She meant nothing to me, as did every other member of my family. I left them. I wanted more and chose the life of the church as the life I fancied I wanted. Life, as I knew it at home, was intolerable, and I got out, leaving it all behind. Now a ghost has risen, awakening a ghostly past. And I feel sick." Rupert ran for the bathroom and vomited, loudly, further embarrassing himself. Ten minutes later he came out, towel in hand, wiping his face. "Sorry about that, but I do feel better!"

He sat down, looked at Sylvia, and smiled. "You know, Sylvia, having you here like this has caused me a greater trauma even than receiving Maggie's letter, and I thought at the time there could be nothing worse. Makes me wonder what's coming next."

He smiled and noticed that she too had a smile on her face.

"I feel like another Scotch, but my rational self now has, I think, got enough control to say no to that."

Sylvia said nothing. She felt like holding him but didn't dare move. She instinctively knew her mothering instinct needed to be bounded.

Rupert used his towel to clean up the spit and saliva that had spilt down onto his shirt. "The dam has definitely cracked, Sylvia, and I can only hope it doesn't suddenly break. If it does, we both will drown in the flood to come."

Sylvia didn't move or blink.

He continued, "Ghosts don't really exist, do they? In Catholicism, spirits float between hell, purgatory, and heaven. Ghosts aren't real, and yet one has come to me as of yesterday and now casts its dark shadow over me. Maggie, that's my sister's name, in real life was needy of attention from anyone but especially from me. But what could I give her? I had nothing but empty feelings and aloneness. I couldn't give. I needed to take something for myself, but surrounded by what felt like a black hole, I grabbed at the church. But the certainty I thought would come from the church has now turned to doubt and uncertainty again. I'm right back where I started as a youth, not knowing and scared.

"Before the massive interruption of Maggie's letter, I never could have owned up to this. But it's all true, true, true, true. I'm feeling all the sorrow, grief, and pain I thought I'd left at home. How could this be happening? This stuff is only supposed to happen to other people." Rupert's head dropped to the table; he sobbed quietly.

Sylvia came over and put her arm over his shoulders. She couldn't help herself, feeling so touched by his outpouring of emotion. People's pain reached deep into her, and she'd gained a reputation in her family and among friends as a soft touch. Most of the time she heard this as it was meant—a criticism—but, through years of therapy, she'd come to learn how to control it and accept it as sensitivity.

Rupert felt threatened by her touch, but he also felt less scared of it. Strange, yes, but what wasn't strange in his life right now? It felt good, comforting, reassuring, and even, he wanted to think, not particularly sexual. He was, however, feeling strange. He had no word for it, but it reminded him of that feeling he had before and during masturbation.

As Sylvia began to softly stroke Rupert's arm, his head came up, and he looked at her. His face was wet from crying and, he felt sure, smeared with dirt. At first nothing happened. They both seemed frozen in place, but they were far from frozen. Rupert felt an agony like he had never felt before. Sylvia was torn by her strong desire to move closer and her quickly diminishing self-control. The tension was becoming unbearable, but neither moved.

Sylvia didn't want to make the first move. Somehow, she knew this moment belonged to Rupert. She could see the sweat forming on his forehead, she could feel his body quivering, and she sensed Rupert was about to burst out in a rage where she might end up on the floor or with a sexual passion so strong she'd be thrown on the floor with him on top of her. Both scared her, but she still did not move.

Rupert tightened his grip, pulling her closer, until finally he tried to give her a kiss. Sylvia started to pull him closer but then remembered he'd just vomited. She hesitated a moment but then thinking, *So what*, she kissed him back, even penetrating his mouth with her tongue. Rupert, instinctively knew what to do. He kissed her deeply while moving his tongue with hers. In time, Rupert relaxed in her embrace and felt an energy flow through him, animating every part of his body. The old alarm bells he used to hear in his head whenever any sexual feelings arose, stayed silent. Their lips flowed together wet and smooth, absorbing Rupert ever more fully into the moment until, from deep inside him, something he tried to stop but couldn't, let loose—a joyous laugh.

That broke the kiss but not the mood. Sylvia began to laugh too. For a moment, he was transported to his perch by the sea, a place where he'd experienced so much joy before. This was different . . . better.

Sylvia felt jubilant herself. Of course, she'd kissed other men, but Rupert's kiss enlivened her in a different way. She dismissed it at first as just kissing a man who'd never passionately kissed before, much like that first kiss between teenagers, but then she just knew this was different. She and Rupert were grown adults, and this passion had years of experience behind it, even if unexpressed. Though her mother had always told her not to go home with strangers, she felt certain that coming here with Rupert had not been a mistake. She felt playful. "Do you think I could have another Scotch?"

Rupert laughed. "Sure." But he didn't get up. He'd masturbated many times before, though he now felt overpowered by his sexual arousal. His penis had hardened beyond any hardness he'd ever felt, overwhelming his embarrassment. The part of his brain telling him this was wrong was getting weaker and weaker. Rupert thought, *This can't be the Devil's work—it's too wonderful.* His body shivered and shook all over, causing him to wonder, for a moment, if he should stop. He wasn't going to stop. He had passed any point of control over what was happening. For maybe the first time, he felt fully alive, hypersensitive, perceiving things he had failed to notice before, and completely immersed in the moment. He thought to himself, *So this is what they didn't want us to do!* Then familiar words came to him and he quietly hummed: "Joy to the world! The Lord is come . . ."

CHAPTER 17

SYLVIA HAD GONE ON THIS TRIP NORTH in hopes of having an adventure. Her teaching had begun to feel dry and uninteresting. She'd taught the same classes too many times. Her department lacked the financing needed to hire new faculty, so everyone there had to teach the same classes over and over. She felt her writing had also begun to suffer. Though doing research helped enliven both her teaching and writing, she had little time for it. She believed she was losing her creative edge and had confided to her friends that she felt depressed. They encouraged her to go on a trip, to "take a break." She decided to try a short trip to Powell River.

It had now turned into more than Sylvia ever expected. Her lethargy had turned into excitement, at least for the moment. She was not getting many ideas for enlivening her writing or teaching, but she was getting aroused. Although she tried to look relaxed and in control, she felt tense and nervous. She had no sense that Rupert was seducing her. In fact, she decided he looked more like he might throw up again.

Rupert couldn't believe what was happening. He'd never felt so out of control, and yet somehow it didn't scare him. He felt like he was in shock but not having a shock reaction—no cold sweat, no dizziness, no confusion. No, even though this was way beyond anything he'd ever experienced, he sensed what he felt now was actually normal.

He wondered, for a moment, how this could be, but his excitement wouldn't let him go there. Rupert knew he wasn't going to stop, but he wanted to reduce the temperature a little, break the tension, and hopefully, halt his growing erection. "Why do you want someone like me? You seem confident, filled with passion. You write books and . . . have sex with men. I've never experienced passion. I've never even had sex, not once! I'm a lost, cloistered, inexperienced man hiding away in small-town Canada."

Saying this may have reduced his tension, but it made Sylvia a little mad. *Are we going to have a discussion?* she thought. *Now?* "You didn't draw me here because of your profession or your small-town life, Rupert. That would not have been a turn-on, quite frankly. I feel an attraction to you because of the open expression of your suffering. You have shown me, even if you did it reluctantly, an honest expression of your pain."

This made no sense to Rupert. Had he accidentally done something right? He knew he couldn't think about that now. The only real thinking he could do in this moment originated between his legs. "Did I upset you with my question?"

"Frankly, I thought your timing was really fucked up, excuse my French!"

"I guess there's a time for talking and a time for doing. Is this one of those for doing?"

Sylvia laughed and shouted, "Yes!"

They both were quiet. The energy had to build again. It didn't take long.

Sylvia spoke up first. "Why don't you come and sit on the couch with me?"

Rupert tried not to stare but couldn't look away. He wanted to see her, to not miss anything, from her long brown hair to the tips of her brightly painted toenails. Her lips were moist and inviting. She wore no makeup, her face plain but soft and welcoming. She had on a floral skirt and white blouse, nothing fancy but attractive, and wore no stockings. He fantasized about women just like this. Sylvia was all he had hoped for and he already knew kissing her was divine. She had invited him. Could he stop thinking and go to her? His head continued to argue vehemently and convincingly with his feelings, but this time his head was going to lose. Rupert let his body do the talking.

He got up and sat next to Sylvia, feeling her warmth but not just physical warmth: he felt the warmth of her openness, her acceptance, her submission. She was so at ease, while he felt stiff, awkward, and scared. What a contrast between them.

"It seems to me you must have done something like this before, Sylvia."

She laughed. "You think so, eh?"

Rupert put his arm around her and pulled her toward him. She received him in a way that helped him let go of some of his lifelong inhibitions and self-restraints. He trusted her to navigate her feelings, but he would have to wing it, improvise as he went. She reached out with her hand and took his to her lap. Rupert moved away quickly, so she gently laid her open hand between them. He took it and they squeezed.

"Wow, this is intense." In no way did he want things to stop, but he needed a little room to breathe. "Mind if I turn on some music?" Before she had time to answer he got up, found his CDs, and quickly chose several he played a lot: *A Fine Romance* by Ella Fitzgerald, *Round Midnight* by Thelonious Monk, and two albums by Joey Alexander, *My Favorite Things*, his first album, and *Countdown*.

"Jazz fan, eh?"

"Yeah. I like this stuff, though now, I wonder if jazz fits the mood."

"What mood are you referring to, Rupert?"

Oh well, he thought to himself, *we're living dangerously now*. "Romantic maybe?"

"In my limited experience, Rupert, romance adapts to any sound. Let it go; we'll see what happens."

His thoughts were invading his feelings again and no wonder. He could feel his hardness, his sexual desire rising. So, again, he shut off the debate he was having with himself by moving back to sit with her.

They sat together quietly listening to the music. Then, rather than just put his hand out for her to take this time, he put it on her thigh and began to caress her leg through her skirt. Sylvia put her head on his shoulder and her hand on his leg. He didn't try to move away.

They kissed, at first gently and cautiously, but then she slowly moved her tongue inside his mouth. Sylvia stroked his head, shoulders, and then his thigh. Rupert caressed her hair and face. She unbuttoned his shirt and moved her hands to his chest. He removed her blouse, struggling some to undo the buttons. She was not wearing a bra, so he could easily caress her breasts. He pulled back from kissing for a moment so he could look.

"You're staring," she said and smiled at him.

He smiled back but felt guilty. Sylvia interrupted that by starting to undo his pants. Rupert stood so she could pull them down, and then he released himself from all feelings of guilt. He was going to enjoy this moment. Slowly they undressed and then lay down on the couch. He was as hard as a rock. They wriggled and writhed around so much they fell on the floor.

"Ow!" Sylvia said.

But they found they could move more easily with more space. She held his penis, guiding him, and he entered her. Then they rolled over and over, taking turns being on top. Their sexual passion was alive and exhilarating. As Rupert expected, he came too quickly, but he had no desire to stop. The moment of enjoyment turned into many moments. His body trembled with pleasure. She was feeling full of joy and wonder. Finally, he had to stop.

"I should have started this when I was a lot younger."

Sylvia laughed. "I did start younger, but I'm still as exhausted as you right now."

How long they lay together neither really knew, but at some point, he again heard his jazz music playing in the background. It had disappeared during their lovemaking. "I can see now why the so-called mood music doesn't matter, Sylvia."

They got off the floor, dressed, and sat back on the couch. Rupert's body continued to tingle from all the excitement. His fear had vanished, but then his thoughts again moved in on his feelings. *You don't know this woman. What if she has some disease? If the diocese finds out about this, they could evict you from this house!* He couldn't stop himself. *Now, you're going to hell for sure!* He then responded to himself out loud, "Shut up!"

This spooked Sylvia but woke him to what he was doing. "What?" Sylvia asked as she began to get up.

"Sorry, I needed to send myself a message."

"Well, could you do it a little more gently and quietly?"

"I'll try, but that means overcoming years of self-flagellating criticisms. I might need some time."

The clock chimed twelve. Neither of them made a move to get up, and they soon fell asleep, exhausted but satisfied.

CHAPTER 18

RUPERT'S ALARM WENT OFF AT SEVEN. He and Sylvia had not moved from the couch, so he had to get up to turn it off. As he did, she said she was cold, and asked for a blanket.

"Sure."

After covering Sylvia with a blanket, Rupert headed for the bathroom, not sure if he would vomit or just pee. Last night had shaken him in so many ways. It all made no sense, but he wondered if it was supposed to and wondered if trying to figure it out would only further confuse things. He didn't vomit but did find himself smiling, which soon became laughter, which then turned to tears. His body began to shake, and for a moment he felt cold.

Sylvia, hearing all this from the living room, lightly knocked on the door. "Are you all right?"

"Yes, I'll be out in a moment."

"No rush."

That again made him smile. *No rush,* he thought. *Doesn't she know we're all rushing headlong toward our end?* Then Rupert checked himself. *How morbid is that? And in a moment when I felt so close to being at peace with myself.*

The toilet seat started digging into his bottom. He'd sat there too long. He got up, washed his face, and went out. "I'm finished if you need the bathroom. I'm going to make coffee."

Smelling the coffee helped motivate Sylvia. Getting up was always hard for her, even though she had had early classes and events her whole life. At one point, while in college, she'd even gotten up to go to the gym with friends. Peer pressure worked in those days. It didn't work later. More sleep always won out.

At this moment, Sylvia wanted coffee, but she also wanted to savor the good feelings she had from last night. So she dragged herself up, dressed, and headed for the bathroom. Immediately she caught Rupert's smell. Odors from his deodorant and aftershave filled the air. Memories of last night flooded her mind. She hadn't had sex like that in a long time, if ever. His naïveté had not in any way hurt her experience. In fact, it may have enhanced it. Sex always left her satisfied, but she couldn't recall it taking over her whole body like this time. *Oh dear, I hope I haven't fallen in love with him! He's a priest, for God's sake*, she thought. *I just met the guy!*

Sylvia stood, looking at herself in the mirror. Her face shone brightly, her hair fell loosely to one side and her lips still looked inviting, even without lipstick. "But you promised yourself you'd never fall for anyone again! Sex, yes, but nothing more," she admonished her reflection." *Oh, but you can't be falling for him so fast*, she thought. *It's not supposed to happen like that, except, maybe in romance novels. It must be just the good sex, nothing more.*

And then, almost to test her theory, she burst from the bathroom and found Rupert sitting in the kitchen nursing his coffee. "Let's do it again."

Rupert literally jumped. Then he pushed his chair back, stood up, and moved toward her. He couldn't stop himself and knew he really didn't want to; he wanted her again. Putting his arms around her waist, he drew her to him. But before kissing Sylvia, he said, "Let's go to the bedroom this time."

He took her hand and together they walked into his bedroom. They gently undressed each other. She stopped him before removing her panties and knelt. She motioned for him to come closer. At first Rupert didn't move, unsure of what she was doing. Sylvia motioned him to her again. When he approached, she gently took hold of his penis and put it in her mouth.

Rupert had seen pictures of this in magazines but never imagined it would happen to him. He let her take him but soon pulled her up, held her in a deep embrace, and tried to carry her to the bed. Definitely not a good idea.

They ended up ungraciously toppling on the bed, which luckily was nearby. Rupert tried to jump up, fearing he'd hurt her, but she held him down. She broke out laughing, which at first confused Rupert, but after realizing he'd not hurt her, he too began to laugh.

He removed her panties and inserted himself into her, this time without her help. They rolled around on the bed taking turns leading and following. Their movements flowed together. They touched each other in ways that both stimulated and enhanced the moment together.

It was after ten when they emerged from the bedroom. Sylvia had put on one of Rupert's robes, but he wore only a shirt and underpants. Both felt relaxed and now ready to finally have some of that coffee. She sat at the table while he poured each of them a cup.

"That really was better than sex," she said.

"What on earth does that mean? I thought we just had sex."

"Oh, we did, Rupert, and it was great. That comment was to myself, a continuation of a conversation I started in the bathroom. Private."

"I see. Well, I was having conversations with myself before too. I must admit, though, mine were muddled, unclear. Clarity seems to have escaped me since I heard from Maggie. Living in the church, we prided ourselves on how well we maintained order. People expected us to not change our clothes or the rituals. But I've fallen over a cliff and haven't hit bottom yet. You met me on the way down, grabbed hold, and helped take the fear from my fall. You've helped me feel—I don't know the right word—*human*? Maybe it's excitement or just surprise. It sounds crazy: I was a priest and now I'm a human. Wow. Now I guess I have to figure out what all that means. Maybe nothing. In the heat of the moment, I could just be making up bullshit. Priests are good at that."

"I wasn't raised Catholic, so it's all hearsay to me, but that's what people say." Sylvia laughed. "I feel more encouraged, more optimistic. Yes, that's the right word. I was pretty depressed when I left Vancouver, thinking maybe an adventure of some sort might help. I couldn't be happier having met you, Rupert. I came here feeling lost, confused, flummoxed about my life and what was happening to me. This morning I still don't have any answers, if there are any, but I feel, well, different. Words escape me, and that's surely new! Maybe the words will come if we do it again!"

"Wait a minute, Sylvia. Let me recover! Remember that was my first time. Well, actually my second!"

They both broke out laughing so hard that Sylvia, who had a mouthful of coffee, couldn't hold it. Coffee flew everywhere. Rupert reached out in a futile attempt to help her and his coffee cup went flying. They were laughing and covered in coffee.

"Oh look, Rupert, I've ruined your robe!"

"My robe! Sylvia, look at me. I may never be able to clean this underwear."

"Guess you'll just have to throw it out."

"Good idea. You know I've never gone out and bought a pair of underwear. We paid for our underthings, but they all came from church supplies in two acceptable colors, white and black. I'm thinking now about maybe pants with colored stripes or a red undershirt would look good on me. What do you think?"

"Sounds quite stunning. Hope you'll show me sometime."

Now he felt mischievous. "I'll see. You know that stuff is private."

"Okay. Really, I think I'm most hopeful that I can just see you again."

"I think you will, Sylvia, but the way my life has gone recently, I'm not sure what's coming next. In a short time, I've gone from thinking I had complete control of my life to now, thinking I can't even say what will happen this afternoon. So, though I truly hope I will see you again, my future feels quite uncertain."

Rupert's comment sobered the moment. They both sat quietly, sipping their new cups of coffee, wondering what to say next.

After a while Rupert broke the silence. "How about we try to at least wipe up this coffee? We can use the towels by the stove."

"Sounds like a plan."

They both grabbed towels and began to clean themselves and the area.

"I think I'll get dressed too, Rupert. This robe needs to go in the hamper, if you have one."

"I do. You'll find it by the door as you enter the bathroom. When you're finished, I'll get dressed too."

When dressed, Rupert came back in the kitchen.

"You know, I really feel very good, Rupert. I meant what I said, that this time with you has been transforming for me. It was so good I guess I got caught in a fantasy that it might go on forever. Your last comment, which was the truth, disappointed me, but as I was cleaning up and putting on these clothes—again—I had time to let reality sink in. Now I have to accept it. You have left a mark on me, which I will continue to think about. It all may even help motivate me in my teaching and writing. I'll keep you posted."

Rupert was happy. In all the years he spent in a parish, he never felt like he'd really affected anybody's life. Sylvia had had a big effect on him as well. While studying to become a priest, no one ever mentioned a quid pro quo aspect of interacting with people. "I have a lot to think about too, Sylvia, but I also hope to stop thinking so much. I've lived for too long in my head. I want to remember this time with you and experience more of life outside the church, beyond sex, of course."

They laughed.

"Maggie has set me on this path I think . . . in fact, I'm sure of it."

They both could feel the mood changing, winding down. Neither wanted to acknowledge this, so they sat quietly looking at each other.

Finally, Rupert asked, "What now?"

"What do you mean by that?"

"What happens next?"

"Well, you could take me back to my car."

Rupert really didn't want to do that. "Okay, but can we finish our coffee first? I know it's cold, but I think I'd like to sit here until it's gone."

"Good idea."

Then Sylvia added, "You know, people always talk about coffee as this great stimulant, but sometimes I find it just plain comforting. Security in the arms of black coffee!"

Rupert smiled. "We're alike in that way."

Sylvia thought he looked as if he'd mentally gone away. Maybe her comment about taking her to her car had stung him. Or maybe he had gone back to thinking about that call he expected from his sister's lawyer. She was beginning to feel some concern about her car, that the restaurant might tow it away if left too long. She also could use a change of clothes. "Do you think you'll hear from Maggie today?"

"No, not yet. I have to wait. That's my job right now!"

"When you do hear, what will you say?"

Rupert didn't answer, but a familiar feeling, anger, rose up inside. He thought about swearing at Sylvia, How the fuck should I know? But then he found his anger wasn't that strong. "Right now, I think I'm ready to say, 'Let's do it!' Like the sex I had with you earlier, I need to stop thinking about my life and start doing my life. Maggie has appeared, or should I say reappeared, and I'm not going to disappear again."

They both pushed back from the table and left to go to the car. Rupert drove Sylvia back to the restaurant. Her car was still there, sitting in a now emptier part of the lot. Before getting out she leaned over and gave him a kiss on the cheek.

He turned to her and said, "I'd like more than that, if you don't mind." Then, putting his hand on her chin, he gently drew her face to him and kissed her on the lips.

When they finally pulled apart, he looked at her. "Nice ending, eh?"

"Great, Rupert. Thanks for the wonderful time."

"Thank you. Could I also have your phone number? I'd like to call and at least let you know how things go with my sister."

"I'd like that."

"I also hope to see you again, Sylvia. My life may be in disarray, but I don't feel confused about my feelings for you."

Sylvia gave him her number, then smiled, and got out. As she turned toward her car, she waved. Rupert waved back and slowly drove away. She turned to watch him go and then got into her car thinking, *What a night that turned into!*

CHAPTER 19

MAGGIE DIDN'T EAT ANY DESSERT, but Jake finished a tiramisu and his sherry. Though she really hadn't eaten anything, playing with her food and taking a taste here and there, she said, "Wow, look at that, Jake, my appetite came back. Wonder if it has anything to do with you."

"Maggie, you ate next to nothing, which may well have to do with me. I've been told on numerous occasions I suppress appetites. My kids especially liked to say I was ruining their meal. Seems they thought I talked too much, principally about things that either irritated or annoyed them."

Maggie smiled at this and then began to feel worried she was beginning to like Jake. She hadn't gone out on this walking adventure to find a guy. Something was happening to her, something so different she couldn't follow her usual pattern of fleeing back to aloneness, to a place where she felt secure, safe, and hidden. She was frozen in time, traumatized by what was happening to her, something possibly too good. "Maybe we should go, Jake."

"I'm ready." He motioned to the waiter, who then brought their bill. They divided it equally, even though Maggie hadn't eaten much, and left.

Once outside, they walked south on the street, heading in the direction of Jake's place. Maggie was struggling. For one of the few times in her life, she didn't know what to say. She just kept smiling. She'd always hated it when she had been with people who obviously didn't know what to say but kept a shit-eating grin on their faces. Jake wasn't saying anything either, but it didn't seem to be bothering him.

Maggie finally had to break the silence. "You seem like such a nice man, Jake. Don't you know what they say about nice men? They finish last."

If she had wanted to anger Jake, it didn't work. He said only, "Oh, but haven't you heard the last shall be first?"

He smiled but she didn't this time. She had to say something, but what? She always knew what to say, how to say it, and when to say it. This time words, accidental, unplanned, and impromptu just popped in her head. Maggie began, "Most men tolerate me, but they don't stick around with me as you have, even though I've been both belligerent and obnoxious in front of you. Maybe they leave because I'm not fuzzy and warm. I'd like to think it's because I have too sharp an intellect or I am too witty or just too good with words. Who knows?"

Suddenly, Maggie felt embarrassed again, and she reddened, stopped talking, and looked away. She forgot about Jake or where she was. In her mind, a little girl appeared, one who was trying to act brave but was only aloof, untouched by what was happening around her. She felt ashamed. Maggie the girl was showing off. She could answer all the questions in school, get all As, had no qualms about telling others what to do. She was obnoxious and seemed unaware of what she was doing or very interested in what was happening around her. Other kids stayed away, ignored her. Now as she watched this little girl, Maggie felt sad and worried. Tears formed, and her head dropped.

Jake saw all this happen. It scared him a little. He didn't want to leave her like this. People in San Francisco were used to seeing crazies on the street, but they rarely tried to help. He knew people were looking at Maggie as crazy and therefore she was vulnerable. "Maggie, do you want me to take you home?"

She didn't answer, she just looked up at him. "No, you leave me."

This made no sense to Jake. He waited for more.

"I've wondered why you haven't left me by now. Why are you still around? Are you staying with me because you feel sorry for me? If so, please don't. I'm a big girl and can take care of myself, sick or not. You came out tonight to relax and hear good music so go and do that."

Jake said nothing.

Maggie finally said, "See I can hardly tolerate you staying, and yet—and this scares me to say—I'm also glad you are here, my accidental friend. If I were still a kid, I might say, I'm happy to finally have a pal."

Jake was amazed by what he heard, but then he'd been in some degree of shock since he sat down next to Maggie back at Jaxson. He thought, *This kind of thing happens only by accident. I couldn't have planned this.*

Then he responded, "Well, Maggie, I'm not leaving yet. I want to stay right here with you. You're right, I did come out tonight for musical entertainment and relaxation because I'm alone now. My wife died from a heart attack two years ago, and now my youngest daughter just graduated from college and left for a job in Denver. I have many friends and work for Levi Strauss as a business manager. I just turned sixty-five with one more year until I can retire with full benefits. I've had trouble adjusting to getting older, and it was made worse by having my last kid move away. I even saw a therapist for some low-grade depression. Nothing serious, no suicidal thoughts mind you, but I still needed to talk to someone. Unlike you, Maggie, I've never been much of a survivalist." He laughed as he said, "I've just had to suffer through."

This comment shocked Maggie. The survival thing again. She didn't know what to say or do. It reminded her of how she felt when the most recent earthquake hit San Francisco. When it hit, she got up from her desk to look outside, wondering what could have driven by big enough to shake things like that. Almost forty seconds had passed before it occurred to her that she was in an earthquake and better get down. This was no earthquake, but it sure felt the same. Was she a survivalist? Well, yes, but no one ever dared to say it out loud, and she felt as if she'd been seen naked before she was ready. She couldn't just drop to the floor as she had done in the earthquake. Instead, she pulled her coat around her and used it to cover herself. "How can you think I haven't suffered?"

"Oh, Maggie, from what I've heard here tonight, I know you've suffered terribly, but you seem to have built a pretty strong fortress of personal protection."

"That's just therapeutic gobbledygook."

Jake laughed. "Yeah, some would call it therapeutic bullshit. However, a therapist once reminded me of how much a farmer depends on bullshit to fertilize his land. When fertilized, crops grow taller and stronger."

Maggie said nothing, but a tear fell down her cheek. Embarrassed by this, she quickly pulled a handkerchief from her pocket and wiped it away. Then, as if on some cue, she ran ahead, raised her hand for a cab, and disappeared into the evening light.

Jake hadn't moved. What could he do? He certainly couldn't stop her, so he just stood there and watched her go. When he felt ready, he turned and continued to walk home alone, trying to enjoy the last of the evening light but mostly wondering if he would ever see Maggie again. *Very unlikely*, he thought, but then exclaimed out loud to no one in particular, "Now this is a night to remember!"

CHAPTER 20

"WORLD NEWS THIS MORNING" BLARED FROM the radio Rupert turned on after returning from dropping Sylvia at her car. He was in the kitchen eating peanut-butter toast and cleaning up.

"Some Democratic governors and congressmen are attending the climate talks with foreign leaders and President Barak Obama."

"Today they buried the first victims from among the many killed in the First Baptist Church mass shooting in Sutherland Springs, Texas, last week. Over four hundred people attended the service presided over by Rev. Frank Pomeroy, who'd been out of town on the day of the shooting and whose teenage daughter had lost her life in the carnage. His message now was 'Darkness will not win. Our faith will bring us through this.'"

Those words befuddled Rupert. How could people come to have that kind of faith? He wasn't even sure about the existence of God anymore, much less the existence of a heaven.

"More reports of sexual abuse among the Hollywood elite. Today Richard Dreyfus was accused of exposing himself to a young aspiring actress many years ago."

Rupert got up and turned off the radio. He'd heard enough. World news was really just about the United States, and it depressed him. At the moment, he felt less down than he had, maybe ever, in his life, so why risk plummeting with the news? He still held a broom in his hand, but the cleaning was done. Rupert smiled as he walked to the closet to put things away. His thoughts were on Sylvia and last night.

The morning sun had come up behind his house making the waters of the Georgia Strait sparkle. He got his coat and went outside, forgetting he might get a call from the lawyer. No rain and early sun. A time when nature painted some of its finest murals.

Rupert went to the path along the water and turned left toward Powell River. He walked. As people passed him, he nodded hello. Everyone smiled, even Rupert. Is this what sex does to people? He didn't want to think about it too much. If that was true, he had spent more than fifty years looking in the wrong direction for peace and contentment.

But is my contentment the result of the sex, or did the sex result from a feeling I already had? It couldn't have. When I accidentally met Sylvia, I was close to hysteria. He'd heard knowledgeable people both in and out of the church speak with such assurance of the source of their contentment, and it had never come from feeling hysterically out of control. Rupert stood still for a moment, staring at the water, thinking about all this. *Maybe my sexual encounter really did baptize me again, this time in the waters of life. Before, I had been focused on how to get away from my life. I obsessively followed every path of escape, but that just left me full of doubt and anxiety.*

Looking ahead, Rupert saw Father Brown, a local priest he knew, headed toward him. It was too late to turn and run, but he found he didn't really want to. "Good morning, Father."

"Good morning to you too, Father. Fine morning for a stroll, don't you think?"

"Oh, yes indeed. A day without rain is a day to enjoy outside. See you around."

After walking about an hour, Rupert remembered the phone call. He turned and, with some anxiety, began a fast walk home. Realizing he might have missed Theresa's call radically changed his mood. The looseness, the openness he had felt disappeared. His body tightened, his head dropped, and his eyes stayed focused only on his feet. He no longer felt like saying a hello or giving a cordial nod to those he passed.

Unfortunately, he saw Father Brown again. *How fucking embarrassing is this?* he thought. *Now I have to make nice again.* His voice dripping with sarcasm, Rupert said, "See you in church, Father."

Rupert heard him respond enthusiastically, "Oh good. It's been a while."

Why doesn't he see me? Rupert wondered. *He hears the words he likes and never thinks about the person saying them.* Yet Rupert knew the answer to his question: for years, he'd been throwing up a smokescreen to keep from being seen. Right now, though, he couldn't think about that. He had to get home.

It took a while to get there. He'd never been a fast walker, and his lack of exercise had left him heavier than he wanted to be and out of shape. The church had a public gym, but he didn't go. He disliked sweaty bodies (his own and others), and though he liked the half-naked women in the gym, he didn't want them to see him in shorts and tee-shirt.

Rupert was sweating when he finally entered the front door and heard the phone ringing. He ran as fast as he could and picked it up, only to hear a dial tone. Whoever had called, probably the lawyer, had hung up. He laid the phone back in its cradle and sat down in his chair. Surprisingly, he didn't feel depressed or mad, his usual pattern. This time he felt disappointed for having missed the call.

He sat back in his chair and thought about the past few hours. Something had changed for him, but he was not sure if it was bad or good. *Maybe I just miss getting mad because swearing and cursing feels more satisfying than just feeling disappointed.* He laughed and said to no one, "Well it's fucking true. Who knows, maybe I'll get used to a gentler, more benign style of living? Only God knows."

Rupert grinned. "Fuck that!"

Now that felt good.

CHAPTER 21

Maggie went back to her spacious and well-equipped condo, sometimes referred to by others as her "castle in the sky." It was dark outside, which matched her mood, but inside the lights burned brightly. She had installed an automated system to turn the lights on at a set time, so now she saw she was standing in an empty room. "Crap, alone . . . again." Her housekeeper, Maria, had come and gone long ago.

"At least I have my Yamaha Home Stereo for company." She turned it on and soon was surrounded by jazz, the music she'd come to love so much. Maggie started to move with the music, her body vibrating with each note. "That's it. . . . I can feel it . . . all over. Now this is good company!" Best of all, the pain she'd started to feel again seemed to go away.

It didn't last. She had unwittingly added a Woody Guthrie jazz version of *Little Black Train*, a tune about the coming of death, because she loved the piece. But now Maggie heard only the words in the song, "death is coming tonight." Her dancing stopped, and thoughts of death flowed through her. *What is it? Where am I going when I die? Is there a heaven or a hell? Would Maggie go on in some other form or just become a pile of dirt?* She got scared. The anxiety flowing through her felt like a drug high but different from the one she'd been on before. Now she started to cry, her body vibrating even more but from the adrenaline building in her system. The music played on, but she hardly heard it.

Anxiety turned to terror. Maggie hit a button, and the music got loud, very loud. The phone rang, but she didn't hear it. She got hot. Sweat began to pour off her. Now she was crying, sweating, and moaning along with the beat of the music.

She kicked off her shoes and went to the bedroom where she undressed. She put on a bathrobe and headed for the kitchen and her liquor closet. The fact that all her doctors had encouraged her to lay off alcohol didn't matter tonight. *I may be dying, but while I still live, I have to survive the night*, she thought. She sat at the table and poured herself a Scotch with only a little ice.

Maggie downed her drink as thoughts about her time with Jake drifted back. What had Jake said? "You've built a pretty strong fortress of personal protection" and then something about how it's locked me in and others out. "Who does he think he is?" she said out loud. "He just met me. The audacity, the nerve."

She poured herself another Scotch, not much ice, downing all of it. The pain she felt come up in her chest made her yell, really scream. She peeled off her robe and started to dance around the kitchen, naked, arms flailing, body twirling in circles, head stretched back, staring straight up into the light above her head. Again, she hit a button on the wall, and the music got even louder. *Who cares?* she thought. *No one is here but me, and if there were someone watching, what are they going to do? I'm a dead woman dancing her way into . . . what? Into hell?* She swung herself around and around and around with increasing wildness until she fell down hard. The so-called softwood she'd used for the floor now felt cold and hard on her bare skin. She moaned and saliva dribbled from her mouth. "I spit on life—my life, what's left of it. Thank God it's almost over, over, over, over."

Maggie got up and took a sharp knife from the drawer. She made a deep cut on her upper leg, then across her stomach, and then started on her wrists, first left, then a swipe across the right.

The doorbell rang.

Maggie didn't hear it. She passed out. The next thing Maggie remembered was being shaken awake by someone yelling into her ear.

"Maggie, Maggie!"

She felt so tired. She groaned but didn't open her eyes.

The shaking and yelling continued.

How annoying, she thought. *Doesn't anyone have any respect for me?* "Leave me alone, will you?"

"No, I won't, Maggie. You have to open your eyes and get up."

Maggie was beginning to feel so relaxed, but the shaking was becoming intolerable. She finally opened her eyes and saw Theresa staring down at her. Then Maggie saw she had towels wrapped around her leg, stomach, and wrists. "What on earth are you doing here?" she said.

"Thank God I came, Maggie. Why? Why would you do this to yourself? Your doctor is on his way over. You need help, but I didn't think you'd want to go to a hospital. That could lead to some bad, embarrassing press for the company."

"Good, wouldn't want to hurt the company, would we?" Maggie's words dripped with sarcasm.

The doctor finally arrived and treated her wounds, some of which were deep enough cuts to require stiches. He noted the blood she'd lost and made the assessment that Maggie probably would not need a transfusion. But it was close, and he hoped he was right. He numbed her arms and legs and gave her something for the pain. When done, he bandaged all the wounds and told Theresa he should report such an obvious suicide attempt. "I know you don't want that and the possible publicity that would come with it, so I won't. But you should know this was serious, and to some degree we are both legally and morally responsible to do something. I also want you to monitor her for a while to see if she has any dizziness, abdominal pain or swelling, signs of problems from the blood loss. If anything comes up, get her to a hospital."

"I will, Doctor, and I appreciate the dilemma you, and I, are facing. It's not easy, but please just hold this between you and me—and then we can both pray it doesn't come back to haunt us! I don't think it will."

"Okay, Theresa, but just this time. If it happens again, I will report it."

"Thanks, Doc. I'll stay with her, and I'm sure we will talk when she wakes up."

"Okay. I'll trust you, but please know I'm quite unsettled about all this, Theresa. Remember you must take her to a hospital if she does anything to harm herself again or if her wounds do not stay closed."

"I'll do that."

They put a robe on Maggie and carried her to bed.

"If you hadn't come over when you did, Theresa, she might have died."

"Thanks for coming out. I'll send you a check."

"Okay. I'll find my own way out."

Theresa saw him shaking his head as he walked slowly down the hall.

CHAPTER 22

Theresa called her husband to tell him she wouldn't be coming home. She slept on the couch, something she'd done many times after a late meeting or if Maggie had asked her to stay over. It was quite comfortable.

The next morning, Theresa got up, made coffee, and went in to check on Maggie who was sleeping soundly. *It's going to be a long day*, she thought. And it was. She found a good book and read, slept, and read some more. Around noon, Maggie finally came out from her bedroom. When she saw Theresa, she only could manage to say hello.

Theresa got her to sit in a chair across from her. "Why?" she asked.

"I saw myself as a dead woman dancing her way into . . ." Maggie couldn't complete the sentence. "This damn cancer isn't killing me fast enough. But what brought you here at that hour?"

"I called earlier to tell you about my unsuccessful call to your brother. You didn't answer, so I decided to talk with you in person. I know how anxious and nervous you are about all this, so I thought a personal visit would be better. When I rang the bell, you didn't answer but I could hear the music. You had it turned up loud enough to wake the dead, excuse the pun. So I let myself in with my key. Then I saw you lying there naked with blood everywhere. Thank goodness you have so many towels. You may want to throw them away. What a job that's going to be to clean up. Does Maria come tomorrow?"

"Yes, she comes often, but I can't remember when she comes next, Theresa." Maggie knew Theresa could manage the situation. *My lawyer,* she thought, *always on the job. Well, that's what I pay her the big bucks for, isn't it?* "I'm not sure how I feel about your saving me, Theresa. Now I'll have to wait until this cancer kills me."

"What happened to make you want to hurry up the process?"

Maggie told the story of her day and night leading up to her attempt—how she'd actually begun to feel good during a part of her conversation with Jake and then how she'd become angry and depressed when he said she "survived" her life. "It was a simple sentence, but it had a big impact! I felt sure he meant to add, 'You were just too scared to live your life.' That's what really set me off." *Live my life. . . . The audacity! What does it mean?* It sounded like something she'd heard in some college psychology class. But she couldn't let it go. "Live my life, live my life. Isn't surviving my life one way to live my life?" Maggie could feel herself getting more and more upset as she told the story.

Theresa was becoming alarmed.

I'm scaring her. Realizing this broke the downward spiral of Maggie's thoughts. She got up, took some deep breaths, and went to get a towel from the bathroom. She was beginning to feel more pain from where she'd cut herself and needed something to wipe the sweat now pouring from her face and arms, but Theresa had apparently used all the towels. Maggie got one from the closet. While wiping off at the sink, she decided her face needed a good wash, and her hands still had dried blood on them. In fact, she had dried blood everywhere.

After cleaning herself some, she felt more composed and returned to the living room. Theresa hadn't moved but looked more her alert, formal self that Maggie was used to seeing.

Neither spoke.

Maggie didn't know what to say, and she assumed Theresa felt equally unsure of where to go next. They were both saved when Theresa's phone buzzed. It was her husband.

"Oh, hi, Guy. I forgot to call you. Maggie and I have been talking, and I lost track of time. Wow, looks like it's almost one thirty. Well, I'm going to spend another night here with Maggie, so I'll see you tomorrow." She knew Guy would accept this, as they both led busy work lives and often had to be away from home for a night or two.

Theresa turned back to Maggie and said, "Guy's learned to be so accepting of my absences I could carry on a very successful affair if I wanted." She laughed.

But Maggie did not laugh. Again, she saw herself in Theresa's offhand comment. She had carried on an affair with her work, and it had taken a toll she didn't even know at the time she was paying. *Maybe I still don't know the full extent of it, and now I'll probably die before figuring it out.* She could have again dissolved into that dark place where death and annihilation welcomed her, but she was determined not to go there. The pain she felt was too great to do that again. She changed the subject.

"I wonder if I should have a blood transfusion to replace what I lost."

"From what the doctor said, you should be okay, unless you experience more symptoms of blood loss. But I do think it would be good for you to lie down, rest, and maybe sleep. Are you wanting anything to eat?"

"Crackers and beef bouillon sound pretty good."

"I'll get some. Just rest here."

"Thanks, Doctor Theresa! Your skills never cease to amaze me!"

Theresa ignored this and went to the kitchen.

After eating, Maggie still felt tired but not ready for bed. "How about we watch a little TV, Theresa?"

"Okay. What do you want to watch?"

"Whatever. I think it's tuned to PBS, so we should find something to kill a few more hours of life."

Theresa heard the sarcasm but decided not to get into it. They watched *Antiques Roadshow* for about an hour, and then Theresa saw Maggie nodding off. "How about I turn this off and you go to bed?"

"Okay."

"I'll sleep here on the couch again so I can hear you if you need help during the night."

Maggie got up and walked to the bedroom while Theresa followed.

"Ow, ow, ow," she said as she walked. "Cutting myself was supposed to stop the pain. Now I not only have to live, but suffer more as well.

These damn cuts really hurt. And I have the worst headache." She gently lay down on the bed.

Theresa didn't know what to say about all the pain so said nothing. She just helped Maggie get under the covers. "Remember, I'm right outside your door, Maggie, and I'm a light sleeper. Call me if you need anything."

Maggie finally slept, but restlessly. In a dream, she saw herself at about her current age sitting on a chair in a strange house. Four sexless entities surrounded her. They had black holes where they should have had faces. Scared beyond anything she'd ever felt, she ran away as fast as she could, not knowing where to hide in this strange house. She could see them chasing her, but she ran fast enough to stay just out of their reach. Maggie ran and ran and ran. If she saw a place to hide, she'd see one of those faceless bodies watching her. So she ran some more. She was sure that they'd kill her. Her fear got worse.

She must have screamed because she felt something or someone shaking her and calling her name. She fought to stay in the dream, refusing to wake up, even with the shaking. Was she sleeping or was she dead? Maggie wasn't sure, but her dream continued. She ran on but was getting tired. The beings moved closer. She finally dropped from exhaustion, and everything went to black, her mind anesthetized and that terrible fear gone. Her body moved with her breath, but she had no other awareness—no pain, nothing. A deep moaning sound rose from her belly and then it turned into crying, which finally woke her. The dream had ended. She was crying but not because she was sad. She knew what it was. Despite her bravado, she was afraid to die. Maggie opened her eyes and saw Theresa standing beside the bed.

The crying was what Theresa had heard. She'd heard no screams and had done no shaking. They were all part of Maggie's dream. Her bedsheets were soaked from sweat. She started that uncontrollable shaking again, but this time felt no fear. What was it?

"I think I'm high, Theresa. Not drug induced but definitely in a kind of frenzy of delight." Not a joyful delight but a delight that comes from seeing the unknown—full, complete, and terrifying. "I was in a strange house chased by four faceless and sexless beings until I could not run anymore."

Theresa said nothing but felt unusually warm and connected to Maggie. Not sure exactly what to say or do, she decided to just sit next to her on the bed until the shaking stopped.

Hardly noticing Theresa move closer, Maggie stayed in her thoughts that continued to be haunted by the dream and faceless beings, chasing after her. What would they have done if they'd caught her? Why didn't they catch her? *Where I'm going has to be scary. It's the unknown after all. Give up, Maggie. You're trying too hard to dominate life. You can't control death.* Thinking like this didn't take the fear away, but she did relax some. One thought just kept coming back over and over, though: *Give up, Maggie.* Unconsciously she reached over and grabbed Theresa's hand.

Theresa jumped but did not pull away.

Soon Maggie fell asleep, lost in the comfort of the moment.

CHAPTER 23

TIME PASSED; THE PHONE DID NOT RING. Rupert sat quietly waiting. He figured the call before probably had not been Theresa. If he remembered correctly, she hadn't yet had all the time she said she needed before getting back to him. But really, he couldn't remember for sure what she'd said.

So here he was, back where he'd been so many times before, sitting in his chair, doing nothing, trapped in his thoughts, and these were fast turning sour. Faint feelings of hope were fading; old doubts, fears, and confusions returned. He tried to sit back and relax, but his body wouldn't cooperate. His hands gripped the armrests, his body stiffened, and he felt himself getting hotter and knew his face had reddened.

He yelled, "No, not again." Rupert fought against his mind and body, pushing himself hard against the back of the chair while trying to will himself to halt his fall into that mental abyss he knew so well. He tried to stand up, thinking that would break the spell. Grunting, he sucked in air and then blew it out while trying to push up on legs that felt dead and unable to move, no less hold him up.

Surprisingly, he kept fighting: David against Goliath, man versus machine, soldier against enemy. Rupert didn't want to surrender, and this time he didn't. The combat between resignation and resistance was fierce. He'd submitted so often to running, masturbating, or some form of self-destruction that now he just wanted to rebel. He had no idea where or how he might end up. *I'm in a battle without end*, he thought. For some reason, he now felt like fighting his easy way of life that had left him so dry, so hollow, so devoid of hope and self-confidence.

Then, it ended. There had been no angry outburst, no destructive explosion, no sense of winning or losing. Instead, something broke like a wire pulled too tight. Rupert burst into tears with what felt like a lifetime's worth of sadness. He couldn't remember any experience before with this kind of deep crying. Anger, yes, but not sadness like this. He hid his anger as best he could and always made sure there were no witnesses to his explosions. To those who knew him, he always appeared calm and even-tempered.

On the inside, however, hidden from view, there'd been many a storm of feeling. But now crying so openly like this surprised and even alarmed Rupert. *Will the tears stop flowing? Was this the start of some sort of emotional breakdown?* He was glad he was alone. How could he ever explain what was wrong?

Then, in the midst of all these turbulent and disturbing thoughts, the phone rang. He wanted to answer it and was, in fact, desperate to answer it. But much to his chagrin and embarrassment, he was unable to move, paralyzed in place, sobbing quietly.

Ring, ring, ring, ring. Finally, the ringing stopped.

Rupert continued to sit in place until, after about a half-hour, he stopped crying. *Why?* he wondered. *Did I run out of tears?* No answer came. No time for reflection.

Instead, without warning, he got angry, and this was a much more familiar feeling. "Lousy timing, God. Why didn't you stop me thirty minutes ago when I could have answered the stupid phone? Oh, I know, you and I never were on the same page. Abandoned, screwed again. Thanks. It's time you and I had it out, don't you think? I'm tired of you not ever being there for me in my life. I gave myself to your church and your service, and all I asked for was that contentment, that ease, that peace you promised if I got to know you. Well, no more. I've had sex, so I guess I broke the contract."

Mentioning sex immediately brought back memories. His dialogue with God ended, and instead Rupert thought about Sylvia, her nude body lying with him, her hair falling in his face, their bodies perspiring as they ground into each other, their hands roughly and gently rubbing every part of their bodies. Just thinking about it all aroused him again. There was no sadness, no anger in him now, just excitement and a firm penis. He looked at himself and marveled. I'm an old man! He laughed. Rupert did nothing but knew something had changed. He didn't want to think too much about it, but one thought was persistent. *This is abnormal, isn't it? But I like it! I've spent too much of my life marinating in the church's ocean of normalcy.*

He chuckled, turned, and left the room. Rupert wanted to move, nowhere in particular, just move. He passed by the phone several times before it hit him someone could have left a message. Lifting the receiver, he listened.

"You have one unheard message."

He eagerly punched in his code and heard Sylvia saying she was getting ready to leave town for a short trip and was just checking to see if he'd heard anything from his sister. Then, before hanging up, she said, "I hope we can stay in touch. Bye for now."

Rupert laid the phone back in its cradle. Then he picked it up to call her. And then he didn't. Something told him to wait.

He felt jumpy, on edge. His house was too quiet. He couldn't even hear the waves crashing against the shore outside. Quiet had always comforted him, like the darkness, but right now he wanted noise. So he screamed, a primal letting go. An inner voice told him to quiet down, the neighbors would hear, but he didn't listen. He shouted again and again. But each successive yell was less intense. He was calming himself. Rupert felt different. The house was still quiet, but he had calmed down. He had no interest in noise or being noisy. Instead, he thought about turning on the TV. Then he remembered he'd destroyed it.

I must get another TV sometime, he thought. *Not sure when I'll get to that.* As he turned toward his radio, a siren sounded outside. He went to look and saw an ambulance go by, lights flashing and cars pulling to the side. It passed. He wondered if it was headed for an accident or to pick up a heart-attack victim. Maybe he'd get called out to do last rites.

Oh, that won't happen. I've retired, he thought. *I wouldn't go anyway, not anymore.* He'd never felt comfortable performing any of the rituals. He had learned to be a priest and performed the role, but he never gave himself to the church or priesthood. He wanted the church to take him, make him, but he had no idea how to take the church as his own.

Rupert was certainly well read in Catholic theology and doctrine. He had bookshelves built into the wall of his living room loaded with books he'd had to read. As he now looked at them, he saw textbooks, periodicals, and journals. His well-used Bible was there next to *The Spirit of Catholicism, Catechism of the Catholic Church, Essay on the Development of Christian Doctrine, How the Reformation Happened, St. Francis of Assisi* by Chesterton, and Dorothy Day's *The Long Loneliness.*

He lingered over those last two. St. Francis's life and words had always elevated his spirit. He felt some sort of power in St. Francis's words and personal sacrifices. They had affected people's lives, inspired them sometimes to some personal sacrifices of their own. St. Francis gave his life to God in a way Rupert never could. Or was it he never knew how? *How could I give myself to God? I don't know who or what he is or who or what I am.*

Like St. Francis, Dorothy Day also seemed to find God and had given her life to his service, helping the poor and needy in New York City. People meeting Dorothy must have felt her presence, her power, because he felt something just reading her words.

These two people had inspired him, and the effect lingered. But Rupert could never let himself do what they seemed ready and eager to do. He never could let go or, as some said, "Let God." Rupert fought God while wanting so much to have God with him. Now staring at these books brought back distant thoughts and memories he thought had died.

Where were his thrillers, mysteries, love and war stories? He'd seen them on book and magazine shelves but never had the nerve to buy any. This made him smile as he thought, *I was too busy sacrificing myself to God not to pleasure. God forbid.* No, he'd read and kept only the Catholic texts. Rupert decided to change this and said, "I've tried the sacred. It's time to open up to the material world, the sensual, the secular." He took a deep breath in and slowly exhaled, letting himself relax and feel the relief that came over him with this thought.

The phone rang. He went to answer it, hoping it might be Sylvia calling back. "Hello?"

CHAPTER 24

THERESA WOKE TO THE SUN streaming through the bedroom window. She could see Maggie was still sound asleep, but Theresa wanted to get up. She gently lifted Maggie's arm from around her and eased herself out of bed. Not as easy as she'd hoped, however.

"Ouch."

That woke Maggie. "What's the matter?"

"Oh, just my back. It must have stiffened up during the night."

"Sorry about that. I feel a little sick to my stomach." Maggie got up and headed for the bathroom. She had thrown up many times during her chemo treatments, but this did not feel the same. "I don't think I'm going to really be sick, but I would like to sit on the toilet a while."

"Sure, go ahead. I'll do some stretches to help me loosen up."

Maggie stayed in the bathroom until she heard Theresa on the phone. She couldn't make out what was being said, but she assumed Theresa had called Guy. She'd started to feel better but didn't want to interrupt whatever was going on. "I'll be out in a moment." A couple of minutes later, she came out.

Theresa hung up and turned to Maggie. "That was Guy. He needs some help getting the kids ready and off to school, so I should go. They have only a half-day at school today, and Guy has meetings he needs to attend. Doesn't the housekeeper come at nine?"

"Yes."

"Well, good. That means you'll have company."

"Yeah, guess I will. Thanks for putting up with me and sorry I scared you so much."

Theresa gathered her things and started to go down the hall to the door.

Maggie didn't want to say it, but she wasn't quite ready for her to leave. She wanted to talk, things she didn't want to talk about with her housekeeper. "Theresa, I think you should know, I wanted to die, and there's a big part of me that still does. The fear I've always felt about dying hasn't gone away, but that fear might not stop me. I have no idea about what happens in death, other than the body turns to dust. But is that it? Everyone has a theory, but in the end, I will face death alone, whatever fears or faiths I may hold at the time. That aloneness and the fact that no one REALLY knows what happens when we die is enough to send me into a panic. Now, death is not so far away for me, and it's the fear I feel about living sick, alone, and unwanted that makes me want to die."

"But Maggie, you aren't alone or unwanted. I'm here and will be here when you need me."

"Yeah, right, when I need you."

"Yes, when you need me. I just tolerated you for years, Maggie. I certainly admired you. I never worked for anyone as intelligent as you. You're an original thinker, imaginative, knowledgeable, and creative. And you are a woman who succeeded in the shipping industry, definitely a man's world. But your reaching out to your brother added something I hadn't seen before—vulnerability, Maggie. If anything, you seemed prideful in your invulnerability." Theresa couldn't continue, but Maggie could see she was crying as she turned and walked down the hall toward the door.

Maggie felt a strong urge to run down the hall and maybe grab her hand, but didn't. Instead, she just stood there staring at her until, finally, Theresa left. Now Maggie was alone again in her expansive, upscale place with all her collections and assorted paraphernalia, none of which could distract her from the pessimistic thinking that would, she feared, soon overtake her. "Oh, won't someone save me?" She lay down on her bed, face down, holding her head between her hands. She squeezed harder and harder, like you would a lemon while trying to extract juice.

"I'm so good at wounding and hurting others. Maybe I can wound myself." This time she couldn't. *Last night it felt good to cut myself. But now something had changed. Last night I wasn't thinking, which probably helped me do it. Now . . .* Maggie shrugged. *But I still could hurt myself . . . or maybe someone else . . . or maybe something else. I know, I'll kick the dog. Oh, but I don't have a dog. Maybe I'll drown the cat. But I don't have a cat either. Here I am surrounded by things but nothing that's breathing, farting, sweating, or smelling—except me. Nothing of real meaning or value to anyone, including yours truly, this pathetic, dying piece of shit that I am.*

The doorbell rang.

Sarcastically Maggie thought, *Oh good, finally a victim!* But she didn't move.

The bell rang again, longer this time.

She still didn't move but thought, *It's probably Maria. I can't kill her. Who would clean the house? That just leaves . . . me. I failed once, probably would again. I can see the headline now: AMAZINGLY SUCCESSFUL CEO FAILS AT KILLING HERSELF.*

The doorbell rang again.

Still Maggie didn't move.

Then the door opened. "Anyone here?"

"Just me, Maria. Come on in. I'm in the bedroom."

She didn't try to pull herself together but did stand up just as Maria entered. "The place is yours. You can pretend I'm not here, which is true, even though you see me. You do see me, don't you?"

"Sure Ms. Callaway. I'm not sure what you mean."

"Never mind. Do your thing. I'll leave you alone."

Maggie left for the kitchen, knowing Maria always started her day in the bedrooms and then did the kitchen. She'd be left alone for a while. *The phone does not ring. No neighbors or friends come to my door. Everyone knows I've been very ill with cancer. Some even know the bleak prognosis I've received. All show sympathy when I'm around, but no one comes. Oh sure, Theresa came by last night, but then I'm her paycheck.* "Now there's a motivator!"

The kitchen actually needed Maria's attention the most. Maggie's blood covered much of the room. *Blood on a white background*, she thought, *good background for a horror movie.* Maggie wasn't going to clean it. In fact, she felt unusually comfortable surrounded by signs of herself, even if it was her blood. *Maybe I am real. I bleed, therefore I am. Not Descartes's cogito, ergo sum, but I like mine better at the moment. Rupert should be here to see me now. Your sister is really there. You can't ignore the blood, can you?*

Maggie sat on the floor in her blood, feeling nothing. *This is what being dead might be like.* She rubbed her hands in the now dried blood. It didn't repel her. Although it felt cold, she imagined it felt warm. She wanted to wrap herself in it, like Joseph's coat of many colors, holding her warm and safe. She was staining her clothes, but she didn't care. *I won't be around that much longer.* Maggie continued her pessimistic thoughts, though she was aware someone else was in the house. Somehow, that made her feel secure, safe, safe from herself. She sat there, listening to the vacuum noise moving through the rooms and feeling reassurance, even relief.

Then Maggie realized Maria was headed her way! And the blood! She pushed through the door, almost knocking Maria over as she did, and grabbed her by the hand. "I've decided I don't want the kitchen done today, Maria."

"What? You always want me in there, even if you never use it."

"I know but not today. Call it a vacation."

Maria saw the stains on Maggie's pajamas. "What the . . . is that blood?"

"Yes, I had an accident last night."

Maria just looked at Maggie. "You know, Ms. Callaway, you might be good at fooling all those bigshots you know, but not me."

Maggie was moved by her honest response. Maria, her housekeeper, cared about her. Maggie was not going to lie to her.

"You got me! I did something to myself last night that I now regret. In a moment of despair, I tried to hurt myself. It saddens me now to share that with you, and you may not understand it, but you deserve to know. Over time you, perhaps more than anyone, have heard me express my real feelings. I trusted you to just listen to me, and that's what you did. "The stains you see on my pajamas came from my actions. There's nothing else I can tell you right now, so I ask you respect my privacy and let me grow into some resolution for the conflicts that currently haunt me. I have felt your concern, Maria, and you have my respect and admiration. Thanks."

Maria, well aware of her tendency to cry at the wrong times said, "Of course, ma'am. I can do that for you. I've come here for a long time now and can't say we really know each other that well, but I've always felt your respect for me, and now I can demonstrate mine. I'll stay out of the kitchen until further notice."

They both smiled.

Maria took her vacuum off to work in the dining area.

Maggie went to the bedroom to get dressed. She stripped off her pajamas but did not throw them in the hamper. She folded them and put them in the drawer for later. She might never wear them again, but she had a strong desire to keep them just the way they were now.

She did want a shower, a long hot one. Maggie jumped in and stood in the middle of all the warm water until she noticed the skin on her hands beginning to wrinkle. She turned it off, stepped out, pulled out a big fluffy towel, and proceeded to dry off.

Maggie had several closets filled with clothes for every occasion, from the most leisurely to full formal. She knew she had too much but rationalized her extensive collection by saying she needed it all to meet the multifaceted demands of her job. Now, though, she didn't care what she wore. Comfort would be her primary guide, but she also wanted to hide her wounds from where she cut herself. She found a long-sleeved plaid shirt to cover the cuts on her arms and old brown slacks that would serve to cover the leg wounds. She didn't want to spend her day answering questions.-

She finished dressing and then left the condo without makeup or spending much time fixing her hair. Maggie did, however, grab her phone and yell to Maria as she left, "Goodbye."

"Bye to you, Ms. Callaway. I'll see you on my next visit, when maybe I will clean the kitchen!"

Maggie smiled. Once outside, she called Lyft. Within minutes a car arrived.

The driver asked, "Where to?"

"San Jose."

"You know that's almost a two-hour ride?"

"Yeah, I know. You have my credit card, so let's go."

"Okay, it's your dime." He did not particularly want to drive all the way to San Jose, but it had been a slow day, and now at least he would make some money.

Maggie asked him to please find a jazz station on the radio. He did, and she heard a piece by one of her favorite artists, Mocean Worker (aka Adam Dorn). She sat back and tried to relax. Although she hadn't told the driver yet, she would also be riding back to San Francisco with him. She just wanted to ride, practice letting go, surrendering.

After about an hour on the road, Maggie's phone rang. It was Theresa, but Maggie didn't answer it. She was eager to hear what Theresa had found out, if anything, from Rupert but right now needed time to recover. Yes, *recover*, that was the right word. She had tried to end her life but had decided to live out this nightmare and not end it prematurely. No, she would recover from her wounds, and then she'd get ready to die.

CHAPTER 25

"HELLO, THIS IS THERESA GALLAGHER, Maggie Callaway's lawyer, calling."

Rupert quickly moved to turn down the radio. "Hello."

"Have you had enough time to read and consider Maggie's letter?"

"Yes, I have. Did you try calling me a little while ago?"

"Yes, I did. Maggie would like to know if you have a response."

"I was surprised to read that Maggie is ill, but I must say I was most shocked by hearing from her at all. We have not been in contact for a long time, and in fact, I hadn't even thought about Maggie in many years. Probably smart of her to have an intermediary contact me first to test the waters. Truthfully, Ms. Gallagher, I'd have preferred to stay estranged. Now it seems cruel to her to not see her, but cruel to me to see her."

"Well, I can assure you, Rev. Callaway, this has not been easy for your sister. She agonized about writing to you in the first place, and since doing it, she has questioned her decision many times. You obviously don't have to meet with her. She, on the other hand, would have to live with your rejection and probably regret having taken the risk of putting herself out to you."

Rupert knew what he wanted to tell Theresa, but the words wouldn't come. Maggie had done the heavy lifting by reaching out. All he had to do was say yes or no. But he wanted Maggie to know how he had suffered, how a torment had resurfaced since her letter had arrived.

"Well, what should I tell Maggie?"

"You can tell Maggie that by unlocking the family vault, she has released all the plagues and mental torment of our past. I like order in my life, and since receiving her letter, I have known only confusion and disorder."

A long silence followed.

Theresa waited patiently on her end of the phone but finally broke in. "Hello, Rupert, are you still there?"

"I'm here."

Theresa was tempted to say something that would put this prick in his place, but she didn't. "Truly, I don't know what you've gone through, Rev. Callaway, but frankly my only job here is to find out your response and to convey it to Maggie. What have you decided?"

Rupert didn't say anything. Thoughts roiled in his head, and he felt himself move from anger to sadness to disgust to despair. He was a mess, inside and out, and was glad she couldn't see how he was sweating. Deep in his heart, Rupert was desperate to see Maggie. "Shit, this is hard!"

Theresa stayed detached.

"Do you need more time to decide?"

Theresa's non-engagement finally cracked Rupert's tough exterior. "No, I don't want more time. You can tell Maggie I will meet with her. She can choose where we meet, but please remind her that, because I live on a small retirement income, I would find it difficult to come to San Francisco where the hotels, transportation, and food might bankrupt me."

"I'll let her know. You will no doubt hear from her soon, probably again through me. Thanks, and goodbye."

Rupert hung up, his body shaking all over. He felt weak and went to sit down. As he did, he laughed, thinking about how he hadn't felt this exhausted even after having sex with Sylvia. That had tired him, for sure, but hadn't drained him. Now he couldn't even muster the energy to go make tea. Instead, he sat where he was, wishing someone were there to make it for him. Rupert thought about Sylvia. He felt sure she would have brewed the tea. At times like this in the past, he might have walked to the jetty where he would sit by the water and think—and probably feel defeated. Now, though, he realized he just didn't want to be alone. He wanted company; he wanted a companion.

On the table next to Rupert, there was an oversized book filled with scenes from nature. It had been given to him by someone, he couldn't remember who, as a going-away present when he had retired. He'd only glanced at it before but now took time to admire every scene. Near the end, he was stopped by a photo of an elderly Native American man, looking directly at him with deeply sunken iridescent brown eyes under thick graying eyebrows. His lips were held slightly apart, showing blackened teeth. Rupert just stared, and the Indian stared back. He imagined the man with that face carved by long years of life was speaking to him, saying, "What? I can't hear you."

Rupert turned no more pages, and for some reason he didn't understand, he started to feel less alone. He relaxed. Soon his head fell back on the chair, and he fell asleep with the book still open on his lap.

Waking later, Rupert sat up, looked at the clock, and saw he'd slept for over an hour. The book he'd been holding had fallen on the floor at his feet. He picked it up, thinking, *Wow, I guess I was tired.* He got up and was about to make himself a sandwich when the phone rang again. "Hello."

"Hello, Rupert, Father Brown here."

"Oh, hello." Then, before he heard any more, Rupert said, "When I saw you on the path to town, I told you I'd see you in church, but that was a lie. Now I just want to see you, so I'll be right over. Bye." He put the phone down and left the house so fast he forgot to lock the door.

Father Brown was left literally holding the phone. He looked down at the receiver, still in his hand, shook his head in disbelief, and slowly laid it in the cradle. "What just happened? I can hardly wait to see what comes next!"

Backing the car out of the garage, Rupert hit the garbage can, sending garbage flying everywhere. "Damn." He got out and started to pick it up but, in his eagerness to get going, decided to finish it later.

The church wasn't far, and he arrived in about ten minutes. *I don't even know if the father's here*, he thought. Rupert looked in his rearview mirror to check how he looked. "Oh my God," he said, noticing he was not wearing the clerical collar. Nor was he dressed in black. He knew since he'd retired, he no long needed to dress like an active priest, but maybe because he was about to have a priest-to-priest talk, he should be in more formal attire. He needed his collar for sure.

Rupert drove back home and discovered the unlocked door, but avoiding the usual self-incriminating comments, he quickly changed into slacks and coat, and then searched for the collar. Not finding it in the house, he decided to look in the car again, and, lo and behold, there it was between the seats. He put it on and got back in the car.

As he drove back, a small plane flew overhead. *Life goes on*, he thought. *No matter what happens to any one of us, nothing stops it. Wish I could tell people nothing matters. We're all just living under a cloud of illusion, thinking someone sees us and cares.* Rupert stopped the car for a moment to watch two people walk hand-in-hand down the beach. He rolled his window down and yelled, "Enjoy it while you can. Soon you too will discover how alone you are in this life." Then he remembered his time with Sylvia and wondered if he might be wrong. He rolled his window back up and drove on to the church.

Rupert knocked on the front door of the rectory.

A woman opened it. "How can I help you?"

"I wonder if I could speak with Father Brown. He just called me, but I hung up on him and drove over to see him in person. I'm Father Rupert Callaway, retired."

"I don't know if Father Brown is even here now, but I'll check the whiteboard we keep in the kitchen. He should have written down where he planned to go and for how long. Come in. You can wait in the library."

The kitchen must have been far away because she was gone about five minutes. Rupert used the time to scan the bookshelves. *No thrillers here either*, he thought. Lots of Catholic texts. Two books filed side by side stood out: *Care of the Soul* by Thomas Moore and *Dark Night of The Soul* by St. John of the Cross. He'd never read either one and had never even heard of the Moore book. He took it out, opened it, and read from the first paragraph: "It is only through mystery and madness that the soul is revealed," and then exclaimed, "Wow!" just as Father Brown strode into the room carrying a cup of tea in his left hand.

"Hello, Rev. Callaway. I don't get hung up on too often. You're the first to do it and then appear at my door. I guess you wanted to talk in person, right?"

"Yeah, I guess so. I don't always really know what I'm doing anymore, but it's all good, I think."

"Well, I have time to talk. I was just letting my tea steep before I chucked the bag. We Canadians know a good cup of tea demands a certain amount of time to reach peak flavor." He held his cup close to his nose. "Ahh, the aroma is half of it. But I'm sure you didn't rush over to hear me go on about brewing a good cup of tea." He went on without offering tea to Rupert. "Why don't we stay here in the library, rather than going into my office? Believe me, it's much less sterile. The architect of this building must have thought we needed austerity to experience God. The library is my refuge from all that." He motioned to a chair for Rupert and sat down. "So, what brings you here? You and I have never managed to talk much, even though I've sat with you at table when some of us got together over at the Zone. You were always so quiet and looked like you were miles away. I actually just dialed you up to acknowledge seeing you on the trail and to say I hope we can connect someday."

Rupert put the book back where he'd found it and sat down. "That's a new title for me. Do you think I might borrow it sometime?"

"Oh, I found that book some years back and put it next to the *Dark Night of the Soul* because I thought it might help anyone caught in his or her dark-night experience. Did you know Moore was a monk before he became a psychotherapist?"

"No, I'd never even heard of him."

"Well, you're more than welcome to borrow it. In fact, why don't you take it with you when you leave today. I lend books out once in a while, but I'll tell you upfront that I give everyone a return date. I started doing that after I noticed I wasn't getting books back."

"Of course," Rupert said, "I fully understand." And he did, but what he was really thinking about was Rev. Brown's forthrightness, not like the priests he'd known. He'd found those priests, like himself, to be more deferential, saying less to leave room for the other person to say whatever he or she wanted and sharing little, if anything, about themselves.

Father Brown seemed more open, but Rupert was not put off. He felt surprisingly comfortable. "As I mentioned on the phone, when I saw you on the trail, I said I'd see you in church, but that was a lie." Then he dropped his head in shame, avoiding direct eye contact. He waited for the humiliation he was sure would follow.

"I assumed that since I don't think I've ever seen you in one of our pews. But I don't particularly care whom I see in church. In fact, I'm not even scheduled to preach this Sunday, so if you had come, you wouldn't have seen me. I planned to be off fishing. I love to fish. Not for salmon, halibut, or anything like that. I'm a fly fisherman. Don't catch a lot, but I really enjoy the time standing in rushing water, listening to the birds, feeling the wind, and of course, waiting for a big trout to bite. I even clean and fry them up myself. Do you fish?"

Rupert didn't know what to say. Part of him still thought he should wait for Father Brown to make him feel bad for lying, but then he thought, *Why, Rupert? Just answer his question, will you?* "No, I have never had any interest in fishing."

"Well, what brought you here to retire then?"

Rupert was confused now. Where was the shame? He wondered if he was being set up for a bigger fall.

Father Brown was also confused, wondering why Rupert wasn't answering his simple questions. "I assume you came to Powell River for a reason."

"Yes, but I'm wondering if you're trying to trick me somehow. I'm used to being punished if I tell the truth, and so far, you haven't done what I expected. Didn't you hear me say before that I lied?"

"Yes, I heard you, and I appreciated you telling me the truth. Remember John 8:32, 'Then you will know the truth, and the truth will set you free.' No punishment, Rupert, but I am sincerely interested in why you came to Powell River."

"Well, truthfully, I came here really only to be near water and because the church offered me a free house." He laughed and noticed that even Father Brown smiled. "Seriously, I love being near water. I don't know why. I didn't grow up near it. It's a mystery to me, but since coming here, I've discovered that listening to waves is addicting.

Sometimes I'm so mesmerized by it, I'll stand on the rock wall in front of my house and not notice the rising tide licking at my feet to the point where I might be in some danger. I don't particularly want to die, but frankly, I find the thought of a powerful wave carrying me away thrilling." Rupert suddenly stopped talking. "Sorry, I got carried away there and probably said too much. I really am quite reserved—always careful and cautious."

"Yeah, I kind of picked that up from our previous meetings at the Zone. Now, however, I'm curious to know more. Have you ever been hit by a wave?"

"No, never where I was really in any danger. Waves have come up to my knees on several occasions, and I've had wet shoes often." Rupert noticed that, as he had done with Sylvia, he had an urge to disclose more about himself. It felt dangerous and scary, but he didn't want to stop. Why? He had no idea, but he knew his life had begun to tumble out of control. He wondered if this urge was from his being out of control or from something else, something new. *Maybe you saw the light, Rupert. This has to be God's doing. Oh, come on. You're sounding ridiculous. Oh, you don't trust God? No, I . . .* Never-ending questions, never good answers, always trapping himself in the endless agony of shame. It would go on and on, usually until he just tired himself out. But his internal dialog didn't get that far because Father Brown cut him off.

"You know, Rupert, I just turned sixty-two, but I don't feel close to retirement. When did you retire?"

"Five years ago, at sixty-three, I moved into the Church-owned home here after spending my whole career in Kamloops."

"No water there, is there? From what you said earlier, I'm a little surprised you spent most of your life inland."

"Yeah, me too! Maybe someday I'll understand the many contradictions I've lived."

"Did you retire to confront or maybe challenge these contradictions?"

"Never thought about it much, but maybe I did." Then, without thinking, Rupert blurted out, "I retired because I was finished with church life." The conviction he heard in this statement shocked him, but he noticed nothing like surprise or astonishment from Father Brown.

His courage grew. He did not get scared; he got excited. Some part of his brain, however, kept trying to tell him to be careful. *Shut up, Rupert.*

Father Brown said nothing, just smiled.

Rupert, with face reddening, smiled back.

Chapter 26

An hour into her ride, Maggie told the driver to stop and turn around. She wanted to go home. Her body had begun to ache, and she was bored and. She had had enough.

"Okay. It's your dime." He waited until the next traffic light and then made a U-turn to begin the return trip.

Maggie's phone rang again, and she still did not pick it up.

Theresa listened to the ringing, waiting for Maggie to answer. After waiting longer than she would have on most any other call, she finally hung up. This was probably the hardest job she'd had to do since she'd been hired by the company as Maggie's lawyer. Since Maggie had been furloughed for health reasons, her time was increasingly becoming occupied by Maggie's personal affairs, much different work from what she had done before. She'd become increasingly entwined in Maggie's life and private concerns. And, in this mélange of business and personal, Theresa had begun to notice her feelings invading her work. She had, in fact, started to like Maggie, even with all her idiosyncrasies, and she feared this could affect her legal judgment. But it was now the way she'd have to be Maggie's lawyer. After all, the woman was fast approaching death and had entered into a complex dance with her long-lost brother.

But, Theresa thought, *I should probably get some extra reimbursement for any emotional pain and suffering I will no doubt have to go through.* She felt that was wrong, but getting paid well was one of those legacy issues that haunted her life. Her parents had always worried about money and never had enough. Theresa had learned from them to always have enough, but they had never defined *enough.* She'd become a successful lawyer, and she and her husband made over four hundred thousand dollars a year. Rationally, Theresa knew that was plenty for them and their lifestyle, but here she was thinking of being paid for compassion.

She remembered what the Dalai Lama had said, "If you want others to be happy, practice compassion. If you want to be happy, practice compassion." You're not supposed to get paid to be compassionate, you just do it. Why did she always fall back into old habits, old ways of thinking? She couldn't answer that, but she knew her compassion for Maggie was growing. This surprised her after so many years doing the company's work and having to tolerate Maggie's quirky behavior along the way, but it made her feel happy. She smiled while writing a note, "Call Maggie again."

Opening the door to her apartment, Maggie heard the vacuum cleaner. Maria was still there. Checking her phone, she saw it was three ten and, of course, she'd still be here. She typically worked till after five. Maggie went quietly and quickly to her bedroom, locked the door, and sat at her desk. *What to do?* she wondered. *Do I call Theresa back or wait?* She trusted Theresa would call again so decided to wait.

As Maggie sat thinking, she was jolted upright by an intense pain in her back. Her cancer had caused aches since it began, but an especially troublesome back pain had developed after the doctors operated to remove her tumor. Now it felt worse than it had in quite a while. She had both Vicodin and Oxycodone, so she had plenty of pills, enough, she knew, to end her life. She'd felt tempted to do so many times, but right now she did not. She took a Vicodin. It eased the pain some, and before long, she fell asleep, head down on the desk and slightly snoring.

The phone ringing woke her. The clock read five fifteen. She checked the caller ID. It was Theresa. This time, though still somewhat sleepy, she felt ready to talk, whatever the outcome. "Hi, what's up?"

"Well, I called to tell you it's time to make arrangements to meet your brother. He will meet with you. He conveyed no eagerness for a meeting, but he did say he would."

"I didn't expect him to show enthusiasm, Theresa."

"Oh, he did ask that you not meet in San Francisco because of the high costs for a hotel and food. He reminded me that he has retired and isn't sure his budget could handle a stay here."

"Okay, let me think about what I want to tell him, and I'll get back to you by tomorrow."

"Good, I'll expect your call then." Theresa thought Maggie sounded okay on the phone, but that could have all been a show. Maggie had honed some good acting skills over the years, although the last time Theresa had seen Maggie, she was not good at all. Theresa decided she would call back if she had not heard from Maggie by three the next afternoon.

Maggie stayed in the bedroom considering what to do next. She'd call someone. Jake perhaps? There couldn't be that many people named Jake Newman could there? She found three, but only one had an address close to the restaurant where they'd had dinner. He'd said he didn't live far from there.

Okay, she decided, she'd try the number, but first she went to the kitchen to get a glass of wine. She found some cold, unopened Chardonnay in the refrigerator. Maggie still wasn't sure she should do wine. She decided not to open it, but would she make the call? She'd liked the guy. Jake was different from other men she'd met, primarily all heavy hitters in the business world. He seemed to be a sensitive man the way he had listened and talked to her. "Sensitive man . . . I don't usually think of those two words going together," Maggie spoke out loud to no one. She wanted to talk to someone. Maybe someone besides Jake? But she had no one else, except Theresa, and she'd just hung up with her. Business people, politicians, and other sycophants who had surrounded her in the past had made themselves scarce after hearing of the seriousness of her condition. In addition to their fear of getting too close to death, she knew they no longer saw her as useful to them. *Okay, so calling Jake would be a risk, but what the hell*, she thought. It was dinnertime for most people. Probably a good time to try. She coughed hard, further delaying her call, but then, after the cough calmed, she punched in the number and let it ring three times. "Not home, I guess."

"Hello?" Jake was out of breath, as if he'd run to the phone.

"Hello, Jake, it's Maggie. Fortified Maggie from Mama Leone's."

"Oh, you mean the survivalist I met in the bar the other night?"

"Yeah, that's me. Sorry I left so fast."

"Yeah, AND without giving me any notice first. Needless to say, I was surprised. How'd you find me now? I don't recall giving you my number."

"I was in the world of business and high finance, remember. We're all sneaky and devious. You must know that. I peeked at your name when you paid the bill to confirm you really were Jake Newman. Then I found you listed in an online directory of San Francisco."

"Good work, Maggie. I'm glad your sleuthing found me. I'm not very clever, so I hadn't found a way to reach you."

Maggie said nothing. She couldn't. Her brain chose that moment to stop working. There was no way she was going to be able to have a conversation now. How embarrassing, and Jake was not helping. He didn't say anything either.

"How about meeting for another go at dinner?" Maggie asked. "Same place, in an hour?"

"Sure. I was about to go out for a bite and would like company. How about we meet around six thirty."

"That'll work. See you soon."

Maggie wiped the sweat beading on her brow but also noticed she felt immediately relieved. *Wow, that's amazing*, she thought. All that angst had left as fast as it had come, and now, she was about to see Jake again. She wasn't hungry and wasn't any surer of what she'd talk about than she'd been before, but she was looking forward to what could turn out to be an adventure, a temporary escape from herself, or . . . what? She didn't know but felt determined to go for it.

She found a simple skirt and blouse she liked and changed. No business suit, no stockings. Out of habit, she went to the bathroom to put on makeup, comb her hair, and brush her teeth. Once there, she only brushed her teeth and put her hair in a ponytail. This would be informal and, Maggie hoped, fun. When ready, she called for a car and headed out to the street. Her preparations hadn't taken long so she knew she would arrive early. She didn't care. This was an unplanned adventure.

Maggie did arrive early, sitting down in a booth at least half an hour before the scheduled time to meet. She started to cough quite hard, using her napkin to muffle the sound, and then asked for a glass of water.

Her thoughts went everywhere but ended up focused on Rupert. *I wonder what he looks like. Probably a graying old fat guy with lots of wrinkles and an overly white, fleshy face with big bushy eyebrows. I see a priestly smile mixed on a flat, expressionless face, meant to convey warmth and openness while hiding his real disdain of and control over the human race*, Maggie thought. *Ohhhh, what makes me want to meet with that? What a horrible experience this is going to be and right before dying. I'll probably take my last breaths seeing those eyes, sunk into and surrounded by fat flesh, staring out at me.* A sense of dread enveloped her. Her mind went black, but then she spoke out loud, "My brother—death—is coming."

People around her tried to act like they'd heard nothing, but one little girl looked at her and then at her mother. "Mommy, that woman looks sad."

Her mother pulled her close and whispered, "Shhh. Eat your spaghetti."

Overhearing them, Maggie said to the girl, "Thanks." The girl and Maggie exchanged smiles.

Maggie pulled a pen and piece of scrap paper from her purse and started to write:

A Nightmare before Dying

He's coming tonight before the dawn breaks.
I can see him, caped all in black with eyes as black as coal,
arms swinging wide to pull me into a wide-open mouth,
a black hole pulling, sucking, hungry to consume me, swallow me, ingest me,
tearing me apart, undoing me.
I cower facing this face, the mask that hides oblivion, nothingness,

the end,
the face of death,
void of all that's human.

When Maggie looked up, Jake sat across from her. "Oh, I didn't hear you. How long have you been here?"

"Oh, I just sat down."

Before she could respond, Maggie started to cough. Jake pushed her water glass closer, but she ignored it, trying hard to cover the noise with her napkin. When she finally was able to stop, she tried to smile and look like nothing just happened. Her acting job didn't work.

"Are you okay?"

"Well, no, I can't say that I am, but coughing has become pretty routine for me. It actually tears me up inside, but I usually don't have the chance to talk about it. Coughing can really disturb people, even make them mad. I don't understand it, but it happens, so when I cough, people who don't get mad mostly just try to get away. I'm glad you stayed. Did you get mad?"

"I wasn't aware of feeling mad, but I have to admit that hard coughing is unsettling. I'm sorry you have to suffer like that."

"Me too, but as they say, that's life. Now, let's move on and talk about something else."

"Sure, I can do that, but aren't we here to eat?"

"I guess at least you are. I'm not sure how much I'll eat. It pains me to admit it, Jake, but I think I'm here primarily for the company. You were all the company I could muster up."

"Oh, thanks, it feels good to be the first chosen, even if the only choice."

They looked at each other and smiled.

"I would think someone with your background would have learned not to tell someone he was your only choice."

"Well, I've never been known as someone with a lot of social skills. Words can flow quite quickly from my brain to my mouth without monitoring. Probably one reason I didn't have a large pool of friends to call upon tonight when I needed company." Maggie turned away, but Jake had already seen the tears start to fill her eyes.

"When I came in tonight, you looked like you had just seen a ghost."

"Yeah, well, I'm about to become a ghost, so watch out. I may come back to haunt you!"

The waiter came by to ask if they were ready to order.

"No," Jake said.

Then Maggie added, "But you could bring me a hot tea, chamomile with lemon, please."

The waiter left to get her tea.

They looked over the menu. Jake was hungry, Maggie, not so much.

When the waiter returned with her tea, Maggie asked if she could get just a small plate of plain spaghetti.

"Sure. You don't want any sauce? We can do something plain." He wanted to add, "and tasteless" but refrained.

"No, just plain old spaghetti, please."

Jake ordered an antipasto appetizer with chicken marsala.

"Okay. No beer or wine?"

"No thanks, that will be all."

He left and they sat staring at each other. Neither knew what to say.

Jake wanted to say, *I find conversations with you, Maggie, strange, unnerving, and confusing.* Instead, he chose something just to break the silence. He knew Maggie was unpredictable, but the silence made him nervous. "I had planned to have chicken tonight but not the plain stuff I generally fry up at home. Now I get a special edition! I've had their chicken marsala before and always leave wanting more." He didn't think Maggie even heard him.

Inside, Maggie was struggling, physically for sure, but at this moment, it was her emotions that were boiling over. She so much wanted to talk about herself, while her whole being seemed programmed to silence, to keeping her dirty laundry to herself. Finally, she let go. "I've gotten the word; Rupert is willing to meet, and I don't know what to say or do. Interesting, isn't it? I must have thought at some level he'd never want to see me. After all, that's our history to date."

Jake waited, not wanting to interrupt her.

Maggie, though, felt his silence as a threat after she had taken this huge risk. She had always had the rapt attention of colleagues and coworkers whenever she spoke, and here Jake, basically a stranger to her, now sat looking unmoved, impassive, and detached as she began to tell her personal story. She felt like exploding but also felt intimidated by other diners quietly enjoying a night out.

Jake could see Maggie's face reddening and fists clenching. He began to fear she'd get up and walk out. "You know, Maggie, I've never been good around women sharing something personal. I always want to say or do something to bring down any emotional temperature, supposedly to help you, but it's really to help me. I am feeling downright uncomfortable right now."

"Feel free to leave, Jake. I felt like leaving myself, maybe because of what I was picking up from your side of the table. I need help right now. I have lived my life in such a way that now I have no one I'd call a friend or an intimate, except maybe my lawyer. I'm about to embark on an archaeological dig into my crazy family, and I'm sitting here revealing myself to a stranger. I'm here, Jake, because you seemed interested in me, and now, I need someone maybe just to stick a dagger into my heart to save me from this slow death I'm living," she coughed again, "and from the terrible ordeal that now seems more possible than it ever did when I first started down this road."

"I didn't bring a dagger, Maggie. Sorry, I didn't realize that was what you might want, and I'm not the man for that job. I think I came back because I felt so aroused when we first met. Not sexually aroused, though you are quite attractive, but intrigued by how you're facing the adversity and challenges in your life right now. You're a curiosity to me, a strong, forceful, tough, firm, big-time executive in the middle of an end-of-life crisis and, above all, talking with me about it. Me, a small-time business manager who lost his wife and then his children to lives of their own, living alone in a small apartment in a city full of important people like you."

Maggie smiled. Jake's humbleness had disarmed her. He wasn't giving her anything to fight against.

Their food arrived. She began to pick at her spaghetti. Jake dug into his chicken. Maggie felt happy for him; he could still enjoy a good meal.

The atmosphere of the restaurant was quite pleasant. Italian opera played softly, and though people talked, it was quiet enough so diners could easily carry on conversations without yelling. Maggie relaxed, sat back in her chair, and watched Jake and people at tables adjacent to theirs. The girl who had smiled at her was busy drawing in a coloring book. The adults at her table were laughing and drinking coffee. This was all so new to her, to be with a receptive and gentle male in an agreeable, enjoyable setting.

Then some regret flooded in. *Too bad it all has come so late in life for me.* This brought tears to Maggie's eyes, which she quickly averted, hoping Jake would not notice. It worked this time. He didn't, and all signs of her anguish soon passed.

After finishing what they wanted of their meals, they began to talk again. It felt like everything that had preceded their meals had only been the prelude, like foreplay before a good sexual encounter. Jake's jitters had eased. He felt eager to talk, his curiosity peaking. Maggie had stayed calm.

"You know, Maggie, I think I'd like to know more about this brother of yours."

"Me too. After receiving the cancer diagnosis, I started to think more about family. All of them have passed away, except for my brother, and as you know, he's been gone from my life for many years. I guess the bond of family got relit, fired up perhaps by my sadness and fear of facing death but also, I feel now, out of my deep loneliness. Something had to change in my life. I had to take a risk not taken before. I have not really explored, Jake. What exploring I've done has been at work to find something predetermined by someone else. I thought I knew everything. Approaching death has a way of breaking arrogance, pretentiousness, and pride, at least it did for me. Death scares me. I feel naked before it, and maybe reconnecting with Rupert will help me be more ready to die."

"Do you think you also might want to meet Rupert because he's a former priest?"

"No, not one iota of me has reached out to him as a priest. If family is where we begin our journey, he's all the family I have left as I approach the end of my journey. You know, though, opening a door into my unfinished past like this scares me too. I even have nightmares about him, one of which was forming in my head just before you got here. I think

I want to follow through with my original plan, but now that he's said he's willing to see me, the fright I had before borders on terror." Maggie stopped. She looked at Jake, and he looked back, appearing to her as if he really was interested, even concerned. And he was leaving her space to talk, saying and doing nothing to draw attention to himself. *Strange*, she thought. She'd always had to fight for space for herself. As a CEO it was easy. Bureaucratic power and authority trump personal power or authority. *I ruled, everyone else followed, and I loved it. Yet I have no power over Jake.*

Maggie's head began to spin. She felt dizzy and feared she might faint. Instead, she got up and ran for the bathroom. "Oh God, where is the bathroom?"

She was overheard by someone who could tell she was in a hurry. "Down that hall in front of you. Woman's is the first door on your left. Good luck."

Maggie had slowed down a little only to hear the directions. She saw the door and pushed it open. Four occupied stalls faced her. She dropped to the floor and started to cry.

All four doors opened, and Maggie found herself surrounded by four very concerned women. Some had their hands on her shoulders, and others stood back a little, but everyone was saying something, though nothing she could make out.

"Could someone please help me up?"

The two women closest to her reached under her arms and pulled her up.

Once up, Maggie found she could stand on her own. "Thanks, I think I'll be all right." She looked at the concerned faces of these four women.

Several other women come in, but they immediately just said, "Oh sorry," and left.

No one spoke until Maggie said, "Thanks."

"Would you like us to call for help?"

"No, you have been all the help I needed."

As they left, they noticed Maggie didn't even go into a stall; she walked out behind them. They all looked at each other and one said, "That was odd." The others nodded their heads and walked away.

Feeling less dizzy and no longer afraid of fainting, Maggie walked back to her table. Jake saw her coming and walked over to meet her. They walked back together. Maggie sat down, looked at Jake and smiled. "Did you miss me?

Jake could see something had changed for Maggie and decided to play along. "No, not much." He smiled but then quickly became serious. "I guess I'd really just like to know if you are okay. You left in such a hurry, at first, I thought you might be running away again and considered following you, but then I heard you ask about the restrooms. So I waited—while biting my fingernails down to the nub!"

They both laughed.

"Thank you for not following. I panicked and only wanted to be alone, away from everyone. The bathroom was my refuge. Yes, stupid. As any rational person would know, a bathroom in a place like this could well be full, and this one was. Every stall taken, closed, occupied. I must have briefly lost consciousness because my mind shut off, and the next thing I remember for sure was walking back and seeing you. I have no idea what happened in there. Did I get into a stall or what? What happened?" Maggie went quiet, like she was suddenly lost in thought when actually she'd lost all thought. She had no answers. "Why do I now feel calm? I remember panicking and then, poof, it's gone. That's impossible, isn't it?"

Jake shrugged. "Maybe you'll recall what happened later."

Maggie stared in his direction, but he had no idea if she really saw him.

He waited for her to say something and then asked, "Are you okay?"

"I have no idea, Jake, but for some reason I want to tell you about my plan for meeting Rupert. Maybe get your feedback. Theresa, my lawyer and my only friend, knows everything. Now I want you to hear it, and to, well, maybe be my second friend."

Jake couldn't think of what to say to that. He knew Maggie as a troubled soul who had drawn him into her life. She knew next to nothing about him, but she seemed to be wanting him as a friend even without that knowledge. He had become strangely attracted to her, her weirdness, for sure, but also her vulnerability. "Maggie, Maggie, you are something else. I've never met anyone like you and probably never will again. I'd be honored to be your second friend."

She smiled at him but said nothing.

"You look happy. What a journey you're on, from the depths of despair to the appearance, at least, of being happy."

"I am, Jake. Now why don't you order some dessert and then I'll continue talking."

He called the waiter over and ordered tiramisu and coffee.

After Jake's dessert arrived, Maggie began. "I thought Rupert and I could meet somewhere like Seattle, not too far for him to drive and easy access for me. I'll rent two hotel rooms. I have no idea what will happen when we actually meet. I've always prepared for a meeting, but how do I prepare to meet someone I haven't had any contact with since I was seven? I just turned sixty-three, and he must be sixty-eight. He's retired, and I'm not far from leaving this earth. I wonder if he ever thought about me, like what happened to his little sister. I wrote him letters but never sent them. I didn't even know where he lived or if he was dead or alive. I can't envision him, though I have had some chilling fantasies of what he looks like. So, I'll go to Seattle and try to be the controlled, sophisticated sixty-three-year-old I'd like to be in front of him. Most likely I will be a terrorized little girl, capable of either killing him or embracing him. Future unknown."

"Sounds like your plan remains fluid, which it seems to me, it must since there are so many unknowns at play here. Anything could happen."

Maggie knew she'd asked him for feedback, but she felt some hostility when he actually gave it. What he said was true and she knew it, but hearing it confirmed by an outsider made it feel almost too real. "You know, Jake, I've always been seen as a super-controlled woman, unflappable, no matter the situation. Since meeting you, I've acted more like a child than an ordered professional, but I think it's good for me, and so I'm not going to throw that tiramisu in your face. Instead, I'll say thanks for the feedback. I'm usually first and foremost an angry and untrusting woman, and as they say, a leopard can't change its spots. But I am trying to at least alter the design. So, though I hardly know you and still don't fully trust you, I am trying. I must try."

"Well, I see that, Maggie. I'm not much of a poet and never the romantic, as I've been told before, but at this moment I feel touched listening to what you have gone through and what you yet face."

They were then quiet for a moment until Jake's discomfort became too much. "I'm done, Maggie. Are you ready to go?"

"If you can't stand the heat, get out of the oven or kitchen, right, Jake?"

Jake blushed but said, "Now I have another word for you to go along with controlled and exact. Sassy!"

Maggie loved it. "How about I add saucy and mischievous?"

When they got up and left the restaurant, they were both giggling like kids.

CHAPTER 27

RUPERT STAYED WITH FATHER BROWN for over an hour. They talked about books, and Father Brown shared interesting information on the history of Powell River. He was no historian but had lived in Powell River and been part of the Catholic Church there since graduating from seminary.

"That qualifies you as an expert in my book."

"Well, thanks, Rupert, but the real experts are the first inhabitants whose ancestors still live here, who aren't afraid to tell the story of how they lost their rights and their land to the white man. Of course, the Catholic Church had a big part in all that. With all our missionary zeal to save these folks, we lost our humanity. In our extreme focus on the First Nation people's soul, we stripped them of their humanness."

"But don't you—and I—carry that legacy of the church by serving it? But . . ."

"But what, Rupert?"

"I like you personally, but you represent the institution that I feel, right or wrong, betrayed me and misled me, maybe just as it did to the First Nations. I was led by this institution to believe it was the path to salvation, to God. I never really had much of a humanity when I entered the Church, so you didn't take that, but then I never found it in the Church either. I found rules to follow but no reward. So, maybe that's my fault, not the Church's, but regardless, I've decided to leave it and am trying to accept that I'm leaving. I admit I'm scared to do the act. I have no experience with making decisions like that, and part of me feels maybe I should start with a less consequential decision like—" Feeling noticeably weak and unsteady, Rupert shook and shifted uncomfortably in his chair before continuing, "I don't know, like where to take my next vacation. But I did decide and have tried to adapt to that decision by saying out loud I no longer want to carry or accept the legacy of betraying the First Nation peoples or others disillusioned by their history in the church. I want to make my own history, but it's hard. Yes, even challenging, but whatever is driving me inside—spirit, heart, or some unknown—my will to live in ways I used to think wrong, blasphemous, or just blatantly ungodly has mushroomed." Rupert became quiet, lost in his thoughts and still uneasy.

"You look sad, Rupert."

"I'm not sad, or at least I don't think I am. I don't really know what I feel, but I think it's a cross between excitement and terror. All this I'm doing could be wrong, the work of the devil, but God, it feels so right."

Father Brown said nothing but got up to walk around the room. He had struggled with his own questions about the Church, its history, and whether it was the right path for him. He still harbored doubts but had decided those doubts helped keep him humble and prevented his thinking too much of himself and his power. Finally, he sat down. "I think I understand what you're going through, Rupert. I have been through my own dark night and may again someday, but so far, I've found my path to be in this role. I am in the Church as priest but living life as a man of the world with all the gifts, shortcomings, and transgressions. I read, I laugh, I cry, I lead, but never do I think I'm special. That, I believe, is the problem of many in the Church—we've come to think of ourselves as somehow saved or special or unique when we're not. It sounds like you were seduced as a child into believing something you imagined from the way some priests treated you. They probably treated you well, which you deserved, but could not save you, Rupert. All I can do too is give you what I have, a place in my congregation, a friendly hand, my library, or even a place to stay in my home."

"Thanks, but your house is not what I need, Father Brown. I think I need you, not as a priest but as a friend! You can't imagine how alone I am in the world. I only have a sister, who was abandoned by me in childhood, a woman who allowed me to ravish her, and maybe a few neighbors who have newly come to know I exist. Nobody too close and all very new, including you."

"Rupert, it's true I hardly know you, but you probably have told me more about your life than you've told anyone. Maybe I can start out as a confidant and work into being a friend."

This was all getting to be too much for Rupert. Though pleased with what had happened so far, he wasn't sure where to go next. He was trying not to get emotional, but as he became more nervous and unsure of how to continue, he could feel himself growing angry and afraid. Whenever he felt those emotions, it always led to him being isolated and left alone.

Father Brown looked up at the clock. "You know, Rupert, I just remembered I have another meeting to attend. Can we continue this at another time?"

This gave Rupert an excuse to get mad, and things changed fast. "No."

"What?" Father Brown was surprised and confused. "I have to go and soon. Sorry I forgot to tell you before, but truthfully, I just remembered it myself. We can continue later."

"No."

Father Brown now remembered his earlier contacts with Rupert. Always quiet, you never knew what he was thinking until, sometimes, he'd just lose his temper and walk out. Well, he didn't have the time now to deal with it. He'd just had enough of this from Rupert. "Look, you invited yourself over here, and now you have the audacity to demand more time? You're troubled, Rupert, and I can't deal with that right now."

"How dare you? Where do you get off telling me I'm troubled? You and your arrogance!" Rupert's face turned tomato red; his fists clenched. He rose to leave, thinking, *Get out before you do any damage*, while at the same moment he heard, *Throw the first punch, Rupert. Surprise him.*

Before he could make a move in either direction, Father Brown surprised him. "You want to hit me, don't you? Go ahead. You've no doubt never had the guts to do it before. Oh, but then you were, or are, I'm not sure which, a priest, and priests don't do things like that, do they?"

Rupert was stunned, momentarily paralyzed. The shame he felt overwhelmed both his words and actions. He stared at Father, but his eyes weren't seeing clearly. The depth of the defeat he felt left him unable to think or move. He just stood there, feeling like the naked, impotent shell of a man who masqueraded as a priest.

Father Brown was now equally caught up in what was happening and momentarily forgot about leaving. "Since I first met you in the restaurant, Rupert, you've displayed this quiet seething toward me and the other priests at the table. So now, go ahead, hit me. If you knock me out, just call an ambulance before you leave." He moved the chairs, stood up and raised his fists. "Go ahead. See what you can do."

"Asshole, pompous ass, addle-brained half-wit, . . ." Rupert sputtered, trying to blurt out more names but couldn't. His mind had shut down, his muscles tightened, his heart rate quickened, and his vision blurred. Father Brown was right, he did want to knock him down, maybe knock him out cold, but also, he didn't. Why was Father Brown deliberately trying to provoke him? Regardless, he now had to do something. He calmly went to the shelf and grabbed the book he'd looked at before and threw it across the room, hitting the wall with a loud bang. The noise sounded like an explosion. He jumped.

Father Brown instinctively ducked. "Rupert, I said fight, not throw things."

Rupert just stared at him. The desire to strike out at Father Brown subsided some, but he still wanted to hurt him. "Rules, rules, rules. Got a rule for everything, don't you? Well, I'm tired of doing things according to someone's rules." As he spoke, his anger came back stronger. Rupert looked for another book, but there was none to grab. *Why can't I hit the bastard? Am I a coward at heart?* His mind vacillated between yes and no. He saw Father Brown just staring at him but not looking terribly afraid. *Shit, shit, shit, he knows, and I know. Shit, shit, shit. This can't be happening.* He got madder and madder, again building up to explode. "You can't do this to me, asshole."

Father Brown just stood his ground.

Rupert suddenly laughed. *He's not backing down. He's not afraid of me.* His laughter turned to sobs, his head dropped into his hands, and he fell back in a chair. He quietly sobbed.

Father Brown stayed standing but did not approach.

He knows I'm here, Rupert thought. *He sees me. I am genuinely here. I know he sees me and feels me.* He pinched himself just to check, and yes, it hurt. *And I can hurt him too.* He stopped crying and smiled. "I'm not going to hit you, Father, or at least I don't think so. Depends, I guess, on what happens next."

"Holding back, for now?"

Rupert laughed hard and long. "Can you believe it? Rupert Callaway, super-priest, out of control, but so far not acting crazy. Or am I?"

"You are a little strange, Rupert, but I suspect you have your reasons." He looked at his watch and shook his head. "Wait here, will you, Rupert? I have to make a quick phone call." He walked from the room before Rupert could answer.

Rupert sat, stunned, debating between the urge to get angry again and some desire to stop fighting. There was a strange new feeling germinating and taking root in him. He didn't even know what to call it—a new delicateness, a vulnerability, what? It scared him, but somehow, he wanted to be more exposed, more open.

"I'm back. I called the person I was supposed to meet and rescheduled our meeting for later. Truthfully, I want to hear more from you, and if you can hold your anger back, I'm here to listen."

Rupert decided not to even think about next steps. He just started talking. "Something happened a few days ago that has opened doors into my past and maybe also into me. A woman from San Francisco came to visit me who, it turned out, was the personal lawyer for my long-lost sister, someone I haven't seen or talked to since leaving for the seminary. And now, out of the blue, she makes contact through an intermediary, no less. She must be some important person to send a lawyer up here to find me. My sister wants to see me. She gave me no reasons for this, just asked if I would meet her." He dropped his head a little and walked to stand next to a bookshelf. "Oh, and the lawyer said my sister was dying."

Father Brown looked like he wanted to say something. His eyebrows rose up, and he wiggled a little in his chair, but he did not get up or say anything.

"In the days since this happened, my life has been transformed, and that's a word I don't use lightly. I think what's been happening to me is the real deal, genuine and profound. Not what I've always sought in the church but authentic and deep. Please forgive me for my inadequate explanations, Father. As you have correctly pointed out, I don't have any experience with talking, only getting emotional." Rupert smiled. "I don't completely understand what's happening, but maybe someday I'll tell you everything, once I fully grasp it myself."

Rupert continued, "I've had several days to consider her question and all that has happened since, and then, just a short time ago, the lawyer called for my answer. I said I would see her, Maggie is her name, and now I await the where, when, and how of all this." Rupert's heart was beating fast and hard. He was sure Father Brown could see the pounding in his chest. Perspiration formed on his forehead, and sweat poured from under his arms. He unlocked his arms and walked to a nearby table where he took several tissues. Waving his arms and exaggerating his movements, he proceeded to wipe his brow before slowly heading back to his original chair.

Father Brown smiled.

"I think I've lost my way in life. Nothing feels secure. I can't even remember some of my old safety rituals. Coming here today to talk is happening without my usual controls. I've lost control, but I feel an energy I've never known. And I wanted to tell someone, but whom? I have no one, and I do mean no one, in my life. I live alone. I have no living family except for this sister, and even she was dead to me until this recent contact. Without the title of priest, I'd probably be called a hermit. Now, my iron curtain of self-containment has cracked, shattered, and a me I am totally unfamiliar with has emerged."

"Listen to this—," Rupert started but then stopped, questioning if he wanted to continue. The energy to tell his story was too much to contain. Rupert knew, though it scared the bejesus out of him, that the dam he'd built to contain himself had sprung a leak, a big leak. In the quiet that surrounded him he could hear Father Brown breathing, hear someone banging dishes in another room, and smell incense coming from somewhere nearby, but none of it distracted him now. "I slept with a woman!" He looked at Father Brown, expecting to see some reaction; maybe his mouth would drop open, or he'd cry out. Instead, he saw again that slight smile come across the father's face. "And I really, really liked it."

"I hear tell, it's beyond words—especially the first time."

Rupert yelled, "Yes, yes, yes!" and then blushed. "Sorry, but I've been holding that for too long."

"You're forgiven, Rupert."

Rupert was now confused. "What?"

"And keep on doing it." He chuckled.

Rupert finally saw Father Brown was playing with him. He continued, "Here I've lived a life of deceit, hiding from others, always expecting judgment, and when I finally choose to speak, I do it in front of someone who just gives me a soft smile. No rebuke, no reprimand, just a smile. Go figure. How did I ever deserve that?"

"I can't answer that, Rupert. What happened to the woman with whom you shared your bed?"

"She's gone back to Vancouver, but I have a feeling I'll see her again. Maybe after I meet Maggie."

"Well, you have surprised me, Rupert. I never saw you as a guy who could ever have let himself have sex. You broke the rules but not in the ways I fantasized. Do you feel guilty?"

"I don't really know. Something is certainly stirring in me over my recent behavior. I probably do feel guilty but not for having sex. I suspect it's because I abandoned my family, running away to the church without much conviction but with way too much hope. I needed a sanctuary, an escape from my feelings or lack of feelings, I don't know which. Rather than get married or join the army, I joined the church, a place I hoped would be an escape from my life. But now I cannot say really what I'd hoped to find, other than trite and meaningless things like happiness or security or maybe even just someone who cares. *God, faith, salvation,* and *sacrifice* were words I might have used, but I had nothing invested in any of it other than how it all might serve me and my needs. Me, me, me, me! What a sham of a life I've lived.

"As a priest, I've had to demonstrate belief. I've had to act like I knew the answers to people's questions of faith, and believe it or not, I could do that. I could act because I learned the words and the rituals, even without them having meaning for me. I've been living my whole life in my own dark night, hiding from myself behind my priest facade." Rupert could hardly believe what he heard himself say. How was he saying all this stuff so clearly, so openly after all these years? People who've lived his kind of life don't just go out one day and tell a different story than the one they've always told.

"Well, Rupert, I agree. It sure sounds like you've lost control, but for something better, n'est pas? Perhaps, you, like your whole family, have been dead to yourself and the world, living like a ghost, seen in body but not really alive. So, hallelujah! I think that ghost is rising, shedding the shroud, the façade that surrounded it all these years. Your sister made herself real and alive before you, and perhaps it has served to shake you awake too. In that book you saw by Thomas Moore, *Care of the Soul*, he says someplace that 'It is only through mystery and madness that the soul is revealed.'"

To Rupert, the air in the room around him was feeling charged with possibility until—

His phone rang.

He looked at the caller ID and saw a name: Theresa Gallagher. "I really hate to interrupt you and what's happening but I have to take this.

"Answer it, Rupert."

"Hello."

"Hello, Rupert. I've spoken with Maggie, and she has proposed that, assuming you can get yourself to Seattle, you can meet her at the Fairmont Olympic Hotel. She'll pay for the rooms, starting on Saturday night, and hopes to see you there next Sunday. It's an old hotel but nicely decorated with plenty of meeting spaces and restaurants nearby. Will that work for you?"

"Yes. I'll catch a train down there this Saturday. How will I know Maggie?"

"Maggie will call your room after you arrive and arrange a meeting place for Sunday morning. I may be accompanying her, and if so, I will, of course, recognize you. If, however, I don't come, she said to tell you she'd wear a brown skirt and yellow short-sleeve blouse to the meeting. It's supposed to be warm on Sunday in Seattle."

"Okay and thanks for helping to set up our meeting, Theresa."

"You're welcome and good luck."

Rupert hung up and turned back to Father Brown, who he knew had listened to the conversation. "It's going to happen. I feel ready."

"Good luck, Rupert, and if you want to talk later, please call. As Moore said, 'We need people in our lives with whom we can be as open as possible.' I think you and I have had a good beginning at that. Don't you?"

"Yes, surprisingly so, given my history of keeping secrets." Rupert got up to leave. But instead of heading for the door right away, he asked if he could keep the Moore book for a while.

"Sure, I'm breaking my own rule here, but for you, there is no return date. Just bring it back when you finish."

Rupert pulled *Care of the Soul* from the bookshelf and then retrieved the book he had thrown, the one intended for Father Brown's head, and handed it to Father Brown as he headed for the door.

"Thanks, Rupert. I'll keep it handy in case you ever want to use it again."

"Good. Maybe next time I'll just take it to read, rather than use it as a weapon!"

"Yeah, we'll see. One thing I've learned, though, is you have a lousy aim."

"I'll work on that, Father." Without thinking, Rupert reached out his hand. Then when he saw what he was doing, he quickly pulled it back and thrust it in his pocket.

"You're forgiven, Rupert."

Rupert smiled and said, "There I go again." He then pulled his hand from his pocket and extended it out. The handshake felt like an embrace, and he didn't want to let go. Finally, he did and whispered, "Thanks. I don't know what I expected when I ran over here, but I'm leaving frankly feeling a little wired and jittery but ready to move on to who knows what."

He then turned and left.

CHAPTER 28

RUPERT WALKED OVER TO THE CHURCH GARDEN with its green manicured lawns and well-managed flower beds. The sun had come out while he was meeting with Father Brown, and everything looked fresh and clean, washed by the rain that had come that morning. He thought a walk would give him some time to reflect on what had just happened. That seemed more important to him at this moment than the upcoming meeting with Maggie, which he did have to think about and prepare himself for, but he would do that later.

First Sylvia and now Father Brown have penetrated a place in me I neglected long ago, a garden left untended for so long I didn't recognize it. Angry me, I know him. Hidden, disillusioned, and alone me, I know him too. But the honest and aware me, him I have resisted knowing, and yet that part of me just took over with Sylvia and now with Father Brown. Bang-bang! The masked man has been unmasked! I hardly recognize him. In the last twenty-four hours, the me I've known and lived with, albeit very uncomfortably over the years, has what? Gone into hiding, died, disappeared, what? All this after hearing from my "dead" sister.

Rupert leaned down and looked directly at one of the red tulips blooming in front of him and said, "Change for most people might be subtle, but for some of us, it is the result only of being hit over the head by the proverbially hammer!"

The Church didn't make me what I am, but it certainly nurtured what I've become, mused Rupert. *No, that's not right. It took me in and let me believe it could lead me out of my suffering, out of life's ordeals. The Church gave me shelter, food, clothing, and a job. It welcomed me in, provided for all my needs, and gave me laws to live by. Now it still provides for me in retirement, still makes me physically secure. Who gets a house with water frontage when they retire? I did. And I pay nothing for all the comfort and security it provides.*

But this care and all the accompanying trappings of belief actually have helped me hide. I became a recluse while living among the community of believers, unable to have what all of them claim to have found. I got no results; I couldn't collect on the promises. I have come to know only the darkness of a solitary, isolated existence—until now.

Again, he leaned into one of the plants, a rhododendron flower this time, and said, "Why? Why is this suddenly changing me?" Rupert waited, still hoping he might hear something, that nature would speak to him. "Okay, God, I'm waiting. Your turn."

Nothing.

But then Rupert grunted, "Oh!" Words failed him, but he felt funny—quiet, peaceful. "What's the right word?" For now, he settled on the word *different*.

He looked down, picked up a few stones from the garden path, and threw them as hard as he could, hoping no one was walking near the trees where his stones landed. He heard no cries, so picked up more stones, bigger ones, and pitched them with true reckless abandon. He kept throwing until his arm began to tire, and then he just dropped down to the ground.

Rupert sat there, trying to answer his question: What's changed? The more he tried forcing himself to come up with something the more frustrated he became. This time, though, his frustration did not turn to anger. Instead, he just gave up; he surrendered to not knowing, stood up, and continued his walk, kicking stones and picking up a few here and there. He didn't throw any, but he tossed them in the air as if he were juggling, which of course he had no idea how to do. As the stones fell, he simply picked up replacements. "What a kick this is," he cried out. He juggled and played with his stones all the way back to his car. Then he threw them on the front seat, got in, and drove off.

After arriving home, Rupert sat in the car and looked at the house. *That's not my house*, he thought. *It's the Church's house! I wonder if stones are allowed inside. Well, I see no one around to ask, and the house itself won't talk, so I guess I'll make my own rule: stones are okay here in the bed, in the kitchen, on the floor, or wherever.*

"You know," he said out loud, "I brought a stone into this place the other night. Her name is Sylvia, and I had sex with her, my first-time, body-to-body, unclothed, kissing and writhing, body-on-body, creating a song of desire, a tune of lust and fascination. All the moves came naturally to this old, unused body, and I loved it. All the masturbating I've done can't touch how it felt to be with her, an alive, warm, and sensual woman!"

Rupert took out his phone and called the number Sylvia had left for him.

She answered formally, "Hello, Dr. Plath here."

He knew immediately he'd reached her at school. He recognized the voice, but the name surprised him. "Hello, Rupert here. Can you talk, or should I call back later?"

"Now's okay. What's up?"

"Well, I'm not sure why I called. I just started to think about you, picked up the phone, and you answered.

"I'm glad you followed your impulse, Rupert."

"This may sound strange and out of place, but a question did just come up when you answered the phone, though I wasn't sure I should ask it." He stopped as if he was thinking and then added, "But I now have a new motto: risk is my reward."

Sylvia laughed. "You've moved from babe in the woods to man of the woods."

"Slow down, Sylvia. Things are moving fast but still—"

"So, what's your question, Rupert?"

"Where does your surname Plath come from? I know it's your family name, but where's it come from?"

"Oh, I'm related to Sylvia Plath," she joked.

"Who's that? Remember, you got to go slow with me."

"Sorry, I told you before. She was a famous writer, and no, I'm not really related, but as an aspiring writer, I'd like to be a relative of hers. Maybe then I'd have better writing genes."

They both laughed at this.

"But, you're right; it's my family name. Our family came from Germany where there are two theories on its origin. Some suggest the origin is found in the medieval German word for a maker of armor breastplates. Others claim the name stems from the German word for *plateau*. Whatever, nothing romantic unfortunately."

"Interesting. Thanks for the explanation, which was more than I expected you'd say. In fact, part of me expected you might laugh, thinking, 'Where'd that dumb question come from?'"

"Rupert, I laugh only at your jokes, or at least your attempts at being funny!"

Rupert smiled before saying, "On a more serious note, though, I wanted to tell you I've heard from Maggie, again through her lawyer, and we plan to meet in Seattle on Saturday."

"Oh dear, Rupert, don't you have to be in church every day?"

"Ha, ha. You should know I can't be shamed quite as easily as you might have suspected. You can keep trying, and maybe you'll catch me dropping into the shame pit again, but for now, no, I do not have to be in church on any day anymore. I could even meet you on a Sunday if you would still like to meet again."

"That would be nice, Rupert. For a priest, you excited, oops, I mean you impressed me more than I would have ever expected. Remember, when we first met at the restaurant, I was looking for livelier and less-inhibited folks than what I'd expect to find in a priest. You've cracked that mold—not broken it, mind you, but certainly started something, though I'm not sure what. I would, though, like to spend more time with you when possible. But right now, your agenda sounds full. You scared?"

"Yes, I am. I have no idea what to expect, and that makes me nervous. However, I feel ready. In fact, I've decided to drive down to Seattle tomorrow, rather than take the train. I told the lawyer I'd get to the hotel Saturday night. I'll get something myself for Saturday. Maggie's getting the rooms starting on Sunday. Maybe, if you're free, I'll leave early enough, and we could have lunch together."

"Sure. How about we meet at India Gate on Robson Street? They have good northern Indian cuisine—not too hot! I love Indian food, but some of the cooking from South India is way too hot for me."

"I've never had Indian food before, Sylvia, but I'd like to try it. Not too hot sounds best for me, as a start anyway."

"Okay, I'll see you then."

"Great. Until Saturday. Bye."

"Bye."

Rupert hung up the phone, picked up one of his new rocks, threw it up in the air a bit too hard, and left a mark in the ceiling. "Oh dear, I guess I've cracked the ceiling!"

CHAPTER 29

When Maggie and Jake came out on the street, he suggested they walk south. She didn't care which way they went.

As they walked, Jake tried to think of something to say. "That tiramisu was great, but I felt guilty when I remembered that you can't eat sweets. I can be an insensitive oaf sometimes!"

"Don't worry about it, Jake. I'm the one who can't do sweets, not you, and frankly, sweets are the least of my worries right now."

Jake didn't know quite where to go next. Why was he trying to be so sensitive? Maggie was quite capable of taking care of herself. "Really, Maggie, I think what I said was a faltering attempt at putting myself at ease."

"Oh, Jake, I guess I just naturally put people on edge, even when I'm not trying. I want to tell you a little of what I'm going through; I don't want to keep everything to myself anymore. Hopefully, I can talk to you tonight without upsetting you too much." Maggie smiled and waited for him to say something.

When he didn't, she continued. "My doctors have promised to let me know soon if the chemo I've done has reduced the size of my tumors, but if it hasn't, I may just opt out of treatments altogether and enjoy my last days. I'm so happy I'm out enjoying your company. Chemo made me feel pretty miserable most of the time but especially right after each treatment. I just stayed home with the shades pulled and the door locked, watching TV, listening to the radio, and reading. I've read a variety of books, including several Lee Child thrillers because that Jack Reacher is a man after my own heart. Then there was a Harry Bosch mystery by Michael Connelly and some of the Ken Follett historical novels. And of course, the books on what people go through when dying. I recently read *When Breath Becomes Air,* written by a young doctor as he was dying from terminal cancer and then Sam Shepherd's last book. He just died from ALS, a horrible way to die. I think having a heart attack is probably the best way to go out," Maggie mused. "No prolonged suffering with that. I don't like to grumble and moan, but struggling with cancer has been hard. Not that dealing with a hard life was anything new for me, but this time, I faced an unknown enemy. Before treatment, I read all about what would happen, and my doctor educated me on what to expect, but then I discovered how knowing all about it wasn't going to make it easy." Maggie stopped suddenly, catching Jake off guard.

He'd been listening so intently that he just kept walking. Jake turned back and saw others on the sidewalk also had been caught by surprise, almost running into Maggie before turning. He moved back toward her. She was crying hard. He wanted so much to put his arms around her or at least to take her hand, but he did neither.

Maggie didn't wait for him to decide. "You know, someone once said, 'Knowledge is power.' Who, I don't really know or care because I've learned myself that it's true. My brilliance gave me entrance into a world that provided me shelter and livelihood, saving graces, for sure, but now I know something else is needed. Something you and Theresa have helped me see. Knowing about cancer was one part, but having a caring doctor, a friend, and someone to sit by you in bed is also imperative." She was crying again.

Jake now had tears in his eyes as well.

Neither knew how long they stood there, blocking most of the sidewalk, but at one point a man yelled, "Can't you two rent a room or something? You're blocking the street!"

This broke the mood for both of them. They stared at each other as if they had just met after a long absence, smiled, and then laughed. Jake still did not touch Maggie, but he no longer felt he had to do or say something special. Instead, they just turned and continued to walk south.

"I need to make a call, Jake."

"Do you want me to keep walking so you can have a little more privacy?"

"No, I want you here." Maggie retrieved her phone from her purse and pushed auto dial for Theresa, who answered after only a few rings. "Hi, Theresa. I've decided to fly to Seattle by myself. You don't have to come."

"Are you sure, Maggie? I've freed up my calendar so I could go."

"Thanks, Theresa, I really appreciate all you've done for me on this matter and so many others over the years. I could never repay you, but this time, I must go alone. I may need to call you while there, but I've also met someone I trust, who will also be on call, so to speak. Neither of you will be there with me, but you both will be by my side."

"Okay, Maggie. I'll look forward to hearing how it goes if you want to tell me."

"Till later then. Bye." Maggie hung up and looked at Jake who was smiling.

"Yes," he said, "I can be on call."

"Thanks. Knowing you're there, I just may reach out to both of you. You can't believe how lonely I've really been all these years."

"Well, if you call, I'll try to just listen. When I change a subject or try to offer advice, I often end up just putting my foot in my mouth."

Maggie laughed. "Well, Jake, maybe if you didn't always want to be so helpful . . . I think you could use a little more of my indifference, and I could use a little more of your compassion."

"Hard for me to be mean, Maggie."

"I don't think you have to be mean. That's just how I come across. I've been deeply affected by your sensitivity. How about from now on, you just trust that whatever you have to say will be mixed with all your sensitivity and caring. Don't worry so much about being nice. That's just who you are. I, on the other hand, wasn't nice to begin with."

Jake was quiet for a minute, thinking about what she said. "Okay, Maggie, I'll be on call while you're away, but I won't *try* to be helpful if you call."

Maggie smiled at him. Then she looked at her watch. "Wow, it's almost nine o'clock!" She didn't want to go home, but she was getting tired and didn't know how much longer she'd last. Her doctor told her she might feel more fatigued as time went on. She had continued to cough periodically, but Jake hadn't commented. *Well, I forced myself to eat something,* Maggie thought. *Can I now force myself to stay out late?*

They passed a bus bench, and Maggie asked if they might sit a while, even though they had walked only a short way from the restaurant.

"Sure. I don't know where we're going, but we aren't in a hurry."

The sun still lingered in the sky, but the air had cooled. Maggie felt the chill, and Jake noticed her shivering. He had worn a light jacket for dinner and now offered it to her. She accepted without hesitation. Her days of acting brave with no need for anything were over. The cancer had worn her down. People had always tried to find vulnerabilities in Maggie, and now she couldn't hide them. She felt needy, but she still hated that word. Her firmness had changed to fragility.

Jake put the coat around her. She leaned toward him and put her head on his shoulder. No one spoke, and soon Maggie fell asleep. Jake couldn't see her, but he knew she was asleep because of her steady, labored breathing.

Her cough jolted her awake. "Oh dear, I fell asleep here on the streets of San Francisco!"

"You must be really tired, Maggie, or maybe just less self-conscious than you used to be. Who knows, maybe both?"

Maggie heard Jake but didn't respond. She wanted to think he might be right that she really was feeling less inhibited. The idea kind of excited her. "Let's walk again."

Together they slowly walked, side by side, down the street. Because of the growing darkness, the sidewalk was less crowded. The rush of the day in San Francisco was transforming into the quiet stillness of a charming evening.

"I have small-cell lung cancer, Jake, I suspect from smoking, though my doctors don't talk about causes. Probably because it's too late to do anything about those. Survival rates for this are not great. I hide my symptoms as best I can. Remember, I'm the survivor, right?" Maggie smiled wryly. "What I try not to show most is my shortness of breath and the chest pain I feel. I had to wear a wig for a while, but now much of my hair has grown back. I never wore it long to begin with. I've lost weight, and I become tired easily. It can be difficult for me to swallow, and I have a fair amount of joint pain, though I get some relief with medication. However, as the disease progresses, I have a harder time hiding all this, which you've probably noticed tonight with my cough and how I just fell asleep on your shoulder. Thanks, by the way. I expect all this and more to just get worse as I reach the end. My life expectancy, since I was a smoker, is probably five years at most, and I'm into year five now. That's the clinical stuff, Jake. Personally, I'm scared but mostly maybe I'm more apprehensive about seeing my brother. I know it sounds like it could be a new beginning for us, but truthfully, I think it's more likely a time for me to say goodbye to my only living family member, soon to become the last of the Callaways!"

"We're not far from my place, Maggie. How about we go there? I'm just thinking we could sit there and be more comfortable."

"Sounds like a plan to me. Let's go. I'm tired, which I tell you as a warning because, no matter how stimulating the conversation becomes, I may doze off as I did there on the bench. It feels good to be with you, Jake. I can't believe I'm saying this, but I trust you. Maybe, because of my sickness, I have to trust more, but whatever the reason, I do trust you."

They walked the few blocks to Jake's place, a comfortable two-bed-room condo on the second floor of a ten-story high-rise.

"Oh, I'm so glad you have an elevator. I'm ready to sit. You probably can guess I never have had to walk much. Lots of cars at my disposal whenever I wanted or needed to go somewhere. I can't recall when I've walked even as much as I have in these last days. It's because of the elevators, not exercising, and going everywhere by car that I became overweight. You didn't see me when I was fat only because I lost most of it after I got sick."

Jake turned on some lights and told Maggie to take a seat. "I have plenty of choices from soft to hard, straight back to sloped back. You can tell I had a fussy family; everyone had a favorite. While you're doing that, I'll make a pot of tea. Any particular type you like?"

"Chamomile if you have it."

"Of course, I have that one. My youngest daughter, who just moved out, drank chamomile almost every night before going to bed. Helped her calm down, she said."

"Well, I don't need calming, that's for sure. Maybe I should have a black tea. No, I'm sticking with my first choice; it's the best." Maggie sat in a big soft chair and put her head back. Soon she heard classical music.

Jake yelled from the kitchen, "Hope the music's okay."

"My second choice after jazz, Jake. Let the music play!"

"Well, we'll start things off with a little George Frideric Handel *Water Music*, a collection of orchestral movements he wrote in 1717. Don't get too impressed, Maggie. I just read that off the label. Sounded good, didn't it?"

She laughed and relaxed into the chair.

Jake returned with tea and a light blanket he tossed to Maggie to put across her shoulders or over her legs.

"Jake, when I first heard that Rupert had expressed his willingness to meet, my stomach tightened. I felt suddenly uneasy, almost dizzy, and doubtful. In fact, when Theresa first called, I didn't pick up the phone. I knew she had news, and I just was not ready to hear it. If his answer was no, I thought I might be distraught. If he said yes, I feared I might just pass out. When she called back later, of course, it was a yes. When my brain came back online, I thought about you, Jake, and that's when I began to try to find you.

"Was it the seriousness of your sickness that made you write in the first place?"

"I guess so, but really I think I acted, surprisingly for a person like me, quite impulsively. I was sick, and I knew I faced a short future. Rupert popped in my head, and I wrote this letter inviting a meeting. This happened after not even having a thought about him for years. What makes stuff like that happen? I guess I need a good shrink to answer that. If I'd taken the time to think a little more about it, I might not have sent Theresa up there to find him. But I didn't think, not that time anyway, and now I understand why I never acted without thinking before. It opens doors to the unknown . . .," Maggie stopped a moment and then continued, "where monsters can lurk, waiting to devour you! Just like in all those children's fables we read."

"Yeah, I remember. But weren't some of those Dr. Seuss books about good monsters?"

"Probably, but right now I'd rather think about other things than monsters, if that's okay. You know how I told you I've had pain since developing the lung cancer? Well, I've actually been in some pain my whole life, stabbed in the heart by a family who didn't, probably couldn't, love or care. To survive, I surrendered my heart for my head, but I've lived with a knife in that heart. Now I think I've opened that painful wound, and I fear the diseased, putrid-smelling pus that could flow out when I meet Rupert. He left home and me when I was seven and he was twelve. He joined a seminary to become a Catholic priest. He never wrote or returned home after that. I wrote many letters to him but never mailed one. I still have some I've carried around with me for fifty-plus years. Mom and Dad went about their lives. Dad worked hard till he died, and Mom, I think, never recovered from leaving the old country and losing her family. She moped around and just tried her best to do the housework and be a mother until she had a heart attack at fifty-five and died. Rupert came home for the funerals, but we avoided each other as if we were strangers who'd never met.

"So, Jake, you see how I, the one who got really good at solving problems for others, have now conceived a project that could blow up my life. My life is almost over, but I'll still have to live with whatever comes out of this until they put me in the grave. And the worst part of it all is that this time I have nothing to escape to. No one wants my mind anymore. I'm basically already dead to those who've known me professionally. I can't escape the aloneness I felt as a kid. I am that alone, lonely child now. All my shields have fallen, and I've done it to myself."

They both sipped their tea.

"Your daughter was right; chamomile tea is calming."

"Good. Still feeling scared?"

"What do you think? Scared feelings, on their own linger long, and my meeting with Rupert is still out there in the future, the not-too-distant future now."

"You told Theresa your lawyer—I hope I got the name right."

"Yeah, you did. Go on."

"You told Theresa you did not want her to go along on Sunday, but I thought that when people get scared, they need others, the company of a trusted friend. Did you dismiss her too quickly?"

"I don't know, Jake. I think I was fantasizing you'd both be with me via the phone, but truly, I'm not really thinking too clearly right now, and I'm quite tired. My batteries are running down and right when I need to be at my brightest."

"Another good reason to have someone there with you."

Maggie shut her eyes and leaned her head back on the chair back. "This chair is so soft. Okay if I just take a short nap?"

"Sure. Let me get another blanket for you."

A tear ran down Maggie's cheek. She wiped it off with the back of her sleeve. Jake returned and gave her the blanket, which she laid on top of the other one. Before he left the room, he saw the next tear fall from Maggie's eye.

He said nothing but picked up his teacup and walked toward the kitchen. "I'm just going to get a warm-up, Maggie. Do you want me to douse the light?"

"No."

When Jake was done reheating the water, he turned off the music and sat down at the kitchen table. Even though it was now close to ten thirty, he didn't feel tired. Nor did he have to get up for work on a Saturday. Besides, this evening with Maggie had pumped him up. *I hardly know her, and yet I've been captured by her,* he thought. *What a life she's led. I always thought the rich had it made, no worries, plenty of friends, sycophants and all, lots of servants. She had all that but still seems to have suffered emotionally while hiding it from others, except maybe from this lawyer she refers to. From the fire of family dysfunction, she entered the fire of American big business. I wonder if being so emotionally damaged helped her become successful. It's interesting to think about . . . at a later time. Maggie doesn't need the burden of my curiosity.*

He sat there quietly for a time, just enjoying his tea. Jake liked tea at night better than coffee. It helped lock out unwanted thoughts where coffee could speed them up. He wondered too if he liked tea at night because of his British background.

Jake got up to add hot water again and picked up a notebook he kept near the phone. Maybe he'd record some of his thoughts, never having found himself in a place like this before. His first thoughts were challenges to himself.

What's wrong with me? I'm no psychologist. I'm not even a social worker. I have no training whatsoever in helping women, or men for that matter, struggling with some deep emotional wounding and death too.

He stopped writing. His mind had shut down. He pushed his tea and notebook aside and laid his head on the table. As he drifted off in a light sleep, he was surprised to see the image of Maggie appear in front of him. She was sitting across from him, her eyes dancing with both aliveness and vulnerability, making her even more attractive than he had thought watching her at dinner. He couldn't see the tough, unyielding, severe CEO she had described to him, making him wonder who she really was.

Jake popped awake after his short nap finding himself staring at the notebook. Picking up his pen he started to write:

I have absolutely no sexual interest in Maggie. Why? She's pretty, the right age for me, and she's a fascinating person. Our meeting was purely serendipitous. I sat down next to her, and now she's sleeping in my living room, worn out by time and circumstance. I sit here with my cold tea feeling happy, satisfied, and excited. Maybe I can't figure out what all's going on right now, but I know I can't wait to see what comes next.

He stopped writing, listening to the silence that filled his little house. Then, he thought he heard Maggie sobbing. *Do I go in to her, or do I leave her alone?* He decided to stay put. After a while, the crying stopped. He checked his watch and saw that it was now midnight. As he passed through the living room on his way to the bedroom, he saw her curled up and looking quite comfortable, *like she belongs*, he thought. *She can just stay there tonight.*

Just before he opened the bedroom door, he heard, "Hello." Turning, he saw Maggie had opened her eyes but hadn't moved. "I was just going to bed, Maggie. Feel free to just stay there tonight if you'd like, or I'll call you a car to take you home."

"I don't want to go home, Jake."

"Okay, do you need more blankets?"

"No, stay here."

He switched on the lamp and sat down. "Would you like more tea?

"No. I've been crying. I feel so tired I can't sleep."

"Okay."

"You know, Jake, I can't remember when or if I've ever cried like this. Even when Rupert left home, left me, I didn't shed one tear. I got mad, and I think I've stayed mad ever since. Mad keeps you alert all the time, you know?"

"I imagine it would, Maggie."

"Did you know I was crying, Jake?"

"I thought I heard you sobbing some when I was in the kitchen."

"I wonder what my parents would have done if I'd cried back then and they'd heard it. From what I remember of them, I'd guess they would have ignored it. But you heard it, right?"

"Yes, I did. I didn't know what to do. Part of me wanted to come in and check on you, and another part told me to stay put. I chose the latter of those two options, again maybe still wanting to err on the side of caution."

"Well, I'm not sure whether I wanted you to come or stay away. I think we all want to know what to do or say at the right moment, don't we?" Maggie was trying to go easy on Jake. She had no interest in confronting him for his style again. The time for doing that was over for her. "You know, I think I will take more tea now if the offer still stands."

"Sure. Still want chamomile?"

"Yes, that sounds great."

It took Jake almost ten minutes to finish heating fresh water and make the tea. It was still steeping in the cup as he walked back in the room.

Maggie had her eyes closed, but when she heard him, she said, "I'm awake. I was thinking about why I cried before, and I came up with many possibilities. However," and here Maggie sat up straight before continuing, "I know I was crying because I'm dying and don't have much more time to live. I know I've said on many occasions I'm dying, sometimes facetiously and other times to hear how it sounds, but I think tonight the truth about my dying really hit home and it made me not scared but sad." She started to tear up again.

"I know we just met, but that makes me sad too, Maggie."

She cried harder. Again, Jake didn't know what to do or say, just watched her closely but said nothing. He set her teacup down on a nearby table.

"I don't understand how I can feel so sad," said Maggie. "I should feel glad this life is ending for me. What will I miss? Who will even miss me? You know I have not heard from any of those who worked for me since I retired, which is the term I use to explain my situation, but actually I'm still on the payroll. I've always thought it had to do with not wanting to be around someone who was close to death, might be catching, you know. But I wonder about that. You said you didn't know what to do after you heard me crying, and I wonder if people who've worked with me ever knew I needed or wanted anything from them. I really made myself unapproachable. Even now, I probably put out that kind of message. So to make myself perfectly clear to you, if you hear me crying and if you want to, I want you to come and sit with me."

Jake immediately moved to squeeze in next to Maggie and laid his arm on the back of the chair. She leaned back and wept. He choked up, tears close to spilling out of him too. The situation was so sad. He made every effort to not make any noise as he began to sob, but he failed. When Maggie didn't jump up in surprise, he let go. The surprise for Maggie was how comforted she felt just sitting with him while he showed so much emotion. She wasn't alone.

When their crying stopped, they both were quiet.

"You know, Maggie, I'm more than happy to keep my arm behind you, but it's gone to sleep!"

This made them laugh.

"Well," she said, "that clarifies something for me. When I dated and even with my husband, the guy would sometimes put his arm around me and then without warning move it away. I always interpreted that as another rejection. Maybe, given what you just said, I was wrong! Another missed opportunity to be cared for." She put her head on the couch and leaned into Jake. Soon she fell asleep again.

Jake put his head back and fell asleep as well.

Around five the next morning, Jake awoke and slowly got up. Maggie didn't move. He went to the bathroom, splashed water on his face, and decided to change clothes and freshen up a little. He didn't have to go to work but couldn't see himself going back to sleep. Maggie had fallen over on the couch and, though she looked like she might be uncomfortable, hadn't woken up. He decided to go out and get coffee and maybe some baked goods. He knew of a good bakery not too far away.

Jake was back half an hour later with two coffees, black, and a large cinnamon roll they could split if she felt hungry enough. Maggie was still in the chair looking like she had just awakened. "Good morning," he said.

"Good morning. What time is it?"

"A little after six."

"Wow, it's a good thing no one expected me home last night. They'd be pissed!"

He laughed at this and asked her if she'd like a coffee.

"Yes, please."

He handed her one of the cups.

"Do you have any cream in the house?"

"Sure, let me run and get some for you."

"No, I need to stand up and stretch. Is it in the fridge?"

"Yeah."

They both went to the kitchen, and he gave her the bottle of cream.

"I have a cinnamon roll too. Interested?"

"No, I'll pass."

They sat at the kitchen table. Jake turned on the news.

"Oh, do we have to listen to news? I only have a short time left to live, and I'd rather not have to hear any more about the many disasters happening around the world."

They both smiled as he turned off the TV.

After their coffees, Maggie thought it best that she go home. She wanted to shower and change. She wasn't very good with endings in a situation like this. "I think I'll call for a Lyft. Thanks for letting me hang out, Jake." She got up, made her call, and headed for the door.

Jake watched her go thinking, *No soft endings for her.* Then he facetiously thought, *Our business meeting must be over.* "Bye, Maggie. Good luck when you meet your brother. I'll be here if you want to call, and you now have the number. Take it with you, okay?"

"Okay, Jake and thanks again. I'll be in touch."

He returned to the kitchen and sat staring at his unfinished coffee and roll, trying to piece together everything that had happened. "Strange! How in the world does something like this happen to me? All the good mysteries usually happen to other people, not me. Not this time, I guess. Well, though I may never figure out how or why this one came my way, I'm glad it did."

CHAPTER 30

MAGGIE FELT LOUSY. Her cough had returned, and her chest pain had grown worse. She decided to get in bed as soon as she arrived back at her place, but now, she remembered she was supposed to meet Rupert in Seattle on Sunday. She knew Theresa would have made the room reservations, but at the moment, she didn't feel up to going. Maggie decided to just let it ride until later. *I'll still have time to fly up there. He wasn't scheduled to get there till after six on Saturday anyway.*

She hoped Maria wasn't coming. Maggie wanted the place to herself all day. The sun was above the horizon by the time she got back. She closed the curtains, stripped off her clothes, and put on a pair of comfy pajamas. Then, after a short trip to the bathroom for pain pills, she fell into her king-size bed, pulled up the covers, and slowly dropped into a deep sleep. Sitting up all night on Jake's couch had not given her the full rest she'd needed.

It was two in the afternoon when she awoke. The cough had abated some, but she still felt sickish and hot. The sun warmed the room, even with the curtains pulled. Maggie yanked back the covers but stayed in bed thinking, not about Rupert or last night. Her thoughts were more on death, her death. No more sunshine, warm weather, daytime breezes, traffic noise, hot baths, meals out, new clothes, awards, accolades, or criticisms. *No more me*, she thought.

Her dread grew. She remembered her empty life with no friends, no colleagues, no partner, no family. She thought, *Maybe it's even too late to try to see Rupert. Nothing could come of it, except make me sadder than I am already.*

But her desire to see him was strong, even stronger since meeting Jake. The light of passion, long dead in her, had been lit. She'd never met a man like Jake. Men had shown interest in her because of her position, her rank, her wealth, or maybe her large breasts. What was there beyond those that made her worth pursuing? She had always thought those were her prime assets. What else is there? Jake had not even asked about her work or anything to gain information about her wealth. So was it just a matter of his liking her body? Men like sex as much as money, maybe more. But then, Jake had not come on to her, even when she spent the night at his place. *Maybe he has a macabre fascination with death, or maybe because I'm dying, he does not have to worry about any long-term commitments.* But none of this felt right. So far, her experience with Jake seemed genuine.

And then there was Rupert who agreed to come to Seattle to meet her. Why? *Well, dummy, you invited him,* Maggie thought. *But I didn't really invite Jake. Oh, maybe I did. He saw my ass on the stool and couldn't resist taking the seat next to me. Many a red-blooded male has fallen for a nice ass.* She laughed at herself. Maggie, *Be real, will you?*

Maggie shook all over from the pain, the cough, and now, running from truths she didn't want to face, that Rupert genuinely wanted to see her before she died and Jake appeared quite concerned, curious, or something like that for her. How could her mind hold it all?

She had to get it together before things got too weird. This time, she wasn't sure she could. Was it because she was so close to death? Lots of weird things happen to people when they get close to dying. They will examine how they lived their lives, even sometimes becoming more caring or loving; never, it seems, do they become more selfish or mean.

"I made my life what it was and became unwanted. Now, it appears I've become more available and am wanted? Crazy, yes, but if true, then dying does have an upside!"

Maggie had always wanted someone to want her, not just as a body or as an accomplished woman but as someone valuable, worthy of respect. *What's happening seems too good to be true.* Tears flowed down her cheeks. Soon they stopped, and she smiled as she wrapped her arms tightly around her body to hold in the joy suddenly flowing through her.

Unfortunately, it didn't last. She was hit with another surprise. Maggie raced to the bathroom. She had not eaten much, but all she had consumed now came up. That was quickly followed by dry heaves, which went on and on until she saw blood in the toilet. "Oh God, I feel terrible." She had perspired so much her pajamas stuck to her skin. Staring at all the blood, she thought, *What do I do now?* She had no idea. Her mind had shut down, gone offline, paralyzed by the stress that had overtaken her.

She looked at the clock to check the time but then thought, *What does it matter? Nothing really matters anymore.* Maggie could feel herself sinking into darkness, away from everything and everyone, until something stopped her. From somewhere and without any explanation, she had a feeling of compassion. *Wow, what's that about?* Then she knew. She had no idea how she knew, but she knew. It was compassion for herself, and it made her smile. Mimicking a ghostly yowl, she said, "Out of the darkness come strange things." She laughed. "Yeah, strange indeed. Even weird."

Then a feeling of loneliness took over, but this time it didn't make her sad. She wanted company and she knew whom. Maggie grabbed her phone and called Theresa. "Come on, come on, pick up the phone."

After what seemed like forever to Maggie, Theresa picked up. "Hello."

"Hello. It's me, Maggie."

"Oh, hi. What's up?"

"I'm exhausted and coughing up blood."

"Have you called your doctor?"

"No."

"Oh. Well, don't you think you should get yourself to the emergency room to get checked out?"

"Okay, I have to get dressed first."

"How about if I come by and pick you up in about twenty minutes?"

"I'll try to be ready. I'm so tired."

"Okay, I'm coming."

Theresa hung up and Maggie got herself up off the bathroom floor but couldn't get dressed. Theresa found her sitting on the bed. She helped her lie down and pulled a cover over her.

"I'm calling an ambulance, Maggie."

Maggie didn't respond. She lay there bewildered and disoriented, her mind in a complete daze.

An ambulance arrived. Maggie's blood pressure was low, and her cough continued, making it hard for her to talk. They decided to take her to the University of California, San Francisco Medical Center because it wasn't far, and Maggie really had no preference of where they took her. Theresa said she'd follow them in her car and meet Maggie at the hospital.

The hospital was in Parnassus. Maggie had been taken to the medical area. Theresa couldn't go in without a family member first authorizing her visit, but she decided to wait anyway, sure that Maggie would tell them she was like family. And sure enough, after waiting around thirty minutes, Theresa heard her name called over the loudspeaker. Maggie had asked for her. The doctors had just left Maggie's room, telling her they planned to admit her for further observation.

"I guess my plan to fly up to Seattle will have to wait."

"Whatever, Maggie. You have to stay here now. I'll call Rupert to tell him what happened and that you'll get in touch with him when you can."

Maggie didn't respond, but Theresa noticed tears forming in the corners of her eyes. "You know, Theresa, besides having this cancer and all it's doing to my body, something bigger is happening to me here at the end of my life. I have no other way of talking about it, but look, I cry. You've known me a long time. When did you last see me cry?"

"That would be never, Maggie."

"Right, and I don't feel at all like telling you to go home to take care of your family. In fact, I would like it if you'd come back and sit with me a while after you've called Rupert."

"I'll have to call Guy too. He'll want to know what's happening and when he can expect me home. Then I'll come back. It will take time for them to move and settle you, so I should get back to your room soon after you arrive there."

Maggie smiled.

Theresa left to look for a quiet place to make her calls. The first call went to Tom, and then she dialed Rupert's number.-

"Hello."

"Hi, Rupert. This is Theresa again."

"Oh, hi, I was about to leave for Vancouver and a late lunch with a friend there. I'm late as usual. After that, I'll leave for Seattle, where I should arrive around seven, well, now more like eight or nine tonight."

"Well, there's been a change of plans, Rupert. I'm calling to let you know that your sister has had a setback and is in the hospital. I have no idea how long she'll need to stay, but she coughed up blood, and now her doctors want to do some tests. I can call you when and if it looks like your meeting can happen, but for now I'd unpack and plan to stay put."

Rupert knew his sister had cancer. Maggie had mentioned it in her letter, but with all he'd gone through since he'd read it, he had forgotten about the cancer altogether. "How far along is Maggie into her cancer diagnosis?"

"Four-plus years."

"Well, I really don't know much about lung cancer or its symptoms, but that sounds like she's pretty far advanced."

"That's correct, Rupert. She was originally given a prognosis of around five years, but those kinds of predictions can really only be the doctor's best guess. No one really knows. Some people live much longer, and others don't make it the five years. Maggie's in her fifth year."

Rupert didn't know what to say. "Okay. Call me as soon as you know more." Before he hung up, he added, "Please tell her I hope she gets better and we have the chance to get together. I don't know how much Maggie has told you about me, but our story is tragic to me now. Since hearing from her, my life has gone into a tailspin, but I must tell you, it does not feel all bad. When I first read her letter, I went into shock. I had pretty much forgotten about all my family members before hearing from her and her surprisingly wanting to do a face-to-face encounter. Now, I feel disappointed we cannot get together, and I'm worried about her health."

"I'll convey that to her, Rupert, and call you back when I have news. Thanks."

Rupert immediately called Sylvia. "Hi, I can still come down, but the planned visit with my sister has been postponed."

"Oh dear, what happened?"

"She's had to go to the hospital."

"How unfortunate for her and you, though, of course, for different reasons. You still plan to come, though?"

"Yes, I'll leave in the morning."

"Okay, we can meet for breakfast."

"Where?"

"Call me when you get close, and I'll give you instructions."

"Okay. See you soon."

CHAPTER 31

MAGGIE HAD BEEN MOVED TO A BED on the cancer floor. Theresa got the room number from the front desk and now stood at the door, waiting. She'd never felt comfortable around sick people, and Maggie was beyond what she called sick. Bottles hung off tripods beside her bed, each with a tube running down into some part of Maggie's body. Theresa took in a deep breath and entered the room.

Maggie turned toward her.

"How you doing?" asked Theresa.

"Just dandy. Like a day at the beach. No, really, I feel miserable, and from what they've said so far, my body is slowly failing. Guess I enjoyed myself too much with Jake! Here I finally have another friend, and I'm running out of time to enjoy the relationship. I think he cares about me, and believe it or not, I care about him." She started to cough.

Theresa didn't say anything.

When she stopped coughing, Maggie told her she had started a new medication. "It has helped, I think. Medication, western medicine's answer to all that ails us, n'est pas?"

"Oh, *bien sur*! Tell me more about this Jake person."

"Oh, Theresa, I don't know what to say, but he talks, he listens, and he even shows interest in me—not just what I do or how I look or how much I'm worth—just me. I don't think I even recognized myself apart from my work and worth before, but around Jake, I began to feel I have some personal value. I started to feel special, as if Maggie Callaway has value on her own. With Jake, I was happy. Happy to be alive." She stopped and then added, "For maybe a little longer, if I'm lucky!"

"I think I understand, Maggie. I've known you a long time and cannot recall a person who cared about you, except in the way you advertised yourself, as a successful woman or boss, who could make or break a career. You never seemed like a woman who needed anyone's care, concern, or interest. We all related to you as our boss. It was our job to do a good job for you, to get your approval. When you got sick and left work, it changed for me. And then you reached out to Rupert. I finally saw a vulnerability hidden underneath the boss persona."

Maggie was crying and obviously looking uncomfortable with it.

"Oh, I didn't mean to upset you, Maggie. Somehow, your comments about Jake made me want to open up with you, and I guess it has upset you."

"No, it did not upset me. It . . . it . . ." Maggie had trouble finding the right words. "Mmm, you've triggered my sentimental side. Geez, that sounds so corny."

"Oh no, kind of mushy maybe but not corny." Theresa laughed.

"I feel regret, regret for what I've done in my life. I know I've achieved a great deal, and for that I feel thankful. But along the way, I see a trail of carnage. Now you said you see something more personal, right?"

"Yeah."

"Maybe my being vulnerable now has let you see the person I am that even I did not see. I believe Jake must have seen the person side too. I don't see clearly what you've seen, but maybe, just maybe, I've begun to look for her. For me."

Now Theresa began to cry.

"What are those, tears? You know, years ago another executive in the company, I assume after he had felt the sharp knife of one of my critiques, innocently asked me if I'd ever considered going to therapy. I think I remember his comment after all these years because it so alarmed me. At the time I just said something like, 'Why in the world would I do that?' If I could have told him the truth, I would have said because the idea of therapy scares me. I feared my own feelings, and by God, I didn't want anyone probing them. Wow, listen to me, Theresa. I'm saying things I don't think I've ever even thought before."

Theresa said nothing but took Maggie's hand. It was cold.

Maggie winced. "Oh, your hand feels good, Theresa. Thanks. I'm starting to feel some pain again. Maybe the meds are beginning to wear off. Could you get the doctor for me?"

"Sure, I'll do that, but while I'm gone, will you consider giving me power of attorney so I can discuss your condition with the doctors? Since I'm not family, the hospital will not talk with me about you unless you give them permission. So think about it, will you?"

Maggie did not answer but felt chagrinned she had not considered Theresa—or anyone—for this, assuming no one would be willing to take this on.

Theresa went off to locate a physician or nurse who could administer more pain medication. She found the floor nurse who said she'd talk to Maggie's doctor and go down to her room as soon as she knew what to do. Theresa went back to Maggie, told her what she'd heard, and then said she had noticed the time and thought maybe she should head back home soon.

"Oh, that's a terrible idea, Theresa."

Stunned by this, Theresa just stared but said nothing. Maggie burst out laughing. They both laughed heartily, not from happiness, but from relief from the terrible gravity of Maggie's situation.

"Go now, Theresa. Say hello to Tom for me, and when you come back, would you please bring me the appropriate paperwork needed by the hospital to discuss my treatment with you?"

"Okay, but before I go, I should tell you about my recent talk with Rupert."

"For goodness's sake, with all that's going on, I forgot about Rupert. Did you talk with him?"

"Yes, we talked, and he wanted me to tell you he felt disappointed that you'd had to cancel and that he was worried about you."

"He said that?"

"He did, and I said I'd tell you."

"Well, right now I can't say when or if I'll see Rupert before I die, but now I'm glad I contacted him. So please do keep him posted on my progress or lack thereof."

"I will do that," Theresa said and then left.

Maggie shut her eyes. She still felt the pain in her chest and hoped her doctor might come soon.

He did. "Tell me what's going on, Maggie."

"Well, I've continued to cough some but not as bad as before, and the pain in my chest has gotten worse. Can you give me something for that?"

"Sure, but first let me tell you the results of our testing so far. Your tumors have increased in size, and from our reading of the blood work, it looks like the cancer has spread to other parts of your body. You also have internal bleeding, which is why you coughed up the blood, so we've given you something to arrest that. Okay? Is that clear?"

"Yes."

"Now I'll adjust your pain medication. I'd like to keep you here at least through tomorrow to assess the effects of what we've done, but if all continues to go okay, you can probably go home. Do you have anyone there to help you? Honestly, Maggie, your days of independent living are going to come to an end soon, if they haven't already."

"Not really, but I'm beginning to have a hunch that at least one person I know, and maybe others I don't know yet, will step forward and offer assistance."

"Good, so let's see how the night goes, and we can talk again tomorrow. I usually come in around one or two on Sunday, so I'll see you then. The nurse will administer the additional pain medication."

He left the room, but the nurse stayed and connected a new bottle to Maggie's IV.

Maggie felt almost immediate relief. "Oh, thank you. The bliss, the ecstasy, the euphoria! Only available to you through modern medicine."

The nurse smiled, but Maggie didn't see it. She was already asleep.

Chapter 32

Saturday morning, Rupert awakened with his alarm at 2 a.m. He'd gone to bed before the sun had fully set so figured he'd slept for about five hours. Not a lot but probably enough. He felt wide awake, happy, and eager to head out, but he still took some time to brew a cup of coffee for the road. With a long ride ahead, he might get sleepy. Then he grabbed a banana and packaged muffin from the pantry, picked up the small suitcase with the toothbrush, pajamas, and few clothes he'd set aside for the trip and left.

Waves were hitting the shoreline, but no birds had started their morning songs. "Smart birds! Stay in bed as long as you can!"

He set his coffee and goodies on the car roof and unlocked the door. He could see the outline of his house, or the house he lived in, in front of him. It was dark. Everything was dark. *No moon this morning*, he thought. *Must be sleeping in too!*

Rupert rarely got up this early anymore, not since his days in the seminary when everyone rose early for morning prayers. He opened the car door, collected his bag, and got in, adjusting his seat for maximum comfort. *Long ride ahead*, he thought.

Suddenly very unwelcome memories hit him. Thoughts of those terrible days in the seminary, filled with prayers, liturgies, and promises, quickly flooded his mind. He saw himself kneeling, his face bright and full of hope, and then he saw himself lying face down on the stone floor, someone standing over him, yelling, degrading, and humiliating judgments of his character and intelligence. Rupert started to feel the pain of that time all over again, pain he'd tried so hard to forget. "No, not now. Go away. Leave me alone," he yelled. He tried his best to ignore it all, to shut down his mind. Everything he tried not only failed but seemed to make it worse. "Why now?" he screamed. "I'm happy! I want to get out of here and head for Vancouver, now."

Nothing worked. Opening the door, he tumbled from the car and fell on his knees. Rupert saw himself surrounded by priests, all praying, recharging the soul, getting ready to face the day. He tried to say the words he'd said so often, hoping for some peace, some relief from the mental bullying that had plagued him since childhood. "In the name of our Lord Jesus Christ, I will begin this day—" He interrupted himself. "No, no, stop it. This can't be happening."

Rupert got up off his knees and back in the car. "Go, Rupert, go, go, go. Get away." He then remembered his coffee was still on the roof and reached through the window to retrieve it. "Well, I must be getting some sense back," he said. "I remembered the coffee."

He put his keys in the ignition but then just sat still, feeling no energy to start it. The darkness that surrounded him seeped into him. "Pray, Rupert. You can do it." He sat there, repeating out loud, "You can do it, Rupert," until finally he just yelled, "NO, I can't. I won't. That was before, and it failed me then and does still." He started to bang on his ears and then on the steering wheel, saying, "No, no, no . . ."

Finally, the banging must have helped. At least the extremely frightful pictures that had filled his mind slowed down. The torment he'd felt slowly began to subside. Then he cried. He felt only the darkness of the night. Unable to move, paralyzed in his seat, Rupert felt like time had escaped his consciousness. Only the familiar sound of waves crashing into the shore could be heard in the distance. The birds remained quiet, probably still sleeping.

His hands fell from the wheel and rested on his lap. Thoughts rushed through his mind, but nothing stuck. He saw people from his past passing by and looking at him with blank, expressionless faces. Rupert thought about Sylvia and the night they'd spent together. He remembered himself preaching and how parishioners had greeted him after a service with their polite smiles, and how he'd met them back with his own polite smile. His tears had stopped, but they'd been replaced by emptiness, flatness.

I should get going, he thought, but he didn't. His thoughts continued to come and go. He could still hear the crashing waves but nothing else until he thought he heard a cry. But from what, from where? He thought he heard pain and sadness in it. Did someone need help? His eyes popped open. Suddenly hyperalert, he was ready for action. But what would he do if needing to confront a dangerous situation? Rupert had never dealt with anything more dangerous than facing down a dead rat. He'd never lifted weights, bicycled, or run for any distance where he might have built up his core body strength. No, he had always been and still was nothing but a mighty weakling. His eyes scanned the surrounding area, but he saw nothing in the darkness.

Time to get going, he thought again, but once more, nothing happened. He continued sitting quietly, staying on alert but not as scared. *I should feel afraid*, he thought, *but I don't*. He heard no cries like before, but thoughts from his past continued to roam through his mind. It was still dark, and although Rupert had lost track of time, he just knew it was past time for him to leave. Yet he stayed with the images passing through his mind.

He saw himself inside an ancient colosseum, one like he'd seen in pictures of the Roman Colosseum. He was standing in the middle of the huge inner theater while chariots raced around the track. Multitudes of what looked to be Romans filled the seats all around, but no one could see him maybe because of all the dust thrown up by the chariots and their horses. The noise was deafening. He didn't feel any fear but thought it strange he was in the center of all this action and no one knew he was there. Rupert felt lonely. He raised his arms above his head, thinking he'd wave them until someone saw him. But he froze, unable to move his arms or cry out, torn between two thoughts: I'm not in any danger, and I'm going to die. The chariots raced furiously, some flying off the track toward him. Dirt flew, hitting him in the face and causing him to gag. *This is it. I'm going to die! Oh, God, not now. I'm not ready. As if you cared, God. You never cared before. Why would you now?* His fear mounted, and then he felt it; he soiled himself.

Someone shaking him. "Wake up, Father. You're having a bad dream."

Rupert opened his eyes. The sun had started to rise.

His neighbor stood next to the car in his jogging outfit, obviously returning from a morning run. "You were screaming."

"Oh, hi, Dave. I must have dozed off. I planned to drive south early this morning, but apparently, I never got underway. Sorry I alarmed you.

"Are you okay?"

Rupert didn't respond at first but then said, "Yes, though I must admit this all must look rather strange." He sat there thinking about his dream. "Did you notice my arms waving while I screamed?"

"No, I just heard you yell. It sounded like you might be yelling for someone, but I couldn't make it out."

"Sylvia, perhaps?"

"No. Frankly, it sounded more like *Mother* if I had to identify it."

"Oh, dear, a grown man calling out for his mother. What would some analyst say about that?"

They both laughed.

"Well, as long as you're okay, I think I'll continue my jog. You know, I hardly ever see you, and when I have, you've been down by the water, staring out to sea and looking quite unapproachable."

"Thanks, so much for approaching me this time, Dave. Who knows, maybe next time we meet, I'll greet you first."

Dave wondered what all that meant but said nothing. He jogged away, lifting a hand to wave goodbye as he went.

Rupert checked his watch. It was 6:12 a.m., almost four hours since he'd sat down in the car headed for Vancouver. He found his phone on the seat next to him and dialed Sylvia.

"Hello, Rupert. You're earlier than you said. I haven't left the house yet."

"That's fine, Sylvia. I'm not there. I'm still here in Powell River, sitting in my car where I went at two thirty this morning, fully expecting to drive to Vancouver. My neighbor just woke me up. Said I was yelling and thought I was having a bad dream."

"Wow. Were you dreaming?"

"Guess so, and I'd like to talk about it, but right now, I need some time just to think about what happened." He didn't want to mention it, but he also wanted to go change his clothes. "I'm going to drink my cold coffee, eat a little something, and then I'll call back."

"That'll work for me. I had no plans for today since, originally, I'd planned to meet you. I could still meet you for lunch, if you want."

"Okay, that sounds good. I'll call you later."

Rupert got out of the car and headed for the house, carrying the muffin and coffee. He threw his cold coffee in the sink, brewed himself a new cup of extra strong this time, and went to change his clothes. Afterwards he sat at the kitchen table, warming his hands on the cup. He sipped it, letting the liquid slowly fill his mouth. *So comforting*, he thought. "Oh dear, I best not shut my eyes. I already lost four-plus hours today!" He laughed and kept his eyes open to be sure he would not fall asleep or dream again. The coffee tasted good.

The packaged muffin sat on the table but did not look very appealing. He opened it anyway and took a bite." Blah, tastes like sawdust with a few blueberries thrown in for show. He threw it in the garbage, put his coffee in his travel mug, and headed out the door toward town. Feeling surprisingly cheerful, he thought, *I'll just go get something better.* He knew of a bakery within easy walking distance and took off on foot. Arriving twenty minutes later, he got in line to order a croissant, maybe even two. *How devious of me*, he thought and then laughed out loud. He saw the other customers watching him, but he didn't care. *How shocking of me, drawing attention to myself by laughing without obvious cause.*

When he arrived at the counter, the woman waiting on him smiled and said, "You look happy today, Father Callaway."

"You know me?"

"Why, yes, we all know of you, living out there on the coast. Property owned by the Catholic Church, isn't it? Powell River's a small place. We know many things, but we say and tell little!"

"Well, I don't know you. Your name is?"

"Elizabeth Singh. Everyone calls me Liz."

"Well, Liz, let me introduce myself. I'm Rupert Callaway, formerly known as Father Callaway. You may call me Rupert, and I'll have two croissants to go, please."

"Coming right up . . . Rupert."

From way back in the line, he heard someone say, "Hello, Rupert."

He could not see who had said it, so he just yelled out a hello.

Liz brought his order and placed it on the counter.

"Careful with these, Rupert, our croissants can corrupt the mind so that next time, you'll order three, then four, then five. You'll keep coming back for more."

"Not me, discipline is my middle name. I'm a practiced resister."

"We'll see."

He paid his money and said, "Thanks, Liz. I hope you have a nice day."

As he left, he heard again, "Hello, Rupert."

"Well, hello, Father Brown. I wondered who'd said that before."

"Yeah, it was me, and I'm still going by the name *Father Brown*. Probably will still use the *Father*, even after I retire."

Rupert couldn't tell if he was being sarcastic or serious. "Well, good to see you again, FAAATHER," he said, exaggerating the last word as he went on toward the door.

Then he heard from off to his right, "Bye, Rupert."

He saw Dave waving to him as he left. "Bye, Dave. And thanks again for the wakeup this morning!"

The whole store heard him. Dave was left to explain.

Back home, Rupert again sat at the table, but this time he enjoyed one of his croissants, and what remained of his coffee. He wrapped the other croissant and stuck it in the fridge. The clock on the living room wall struck eight times.

The phone rang.

"Hello, Rupert. It's Theresa again with an update on your sister."

"Hi."

"You should know Maggie's still in the hospital undergoing tests. It does not sound too promising for her. It seems her tumors have grown, and she's experiencing a good deal of pain. They have her on OxyContin now, but soon she may have to go on morphine. She still wants to meet up with you, but at this time I cannot tell you how or when that might occur. I'll continue to keep you posted regarding her situation."

"Thanks for calling, Theresa. I didn't know lawyers did this kind of personal work for their clients. I assume Maggie pays you well for all the time you put in for her. God, with all you're doing for her just in contacting me, it must cost her a small fortune."

"Yes, I am expensive, and Maggie does pay me well. But you should know, since Maggie has contacted you, her life has changed. I hope I'm not talking out of turn, but as far as I know, Maggie's never been a woman who endeared herself to anyone, but in these last few weeks she's shown a side of herself I've never seen. No one liked Maggie. They just obeyed and served her, hoping what they did would meet with her approval, and believe me, Maggie always let you know if you didn't have her approval. Inside her office, she lived like the diabolical Miranda Priestly, that character in *The Devil Wears Prada*, a real bitch of a boss, to put it bluntly. But now I think she's writing her last chapter. Where her armor went, I couldn't tell you, but it's gone. Now I like her. I have no idea how much longer she'll live, but I have fond thoughts about her and will even miss her, something I never thought I'd say."

Rupert listened carefully.

"I'm going to catch a flight to San Francisco. Can you tell me where to come and maybe some directions? I've not traveled much, and I don't know how to use Google, Uber, Lyft, or any of that new stuff. I'm thinking I should head down to California. Maybe I've become more daring since I got Maggie's letter, but I want to come. I'm ready to see my sister on her home turf. See, I have no home turf, Theresa. Since leaving home, I've lived all my life on Rome's dime. Only now, I am beginning to see myself as distinct from the Church. I'll call you back before I leave."

He put the phone down, thought a minute, and then immediately dialed Sylvia.

"Hello, Rupert. I have a feeling you haven't left yet."

"How'd you know that?"

"Well, obviously you couldn't have driven to Vancouver in the short time since we last talked."

"You're right. I'm still at home, and I'm not coming. I just talked to Maggie's lawyer again and have decided to catch a flight to San Francisco as soon as I can. Maggie's health has taken a turn for the worse. I do hope I can see you again, but not right now."

"For sure, Rupert. Call me when you get back, and know you have my best wishes for this reunion with your sister. What you're going through is so intense. It reminds me of an Anne Tyler novel. She's an author you might want to pick up some time." Sylvia stopped herself, aware she had again dropped into her teaching role. "Not right now, of course. Seems to me you have to live *your* story now. Take care. We'll talk later." And she hung up.

Sylvia's last comment stuck in Rupert's head: *You have to live* your *story now.* Was he living? He'd always felt like someone living on the outside of real life, trying to figure out the mysteries that would allow him entrance into it. He'd lived his life doing prayer, penance, and physical sacrifice in hopes of finding what would bring him to some feeling of being loved, of belonging, and the peacefulness that "passes all understanding," as he'd read in Philippians 4:7: "The peace of God, which passes all understanding, shall keep your hearts and minds through Christ Jesus."

He'd worked more than lived his life. Rupert had learned to live only with the punishment and abuse that was designed to help him become a good priest. *Now Sylvia says, you have to live your story. I must ask her more about what that means.*

Rupert felt freer of duty at this moment than he could ever remember. He'd noticed changes happening since shortly after retirement, but he'd done all he could to organize his life to maintain discipline, prayer, and Bible study. He'd not been so good about church attendance and performance of the sacraments. The church remained his sanctuary, but now he could add his curse, maybe even his cancer. It was, he thought (and hoped), losing its power over him. The protection and safety it had given him had diminished, which was both good and bad.

As Rupert faced a trip to California to see a sister he had not seen or talked to since he was twelve, he was bordering on feeling a profound sense of powerlessness. Without the Church behind him, he knew he had to do something to counteract this growing sense of impotence. If he didn't, he worried he'd soon be overcome, stuck, and unable to act.

From someplace inside, he felt a craving arise, and surprising him, he recognized it. Rupert had experienced it before, but then he had called it lust. He had felt it when he'd become sexually aroused, but now it was different. This time *craving* seemed like a more accurate word, even though it described the same thing, a feeling he couldn't resist. He was having a craving to see his sister.

Rupert called the airlines and made a reservation on United from Vancouver for tomorrow, Sunday, at 10:30 a.m., direct to San Francisco. He would arrive in the early afternoon. To avoid figuring out how to do Lyft or Uber, he reserved a car and then a hotel room. "Wow, I'm on a roll."

Later, he would wonder, given all the fluctuations in feeling he'd had lately, how long could this one last?

CHAPTER 33

MAGGIE AWOKE AROUND THREE IN THE MORNING. She had a private room, but noises still came from the hall and a nurses' station nearby. Several nurses walked by, but none looked in or entered her room. *More urgent business to attend to than me right now*, she thought. *How long before I become the most urgent business?*

Even though Maggie had been diagnosed with cancer over four years ago, she had not really thought much about dying, at least not in a way that caused her much anxiety, till now. Growing up Catholic, she'd had to attend church at least once a week. Her mother liked to take her along to early-morning Mass, but after about the seventh grade, she'd abandoned all church activities. No more church anything for her. Maggie had nothing but herself to believe in; she could really only depend on herself. Now, though, she faced the end of herself; the one she had depended on would be no more. Death was coming—maybe soon—and it scared her, though she still hoped it was far off. She asked herself if she was afraid of dying, hoping that thinking might distract her from the reality of it all. Now, as she lay in the hospital, not even focused thinking worked. Maggie only kept feeling death coming. The questions that came up made her even more scared. *What happens after I die? Is heaven real or not?* Part of her wanted heaven to be real, but then she remembered how the priests had described it and thought, *Oh, no, everyone living in a state of bliss for eternity.* "Bad. Surrounded by a bunch of junkies for the rest of time. No way." She smiled at the thought.

But her relief was not to last long because at that moment she was seized by severe chest pain. *Is this it?* was her only thought now. She buzzed for a nurse. Within minutes, the nurse who had looked so busy before entered the room.

Maggie screamed, "It hurts," and let loose an insane laugh, releasing pain and surprise at once. "It hurts so much! Is this it? Am I dying?"

The nurse adjusted Maggie's IV and waited by the bed until Maggie reported some relief. When Maggie had calmed down, the nurse asked, "What happened?"

"I just had a jolt of extreme pain. What's going on? Do you know?"

"Really I don't, but you can talk to your doctor about it in the morning."

"Okay. But what happens if I die before he arrives? I'll never get to know what happened."

"True. I guess you'll just have to think of it as one of life's little surprises."

With the increased medication, Maggie's pain did subside and was followed by a peaceful quiet. Her mind focused on the word *surprise.* *You're about to face the last surprise, Maggie. When, where, how? Well, that's to be revealed. Be ready, Maggie.* "How?"

Nothing came. No answer to her question.

Maggie started to get angry, but maybe because of all the medications being pumped into her, she did not yell out. Another word then popped into her mind: *surrender.* "No, no, no, never."

But again, nothing. No pain, but also no insight.

Maggie began to cry. She cried and cried until a nurse came to her bedside, smiled and put her hand on Maggie's forehead. Maggie's tears then flowed even harder. The nurse took some tissues, leaned down to be closer to Maggie and gently wiped her face. She had that soft, welcoming smile.

Maggie couldn't explain what happened next, but it was like she fell into that face and things changed. Somehow, she too began to feel warm and accepting of herself. All thoughts stopped, leaving her feeling something strange. What was it? She did not try to name it, nor did she resist, and soon, even with her eyes wide open, she saw herself being held by this nurse in a manner she'd never known before.

The nurse was so accessible, reachable. Maggie almost felt as though she'd become one with the nurse and lost any sense of the other, feeling only like she'd been surrounded by welcoming arms that had no judgment, no assessment, no evaluation. She opened her mouth as if she were going to speak, but nothing came out. The room was silent, and soon Maggie fell into a deep sleep.

While sleeping, Maggie looked up toward the sky. A giant bird appeared above her head, sitting regally on the branch of a large oak tree. She'd never seen such a large bird. What was it? An eagle? No, it didn't have that distinctive white head with large protruding beak. This looked more like an enormous owl, big eyes, big head, sitting straight up and staring down at her.

"What are you staring at?"

It said nothing.

"Are you trying to tell me something?"

Again, she heard nothing, but from somewhere, she thought maybe from inside herself, Maggie heard her name. Filled with excitement, she reached up to touch the owl. It didn't move, so she reached higher until her hand brushed the soft body, nothing hard or sharp anywhere. "Wow, so big, yet so delicate."

After she said that, the owl spread its wings, apparently getting ready to fly away.

"No, don't leave me." Maggie grabbed a leg just as it took off.

The owl did nothing to shake her off. It flew higher and higher.

"Beautiful. Where are we going?" It really didn't matter since Maggie knew she couldn't hold on for too long and that she was going to fall. *But why aren't I afraid?* Before she heard an answer, she lost her grip and fell toward . . . what? She didn't know and didn't care. She watched the great owl fly higher and higher with its wings spread wide, and she was sure it was calling her name. As she continued her fall, Maggie had only one thought, *I've heard the owl call my name.*

Maggie felt nothing until she was aware of the pillow under her head and she opened her eyes. It was still dark. No nurses were in her room or walking the halls. It was quiet. *Geez, it must be the middle of the night.* She shut her eyes again, thinking she'd go back to sleep and maybe return to her dream. She had no idea if she actually did or didn't but was sure she heard an echo for the rest of the night.

"Maggie, Maggie, Maggie . . ."

When she woke the next morning, she felt alert and fully refreshed. She remembered her dream but not much that had happened before that. She exclaimed, "Wow," to no one in particular. She just wanted to hear it herself. It was all that came close to describing the feeling of encouragement that filled her every cell, organ, orifice, her complete being, not because she'd accomplished something but this time because she'd completed something.

"Wow!"

CHAPTER 34

ACTIVITIES IN A HOSPITAL ON A SUNDAY MORNING aren't any different from any other day. The night shift leaves at 8 a.m., and the day shift starts. The new staff reviews charts and checks in on the patients.

The noise created by all the activity drew Maggie's attention. *Oh, guess I'm not dead yet.* The thought made her smile. She felt amazingly relaxed, so much so that the word *death* had no effect on her mood. *Interesting*, she thought. She had some vague memory of having had a dream about a large bird. She couldn't remember the details, but she knew she'd made an important friend.

Maggie still had some pain but nothing she couldn't tolerate. She lay with her eyes open, watching the nurses and their assistants go by her room. She wondered when visitors started coming. *I hope someone comes to see me. Maybe even Rupert will come*, she thought briefly. *No, no way, he's still in Vancouver, Powell River, or wherever up there.* A big smile appeared on her face, so wide it almost turned into open laughter.

Nurses continued to hurry past her room. Most of these, she noticed, were women. In her management position, Maggie had hired both men and women. Their sex didn't matter. She only was concerned about their competence. She hired people based on educational background of course, but she paid more attention to their work experience. How successful had they been at getting a job done?

Now, with nurses, she thought, *they have to be competent and probably good mothers to us, their patients, and maybe women are more competent at that.* Then she remembered her own mother and thought, *No, maybe not. Do these nurses care because they get paid to care? After all, they go on strike if they don't like their pay.*

Right now, though, Maggie didn't really care if nurses did their jobs for money or altruism. Since becoming ill and feeling so vulnerable, she had found that a nurse's care, female or male, feels welcoming and very, very good. *That's strange,* she thought. *Maybe I had to get cancer before I was worthy of nurturing.* Without thinking, she pushed her call button. A nurse she recognized from yesterday came in.

"Do you need something?"

Maggie looked at her name tag, and said, "This may sound strange, Darlene, but I think I just want attention."

Darlene smiled and took Maggie's hand. "I read in the chart that you'd had bad pain last night. How do you feel this morning?"

"I still have some pain but not like last night. Do you know when I might see the doctor? The nurse last night—sorry, I don't know her name—said I could discuss my situation with my doctor this morning."

"Dr. Wright should come in by one or earlier, and I'm sure he'll answer any of your questions. I'll tell him to come in straightaway, but for now, are you hungry?"

"Not really."

"Well, Doctor has written in a 'light breakfast' for you, which means probably toast, a banana, and a flavored yogurt. Yum, yum."

Maggie laughed. "Okay, bring it on. I wouldn't want such a good meal to go to waste."

"I'll come back in a bit to check on you, Maggie. Okay?"

"Sure. Thanks for stopping by."

Darlene left Maggie alone but satisfied. She had received the attention she'd wanted. After a short time, she heard a light knock on her.

"Breakfast time, Maggie."

Maggie took a minute before answering while she tried to read the young woman's name tag. "Thanks, Molly. I heard through the grapevine (or the nurse-vine) that you would come by with a delicious meal. And here you are."

"I'm afraid someone might have been pulling your leg, Maggie. What you have here I'd call 'hospital food to endure.'"

"Oh, darn. Well, leave it anyway. I'll try to force it down."

Molly smiled and put the tray in front of Maggie.

"Bon appetite. I'll come back for the tray later."

Maggie looked at her meal.

"Try, Maggie."

She just couldn't. The tray remained untouched.

Theresa came back before Maggie's doctor got there.

As she entered, Maggie smiled. "Hi. I hoped I might see you today."

"Well, I told you I'd be back and so here I am. How you doing?"

"Right now? Well, strangely, close to death. Sit down. I'm glad to see you."

"Thanks, Maggie. How was breakfast?"

"Honestly, the toast tasted burned, the blueberry yogurt had no blueberries, and the orange juice was colored water. Overall, I'd have to say, delicious! But I lie. Actually, I didn't touch it. I've lost my appetite."

Theresa didn't really know how to respond to that. Maggie seemed different, even weird. *Maybe it's because of the medication,* she thought. *She has to be taking some powerful meds.*

Maggie interrupted Theresa's thoughts. "I'd like to call Jake. Would you please see if you can locate my phone book? Look here in my nightstand. I think that's where they put everything I brought to the hospital."

Theresa found the number and gave Maggie her phone, noting Maggie hadn't asked her to make the call.

Maggie looked up at the wall clock. "Ten o'clock. If he's not up by now, he should be." She dialed and he picked up.

"Hello."

"Jake, it's Maggie. I don't want to shock you, but I had to go to the hospital again. I just wondered if you might come by for a visit later today. My doctor is supposed to see me this morning, but maybe you could come by sometime this afternoon."

"Oh, Maggie, so sorry to hear that. Of course, I can drop by. I'd love to see you. Baseball, my usual Sunday fare, can just wait. How about around three o'clock?"

"Sure, that sounds like a good time."

"Give me the name of your hospital."

Maggie gave him the name and her room number.

"Great. See you later."

Jake hung up but didn't get up. He sat in his chair, thinking about what had just happened—Maggie, calling from her hospital bed but sounding to him like she was making a business call! She was so different from other women he'd known, but maybe that's what made her so interesting. Maggie would probably die with her boots on!

Theresa listened to the call with great interest. Now seemed like a good time to tell Maggie about her talk with Rupert. "I called Rupert to cancel the plans for the two of you to meet in Seattle. He seemed very interested in your condition, so I filled him in the best I could. Then he said he wanted to come to San Francisco."

"But I thought he said he couldn't afford that."

"Yes, he did. Something must have changed. He sounded highly disappointed that he couldn't see you as planned. I really can't speak to what's going on with him, but I'm pretty sure he's coming here."

Maggie picked up her phone. "Now, what's Rupert's number?"

Theresa gave it to her. "Do you want me to step out, Maggie?"

"Nope, I want you here as a witness to this call, my first contact with my older brother in fifty-six years. Can you believe it?"

Theresa didn't respond.

"Hello."

"Rupert, this is Maggie."

Silence on both ends. Even their breathing seemed to stop as if anything that happened might upset the world order.

After what seemed like minutes, Rupert spoke. "Hi, Maggie. It's been a while."

Long silence again.

"You know, of course, I've been talking to Theresa. I'm glad it's you this time. I never expected it, but then I feel more ready for this surprise.

The letter you sent hit me like a tsunami. I've been rolling around in that wave ever since. The foundation on which I built my life was torn apart. Part of me is mad about it all, feeling like I'm too old for this and this is terrible timing. However, Maggie, I want to say I feel more alive right now than I've ever felt before. I feel like I am no longer living in the shadows where the air is thin and breathing is hard. Suddenly I feel I can look forward to a future. I want more than anything to see you. And I want to say thank you for reaching out. It took a lot of courage to reach out like that after all the time we've been apart. It was a cowardly thing I did, disappearing from your life. It's taken me a long, long time to find the courage to say that to you, but you set the stage by reaching out first. Thank you so much, little sister."

Maggie said nothing through all this, but tears flowed down her cheeks. She felt so much emotion; she couldn't have talked even if she'd wanted to.

Rupert wondered if she had hung up the phone. "Hello? You still there, Maggie?"

Theresa spoke up. "Yes, she's here and listening, Rupert."

He was surprised to hear Theresa's voice, but continued. "I know you're too sick right now to travel, Maggie, but I really want to see you, so I've made plans to come to San Francisco."

There was more silence on Maggie's end, but then she found her voice. "Wow, Rupert, and I'd like to see you too. However, I am currently indisposed. As I mentioned in the letter, I have lung cancer, and I'm in the hospital for emergency treatment. The doctor said I probably can go home sometime soon, but he's keeping me here until he sees the results of my latest tests. I've endured test after test, followed by analysis and assessments, inspections and experiments. What an ordeal it's been, and it goes on interrupting my life and now yours. Sorry, but that's my story, and I have no choice but to stick by it."

Rupert assumed Maggie was trying to be funny. It helped him. "This has all unfolded mysteriously for me, Maggie. I've lived a programmed life from the day I left Hazelton, really, until I got your letter, from one planned event to the next. No changes. No surprises, nothing astonishing or amazing, all same-o, same-o. Now, a big unexpected change has come to me, and I feel certain I need to come to San Francisco, even if I just stay in a hotel until you get home and feel ready to meet."

"But can you afford that? From what Theresa told me, you are retired and don't have a lot of money."

"I did say that, and money is tight, but I plan to rob a bank later today, and then I'll be flush for a while." Rupert smiled. "No, of course not. Really, I haven't led a very active life. I've mostly lived off the Church all my life, and though we priests have little money of our own, what I do have just sits unused in a bank. I think it's certainly enough to cover my trip. How about I call you when I get settled in a hotel?"

Maggie felt like asserting her CEO side and saying, "No, Rupert, you stay put until I call and let you know you can come." Instead, she said, "Maybe, after I get home, you could stay with at my place."

Rupert paused and then said, "We'll see later."

Maggie just said, "Thanks, I'll see you soon . . . finally!" She hung up.

Theresa watched Maggie as she wiped away the residue left by all the tears she'd shed. She looked so sad and so happy at the same time.

"I think I've realized something, Theresa. If I am to die soon, I'm glad my ending will be so full of what I never had in life. Yes, at first, I found this radical reversal of fortune confusing and overwhelming, but now, though still not satiated, I am satisfied. I'm disappointed and a little bit annoyed that I'm dying, but I do feel thankful for this ending I'm living." She stopped a moment and then said again, "This ending I'm living. Not words I remember ever putting together before."

Theresa could find no words. What was unfolding in front of her reflected something bigger than her little courtroom—this was the real versus the legal! She smiled.

CHAPTER 35

Aﬀter talking with Maggie, Rupert just stayed in his chair. For now, he had nowhere to go, nothing more to do, and his chair was so comfortable. He thought he might take a nap though he wasn't really sleepy.

Outside, a steady rain was falling. Appropriate, he thought. A cleansing of heart, soul, and earth. He watched the rain for a while but did not go to sleep. His mind raced from one thought to the next. *What would happen next?* he wondered. *What's the next chapter of my story?* Rupert felt both scared and happy, an unexpected combination. He expected anger, his and his family's emotion of choice.

The pull to anger was certainly still there. When fear transformed into anger, all his feelings of vulnerability would disappear. Magic. That was what he was accustomed to. It never resolved any problems, but neither did fear, loneliness, or sadness. All those emotions just added to family and personal instability.

Rupert laughed to himself, thinking about how stable his angry family must have looked to others. He also noticed he had begun to feel sad, not about Maggie but about their parents and all their anger. But what fear and loss they must have felt coming to Canada, a new and strange land, to escape their lives in Ireland, trying to survive and raise a family, separated from everything they'd known, loved, and recognized. *Mom and Dad were definitely survivors,* Rupert mused. *And Maggie and I were NOT their focus.*

In the end, Dad probably survived the best of the two though he died on the youngish side. He sold his soul to the lumber mill and died at sixty-eight. He was not there for Mom, our so-called caretaker. He left her to survive on her own. A heart attack killed her, also not that old, Rupert thought. *She spent her life feeling sad, missing the old country, and sulking when she should have been there for us. I was mad, everyone was mad, but now,* Rupert realized, *I am definitely less mad.*

Rupert mulled how having anger was at least juicier than just having the dull belief the Church handed him. He had to smile. He'd never had a positive feeling about his anger before.

Suddenly Sylvia popped in his mind. His plan to see her had fallen through, but now he had time before going to San Francisco when he could still visit her in Vancouver. "I'll even be closer to the airport. Wow!" Rupert jumped from his chair to find the phone, then stopped, and laughed, realizing it was on the table right next to his chair. He turned around and walked back to the phone, but this time he didn't sit down. He dialed.

"Hello."

"It's me, Rupert. I have a flight out of Vancouver for San Francisco on Sunday morning. Do you have an extra bed at your place where I might sleep or . . . sleep with you! I know I might be pushing my luck, but I am close to seventy and a sexual novice, eager to make up for lost time if I can."

Sylvia didn't know what to say. Since meeting Rupert, he had continually surprised her with the unexpected. "You are pushing something, Rupert. First, we meet in a restaurant, then we have sex, and now you want to sleep in my bed?" she laughed. "Oh hell, I may regret it, but come on down. I have plenty of room here with extra beds if we end up deciding not to sleep together."

"Thanks, Sylvia. Maybe someday I will even come on a weekday, and I'll be able to attend one of your classes too. You know, I've had a pretty narrow education, focused on religion. But maybe another time. I'll leave here within the hour and be there before dinner. What's your address again?"

CHAPTER 36

IT TOOK MAGGIE SOME TIME TO RECOVER from hearing her brother's voice. She looked up at Theresa. "Funny, here I am trying to survive cancer while also opening the door to old and not-yet healed wounds from earlier battles. I'm about to face death and family at the same time."

Dr. Wright stuck his head in the door. "Okay to come in?"

Theresa and Maggie looked at each other.

"Sure. Do you mind if my lawyer sticks around for the consultation?"

"No, that's fine."

He entered followed by his nurse, Darlene, and a second nurse Maggie didn't know, who carried what looked like a box of supplies. Theresa moved her chair away from the bed, pondering Maggie's use of the word *friend*.

"Well, we have results from our recent tests, Maggie. A lot of what I'm about to say might be hard to hear. I can stop at any time so just say the word."

"What word, Doc? Like *STOP*? Would that do the trick? Or maybe you're looking for something more aberrant like 'Oh, Doc, give it to me harder.'"

Theresa jumped up. "Oh, Maggie, that's so crude." Then to the doctor, she said, "I think Maggie might have just heard some family news that could have dazed her. I think joy and happiness have replaced her normal good sense."

"Theresa's right, Doc. I'm happy, and you're about to tell me the end is near. If I embarrass anybody, I'm sorry, but I don't have much time left, and I want to break a few rules. Maybe I'll sound like a teenager, something I never sounded like when I was a teenager." She stopped, closed her eyes, and leaned back on her pillows. "Seriously, I know I might have to make some big decisions." Maggie stopped herself again.

The room went quiet.

"I'm sorry. I'll be more serious. I lost my teenage years, and I can't relive them now. I'll listen to what you've learned from those tests and then tell you what I plan to do next. Okay?"

"Well, Maggie, you surprised me. But I think it's safe to say a simple *stop* will work for me. Please feel free to be nice or nasty at any time, though. In fact, I prescribe it."

Everyone stood around, looking surprised until Darlene started a soft clapping. That broke the mounting tension in the room. Everyone started to clap and laugh, except Theresa, who was the last to join. Soon other nurses came to join in what looked like people having a jolly good time.

Maggie didn't want it to stop, but she knew she had distracted the doctor and others from their tasks. "Thanks, thanks for that moment, folks. I think you have some things to tell me doctor."

"Yes, Maggie, we should talk about your tests." With that, all the extra personnel left, and things calmed down. Let me just start by reminding you, if you've forgotten the technicalities, that you have what we call non-small-cell lung cancer. We discovered it about four years ago."

"I think about four and a half years ago, Doctor."

"Okay. At the time of discovery, the tumors were increasing in size, so we operated, and you've gone through radiation and chemotherapy. This new pain, fatigue, and nausea is because the cancer has spread to your lymph nodes, and we see new growths developing in your chest. These will cause you to experience more coughing, loss of appetite, and more chest pain. You can elect to do another round of chemo, or and I have to say this, you can elect to do nothing. We've found that, if treated further, a small percentage of patients in your late stage of cancer live a few extra months, but without treatment, you may have a better quality of life."

"What does that mean?"

"Only that you won't have to put up with the side effects of the extra treatment."

"What *will* I have to put up with then?"

"Mostly increased pain, but we can control most of that with medication."

"Won't I become a zombie? Zoned out on morphine?"

"Morphine does have some side effects, like nausea, tiredness, and constipation, but we find that these decrease as the body adjusts to the medication. You will not be zoned out, nor are you likely to become addicted. Very few patients who take morphine become psychologically dependent on it. It is likely to help you a great deal as you enter, what I must say, is the last stage of your life."

"Wow, Doc, that's putting it all out there. What about those patients who beat this stuff and go on to live long, healthy lives?"

No one spoke.

"Just trying to add a little levity to the conversation. Ha, ha."

Nobody laughed.

"How about I think about this for a bit and get back to you? Do I need to stay hospitalized, or can I go home?"

"You can go home. The nursing staff will let you know about nursing programs that do home visits. They can provide all the help you will need, and later we will assign hospice to your case."

"Okay. Thanks. Anything else?"

"Not now. Darlene will adjust your medications. Call me when you feel ready to talk further. And, oh, stay happy if you can. It's addictive."

"Will do. I might even be bawdy once in a while!"

Dr. Wright took her hand and laid his other hand on top. "Sounds like a plan, Maggie."

The doctor left, and Darlene adjusted the medications. An eerie quiet enveloped the room until after she'd left.

"I'm glad you stayed for all that, Theresa. You probably need to get home to your family. I'll sit with all this and probably talk with you before I call Dr. Wright again. By the way, I think he has a good name. Imagine how a doctor named Dr. Wrong would be received!"

"Yeah, tough to generate much confidence from your patients start-ing with a name like that. Do you want me around when Jake comes?"

"No, I feel safe with him, and if he surprises me and attacks, I . . . I might even like it!"

"Maggie. I hardly recognize you anymore." Theresa smiled. "You've become quirky and unpredictable . . . maybe fascinating and appealing too. I'll be back later. Call if you need me before that."

"Wait, Theresa. I just remembered you haven't submitted a bill for your time in quite a while. Better get your money while I'm still alive. Who knows how long it will take after I'm gone?"

"Thanks for reminding me, Maggie. I'll do that." Then she was gone.

Maggie looked around her empty room and started to yell. "Ding dong, the bitch is dead! The bitch is dead!"

She got louder until Darlene stuck her head in the door. "What are you talking about, Maggie?"

"That was me, the bitch. No one dared call me that to my face, but I know that's what they called me. But that's over. The bitch is dead, Darlene, and you're the first to know."

"Congratulations.

"Thanks."

Darlene left Maggie alone again. This time, though, she did not feel lonely. She felt as though she had discovered her inner champion, some-one who would carry the flag into battle for her. She wasn't alone now. People would not define her simply as successful anymore. She was bold and gutsy too. "Yes, I like it." She wanted to get up and dance around the room but didn't. She was just too damned weak. "Good idea girl but maybe later. For now, I think I'm stuck with this bed and the TV."

She flipped it on but found nothing of interest. Just Sunday morning TV viewing, mind-numbing crap together with talk shows analyzing, dissecting, and scrutinizing every bit of last week's news. "I don't need that anymore." Maggie switched off the set and lay back, just enjoying the opiates dripping into her body.

That, however, was not to last. There was a knock on the door. Jake had arrived.

CHAPTER 37

WHAT TO PACK? HOW LONG WILL I BE GONE? Will I even return to Powell River? Rupert stood in his bedroom, unable to decide where to start. *Suitcase . . . I know I have a larger one. Where is it? Where did I leave it? When did I use it last? The movers brought all my belongings here when I came from Kamloops. I don't even remember that move.* He tried hard to remember the suitcase and suddenly felt weak in his legs. He sat on the bed where he had a scary but familiar feeling.

"Oh no, it can't be happening again, can it? I can't move, just like that morning in the car, paralyzed but not numb. Don't go to sleep, don't dream, Rupert. Move, move, move; get up, get up . . . I can't." He remembered how Dave had brought him back. "This can't be happening. What's happening to me? Think of something, Rupert. Think, think . . ."

He waited for something to come to him, fell back on the bed, hands holding his head, but still nothing happened, no thoughts, no dreams. Not even a wraith came carrying some ominous or optimistic message. Only one image emerged, not scary but definitely real: an old man lying flat on his back, face up, and totally naked.

Three hours later the phone woke him up. "Hello, who's calling?"

"It's me, Father Brown. I wanted to let you know that a local psychologist and I are going to do a ten-week group discussion on The Immigrant Family: Effects on Child Development, starting next month.

I thought you might want to come. You can come as Rupert if you'd like, no 'Father' required."

A smile crossed Rupert's face. "No thanks. I'm about to leave town, but your call was timely."

"How so?"

"Have you ever experienced what I can only explain as a major brain fart?"

They both laughed at this.

"I was trying to locate my suitcase for a trip to San Francisco to see my sister when I became paralyzed. I must have fallen asleep then because I had this strange dream, you know, strange like naked man, prone, and ready for sex. I saw no woman, though." He had to laugh. "Could have been a lot more interesting if this old man had had a young muse with whom he could play. I might not have minded being paralyzed so much, eh?" Then he remembered to whom he was talking and said, "Oh, sorry, Father. Now I've gone and embarrassed myself."

"Don't worry about it, Rupert. I'd like to hear what else happened."

"Nothing this time, but the same thing happened this morning while I sat in my car intending to leave for Vancouver, for a visit with . . ."

"Yes, please continue."

"To visit the woman with whom I recently had sex."

"Oh, I see. I understand your hesitation, Rupert. But please know, I stopped doing what I call 'Catholic shaming' some time ago. I discovered it helped in conversations with my parishioners. So, this brain fart of yours sounds a little like something I read about in *New Scientist*. Yes, I try to keep up on the latest. It's something called traumatic paralysis of the brain."

"And you're a priest? You don't sound like any priest I've known. But please tell me about this paralysis."

"Well, it seems sometimes, after trauma, the brain can give contradictory messages, causing a temporary inability to act. With the little I know about your history, Rupert, you could be carrying some traumatic memory, but more likely, your temporary paralysis is caused by some recent event. For example, you've lived most of your life as a priest with all its rules and proscriptions, and not having sex is a big one. Then you go and have sex and dream about the potential of it happening again. Those might qualify as traumatic events for you. Recovery takes time and will require acknowledging all the new things happening in your life. I think, however, you've tried to hide from things you don't want to accept or just don't understand."

"What do you mean acknowledge the new?"

"Well, remember how I heard you call yourself Rupert in the bakery, not Father Callaway?"

"Yes, and I felt very embarrassed that you heard it."

"Calling yourself by your given name and not with a title affirms now you are not just retired from the priesthood; you have also left the priesthood. Recovery lies in stating that truth. Maybe another example is acknowledging you have a sister and are trying, probably for the first time, to act as a brother might, not as a man escaping his family or little sister but as a member of the Callaway family where only a brother and sister remain."

"Acknowledgment, eh! Telling the truth, you say. Frankly it's all a little abstract for me."

"Well, so be it. Good luck, Rupert. I'll say goodbye for now, but feel free to call again with questions or just to talk. In fact, I may call you to find out what's happening."

He said no more, but Rupert did not hang up. It felt to him like Father Brown hadn't finished with what he really wanted to say. After a short wait, though, the silence began to feel awkward, and Rupert said, "Bye."

"Bye, Rupert."

The phone went dead in Rupert's hand, but he didn't put it down right away. The conversation he'd just had continued to rumble around. It had piqued his curiosity but hadn't really given him any answers, anything, as they used to say, on which he could hang his hat.

Rupert pulled the phone from his ear and stared at it. He just couldn't understand why this hadn't angered him. Something was wrong. What? No answer came, but then strangely he felt encouraged, even eager to get going. He hung up the phone and began again to search for his large suitcase. He finally found it hidden in the attic among the many items the diocese had stored there over the years. He must have put it up there after he'd arrived in Powell River, thinking he'd never have any use for it again. Now it needed cleaning, so he quickly dusted it off and carried it to his room.

What to pack? He didn't have much, and what he had was either black or white, black for suits and white for shirts and underwear. Ties brought a little color to his look, but even those colors were funereal. These were really all the clothes he needed before, but now he wished he had something more colorful to wear. He committed himself to rectify this problem soon but knew that without much extra cash on hand he'd no doubt be stuck with this wardrobe for some time. He packed quickly, leaving out all his old church collars. "I won't need them on this trip."

Rupert put his packed suitcase in the car and pulled away, relieved he had finally been able to leave Powell River. Roads between Powell River and Vancouver were made to accommodate sightseeing tourists and were not built for speed. No freeways. *Looks like I'll have ample time to think about what lies ahead and maybe sort through some more of the debris I'm leaving behind.*

It was Sunday afternoon when he left Powell River. The day promised to be hot, 18°C. As he drove south toward Vancouver, his mind raced through all that had happened. As he did, he remembered a book, one of the few non-Catholic books recommended to him that he'd actually taken the time to read. It was a story about a woman who wanted to hike the Pacific Crest Trail alone and without proper preparation. She was flying by the seat of her pants with her life on the line. That felt like his life now. *I'm not hiking a trail, but I am trekking, unprepared and alone, into the unknown. And it was Maggie who provided the push, the stimulus for the journey.* "I wonder how my journey will end. Maybe I'll write a book too." He laughed. "I truly am losing my mind. I knew it."

Rupert had always been pessimistic, even though he longed to escape that dark, cynical, and malevolent thinking. He had consciously chosen a life in the church, thinking it would help him escape the darkness. Though he had to preach about hope, love, faith, and redemption, his thinking mimicked more the pessimistic philosopher Arthur Schopenhauer than any Mother Teresa. Suicidal thoughts had been his constant companion.

Now, as he drove, he felt buoyant and hopeful. For the moment, those dark thoughts were gone. He was excited to see Sylvia again, but that excitement was laced with fear and uneasiness. He'd only ever imagined having a female companion, never dreaming it might come true for him. *Is she my girlfriend, my lover . . . my what? And if she's my lover, how can I be a priest? Am I still a priest? And then, we've had sex.* He couldn't help but smile at that thought. "Mind-blowing sex." His eyes closed as pictures of his time in bed with Sylvia flashed in his mind.

Suddenly Rupert felt the car swerve off the road. His eyes opened just in time to see he was headed straight at a large tree. He hit the brakes hard and tried turning the wheel back toward the road. The car turned but kept sliding toward the tree. He couldn't see as dirt and stone flew up from the median. Finally, the car came to a stop without the great crash he had been sure was coming. "Fuck me," Rupert said as he looked out and saw how close he'd come to crashing.

Rupert got out of the car and looked around, but there was nothing to see except a few cars that had slowed to see what was happening. Embarrassed by all this unwanted attention, he returned to the car, turned on the ignition, and pulled back on the highway.

Any uneasiness he'd had about seeing Sylvia was gone. Only the scare he'd felt going off the road lingered. He saw a gas station ahead and decided to stop, even though he really didn't need gas. He did have to pee, so he pulled in and drove around to the side hoping to find an outside bathroom. He didn't so he parked. He always hated having to go in at gas stations because he felt he had to buy something.

Back in the car with his bladder empty and a Mars bar in hand, Rupert drove off toward Vancouver. Traffic was heavy, and he reminded himself to keep his mind on the road and the business at hand. He'd see Sylvia soon enough, and then he'd find out what comes next, if anything, with her.

Of course, with everything apparently changing in his life right now, his mind soon wandered off again. This time, though, he kept it mostly to brief mental excursions into what it might be like to see his sister after all these years. *Funny how this excites me now when it used to scare me.*

Rupert drove on, knowing the verdict on how all this would yet unfold was still out there. Maggie was directing the play now, and it would to take him through Vancouver and Sylvia.

After Sylvia, my sister awaits. What will that be like? Not only was he seeing her after all the years but also doing so as she faced death. What would that bring up for him? Rupert drove on, encouraged but also full of anticipation and angst, hopeful that maybe he really did have a future.

He flipped on the radio, but instead of searching for a jazz station, he began to scan the dial for something different. So many genres of music—a little rock, a little rap, a little country—and then he hit upon classical. That's where he stayed. Rupert knew nothing, or nearly nothing, about classical music, but the cadence, the flow of sound, fit this moment better than the pulsing, sometimes discordant sounds of jazz. He'd found a good companion for the remainder of his trip. He noticed, however, that he had to fight a small urge to go back to that rap music he'd heard briefly while changing channels. *What's that about?* he wondered. *Oh well, I guess that will have to wait for another time, maybe another road trip.*

CHAPTER 38

RUPERT'S MIND RACED but not in the usual negative, self-condemning way that left him anxious and depressed. On this drive to Vancouver, he was again assessing his past life.

I went to seminary, joined the priesthood, gave up a normal life to find security, serenity, and sureness. What a disaster all that turned out to be. After fifty-one years in the Church, I'm still insecure, disturbed, and unsure. Geez, talk about a waste of time.

But what path am I on now? Not one I chose, that's for sure. Is it a path at all? If it is, I don't know where it ends. But who's stupid enough to go down some path without knowing where it ends? Me?

His cell phone rang, startling him. He pulled to the side of the road. "Oh, hi, Sylvia. What a surprise to hear from you again."

"Surprise? Why are you so surprised?"

"Oh, nothing. Forget I said that." Instead, almost like he had placed the call, Rupert started to share some thoughts he'd been having on the drive. "I've been thinking about my life and how things have changed since Maggie re-entered my life. It's all shocking for sure, but I do not feel angry toward her. No, no anger, no violent fantasies toward Maggie."

"Violent fantasies, Rupert?"

Rupert felt immediately embarrassed.

"You never told me about those."

"Sorry, I misspoke."

"No, you didn't. You can't get out of it that easily, Rupert. Don't worry. Who knows? It might turn me on."

"Really!"

"Oh, never mind."

He was quiet. *How do I get out of this?* Then he exploded. "Fuck it, Sylvia. I can't answer for everything that's happening or that I might be saying right now. I'm sick, okay? I think it's mental, but who knows? I could just have come down with some serious illness that I can't control. It's driving me in directions I hadn't planned to go. So here goes. I have always had violent fantasies, mostly of hurting someone, but I've also had thoughts of killing someone, never about whom or how I'd do it, but the prospect of doing it has scared me enough that I've often wanted to talk to someone about it."

"Did you?"

"Well, no, not until this very moment."

He stopped. It was like he'd run out of words.

"Don't hang up, Rupert, if that's what you're thinking."

He actually wasn't considering hanging up. He wasn't thinking anything. Then he tried to remember what Sylvia had called him about. "Did you call me for something, Sylvia? I feel like I haven't answered your question."

"I never said, Rupert. You took the conversation in another direction from why I called, and I found it quite interesting, even fascinating. Most of us don't have the courage to say anything about our violent feelings."

"I'm not sure it was courage that drove me, Sylvia. I'd really like to blame you for pushing me into talking about that stuff, but whatever. The secret is out. I have violent thoughts.

"Me too, Rupert."

"What?"

"Yeah, I've even thrown things when I've been angry. Thankfully I throw like a girl and couldn't hit the side of a barn, but a projectile has left my hand in anger."

For some reason that made Rupert laugh. "I'm sorry, Sylvia, but the way you said that struck my funny bone."

"I can laugh now too, Rupert."

"But what did you call me about? Pretend I just picked up and you wanted to ask me something."

"I can't do that Rupert. In fact, I don't want to forget what we just shared with each other."

"Now I feel embarrassed."

"Blushing?"

"No. Guess I'm not embarrassed enough."

"Good. Well, I just called you to find out more about when you hope to be in Vancouver."

"Well, probably sooner than you think. I pulled over when you called, but I'd say I'm only a half hour to forty-five minutes away."

"Wow. I wasn't sure you'd ever get south of Powell River."

"What's your address? You probably gave it to me already, but if you did, it's left my memory bank by now. Can I please have it again?"

"Sure. You ready?"

"Go ahead. I've got paper and pen in hand."

"It's 1707 Davie Street. I'm in West Vancouver, not really close to the airport, but you can still get there in a half-hour or so, since you're going there in the morning. You can Google my address on your phone, Rupert."

"Can I? Since I haven't traveled much, Sylvia, I don't Google like everybody else, but I have the app on my phone and will see now if I'm smart enough to figure it out. All these new things I'm doing with you. First, I have sex for the first time, I mean sex with a woman, not just sex with myself, and now I'm about to Google. My God, what will happen next!"

They both laughed.

"I'll see you soon, I hope."

They hung up. Rupert thought he'd try the Google thing before he took off again. He opened Google on his phone and put in the address. To his surprise, the directions popped right up. "Wow. That was easy."

Now full of pride, Rupert pulled away, heading south and to Sylvia, at last.

CHAPTER 39

MAGGIE TRIED TO SIT UP BUT COULDN'T.

Jake said, "Don't get up on my account, Maggie. No formalities required, especially when you're flat on your back in blissful sedation, I'm sure."

They both laughed as Jake pulled a chair over near the bed.

"Is this seat taken?"

"No, I've kept it free since I knew you might stop by."

"Oh, thank you."

Maggie stared at him and began to cry. "Oh, Jake, I didn't know I could ever feel happy, but I do."

"Wonderful. I feel happy you called, Maggie. Frankly, I was surprised. I haven't known you long, and yet you invited me to visit you here in the hospital, a place where I would think you'd want only your closest friends."

"Well, Jake, this may surprise you, but I have few of those. In fact, I can think of only one, and she's my lawyer. I wanted you to come because, even though I have not known you long, you reached out to me in a way that feels different from what I've experienced throughout my life. It always felt people wanted something from me. You, on the other hand, appear to actually care about me, maybe even like me. I have asked myself, why, what does he want from me? But no, it feels so much better to just feel cared about. I've tried to stop asking my usual mistrusting questions. If I weren't lying here chained to this bed by all these tubes, I think I'd ask you to hold me. Wow! Did I just say that? Who is this masked woman?"

They both giggled a little.

"I've hugged people before as a formality, you know, professionally or as a show of affection I didn't really feel. Fake, but it looked good. What I feel now actually scares me some. Is hugging with affection and admiration a prelude to having sex? Men I've known seemed to associate any attention from a woman as an interest in them sexually. Do you? No, don't answer that, Jake." She stopped for a moment and then continued. "No one in my family hugged. We actually didn't touch. Not even a good spanking happened." She paused another moment. "But, alas, maybe I feel safe telling you all this because currently you couldn't even get close to me if you tried!"

"Do you ever stop thinking, reflecting, on this stuff, these questions you have?"

"You know, probably not, but I don't usually say it all out loud either. You've been cursed to listen to it, Jake."

"Cursed or blessed, Maggie, I don't care. I just meant that maybe you think too much, but then maybe that becomes more important at the end of life, even to the non-curious, the non-analytical, or just the non-nosy among us. Wouldn't you say?"

"Can't say, Jake. This is my first 'end of life' experience."

"That's fair. Apart from all this, though, Maggie, I was wondering why you are here in the hospital."

Maggie grinned, but then became serious. She launched into her cancer story and how she ended up here now.

Jake listened. "That's why you told me at the bar you were dying, right?"

"Yeah. I was telling you the truth but edged it with humor, maybe to put you off."

"Oh, Maggie, I'm so sorry."

"Sorry for what, Jake? Sorry for me, sorry for not knowing what to say to a dying person, or sorry for the nature of this life we all have to live?"

"I feel sorry for my loss, the loss of my blossoming affection for you. I have started to like you, Maggie!"

Maggie felt so much sorrow she couldn't speak. Why couldn't this have happened to her earlier in life? Or did it, and in her hurry to meet all the goals she'd set for herself, did she just miss it? How sad. Finally, she could speak, words stumbling out of her mouth. "Thanks. You don't know how much that means to me. I really don't know how much time I have left, but I'd like to milk that time for everything it has to offer. I want to cross the finish line totally out of breath."

Her voice now became stronger. "How would you feel, Jake, if the doctors here let me go home, about coming to live in my condo? It strikes me that this would help us both live what time I have left to the fullest."

Jake's mouth fell open.

"Oh dear, it looks like I shocked you."

"You could say that. Maybe as a CEO you learned to act decisively, but I'm not used to that. I guess I act slower, maybe even think slower. How can you ask me that so fast? Neither you nor I could possibly be ready for that. I only just got here. We've only touched on how we feel, so I'm sorry, but I have to say no for now."

"Jake, I'm sorry. Please be patient with me. I have so many things to learn. For one, as I said before, I haven't really felt much in the way of affection before. Sexual attraction, yes, but affection or love . . . I don't know. Maybe I learned to ignore it, even if it was there. I know, though, that when you just said you felt affection for me, I felt like I'd been punched in the gut, not in a bad way, mind you, but in a highly disorienting way. Maybe that's why I suggested action, like a CEO. It's automatic. I take control when threatened, and I always feel threatened by vulnerability. And now, here we are talking about death and feelings, things I have no understanding of or control over. What to do? Take charge, set the scene, so I did . . . and, even though it was abrupt, I meant what I said. I feel something wonderful about you, Jake. You're so different. I know there's probably affection, maybe even love, though I can't say I know what that last word really means. I'm feeling something strong, and frankly, it leaves me somewhat—no, a lot—bewildered."

Jake got up. He moved to the side of Maggie's bed, reached out and took her hand in his. She grabbed on. No one spoke, but she could feel herself choking up, and deep sobs welled up inside her. It scared her. She grabbed for tissues to cover her face, but the cat was out of the bag. Maggie sobbed.

Jake found himself tearing up, but said nothing. They cried together, holding hands so tightly that they felt each other's rapid heartbeats.

Slowly Maggie's sobs turned to soft crying. "I'm happy, Jake, not sad, and I feel full. Full, that's a funny word, isn't it? After all I haven't hardly eaten a thing all day!"

They laughed.

"It's an amazing feeling. How can I hang on to it forever?"

"I don't think you can, Maggie. And you don't really have to hang on to this one moment since I plan to stick around."-

Maggie said nothing.

"I can see satisfaction carved into your face, the kind of satisfaction that's born of suffering."

Maggie stared at him. "You sound like you've had some experience with all this, Jake."

"Yeah, I suppose I have. I've suffered from pretty severe depression really since college years, but later on, after my wife died, I was left alone to raise my children, and then I definitely felt worse. I never wanted to admit it, but at one point, suicide was a real possibility. As you can see, I didn't end up killing myself but really only because I went to my doctor who immediately put me on antidepressants and got me started in therapy. I came out of those experiences not feeling exactly happy, but I was less discouraged about my life.

"Then I started talking to close friends about my history, and that helped even more. A good friend shared some things he'd gone through in his life, all new to me, and invited me to attend a meditation program with him and his guru. Far out . . . and pretty brave, don't you think? But I trusted my friend, so I went. And I found I liked it. That was at least five years ago; I have the same teacher, and I meditate regularly. It helps."

"Very interesting. How in the world did we happen to meet now, Jake?"

"Indeed, Maggie, that's a mystery and probably not for us to know, nor for either of us to spend time trying to figure out."

"Sounds right. What I do know, though, is I feel even more convinced I want to share my last days, weeks, months, whatever I have left with you. Will you come to stay with me in the condo? I have plenty of room. My God, there are four bedrooms and four baths in the place. My kitchen is large enough for twenty people, and I know that because I've had that many people in there. You could get lost in my place. You're almost retired, and all your kids have left."

"You make a convincing argument, Maggie, but my answer is still no. I will see you often, and I'll introduce you to meditation, if you'd like, but I won't move in with you. Death is close, and I think your relationship with it seems most important. You and death need to dance together. People who care—me, your lawyer, your brother—will be there with you, but right now, the main event in your life is what's right in front of you."

"Oh, my brother. I totally forgot about him."

"Your plate is full, Maggie."

She knew he was right but still felt disappointed. Maggie was surprised that mentioning death didn't really frighten her. She knew it was close, that it would take her when the time came. This death was hers, her burden, no one else's. And maybe a blessing? "Okay, Jake. You're right. So I now give you permission to come over as often as you like. We can visit, maybe play games, listen to music, or do anything else that comes up, though I probably won't be sharing many meals, unless my appetite comes back. And to help encourage you to make the trip from your place to mine, how about if I help with the taxi or Lyft fares?"

"Thanks for the offer, Maggie. I might take you up on it, but I plan to come with or without your financial help."

"Deal."

"Deal."

They shook hands.

The nurse who came in saw them shaking hands and smiling. She wondered what had been going on but didn't ask. She was there to give Maggie a sponge bath and change her sheets.

"Bath time, Maggie."

"I think I'll mosey along, Maggie."

"Wish I could mosey along out of here with you, Jake, but that's not going to happen today. Thanks for coming." She watched him gather his things and head for the door. Waving goodbye, she surprised herself and blew him a kiss.

He waved back and smiled.

The nurse started to change the sheets.

Maggie marveled at how she was able to do this with her in the bed. "Did you have to take classes to learn how to do this?"

"I had what you'd call on-the-job-training. My supervisor did it once while I watched, and then she turned it over to me. Of course, the first few times were rough for the patients, but now I think I have it down."

"You do." Maggie was just letting her move her around, and then she lay back to receive the sponge bath. That was nice, but Maggie didn't pay much attention. She couldn't relax. She had started to think about Rupert's visit and was feeling more and more nervous. My stomach! It never churned like this before I gave speeches or had big events to lead. Guess I'm not as numb as I once was. She smiled and asked the nurse if she could have a pen and some paper.

"Oh, for sure, Maggie. You planning a big speech?

"No, something even more demanding. I have to get ready to meet, actually re-meet, my older brother whom I haven't seen in a long time."

"In that case you probably need more than paper. You need to see a good shrink."

Maggie laughed. "Thanks for the advice, but I think it's too late."

The nurse finished her job and left to find paper and pen. Maggie waited, trying to stay calm, but that felt like something she could no longer do.

CHAPTER 40

R UPERT ARRIVED IN VANCOUVER LATE IN THE AFTERNOON, the sun
still strong in the sky. With the car windows down, the warm air
rushed in to surround him like a warm blanket. He had turned off the
music to help him focus on locating Sylvia's place. New at using GPS,
Rupert needed to concentrate. He had come to Vancouver a few times
for meetings but had always been with others who knew where they
were going. Now everything looked strange and unfamiliar.

It took almost an hour before he finally had to admit he was lost. He
pulled the car into a parking space and called Sylvia.

"Hi, Rupert. Are you calling me to announce you turned back to
Powell River and are not coming or what?"

"No, actually I just arrived in Vancouver, but I'm lost."

"Tell me your location and I'll direct you here."

Turned out her address wasn't far from where he'd pulled over. As he
drove the short distance, he couldn't help thinking about how strange
this all was. Rupert, the recluse, the misanthrope, approaching the home
of a woman he'd only recently met and with whom he had had sex for the
first time ever in his life.

At four forty sharp, he rang Sylvia's doorbell. The door opened. She
stood there, looking shorter than he remembered, wearing a very colorful skirt-and-blouse outfit. Her hair was tied back in a ponytail, and he

could see she'd put on lipstick.

He stepped back a little "You look wonderful, Sylvia."

She smiled. "Come on in. It's good to see you, Rupert. For a while there, I wasn't sure you'd ever make it."

"Me either. You look great, Sylvia."

"Thanks. You can stop telling me how wonderful and great I look now. It's a little embarrassing."

He followed her into the kitchen.

"I left the teapot on in case you wanted tea, but I also have beer and wine if you'd prefer that after your long drive."

"Thanks, I think I'd prefer tea for now. Are you having any?"

"Yeah, I'll join you, but let me show you around the place first. I don't see any luggage. Don't you plan to stay tonight? Your flight is tomorrow, right?"

"Well, I do have a bag, but not knowing the protocol for these sorts of things, I left it in the car. You know I've lived a pretty isolated and sheltered life up till about two weeks ago."

"I want you here and would like to share a bed with you, but as you can see, I also have an extra bedroom if you'd prefer to have a private space."

Sylvia's frankness still shocked Rupert. He loved it, and he did really want to sleep with her again, but he could never have said it with such directness. Whatever happened to that old practice of seduction? From the back of his brain, he heard, *Once seduced, Rupert, there is no longer any need for formalities.* "I'd prefer to sleep with you tonight, Sylvia. But remember, since I never had sex with a woman before you, I could get a little wild!" He laughed out loud.

Sylvia smiled. "Fine with me. Want to start right now?"

Rupert blushed. "Oh, did I sound eager?"

"Yeah. It might be better, though, for you to settle in first."

"Okay."

"How about you go get your bag or bags, and I'll make the tea. I have lemongrass, chamomile, Earl Grey, and several others I can't remember right now."

"Lemongrass sounds good. No caffeine. I think I'm high enough already!"

By the time he returned with his bag, Sylvia had their tea on the coffee table.

"One bag, eh?

"Should I have more?"

"No, just kidding. Come on. I'll show you to the room."

Rupert dropped his bag at the foot of the bed, and they both headed back for their tea.

"So, tell me what's happened since we last talked."

He didn't say anything for a minute until, "Oh, not much!" and laughed. "That was a joke, Sylvia."

"I know."

He sipped his tea. "Maggie has brought back memories long hidden away in my brain. I'd put them so far back I felt sure they would never return. I thought I did this because of what I had to endure at home, but it had more to do with guilt. I naïvely thought I could completely escape it all through forgetting. One letter changed that. What had I done to her and ultimately to myself all those years ago? I felt for the first time the magnitude of the tragedy I'd perpetrated on my sister. How could I have left her so alone? I've lived in a fantasy. For whatever reason, Maggie found the courage to reach out, a move that actually helped me. . . . Is this really me here with you, without clerical collar, excited . . .," Rupert went silent and then, with hesitation in his voice, continued, "about having sex tonight." He watched Sylvia's reaction—a look of delight and what he would call smiling eyes. Rupert smiled and started to breathe again. "For the first time I've had conversations with neighbors in Powell River. And tomorrow I'm getting on a plane, off to San Francisco, California, the land of sun and fun, right? After that, who knows what? Wow, is this the Rupert Callaway I've always known, the unwanted, the unloved? That's some of what's happened to me since we last met." As he looked at Sylvia, he saw something that surprised him. "Are you crying?"

"No, but when I first asked you what's happened since we last talked, I thought you'd say you'd gone fishing, read a good book, eaten another meal at the Thaidal Zone, or maybe taken a ferry ride. I should have expected it I guess, given the short comments I've heard over the phone, but God, that's a hard thing to hear from someone you've started to care about." Sylvia stopped, saying no more.

Rupert just stared.

After a while, Sylvia finally broke into the stillness. "And now my tea's gone cold!"

They laughed.

Rupert had never spoken so intimately to anyone, much less a woman he hardly knew. His heart pounded in his chest. He felt hot, and his face turned bright red. "I think I need to go for a walk."

"Do you mind if I come along?"

"I don't know. Talking to you has made it all feel more real. Things have happened so fast, maybe too fast. I don't know, but right now I feel like I've passed through some kind of wormhole and entered the future. My future."

Sylvia didn't respond. What could she say? She thought, *A professor of literature at a loss for words!*

Rupert leaned back in the chair. The quiet felt comforting. He really did wish his heart would stop pounding, though. *Maybe if I just close my eyes and sit here a bit, I'll calm down.* After about five minutes, which felt like fifteen to him, he sat up and asked-if she'd warm up his tea.

Sylvia had been watching him closely. She'd grown a little alarmed when he became so quiet after such an explosion of feeling. When he finally asked for tea. it reassured her. "Of course, Rupert. Warm tea coming up."

While Sylvia made tea, Rupert scanned the place. His body tingled with energy. Though his heart had slowed some, he could still feel it beating. He got up and walked around. Furniture filled the room, and he noticed she had books everywhere, on the floor by his feet, on tables, on top of the TV, which looked like an antique. *She must not watch much TV,* he thought. Rupert had never been much of a reader. But since his life had changed, he noticed how attracted he'd become to book collections. It happened while visiting Father Brown and now it was happening here. He picked up the book closest to him, a book of poems by Emily Dickinson.

Sylvia walked in carrying two warm cups of tea. She was glad to see Rupert holding a book. "I see you've found my books."

"Well, I've found the one on top of this pile, but it does look like you have a large collection."

"Whaddya find?"

He held up the cover.

"Oh, that's a favorite of mine. Emily Dickinson was a poet of some depth and understanding about life and death. Lived mid-1800s until 1886, only fifty-five years." Sylvia went on to talk about Dickinson and what she had written until she saw that she'd lost Rupert.

He was staring at her with a blank face.

"That's enough trivia, I think, for now."

Rupert, acting the role of the pastor, tried to save her from her embarrassment. "Maybe I'll read her poems sometime, and then we can talk more about it."

Sylvia realized, that in her excitement at having a comfortable topic, she had moved the conversation to a less personal place. She had turned their animated exchange into a lecture on a dead poet. Sylvia inwardly rolled her eyes. *Again, my fear of intimacy rears its ugly head.* This was getting awkward. "I bought a few things for dinner, Rupert. Hungry? I know I am."

"Yeah, I haven't eaten since breakfast, and even then, it was only a croissant. I'm not much of a cook, but I can help in the kitchen, maybe act as the sous-chef." This was not just an altruistic move for him. Rupert was still feeling antsy and had to get up and move around. He wasn't ready to just sit and talk again.

They jumped up and walked toward the kitchen together. She feigned running, and he passed her, but soon stopped and turned around.

"Where's the kitchen?"

CHAPTER 41

Maggie left the hospital later on Sunday. She wanted to go home.

Theresa picked her up and drove. On the way home, Maggie told about Jake's visit. As Maggie talked, Theresa marveled at the change she saw and heard. Maggie seemed comfortable with a man. Her usual controlling manner had softened. She reported she felt happy. And now as they drove, Theresa couldn't help but feel happy for her. There was sadness too as Maggie spoke with affection and enthusiasm for her life, now that she was going home to die. The doctor said she could live another six months, maybe longer. But he had not said it with a lot of enthusiasm or optimism in his voice.

Arriving at Maggie's place, Theresa pulled in the garage near the elevator that could take them and all the medical gear up to her condo. A nurse was to come by that afternoon to help set it all up.

On the way up the elevator, Theresa thought she should remind Maggie about Rupert's visit. Maggie had really always kept good track of her schedule, but she also depended on Theresa to go over it with her each morning. So, partially out of habit but also now out of consideration and respect, Theresa started to review the schedule, which on this day really had only one upcoming event.

"Thanks, Theresa, but I hadn't forgotten all that. How could I? I know

I might see Rupert tomorrow. How many years has it been?" She really didn't expect an answer so went right on. "By my getting home today, he won't have to find a hotel when he gets here. He can stay here." She walked to the dining area and sat in a chair by the table. "I think I'll just sit here until everything gets set up."

Theresa was a little shocked that Maggie would have her brother stay at her place, but then much that had happened already had more than surprised her. She let it pass and said nothing.

The nurse arrived soon after Theresa had everything piled into the condo. While Theresa helped set up all the equipment, she introduced herself and Maggie.

"Nice to meet you both. I'm Lively Thornton." After Lively went over how and when to use everything, Theresa left. Maggie had no trouble understanding the directions, but the nurse said she'd visit twice a day to help her in any way she could. Maggie heard how all this treatment was tied to her expected imminent death. *It's okay*, she thought. She felt more content about dying. She had stopped telling others she was dying. It had become too real.

After Lively left, Maggie went into the bedroom. She stood in front of a full-length mirror staring at her body. She moved in as close as she could without bumping her nose on the glass. She scanned her face. She wore no makeup, and her skin was sallow, the color of mixed white and yellow paint. Her eyes were sunk deep into their sockets. Her hair, what there was left, was turning gray and looked messy. She hadn't combed it at all while in the hospital, and though the nurses had made some efforts to disentangle it, it now made Maggie think she'd better tell someone to be sure it gets fixed up before they put her out for viewing in the casket. Her face looked shrunken, her nose and ears noticeably sticking out. *I look so old, and yet I'm too young to die.* "Not true. We all die when it's our time."

Saying that sent a tremor through her, and she went to sit down. Maggie knew she'd have to delay thinking too much about death for now since she needed to focus on Rupert's visit. She decided to try calling him.

Rupert was in the middle of preparing dinner with Sylvia when he heard his phone ring. He answered on the third ring.

"Hello, Rupert. It's Maggie. Just thought I'd check to see if you still plan to come down."

After a short silence, he answered her. "Oh, yes, I'll be there, but I must say I feel a little nervous about it all. It's been so long that we've been separated. And now you're sick, and I'm in a kind of discovery period, moving from a life of dependence to one of independence. But, yes, I'm coming. I'm curious about where life is going and what happens next."

"Well, it looks like you'll be catching me close to the end, Rupert, so as we met at the beginning of my life, we will now meet again at the end. Poetic, isn't it? Tragedy or comedy, we have yet to find out. When you arrive, come to my house. They've set me up here with all the medical paraphernalia you can imagine to keep me comfortable, maybe even alive. I'm still mobile, so when you get here, just ring the bell and I'll come to open the door."

Again, Rupert paused before speaking. His heart pounded, and he began to wonder if he was up for all this.

Maggie waited on her end as her hand gripped the phone ever tighter.

"Thanks, Maggie, I'll see you soon."

They both hung up.

Well, I know he's coming. She wondered if she'd called to find that out, or did some part of her hope he might cancel the trip. *He ran away once, why not do it again?* she wondered. But now, even if she'd secretly hoped for him not to come, they would have to face each other.

Her phone alarm rang to remind her to take her pills. She took care of that and then went to lie down. Maggie didn't wake up until the next medication alarm went off, three hours later. The phone read 7:48 p.m. *Wow,* she thought to herself, *I really went out for a while. I guess that's what death will be like, only, I won't wake up. Or will I?*

Out of habit Maggie called Grub Hub to order dinner. She had no appetite and would not really eat much of the order they said would arrive in about forty-five minutes. Dinner was not the primary thing on her mind, though. The house was quiet. She really hadn't been home much with all her meetings and trips, and when she was home, she did a lot of paperwork, talked on the phone, and entertained. It really was never quiet, even though she lived alone. Now, though, she felt the aloneness. She had no board meeting to prepare for, no speech to write, nothing to distract her. So she sat, her only company, her thoughts.

It struck Maggie that her situation was probably much like what a soldier faced sitting in a landing craft on D-Day. Though surrounded by other soldiers, he was, like her, alone with his thoughts and fears. Sure, others would have to go through the upcoming battle, but each of them had to live that out alone, face his destiny alone. Even though she'd had to face many battles in business and life, she felt unprepared-thinking about this one. There'd been no way really to get ready, no course she'd taken, no lesson learned from experience, nothing to draw on from her quiver of experiences. And she only would have one shot. Her last. The quiet of her mind got noisier.

The doorbell rang. She answered the door and took her dinner to the table. Maggie stared at the mashed potatoes, green beans, and fried chicken. Oh, how she had loved this particular dinner, but now she ate nothing.

A quote from Pooh Bear, a favorite story of hers when she was little, intruded on all the dark thoughts: "Always remember, you're braver than you believe, stronger than you seem, and smarter than you think." Oh, Pooh, I'll try to hang on to your wisdom!

CHAPTER 42

After Rupert finished talking to Maggie, he felt a little light-headed, so he sat down at the table in Sylvia's kitchen.

"Everything all right?"

"I don't know, to tell you the truth. I think I've lost touch with what *all right* means. My life always felt true and right. I tried to do good things, do the right thing, and be a man of good faith. Now I don't know what the right thing is anymore. My life is ruled by doubt. I've wondered if it's the devil leading me astray, but it doesn't feel bad or wrong. I feel happy, really for the first time in my life. But is that what you call *all right*?"

"I can't answer that for you. Does life have a program to follow? We may want one because the structure makes us feel safer, giving our lives meaning that we may realize later really had no great meaning at all." When Rupert didn't respond she thought, *Oh, shit, there I go again, teaching/preaching.* She found an escape from her embarrassment by returning to her dinner preparation.

Rupert again wondered if he was up to the task at hand, whatever that was. In this moment, all he knew for sure was that he was standing in Sylvia's kitchen and that he had a ticket to fly to San Francisco tomorrow. He knew everything else was open, yet to be revealed. *But that's crazy. I have to know something about what I should be doing, don't I?* He turned to

Sylvia. "You know, we could have sex here on the kitchen table, or I could continue to help you prepare dinner, or I could get in my car and just drive east, maybe all the way to New York City. Or I could go upstairs and take a bath, or on and on, endless possibilities. Who's to tell me what's the right thing to do now? How does one live a life without directions?"

Sylvia, determined not to turn teacher again, said, "I'm hungry, so I think that should be our guide for right now."

"When all else fails, eat!"

They sat down to a cheese omelet, fried potatoes, and green beans. Earlier, she'd made an apple pie for dessert and set that off to the side. The smell of food triggered Rupert's appetite, but his mind was not on the food. He ate simply because everything smelled so good and he was hungry from the long drive.

After cleaning up the dishes, Rupert and Sylvia went to the living room and found chairs. Sylvia didn't seem to have a special chair as he did at his house, so he chose one that looked comfortable. He sank into it, wondering at first if he might go all the way to the floor. He didn't. He felt held, surrounded with softness. Rupert looked at Sylvia and smiled. "I guess I chose the soft one, eh?"

"Yeah, I call that my *nap chair* because I always go to sleep if I try to read or write while sitting there. It's definitely not a chair from which great ideas sprout."

"In that case I think I'll move over to the couch if that's okay. Right now doesn't feel like a good time for sleeping."

"Tomorrow morning I have to leave for school around nine. What time do you leave for the airport?"

"My flight goes at ten, but I think I should get there at least an hour earlier."

"You may want to get there two hours ahead, Rupert. You haven't flown in a while, and there have been a lot of changes in security that require more time to navigate."

"That's fine with me. How about I catch a taxi around seven? I'm not driving to the airport. Not a good time for me to get lost."

"That should work fine. With traffic, it may take a taxi an hour to get there. Do you have any idea when you might return?"

Rupert really had no idea. "See, Sylvia, this is one place where things get really difficult. I might never return. I could come back on the next plane out of San Francisco, or I could . . . I don't know what. It all makes my head spin. What's going to happen when I meet Maggie? I feel like I'm on an emotional roller coaster with no sure place to get off." Rupert sat silently lost in thought. Since I don't know what I'm doing, I think I'll leave my car in a long-term lot I spotted in walking distance from here. Whatever happens, you won't have to concern yourself with that."

Sylvia stared across the room at him. "So be it, Rupert. When do you plan to drive to this lot?"

"Now," Rupert said and left the room. Her comment had angered him. He wanted to get out before she could say anything else.

When he returned from parking, she was standing at the door and said, "You looked before like you either wanted to hit me or fuck me, Rupert."

Rupert just stared. Her comment, her observation, broke through something. What, he didn't know, but his anger unexpectedly subsided. "Sylvia, I've worked so hard and failed to hide my anger because all it did was create distance and keep me from making friends. They couldn't kick me out of the priesthood, though I know they wanted to get rid of me because, heavens, I was so unpleasant, unbearable, downright insufferable to have around. But no one was kicked out, even those who we now know were sexually abusing kids or nuns. When I retired, they shunted me off to a house they owned in Powell River, far away from any of them. They knew the only way they or others might be safe from my explosions was to not have me around Sad, eh?" Rupert didn't expect Sylvia to say anything, and she didn't, which left time for his sadness to emerge. Finally, after all the years he'd lived feeling rejected and unaccepted, he was sad. His head dropped, and the decades of heartache, hopelessness, and heartbreak rose as Rupert cried,

Sylvia just stood by, watching, and waiting.

Suddenly it was like he'd cried enough, and he felt calm, composed, and quiet.

Sylvia still said nothing, even though she was tempted to throw out a few choice quotes that had popped in her head. She just waited to see what would happen next.

"Anyway, you were right. I'm sure some very old part of me did want to either hit you or fuck you. Anger, an anger that could hurt and wanted to hurt, was still lurking there, just like so many times before. I never allowed myself to act on those feelings and wouldn't have now. But they were there, like always, deep and hungry for prey." Rupert stopped a moment before continuing. "Turns out I was the only victim of all my anger, but now, something's changed. A little." He smiled and then added, "I still would like to fuck you but NOT in anger. This time I think, or at least I like to think, it's coming from some feelings of warmth, affection, and passion. I hope anyway."

"For sure, Rupert, though let's change it from fuck to having intimate and wild sex." She then quickly added, "Later."

"Okay."

Sylvia took a deep breath. She'd been holding her breath, not sure if Rupert might get really mad or upset again, sensing the strong feelings coming from him. It filled the room. Sylvia had watched him after her comment, "So be it." His face had reddened, his body tensed, like he really did want to hit her. The air was full of violence, anger held in, like the energy from fission, but held back, contained behind some wall Rupert had built. Though she saw no explosion, she did feel as if she'd been penetrated through the heart. The depth of his emotion, be it irritation or fury, sadness or grief, reached deep inside her and touched her soul. *Why*, she wondered, *did a country priest, massively screwed up in his life, touch her so deeply?* She too felt she had always tried to hide her intense emotions. Being a college teacher of literature and language, she had focused on the intellectual material. *That has to change*, she thought, *starting now.*

"I'm feeling more determined than ever, Rupert, to release my inner beast. No more words trying to display my intellect and acuity. I want to convey what's happening to me, the uncooked, unprocessed truth. I think I'm falling for you." It took a lot for Sylvia to put that out, but it went seemingly unnoticed. Reason told her Rupert had the stage, and right now, she felt okay with that—for now—maybe even a little relieved.

Rupert heard what Sylvia said but ignored it. He didn't want to acknowledge it. Without even thinking, he knew that to recognize it would change the course of their conversation. Right now, he wanted to feel, not think. His passions ruled; his body shook, not wildly, more like the mild vibration of an idling vehicle. It felt good, but he would have been embarrassed if he thought Sylvia could see his body humming like this. He wanted to say more—he had so much to say, things never said to anyone. "You know, Sylvia, I sometimes wonder why I never considered suicide. I felt so out of place, so unwanted, but I also felt an aversion to others. I hated my life. Surrounded by people every day, I felt only loneliness and despair. I sought solace through private prayer, but I never found the peace I sought. I punished myself with self-flagellating thoughts and tried to throw myself into work. No peace came; only lots of anger, sometimes with the least provocation. People shunned me. They avoided the Masses I led. Thank God for those Catholics who felt they had to attend Mass to save their souls. Otherwise, I believe I would have preached to empty pews. What a disaster, eh?"

"If you had killed yourself, Rupert, we wouldn't have met."

"Somehow, right now, that feels like a terrible loss." He went silent again as what he had just said bounced around inside his head. Then he continued, "Loss, like many feelings, has been hidden, cloaked in anger and despair, hidden from me and others. Maybe facing the prospect of a reunion with Maggie, a person lost to me so many years ago, was enough to crack the shell around me. Since hearing from her, I've had this urge, unbidden, unprompted, and unconscious, to connect, to relate, to engage with the world. You were the first person with whom I gave into this urge, but you probably remember I was still needing your encouragement to do it. Then I connected with a neighbor and a local priest, whom I knew but had avoided. And still to come, who knows, but first I have to face Maggie."

Rupert looked at his watch and saw 10:48. "Wow, it's almost eleven."

"I better hit the sack pretty soon, Rupert. I have three classes to teach tomorrow." Sylvia wanted to go on listening to Rupert and to talk more herself, but truly her energy level had dropped into sleep mode.

"Okay, I guess. I'll just curl up here on the couch, if that's okay."

"It is okay, Rupert, but you can also sleep with me in my bed."

Rupert said nothing but walked over to her and pulled her close.

They stood together in a close embrace that was now full of affection and tenderness. They kissed, and Rupert gave her an affectionate pat on the bottom.

"Rupert, you naughty boy!"

"Now, that's a first. 'Naughty boy.' I think you just made my day, maybe my year. Oh hell, maybe my life!"

They both laughed as she took him by the hand and led him into the bedroom. He came out about four hours later. Sylvia had fallen asleep a while ago, but he was wide awake. The sex they'd shared had been great, wild but full of tenderness and care.

Rupert turned the light on next to the couch and sat down, hoping to read. It might help him fall asleep, and besides, he was hungry for words to help him understand the world he now willingly inhabited. He picked up one book he thought might entertain and distract him, perhaps helping him also calm down for sleep. It was *Upstream*, a collection of essays by Mary Oliver. Rupert didn't like poetry very much but hadn't mentioned that when Sylvia told him about Emily Dickenson. Father Brown had told him to try reading Mary Oliver. He said she encourages the reader to live a bold life, certainly not the kind of life Rupert had followed so far.

One tree is like another tree, but not too much.
One tulip is like the next tulip, but not altogether.
More or less like people—a general outline, then
The stunning individual strokes.

Rupert liked this beginning and read on, as it turned out, for almost an hour before he reached up and turned off the light. He slept soundly, not waking until he heard Sylvia in the kitchen making breakfast and he hoped some good strong coffee. He had a big day ahead.

CHAPTER 43

MAGGIE WOKE AFTER A RESTLESS NIGHT. Pain plagued her sleep, but she also had Rupert's visit on her mind. She didn't feel much like getting up, but remembering the nurse was scheduled to arrive around ten and since it was already after nine, Maggie dragged herself out of bed. Her pain felt worse, so much so she wondered if all the meds she took were working as well as they had in the hospital.

Then the nausea hit. She managed to get herself to the bathroom just before she threw up, actually gagged, trying to throw up. Blood was all she had to come up now. Thoroughly exhausted, she went back to bed and stayed there until Lively rang the bell. She had a key, so Maggie didn't have to open the door, thankfully.

"How do you feel this morning?"

"Truthfully, like roadkill or close to it. My brother arrives later today, so I hope you brought your miracle drugs."

"Did you eat last night or this morning?"

"Nothing this morning—I've felt sick to my stomach—and really nothing for dinner last night either. I really haven't felt hungry for a while now."

"Okay. And when does your brother arrive?"

"He should be here by dinnertime, but the actual ETA remains unknown. I do know my brother, whose name is Rupert, has not traveled much or far in his almost seventy years, so travel snags could cause a delay or, I suppose, even a cancellation." Maggie didn't like realizing that. *After all this and I don't get to see him before I die because of some travel snafu.*

Lively had begun changing out bags of intravenous fluids and pain medication and installing new ones. "Well," she said, "I hope he calls first. You could get sleepy and go back to bed before he arrives."

Maggie walked into the living room and sat down.

Lively followed behind.

"How in the world did you get a name like Lively?"

"There's nothing profound about it at all. It simply came from an ongoing dispute between my parents over what to name their only child. Both were avid readers, and so they chose names from literature. It seems my mother preferred Alice—ugh!—from Lewis Carroll's *Alice in Wonderland*, a favorite of hers from childhood, and from the author Alice B. Toklas, another favorite. My father wanted Anna from one of his favorites, *Anna Karenina* by Tolstoy. They couldn't agree. This name battle went on for about three to four months, and pressure increased from both family and friends to decide. Well, they finally did but not from literature. They named me after what they saw, a lively, energetic, and high-spirited little girl. Hence, I became Lively. "It's so unusual you might think I wouldn't like it, but actually I've always liked it. I had a different name from other kids in school, I stood out from the crowd, and it reflects the kind of hyperactive person I've always been."

Maggie found all this fascinating, thinking about how wonderful it would be to know how your parents had picked your name. For her, this was just another thing she'd never know. "Thanks for sharing. I found it very interesting."

"I need to leave soon, Maggie. Would you like me to help you put together some lunch?"

"No, I'm not hungry."

"Well, I want you to try to eat something, even if it's just applesauce. I brought along crackers and cheese and a few oranges I'll peel and put out on the kitchen table. You can nibble on them all afternoon."

"Thanks." Maggie watched Lively go but didn't follow. Soon, if all went according to plan, Rupert would arrive. A shudder of excitement passed through her.

CHAPTER 44

SYLVIA DID HAVE THE COFFEE POT ON AND EGGS AND BACON IN THE PAN. Rupert breathed in the wonderful aromas. In seminary, everyone ate together in a large hall off the kitchen, and in his parish, they had what felt more like a dining room for meals. In both places, though, large air vents over the stoves sucked any wonderful cooking odors into the outdoors. He had not cooked much for himself since retiring mostly because he didn't know how to cook, other than canned soup, tuna, or something he pulled from a box. Now, he knew what he'd missed for all those years. Finally, he rose, put on a bathrobe and entered the kitchen.

Sylvia smiled as he came in and directed him toward the table. "I put together some breakfast for us before you go."

"Smells great. Bring it on."

She piled his plate high with eggs, bacon, and potatoes.

"Wow, potatoes too. Didn't smell those cooking."

"Coffee?"

"Right here."

She filled his cup.

"Oh, the smell and then the taste of good coffee." Rupert started to sing.

I'm feeling' mighty lonesome
I haven't slept a wink
I walk the floor and watch the door
And in between I drink
Black coffee

"You know that tune? Ella Fitzgerald, among others, recorded it. Listening to jazz while alone was one pleasure I always had while living in the seminary and later in the parish. Thankfully, I had something, eh? And of course, it was even better when accompanied by a strong cup of brew, one of the few things I could make myself!"

When they'd finished eating, Sylvia reminded him that he'd have to leave soon and got up to start the dishes.

Rupert looked at his watch, and jumped up. "Oh my, I can't believe it. I really do have to go." His ride to the airport was scheduled for seven, and it was already six forty-five.

"Well get going, man," Sylvia said as she patted him on the bottom.

He took his dishes to the sink.

She got ready to wash them but quickly turned off the water. "Oh, these can wait until later."

Rupert went to get his bag, and Sylvia headed off to finish dressing and collect her books.

At seven, a horn honked out on the street. His taxi had arrived. Rupert started toward the door but then stopped. He put his bag down, walked over to Sylvia, and kissed her on the lips while hugging her tightly. "Not bad for someone who really hasn't had any practice, don't you think?"

"Oh, yeah, come back soon," she said while smiling.

"I'll call when I know more about a return time. Hard to say when that might be, but the way I feel right now, I'm thinking you might have me as a guest again soon."

Sylvia said nothing, knowing the future was very open and unknown for both of them. "It's been a great ride so far," she said. "Bye, for now."

"Goodbye, Sylvia." Before closing the car door, Rupert looked back and blew her a kiss.

Sylvia stood there waving as the car pulled away. She was crying.

Though sad, Rupert couldn't cry. He had too much excitement about what lay ahead.

CHAPTER 45

No MUSIC, NO PHONE RINGING, NO SOUNDS wafting up from the street below, no TV blaring in the condo as she lay on the couch following Lively's visit. The quiet stillness surrounding Maggie felt oppressive and suffocating. Though she'd never run a foot race in her life, she felt like she'd just finished a marathon. Was this the illness, or was this all just her imagination?

Whatever, she didn't like the feeling so forced herself to get up, open the shades, and turn on her CD player. It really didn't help much. She still felt like the walls of the condo were closing in on her. Maggie looked around for her watch, wondering how much time had passed since Lively had left. Finding it, she saw that it was only one in the afternoon, and Rupert wouldn't arrive until dinnertime or later, if he came at all. She went back to the couch and sat down.

Jake had told her about his meditation practice, but she couldn't remember what he'd said about how to do it, if he'd said it at all. *Too bad*, she thought, *since right now it might come in handy.* The pressure she felt caused her to start saying the word *help* to herself over and over. How long this went on, she didn't know, but suddenly she became aware that the compact disc she'd turned on was no longer playing, which surprised her since that disc had always played until she turned it off.

The quiet was back, but now she noticed her breathing had calmed and the weight she'd felt pressing on her chest had lifted. Maggie closed her eyes and saw herself floating in a large body of warm water. She was doing nothing to keep herself afloat, but she didn't seem to need to do anything. Her mind raced with multiple images, some disturbing and some downright scary. The feelings that accompanied this caused her to shudder and shake. Held by the warm water, she still felt secure and safe—until—BANG.

Startled, Maggie jumped, and everything stopped. Her eyes flew open, and she saw Theresa standing over a broken teacup with tea flowing across the floor.

"I'm so sorry, Maggie. I came in just now and didn't see you at first, so I went into the kitchen to fetch you a cup of tea. Then looking through the house, I saw you lying on the couch, and I'm so sorry to say it, but you looked dead. That's when I dropped the teacup and you popped awake. How stupid of me. I'm so sorry."

Maggie smiled and said, "Well, I guess everyone assumes I'm dying, so you could have been right. Not yet, though. Before I heard the cup fall, I was having a very interesting dream or hallucination, I'm not sure. I was thinking about meditating but didn't know how. Then I must have fallen asleep and ended up in this strange place, in some dream. Weird! I felt like I was being held safe while in mental turmoil. What time is it?"

Theresa was still cleaning up the mess but stopped to check the time. "It's after three o'clock."

"Wow, that went on a long time, and look at my shirt, it's soaked. I must have sweated out a gallon of water."

"Yeah, now you have wet clothes and a wet floor. Do you want me to get you a fresh shirt?"

"No, I'm going to go take a shower."

"I can't stay long, Maggie. I need to get back to the car where the kids and Guy are waiting for me to take them to the store. We just stopped here on the way so I could see how you were doing. They must wonder what happened to me."

"Oh, Theresa, how thoughtful. Be sure to say hi to everyone. I'll call you later. If Rupert comes, it could happen anytime between five and whenever. I at least want to look good when and if he comes."

"Sure, okay." Theresa finished cleaning up and then, just before leaving, she yelled back toward Maggie. "Sorry, again. Call me. Bye."

Maggie took a long, hot shower and then heard the phone ring while in the shower. When she finished, she checked to see if anyone had left a message. She heard Jake asking about how she was adjusting to being home and to call if she wanted. *Oh, yes, Jake, I want to*, and she hit the callback button.

"Hi, Maggie. Guess you got my message."

"I did. You called while I was taking a shower, cleaning up, getting ready to meet my long-lost brother."

"Sounds good. I just wanted to say I'll be thinking of you and wishing you well. Of those standing behind you, be sure you count me."

"I sure will, Jake. I hope I can see you again soon, but as you know, my future right now can't be planned." Listening to Jake made Maggie reflect on her dream, that feeling of being held. Tears formed in her eyes as she said goodbye and hung up.

My next big adventure awaits, and I feel ready and alive, she thought. Then the phone rang. She read the caller ID on the phone: Rupert Callaway. Despite thinking she was ready for this, Maggie just stared at the phone. She couldn't pick up. Finally, the ringing stopped, and he didn't leave a message.

CHAPTER 46

RUPERT'S RIDE FROM SYLVIA'S MADE GOOD TIME. Traffic was lighter than usual with none of the slowdowns or stops he'd expected. He'd left his car in a long-term parking garage, having decided it wouldn't be fair to ask Sylvia to take responsibility for it, especially since he had no definitive return scheduled.

Sylvia was right. Airport protocols had indeed changed since his last visit, which had been so long ago Rupert couldn't remember where he'd been going. After checking his one bag, he was told to go to security. He found a sign that said Security, got in line, and then waited over forty-five minutes to negotiate the process. Then when he went through the x-ray machine, it buzzed.

"Did you take everything out of your pockets, sir?"

Rupert found car keys in his pants pocket. After removing them, he got through this final challenge and headed for Gate 12 where he'd have to wait about an hour before takeoff.

That hour went by too slowly. Rupert passed the time watching people as they read, worked on computers, or slept. Some stood at the airline kiosk arguing with staff about seat assignments. One middle-aged gentleman, dressed quite formally, insisted he should get a seat in first class. Seems he'd gotten bounced for some reason and was quite upset about it. Rupert could hear the man arguing his case. *Interesting*, Rupert thought, *entitled, pompous, asshole.* Then it hit him. *That sounds like me.* Rupert moved away as quickly as he could and took a seat near one of the many TVs where he stayed until they called his flight.

He felt nervous as he boarded the plane and walked down the aisle toward his seat in the back. Rupert had booked an aisle seat so he wouldn't have to climb over people if he had to pee. He put his book in the pocket on the back of the seat in front of him, put on his seat belt, and settled in the best he could.

A half-hour later, the plane took off. As it moved down the runway, Rupert tried looking out the window but could see little. He was still nervous, not because he had a fear of flying but from the fear of what lay ahead. Rupert had no idea what was coming, and even though he had hopes, he knew it was all out of his control. Some might have called what he was doing an adventure, but for him it felt like a big gamble and his life was on the line.

He decided to try watching TV. It looked easy enough to operate, but he saw no on/off switch. Rupert tried pushing every button he saw but to no avail. Help came from the woman sitting in the window seat. The middle seat was empty.

"You'll find what you're looking for in the armrest."

"Thanks." He tried to open both sides, pulling and pushing on each one in turn, but they just would not open for him. Confused and getting frustrated, he looked back at her.

"Lift the top of the one on your left, but from the side not the top."

He did, and to his amazement, it opened. "Wow, technology for better living. Thanks, again. Guess, the world changed when I wasn't looking."

She smiled. "You're welcome. I had trouble finding it when I first looked too. Are you staying in San Francisco, or do you have another destination?"

"Staying."

"Me too. I have to attend a conference downtown."

"What conference is that?" His TV was now on, but he ignored it. Rupert was instead starting to enjoy this talk with a stranger.

"Oh, a conference of social workers." Instead of saying more about the conference, she said, "If you want to hear the TV, you will have to purchase headphones, unless, of course you have some of your own."

"Just one more thing I didn't know. I haven't flown in a long time, as you can probably guess."

"Yeah, but we all have to start at the beginning when we're ready. Next time the flight attendant goes by, you can ask. They'll be more than happy to take your money."

"Thanks. You're very helpful. Must be a social worker, eh?"

"Yeah, I guess I can't hide it. But, then again, I don't want to either."

"I'm not a social worker. In fact, I'm in between a former life and a new one I have yet to discover." Rupert could see she wanted to ask him about this so he added, "It's so new I don't think I'm ready to talk about it."

"Okay." She turned away and left him alone, which she assumed he wanted.

Rupert didn't but understood her move away. *What now?* he wondered. He'd lost interest in watching television, and besides he didn't really want to put out any more money, especially to buy something he might use only once. So he put his head back, hoping to sleep. But after about five minutes, Rupert knew sleep was not an option. His mind would not let him. A deluge of thoughts about his life and what he had ahead of him took control until the plane began to bounce around. *Now more to worry about. Is there no end to all this? My life has been a continuous flow of personal tumult and fear. And it goes on.* Finally, the shaking stopped, but his thoughts did not.

He picked up his book and got as comfortable as he could with Mary Oliver. She spoke to what he now realized as his predicament in life. Rupert read, "In the beginning I was so young and such a stranger to myself I hardly existed. I had to go out into the world and see it and hear it and react to it, before I knew at all who I was, what I wanted to be." That made him wonder how it could have taken him so long to go out into the world in all its fullness. He'd spent so many years exploring how to limit himself, his impulses, his desires, his inclinations, his spontaneity and, yes, his lust.

Losing himself in his thoughts, his book fell on the floor. Rupert reached down to pick it up but couldn't maneuver his body to retrieve it. He undid his seatbelt, but before he got far, the woman in the window seat reached down, picked it up, and handed it to him.

"It fell way over here by me. Thank goodness it didn't go too far under the seat in front of me. I've dropped things on planes before that roll two or three rows up ahead before stopping. Bizarre but true."

"Thanks so much." This time Rupert felt an appreciation bordering on being in love. He stared at the woman trying to make it look like he only was looking out the window. She wore slacks and a nice blouse covered by what looked like a warm and well-made sweater. He thought, *She knows how to dress for traveling.* She looked to be of average height and was maybe in her mid-sixties. She was reading a book, but he couldn't see the title. If she noticed him staring, she was not letting on.

After a short time, though, Rupert felt guilty and turned back to his reading, or at least to look like he was reading while he was actually still thinking and fantasizing about her. *She must be married. At her age, she's probably been married a long time, or maybe . . .,* he stopped a moment and then went on, *maybe she's divorced. I've heard social workers can be pretty liberal with their morals. Probably attracted some man on a plane like she's done me, and they had an affair.* He knew he was blushing, so he pulled his book up to hide more of his face and to maybe really get back to the reading, where his mind should be anyway. *At my age, I'm still easily distracted from where my mind should be. But should it?* Rupert thought about this but couldn't come up with an answer. He started to think about how easy his life was before he questioned things. But was it really easier? *I always resented the easy directions I was given, but I also never spent any time trying to figure out what I wanted instead.*

His thoughts were interrupted by a flight attendant asking him what beverage he would like. Stunned by her interruption, he couldn't even respond for a moment. "Oh, sorry, lost in thought. What do you have?"

She went through the list, and he ordered an orange juice.

His seatmate ordered beer.

As Rupert held the beer, he leaned forward for a better look at the woman he'd found so alluring. He now could see the white teeth behind her smile and the emerald green eyes set into a most inviting alabaster-colored skin, a face that seemed to penetrate straight into his heart.

"Are you going to pass me that beer? It looks so good I'd like to drink it."

"Oh, sorry. I got distracted." He handed the beer to her. "Thanks for finding my book before. It's really a good book, but I'm having trouble getting into it here on the plane."

"I do that too, bring a good book but then either fall asleep or get talking, and the book waits till later. The nice thing is books don't complain. They stay neutral, leaving us free to open or not. Nice, eh? People judge, books don't."

Rupert looked at her wondering if she'd listened in on some of his thoughts. He leaned back in his seat, feeling surprisingly relaxed. *Where's my embarrassment?* he thought? This brought a smile to his face.

He spent the rest of the flight staring into space. As they got closer to San Francisco and to his rendezvous with Maggie, his mind went blank. Rupert mulled over the buildup to this, everything that had happened after the lawyer showed up at his door carrying the surprise document. He was flying alone into something, but he didn't know what.

The 737 began its descent, and in half an hour they touched down.

Rupert had arrived. His life was about to change again.

CHAPTER 47

Rupert called Maggie as soon as he landed, but no one answered, and he didn't want to leave a message.

He'd never been to San Francisco International before. It was so big. So many souls in one place. He hadn't worn his cleric's collar, and wasn't sure if he would ever put it on again, so he got treated like every other person around him. No one said, "Hello, Father" or "Welcome to San Fran, Father." No one spoke to him at all as people jostled along in their apparent eagerness to retrieve their bags. He kind of smiled to himself. Rupert had never really liked how he had stood out in his clerical garb. *At least now I don't feel like a fake*, he thought, *and I'm finally getting pushed around like everybody else!*

After retrieving his bag from one of the many carousals, Rupert began to look for his exit and then the sign to rental cars, but didn't see it from where he stood. He turned left and started walking. Soon he saw it and walked out into the midday California sun, beautiful and bright but not what he would call hot. *Glad I brought a jacket.* Maybe the surprise of seeing the bright sun did it, or maybe something else triggered it, but as Rupert exited, he suddenly felt faint. His vision blurred, and he felt himself getting weaker and weaker until he fell down, face first, on the sidewalk. He must have lost consciousness for a moment because when he came to, he saw all these faces looking down at him. His first thought was, *Wow, finally attention for something genuine,* and he burst out laughing.

"Are you okay, sir?"

Stupid question, he thought. *If I were okay, would I be lying here on the ground in front of all these people?* "Well, I feel a little woozy and could use a hand over to that bench."

Almost immediately, large strong hands lifted him up and guided him to a nearby bench. "Should I call for help, sir?"

"No, just let me sit here a while. I'll be okay." Rupert wondered what had happened. He felt better but questioned whether he should drive. Had he had a heart attack? He was in his late sixties now and had never taken care of himself. Exercise had never been a priority, and he'd eaten pretty much whatever had been put on the table. Now, however, as he sat on the doorstep of his only living sister, he really hoped he was not having a heart attack or stroke. After sitting a while, stress building, worried about what might be happening to him, words came unbidden, strong, and clear: "Please let me have some time with my little sister." Then he thought, *Wow, did I just pray?*

Rupert took out his phone and dialed Maggie's number again.

"Hi, Rupert. I assume you have arrived in San Francisco by now."

Her voice sounded frail, not strong and commanding. But then she had cancer, probably more advanced since he last spoke to her. "Yes, Maggie, I've come to see you. I'm outside the airport now and was on my way to rent a car when I had a slight dizzy spell. I'm not sure if I should drive."

"Don't worry, I'll ask Theresa if she'll come by and pick you up. You remember her, I assume."

"Sure, I do."

"If she's not available I'll call a Lyft for you. Where are you?"

He told her his approximate location.

"Hang tight. I'll call you right back."

It turned out to be ten minutes before his phone rang, and it was Theresa. "Hi, Rupert. I've been out shopping with my family and am not far from you. I should be able to get there in about ten minutes. You will have to squeeze between my two kids, but they won't bite. I think you'll find them quite pleasant."

Rupert heard murmuring in the background and then said, "Okay, I'll watch for you."

"We're in a blue Acura SUV. See you soon."

He spotted an open bench closer to the street and walked toward it. Rupert continued to feel better but still thought it a good idea to sit. After all, he had no idea what had caused him to faint. *What if it happens again? I may not recover so quickly next time.* He didn't have to sit long.

Within five minutes the blue Acura pulled up, and Theresa jumped out to greet him. "Hi, Rupert."

Her husband got out of the car when she did and stood next to the driver's side door.

"Guy, let me introduce you to Rupert, Maggie's brother."

"Hello, good to meet you."

"Hello, it's very good of you and Theresa to come out of your way to pick me up. Thanks."

"No problem."

"And in the car, my two kids, Charlotte and Alex."

They had the window open and said, "Hi."

Guy opened the back door and told the kids to make room. They did, seating Rupert between them.

"Never sat in an SUV before. These things are as big as they say in the TV ads."

Theresa said, "I called Maggie and told her we should arrive in about an hour."

"Okay, I think. Frankly I'm a little, no, a lot, nervous. What can you tell me about her? You're her lawyer, right?"

"Yes, I am still, even though she's on furlough from the company."

"What can you tell me about her job? You know, I heard she was a CEO and I'm not sure I even know what is meant by the letters CEO. I've heard of Continuing Education Online and Catholic Education Officer, even Code Enforcement Officer in regard to someone who came to check out our seminary and church buildings."

"Maggie was the chief executive officer, the head person, for an international shipping company based in San Francisco and in Hong Kong. She ran the day-to-day operations of the American arm of the company, but she really oversaw the whole operation from Asia to New York. Even the board of directors, who, on paper, had responsibility for overseeing her work, really did whatever she wanted them to do. Maggie did a phenomenal job. She continues to hold her position in the company, but another person serves as acting CEO in her absence. I don't think she'll go back, even if she returns to good health." Theresa paused and then went on. "I have to say that, although effective, Maggie was not popular. She could be, and often was, politically incorrect. Many in the company disliked her, but everyone respected her."

Guy spoke up, "Though I heard about Maggie a lot from Theresa and her co-workers, she never welcomed me into her home. She wasn't a very welcoming person."

"Geez, I can hardly wait to meet her."

"But Rupert, Maggie has changed with this illness, mellowed. I now call her my friend, and she says the same of me." To Guy she said, "I think you'd find her much more likable, engaging, and good-natured, Guy."

"That helps, Theresa, but she still sounds intimidating," Rupert said. "I think we have some things in common, though. She must have lived a life as aloof, emotionless, and solitary as the one I've lived. Not surprising, I guess, since we did come from the same seed and probably adopted similar behaviors to hide our true feelings. Though I never thought much about this, I now think we both may have wanted to only feel safe. I know I did, even though now I believe the detached, dispassionate life didn't work for me. I wonder what Maggie might say about this for her."

Theresa jumped in and said, "Maybe another ten to twelve minutes."

Rupert remembered how accurate Theresa had been on her arrival time at the airport. His anxiety began to spike. The back seat suddenly felt crowded, and he wanted to jump out and run. He began to sweat and felt embarrassed. "Can you slow down a little, Theresa?"

Theresa and Guy looked at each other.

"If we slow down too much right here, we'll have cars honking and lots of angry drivers. We can slow down when we get off on the side streets that are coming up."

"What if I don't meet her expectations? History repeating itself, me letting her down again."

Then Alex, who had not spoken since Rupert got in the car, said, "Courage, Mr. Callaway. We've been discussing courage in my high school class, and I'm writing my thesis on this topic." He opened the book on his lap. "Do you know who Nelson Mandela was?"

"Sure, the anti-apartheid revolutionary and political leader of South Africa."

"Okay. Well, he said, 'I learned that courage was not the absence of fear, but the triumph over it. The brave man is not he who does not feel afraid, but he who conquers that fear.' Or there is Winston Churchill, who said, 'Success is not final, failure is not fatal: it is the courage to continue that counts.'"

Rupert eyed Alex and everyone else in the car. The quotes certainly meant something to him, but he felt more moved by the courage this quiet boy demonstrated in speaking out to someone probably six decades older whom he didn't know at all and sharing something so meaningful to him.

The car was quiet after that until Theresa looked out and said, "We've arrived, Rupert."

"Really. Where's her house?"

"It's not a house, Rupert. She lives in that large building directly to your left."

"Oh, that's big.

"Yeah, her apartment takes up most of one floor. You'll see."

Alex exited the car to let Rupert out.

"Thanks, Alex, and good luck on that paper. I think you'll get an A."

Theresa asked, "Do you want me to come up with you, Rupert?"

"No, just point me to the right door."

Theresa did, and the car pulled away with everyone waving.

Rupert walked to the door, reached for the bell but, and then heard a buzzer unlocking it. "But I haven't even rung the bell yet. She must be able to see me. Or maybe there's a doorman who was told I'd be arriving and now was opening the door."

The door buzzed again.

He moved closer. Now he stood where he could reach the door but didn't open it.

Maggie spoke over the speaker phone. "Welcome, Rupert. I'm in the living room at the end of the hall."

He stood at the door, unable to move. *Courage, where are you?* Now beginning to feel embarrassed, he thought, *Act, Rupert. You can do it.* Then he thought, *No, you can't, you coward. This is real life. You're facing the real trials of man, what you tried to avoid for the glories of God.* Though he never thought of it before this day, at this moment, he realized fully that he had to have courage to face this journey toward possible family reconciliation. But he still just stood at the door, unable to move, feeling paralyzed.

Then from the voice box in front of him came, "Open the door, Rupert."

CHAPTER 48

RUPERT ENTERED MAGGIE'S APARTMENT feeling as if he were entering a dragon's lair—alone, uncertain, apprehensive, and like he was about to sully himself. His feet felt like someone had attached one-hundred-pound rocks to them. Sweat beaded on his face and trickled down from his armpits. Time stood still.

Maggie, or someone he assumed was Maggie, was sitting in a large chair directly in front of him. She seemed small, almost hidden in the chair, encircled by tubes and wires. She said nothing, but had a big smile on her face.

Rupert thought if his heart beat any harder, it might just explode from his chest. Pressure built up around his eyes, and then tears flowed like a river that had been dammed up for a long, long time. Scenes from his childhood passed like lightning through his mind, too fast for him to catch. He saw only a blur, like a train speeding by a stationary camera. Rupert moved into the room but said nothing.

The smile had left Maggie's face, replaced by firmness, a steady resolve, that betrayed nothing of what lay behind it.

Neither spoke as Rupert continued to enter. Silence filled the room. They both seemed to stop breathing. Both were facing a raw moment without precedent.

Then Maggie exploded. The yell coming from this small woman filled the universe with sounds of agony, pain, and sadness.

It was too much for Rupert. He too let loose with his own ancient, primal cry that would have scared anyone hearing it, except Maggie who had also sunk into some ancient place within herself.

Both had fallen into some part of their psyches, not often reached in anyone's lifetime, and the sounds they made could have curdled the skin on any innocent listener. They, however, were deep in themselves, lost in their own moment of uncovering parts of themselves that had been lost or concealed long ago. Something was happening beyond their understanding that neither one tried to stop. It all continued until they both seemed exhausted. But neither felt tired. Instead, they felt exhilarated, full, complete.

Maggie knew this meeting might be terrifying. Even the feelings leading up to it approached the unbearable, but now she thought she felt the walls she had built, the charade of power and knowing, tumble down around her, the pieces scattered like the splashes of a Jackson Pollock painting.

Rupert, sobbing uncontrollably, fell into the nearest chair with his head down like he was trying to hide his nakedness. It didn't work. He needed to look at the sister he'd left so long ago.

Maggie sank more deeply into her chair. She moaned and cried, sounding like she might be in some pain. She was, but it wasn't physical. All thought abandoned her, replaced by some primitive urge to just stare in wonderment.

Each of the siblings glared at the stranger in front of them. Neither spoke. Rational speech had left them. Time passed. Both felt fulfilled yet tentative. Politeness and formality had been overtaken by fear. How much time actually passed neither knew until another natural function took over.

Rupert asked, "Where's the bathroom?"

Maggie smiled at the elemental nature of his question. Surprising herself, she said, "I don't have one."

"Well, then you're about to have pee all over your chair."

"What fun. Mom and Dad would be so mad."

"Yeah, no dessert tonight."

They both laughed until, as if they had become conscious again of where they were, the laughter abruptly stopped.

"Come on, I'll show you where you can find a bathroom." But then Maggie remembered she was again tethered to multiple IV tubes. "Oops. I guess I'll need to just tell you where to go."

"I'll try to follow your directions, but given my current mental state, you may have to remind me."

She told him where to go and then laid her head back to rest. On top of everything else, she must have aggravated something that made her chest pain worse.

After what seemed like a long time, Rupert returned. "What a bathroom, Maggie. I could almost live in there. I didn't know people needed that much room to pee!"

Maggie thought he might be trying to be funny, but she got defensive anyway. "Well, Rupert, you may not know it, but you're supposed to pee in the toilet and then use the rest of the space and furniture for sitting, talking on the phone, and primping. I also have to store all the creams, soaps, and assorted paraphernalia needed to keep me looking beautiful! You may not remember, but we Callaways were not blessed with natural attractiveness. Just look in the mirror. Oh, I'm sorry, that was not nice."

The room filled again with awkwardness and rawness, neither knowing what to do next until a simple question broke through their uncomfortableness.

"Do you like music, Rupert?"

"Yes and no. I used to like certain sacred pieces of music, but truth be told, I generally hated most religious stuff. Gregorian chants always lightened the weight that bound me into moody knots, and certain Christmas songs like 'Silent Night' and 'Hark! The Herald Angels Sing' made me feel a peacefulness inside, but 'Joy to the World' made me want to puke."

Maggie laughed, which encouraged Rupert to continue.

"But when by myself, I listened to jazz, mostly on my own CDs because I didn't find a lot on the radio. I still listen to those old CDs. That's the music that comes the closest to making me feel alive."

"I'm shocked, Rupert. You left to find the land of milk and honey, not one of disquiet and depression. Sounds like your music did more for you than your church."

"I've never been happy, Maggie."

"If you felt like that for all those years, why didn't you ever reconnect with me? I must not have been the cause. My God, you're saying your unhappiness has been with you for all the years after you left our home." She waited and then added, "Honestly?"

"Yes, honestly. You may not like hearing this, but here goes. You had died to me, Maggie. I had wiped my past clean. Mom and Dad couldn't help me, and at that time I was sure they didn't even really want me. You became collateral damage. I just couldn't see or accept you as anyone with whom I could share my life; too young, too needy." As he talked, Rupert felt ashamed but also proud of himself. He was speaking, out loud, about things he'd hardly admitted even to himself. And he had no desire to stop, but Maggie got this painful look on her face as she began to cry.

"I think I need a break, Rupert. Would you help me to the bedroom? I need to lie down.

"Sure, I can do that. Should I wait here?"

"Yes." Then she smiled and added, "Don't move!"

He had no idea the protocol to follow so just stood there, paralyzed, until Maggie nodded in his direction and reached a hand toward him. He took it, and together they walked into the bedroom.

"Don't leave, Rupert."

"I won't, Maggie."

She looked at him with questioning eyes and a slight smirk on her face.

"But of course, why would I ever assume that you'd trust me? How about I sit right here in the room while you rest? That way you'll know I haven't left."

"You're right, I don't—can't—really trust you, Rupert. Our history is one of absence, abandonment, and what I'd call desertion. You are, though, now in my private space, and I really need it for myself if I'm to get a rest, so please wait for me somewhere else in the place. It's big. Wander around. Even if I don't trust you, Rupert, I can't keep guard over you."

"Till later, then." He quietly eased his way out of her room, gently pulling the door shut behind him.-

Truly some part of him did want to run. Rupert had had that impulse since this whole family resurrection journey had begun. He had been running away, escaping, his whole life. But, to what? Had he really been running away or toward something he had to find—family?

Once he got back to the living room, Rupert did not sit down. He decided he'd explore Maggie's place. *What a place, apartment, or house or whatever you use to describe a place like this! One person lives here. And I thought the bathroom was ostentatious.*

The group of suites that made up Maggie's home lacked for nothing. She had at least two televisions, comfortable furniture, books (mostly the classics) and views of downtown San Francisco that most people only dream about. Everything was clean and orderly too.

I wonder if she had a designer, Rupert mused. *I couldn't have done anything like this, even if I'd had the money and the interest.* "Sis, I guess you made it."

She had paintings on all the walls; several looked like they could be originals by Andy Warhol. Other large pieces hung around the apartment by painters Rupert didn't recognize. One he liked depicted a pastoral country scene that reminded him a little of their home in Canada.

Rupert looked in the study, where he saw three computers, two large desks, and several chairs. She also had several small expensive-looking paintings of nudes, one fully undressed and the other undressed but draped in a see-through scarf. Those really drew his attention, so he got closer to see titles: "Venus Rising" by Jean-Léon Gérôme and "The Dancer" by Gustav Klimt. *That one's more tasteful*, he thought of the latter, *but not the one I find the most stimulating.* He couldn't tell if these were originals or copies but still walked back for a closer look at the nude piece.

He checked out all the rooms, stopping only to admire the great view. "Nice place, Maggie. No priest ever gets to live like this," he sighed, "except maybe the pope. But how would I know how he lives? Never got invited!"

"Rupert? I'm ready for you to come back."

"Sure. Be right there. Just looking around your place." Even though she'd called for him, he still knocked lightly on her door before entering.

"Welcome back, Maggie. Some place you have here. Wow! That's really all I can say."

Maggie had no interest in talking about the beauty of her place. "Help me up, will you? I'm ready to get out of this bed. I'll have plenty of time to lie around soon enough."

Rupert missed entirely what Maggie was alluding to, responding only to her request for help. "Here, grab my arm." He put his other arm around her back and gently lifted her up till she stood next to the bed. "Easy now."

"Thanks, I can walk by myself, I think." Maggie shuffled off toward the living room where they had been before.

He followed close behind and was surprised to see Maggie begin to do a little dance.

She moved right and then left while singing, "We go to the right, to the right, to the right; then we go to the left, to the left, to the left. Now kick, now kick, now kick. Now walk it by yourself." Maggie shuffled off on her own and then said, "I heard some song like that on the radio recently, and it stuck with me."

"Can't say that one sticks with me, Maggie."

"Oh, me either, silly. I'm just being a little foolish. Or just a little freaked out by all this."

For a short time, neither of them spoke. Rupert was still trying to calm down, and Maggie was trying to get used to him being there at all. Soon the silence became awkward.

"Well, Rupert, I have to say I didn't expect the power of feeling that showed up when you entered nor the high that came after."

"Me either, Maggie. How do you follow that up?"

"Don't try, Rupert. You've heard I'm sick and probably dying. That was stressful enough. In fact, the nurse will probably return around five or five thirty to check on me. It's probably best if I look my finest for her."

Rupert looked at his watch. "Okay, I'll try. As many would say, I've always been good at keeping the lid on things. Not this time though, eh? Believe me, I had no idea what would happen when I got here. I just know I felt the time had finally come for me to rectify what I'd done. I tried thinking ahead about what I'd do or say and even had some good ideas. None of that happened. I guess seeing you after all those years was just plain heartrending, almost beyond what this human could bear. Pretty primitive stuff came out of me . . . and you.

"The letter you sent surprised the hell out of me. No, it shocked, startled, astonished, oh what's the right word? Nothing seems strong enough to express my amazement. Honestly, I'd forgotten about you. No, no, I never forgot you entirely, but more accurately, I hadn't thought about you in, I bet, fifty years. We never spoke at our parents' funerals, so seeing you there never really registered as a meeting or homecoming for me.

"You know, I left home to join the church community, but I did more. I left my family. I tried to end what I had. I was terribly unhappy, felt unloved and unwanted by our parents and kids at school and in the neighborhood, and fell for the romantic tales spun by the local priests about life in the Church. Signing up for the priesthood gave me hope for a future and, of course, salvation. What I really found in that life left me disillusioned and disappointed, though truthfully, I lacked the courage to face this. I had left everything behind. I just didn't have the will or fortitude to leave something else, this time a choice I had made and not a family I'd been born into. The Church fed me, clothed me, and generally took care of me; at least I had that. Then I also had the title of priest and now it's retired priest. I still take their money and live in their house, even though I feel spiritually shattered and emotionally bereft. Pretty duplicitous life, eh?

"Your letter, for some reason, broke my self-destructive journey. Fear has replaced my depression, and some moxie has spontaneously emerged in my life. Suddenly I'm willing to risk rules I faithfully followed my whole life. I feel not brave but driven. Before, I accepted the form of life given to me by authority. Now I struggle with the form those authorities imposed on me. No one forced me into it. I willingly accepted what I was given. The formlessness I felt at home with our parents frightened me too much. At that age, in that place, I connected the formless with death." Rupert got up out of his chair and started to pace. "But you know what? I felt like I did die, spiritually and emotionally, in the Church. I had the form I sought but not the substance. Now, without knowing why or what I want, I've made friends in Powell River, had an affair, and ended up here with you. Something has definitely changed, but part of me still wants to run home to my little refuge by the sea, lock the door, and just hide again."

Maggie had not said a word while Rupert shared his story. When he stopped talking, she still said nothing. He looked deep in thought, unaware even of her presence. She turned to listen to herself. Unfamiliar feelings welled up. The sickness that had overtaken her life for so long, that had seemed the only thing happening, now felt like just one thing among many informing her life. She thought she was experiencing what might be love but wasn't sure she could define the word if anyone asked. Maggie had never thought of herself as having experienced what others called love, nor had she given or expressed it. She had only ever demanded, commanded, insisted, or required obedience from others. But now she felt something different, maybe love? Who knew? But that feeling was growing.

It couldn't have a connection to Rupert, could it? she thought. *I don't even really know him or that much about him. He sits over there looking unhinged, and I sit here more assured but perplexed.* Maggie checked the time. She hoped this moment would not get interrupted by a visit from Lively, but it was now time for her scheduled arrival.

And then, without warning, things changed for Maggie. She felt herself stiffen and her mind readjust to the well-tuned sick program much like a computer changing programs. All this was happening to her without any conscious command. She felt sick and helpless again. Although she knew she was ill, very ill in fact, this command to return to sick mode angered her. "No, goddammit." But her anger outburst had no effect (not even on Rupert who didn't seem to even hear her). Maggie wasn't used to not having control over people and events. She was always in charge. Her successes in life depended on it. Loss of control equaled failure, a word akin to death. At this point Maggie experienced intense fear overwhelming everything else, including the anger. Helplessly, she felt her heartbeat speed up. Sweat poured from her pores. She must have spoken because within a minute Rupert was sitting beside her. If he spoke, she didn't hear what he said, but his vibe was strong. She was so scared, and the pain hurt so much.

No one had noticed, but Lively had rung the bell and knocked, but no one had answered the door. After a time, she finally let herself in and saw Maggie sitting on the couch with a man she didn't recognize sitting next to her. He had his arm holding her head from behind. Lively wasn't sure they even knew she had entered the room. Their eyes were closed, but she could see neither of them was asleep or, she thought, dead. Maggie had the color of white satin and he a fire-engine red, colors sometimes signaling distress, but Lively, an experienced nurse, decided against intervening. She sat in a chair nearby and waited.

Rupert was thinking, imagining things, not fantasies exactly but thoughts he'd never strung together logically before. *What are we doing in this life except discovering? We search the skies; we dig and probe into anything at any time. The young child finds a stick to poke in the hole to see what's inside. The schoolboy explores the stream running through town to see if he can rouse any kind of life. The scientist, engineer, housewife, father, gardener, builder, CEO, worker, everyone asks why? How we discover the answers determines how we live and opens us to the experiences of love and hate, success and failure. . . . Boy, I could really write a good sermon from some of that!'* Rather than think of good sermons before, Rupert had generally succumbed to platitudes and niceties, aiming to please the congregation. Now he was not writing a sermon, but the rudiments of a good one flowed through him.

Maggie too was now in the throes of a mental exploration. Hers was really the result of two things: her brother's coming and the pain currently causing her so much distress. The clarity of thought she'd always known was apparently gone.

Sermon ideas left Rupert as fast as they'd come. The old anxieties returned, and he found himself in the throes of fears he'd hidden from since childhood and the emptiness he'd carried locked deep in the attic of his mind since childhood. *How much of this can I take? Truthfully, I'd rather go back to having sermon ideas than going through this emotional trauma.* But that wasn't to be (at least not right now).

Maggie finally uttered one word. "Help." At first it emerged so softly that no one heard it. She kept repeating it, however, and slowly it got stronger.

Finally, Rupert heard it. He opened his eyes, and looked at her. "I'm here, Maggie."

She opened her eyes. "Who?"

"Rupert, your brother."

"Rupert."

"Such profundity we're showing, Maggie. Where can we go from here?"

This made her smile. "Never thought you were smart enough to be profound, brother."

"I wasn't, sis, and still am not, but I think you confuse simplicity for the profound."

"Wow, big brother, after so many years, you finally have some guidance for your little sister. I feel . . . accepted. No that's not it, maybe received? Yes, that's more like it. But working on feeling wanted."

At this point, Lively made her presence known. "Well, folks, I'm here too."

This somewhat alarmed them, especially Rupert, since he didn't know Lively or how she could have gotten in the house.

Maggie, took over, just as she used to do in awkward moments. "Lively, I'd like you to meet Rupert, my long-lost brother."

"Hi, Rupert. Glad to meet you."

"Rupert, this is Lively, my nurse tasked with making my final days, hours, or whatever as easy as possible."

Rupert nodded hello. "I'll just move over here while you two do business. Carry on." He moved to a chair across from them, watching while Lively examined Maggie. He shut his eyes and let his mind drift back in time to where he saw Maggie as a young girl, sitting alone, cross-legged, and fully absorbed in some book. He saw her at the kitchen table, sitting alone, eating what looked like breakfast before school. No one else was there. Next, he saw her sitting on her bed, again cross-legged, reading a book while listening to one of her Buddy Holly or Johnny Mathis records. He couldn't see what she was reading, and he had never stopped to ask her about titles or content in all the times he'd seen her with her head in a book. Why? He knew it was not really sibling tension but more to do with his lack of curiosity about people and about life around him. He opened his eyes and heard Maggie forcefully commanding Lively.

Until recently, Maggie had accepted that she was in the final stage of her life. But now things had changed. Before, she believed she had nothing to live for, that she'd accomplished everything she ever wanted, that she'd become as wealthy as she would ever want to be, and that no one would really miss her once she was gone. Now she felt encouraged about a possible future. She imagined the family portrait, rent by the circumstances of her past, reconnected and renewed in the present. So, when Lively tried to advise her about taking care of personal affairs, Maggie told her to leave. "I know how to act responsibly, Lively. I've done it my whole life. Right now, I want to live free of all that, the tumors and your treatments be damned."

Rupert had to smile at the resignation on the nurse's face as she turned to leave. He had lived a passive life, but here he was watching his sister showing determination and toughness. He'd always seen the Callaways as quiet survivors, certainly not gutsy and daring. He now thought he'd been wrong. And it made him feel happy and hopeful for his future. "Hot damn, sis. I'm beginning to see what I've missed, a strong, determined, and confident woman. I certainly never saw any of that in our parents, and though I feel a little embarrassed to say it, I've never experienced it in myself."

After Lively left, Maggie felt better. She knew many people would have agreed with Rupert's assessment and seen her as strong and confident but also generally unlikable. But Maggie had used her strengths as shields to hide underlying feelings of insecurity, doubt, and uncertainty. She had hidden these well, and now that's what she wanted to talk about with Rupert. "When I wrote my letter, Rupert, I had two goals. Both were personal and selfish. First, I'll be frank, I wanted to shame you, embarrass you, and inspire your Catholic guilt. I wanted you to suffer through your last years. I feel I had suffered my whole life. I didn't want you to get away with living happily in blissful amnesia, forgetful and brainless in the hermitage of the Catholic brotherhood.

"My second goal was more mystical and arcane. You left to join the priesthood for what *I* believed to have been a very selfish reasons, to find your God. I'm not sure that searching for one's God is selfish, but that's what I felt. And now, my selfish goal was to discover if you'd found him and to take whatever benefit there might be for me in your discovery. Basically, I didn't want to go out, leaving anything on the table I should have discovered from you. So I wanted to hurt you and maybe, in some mysterious, magical way, save myself."

"Sorry, I have no magic to impart, Maggie. I bring only the story of what has happened to me and what I've learned since you sent me your challenging letter. The Church did teach me theology but failed to provide a context for me to experience its truth. I cannot assure you in death so am pleased to hear that somehow you have overcome the mystery and are not facing it now with fear. I'm still afraid but frankly less so now that I've been shocked out of my complacency and rigid lifestyle by you."

Rupert had brought Maggie's letter with him and at this point went to his suitcase and pulled it out. He reread the whole thing before speaking "You asked me to make a decision, to choose you or not, the same decision I faced as a boy. Back then, I chose the Church, not you, not Mom or Dad. But when you asked now for a decision, I came to realize that my childhood decision was erroneous, a mistake, just wrong. I cut you out of my life. No fuss, no struggle, no agony, all things I realize now would be necessary for a genuine decision-making process. Remember, I was a child, immature and unhappy. This time your request that I choose stimulated a difficult and distressing personal wrestling match between myself and the Church. I had to accept that I had failed to find anything in my church life that filled my soul and that, after all the years of trying, I now lived only an empty life in an empty, cold house that I couldn't even call mine.

"You gave me a chance to choose again, and this time to make my choice without fantasy and delusion, make it in real life. You offered a choice to see you, dialogue with you, enter an unknown and insecure future. A lot of personal struggle has gone on since that request for a choice, and so far, I have discovered more joy, hope, and promise than I've ever known. I've experienced highs and lows and been opened up to new intellectual and personal stimulation.

"You know . . . no, you couldn't know. How could you? I never let myself read books. Now I know the poetry of Mary Oliver, I have opened the door to mindfulness, I have read Thomas Moore, and I've even heard of Anne Tyler and Margaret Atwood but have not yet read them. When I joined the Catholic Church, I expected it to conquer my suffering and provide me with answers to all questions and quandaries. It sounded so easy. No wonder I went for it. Any reasonable person could fall for that line, and many do, as seen in today's advertising—'finances made easy,' 'baking made easy,' 'Russian made easy.'

"Once I joined the brotherhood, I was stuck. I'd committed myself and then convinced myself that the promised easy life didn't happen only because of my own inadequacy, not because I'd bought into a fantasy. I do believe those two priests back in Hazelton wanted to help me and offered something they thought would really guide and support me. I want to think they really believed what they told me because it had been real for them. It wasn't true for me, however, and I knew it within the first five or six years of my priesthood. I kept trying to make it work and failed.

"Believe it or not, you played a key role in my finally breaching the divide between what these other priests believed and what I knew was the truth. Maybe I was ripe, ready for your push. I was ready to jump into something unknown to me. That's all I can say. Then you came out of nowhere, a voice from half a century ago. All you said was you wanted to connect. Jesus, how simple, and yet it served to kick-start me, push me out of my self-styled nest. And now, like any bird flung from his nest, I'm falling headlong into unknown territory, but already I've found out I'm not alone. First there was you. Then others appeared with something for me. Weird, eh?

"Maybe I'm about to get crunched. I don't know. All I know is that I'm anxious as hell and suddenly also feeling self-conscious and on alert, like something's going to happen."

Suddenly Maggie burst out laughing.

"Are you all right, Maggie?"

"Yeah, never better! I was just thinking about how I've surrounded myself with monkeys, not people, Rupert. Monkeys perform; people are capricious, erratic, changeable, and yes, unstable." She laughed. "Don't be my monkey, Rupert. I'm starting to like you, as you are, brother."

"Okay, sis. I'll do as you have commanded!"

Now, they both laughed.

"Maggie, I want you to know there is one thing I'm sure of. I don't want you to die for many reasons, not the least of which is that I couldn't do the last rites for you."

They laughed some more.

"Well, I prefer not to die too, Rupert, and in fact, I don't plan to die anymore, at least not for a long time."

CHAPTER 49

Now what? Neither Maggie nor Rupert knew what to do next. Both felt more comfortable together but knew they had just begun their reunion, reconciliation, recovery, restoration, recovery, or whatever—neither knew what to call what was happening between them. They had just wanted to meet. Everything was unknown. Now they both faced something they hadn't even thought about but confronted: feelings of tenderness, of closeness. What do you say? What do you do?

Silence ruled the air. Heads were bowed, embarrassed, speechless until Maggie launched: "I don't want to die, Rupert, especially now when I'm beginning to feel different—happy, I think."

Rupert didn't want Maggie to die either but assumed she was really sick and probably near death. He still hesitated to say anything, unsure, not wanting to say the wrong thing. This time the danger did not stop him. He leapt in, took the risk. "I think it might be best if we try to enjoy this time together for as long as we have it."

"Enjoy? Maybe, though that sounds like something a priest might say—try to make things pleasant and agreeable—but that's not my goal. I hope to milk everything I can from your being here, Rupert. Who knows where I'm going, but this time, you can't go with me. This is it for us. our last chance to be sister and brother. I may or may not enjoy it, but I will do it."

"Can we really be sister and brother after so long apart? Or can we only be strangers, trying to find something we have in common?"

"Rupert, don't get abstract on me now. Priests may live in the metaphysical world, but I, as Madonna sang, 'live in a material world.' I am earthbound. In my world, I *am* your sister, Rupert, and you *are* my brother. I may be a stranger now, but first I was your sister. We came from the same womb, the same family with the same history. Our paths diverged, for sure, but our paths have crossed again. The only question, I think, is are we going to recognize each other for who we are? That may be all we can achieve, but wouldn't that be marvelous?"

Rupert's mouth had dropped open as he listened.

"Shut your mouth, Rupert. It's quite unflattering."

"Oh, sorry, I think I zoned out while you were talking. Not in a bad way, though. I went someplace familiar and comfortable but felt unreachable. You've touched something I want to think about, Maggie, and I think I'll need to be alone to do that."

"Well, there's something I need to do too. It's now past time for dinner, so maybe you can go out and get something for yourself and come back later."

"Okay, but where?"

"There's not much around here, but I can call a taxi to take you into the city. There's a diner I know there that's not expensive but good."

"Great, but aren't you going to eat?"

"No, I'm not real hungry, but if I want, I can just open a can of soup for myself."

Ten minutes later Rupert was in the taxi headed to the diner.

Even without Rupert there now, Maggie didn't really feel alone. This time her place felt full of life, not the empty shell that had always been simply a refuge for her. She'd been surprised by Rupert's need for time away, though she understood it as a way he could escape, take some time with his thoughts, without running away. *Old habits don't change easily*, she thought, *but at least he's trying*. It took a minute or two for that thought to sink in, but when it did, she added, *We both are trying*.

Maggie had something to do anyway, and this would give her the time she needed. She turned back to the phone to make a call to her personal lawyer, not Theresa.

CHAPTER 50

O N HER WAY OUT, MAGGIE'S PERSONAL LAWYER usually wouldn't have answered her office phone but did when she saw a familiar name on caller ID. "Hello, Maggie. You just caught me. How can I be of help?"

"Well, Sarah, first, thanks for picking up. I realize I haven't been in touch in a long time, thinking I had finished all my work with you, but something's changed for me, and I want to change my will."

"Really? You're a planner and have never, to my recollection, ever acted spontaneously. Have you lost your mind?"

Maggie laughed. "No, not yet, though I can understand how you might think that."

"Well, convince me."

"The moon is blue, the Earth is flat, our president is a rooster, and the rivers all flow either north or south. Convinced?"

"Okay, I was right. You have lost your mind."

"Sarah, I've never been saner. Think of it this way. You've known me only as the company woman, professional and detached. Underneath all that lurks genuine, authentic, me."

"And what you just told me is the real you?"

"Well, not really, but I now have, let's say loosened up, allowed myself to even try to be spontaneously funny."

"Okay, I'm ready to hear what you want. I need to get going too. I promised some friends I'd meet them for dinner at Shaw's, and I'm now already going to be late."

"Shaw's, wow. That's a great place.

'Oh, in my rush, I forgot to ask you how you're doing. So sorry. I can really be an insensitive oaf sometimes."

"Too bad I won't have enough time left to get to know your more insensitive side, Sarah. I'm discovering now just how much of life I've missed."

Sarah didn't know what to say next. This conversation was either devolving or evolving, she didn't know which, to something beyond with which she felt comfortable, especially with a client, even a very special one. Thankfully Maggie changed the subject.

"As I said, I need you to amend my will. I want to add my brother, Rupert Callaway, to my list of beneficiaries. I won't be able to stay around physically much longer, but I want him to have money to take with him wherever he goes. There's nothing else I have, and money is what I've spent my life living for, rightly or wrongly."

"Okay, Maggie. How much?"

They spent a few minutes going over the details, and Maggie was about to hang up.

"Wait a minute, Maggie. After I make these changes, I will need you to sign it again. How about if I come by later tonight, probably around ten. Okay?"

"I'll figure out how to make that work, Sarah. Rupert's staying here, so I'll make an excuse to see you privately."

"Great, see you later."

Maggie knew she'd just closed a chapter of her life but opened up more options for her brother to continue with his. She smiled and felt relieved.

Chapter 51

MAGGIE HAD JUST PICKED UP A BOOK to read when she heard a knock on the front door. She knew it must be Rupert. "Come on in. The door's open."

He came down the hallway toward Maggie, looking comfortable and content.

"Well, don't you look happy. Have a good meal?"

"Sure did. The food was great but expensive. Remember, I live on a retirement income, paid by the Church, an institution of sacrifice and renunciation. But I really enjoyed it this one time."

"I'm glad you did—this one time." She smiled up at him.

"Did you finish what you had to do?"

"I did, though I may need more time later to finish."

"That'll be fine, Maggie. Just let me know when to vamoose. Maybe I can unpack while you're busy."

"Sounds like a plan, Rupert"

With that all in place, Maggie was eager to continue getting to know her brother again. She knew she really had nothing to lose, and she'd never been one to beat around the bush, but still she hesitated. Why now? *Who knows how much time I have left?* she thought. Her time with Rupert felt precious, even if their relationship still felt precarious. But how to begin? Maggie had years of experience kickstarting meetings and manipulating people toward her goals, but now with Rupert, something held her back. Was it concern, personal regard, respect, what? She stopped to think. Her head dropped down, her eyes closed, and her body went limp, not from feeling beaten as it might look but from feeling resigned. Maggie felt she might be finally letting go of that long-held compulsion to order and arrange everything, which ultimately had controlled her.

Rupert couldn't help but notice all the faces Maggie was making as she sat quietly across from him. She'd gone from looking mad to sad to curious to relaxed and . . . now to , , , he wasn't sure what. Did he see happiness, satisfaction, or delight on her face? "Maggie, have you always made faces like that? Pretty revealing for a schemer like you, don't you think?"

Maggie heard him say something but had no idea what. Her thoughts continued bouncing around in her head, maybe just waiting to escape because, without warning, she said out loud, "Amazing," followed immediately by, "unbelievable."

Rupert waited for what would come next, but nothing did for the longest while.

Then Maggie started laughing. It was an easy, delighted laugh. "Talk to me, Rupert, about anything. Tell me what you want me to know. Make my day, will you?"

Rupert had no idea what that last sentence meant, but he saw her smile, so he let it go. "Okay. You know as a priest, I was pretty much a failure, but as a person, I was not very well liked either. I've heard that you also weren't liked much, Maggie, though you were a success at your job. You seem so gentle, warm, and welcoming now. Confusing but much appreciated."

"You too, Rupert. Hard to believe people didn't like you. But then you already told me you've changed. Well, me too. Facing death can do that, but for me I think it had more to do with facing you!"

"Wow, same for me. The idea of facing you traumatized me."

Maggie laughed. "Well, you've already heard that I'm one scary bitch."

"Tell me about that, will you?"

"It's simple, Rupert. Liking me was never important to me. Performing well on the job was. I knew how to make people do well, be successful in ways that surprised even them. I think people appreciated me for my skills. I know my board members did. I ruled with a big stick, not by speaking softly or being particularly nice."

"Were you mean then?"

"Not intentionally. I never really thought I was mean, but maybe I was through my silence and withdrawal. Doing it like that allowed me to lie to myself that I was the good guy and others were the meanies."

"Well, what do you know? We both be bitches."

They started to laugh, but then Maggie stopped. "That's nothing to be proud of, you know."

"Yeah, I know."

"Maybe it's how we live now that will matter."

"I'd drink to that, if I had a drink, that is."

"Me too."

Rupert got up and walked to stand beside Maggie. He raised his hand, and she raised hers. They clapped them together.

"To friendship and good will forever."

"To brother and sister," Maggie added, and they clapped hands again. "That felt amazing, Rupert. Thank you.

He smiled. "Anytime, sis."

Maggie didn't smile back. Instead, her face suddenly turned red and contorted in a grimace of pain.

"Maggie!"

He jumped and moved toward her, wanting to help until Maggie's hand went up to stop him. "Are you okay?"

She didn't answer at first but then asked, "Do I look okay, Rupert?"

Now his face turned red. "No."

"Well, just wait a minute, will you? This will either kill me on the spot or, I hope, go away soon."

Feeling humiliated, Rupert continued standing but moved back a little.

Maggie started talking to herself. "Pain, pain, go away, and don't come back another day!" Her hands now gripped the seat cushion, and she yelled: "You can't have me yet, not yet! Stop!" Her whole body now jerked and twisted violently as if she was trying to fight off an attacker.

Her words were strong and forceful. "No, no, NO!" Maggie tried to stand up but instead fell back on the couch.

Rupert was in a battle of his own. How to stay away while seeing her in such obvious pain? Slowly and hesitantly, he moved closer, ready for anything she might say. But she said nothing. Instead, she placed her hand on the couch in a gesture that welcomed him to sit next to her, so he did. He didn't ask her if she was okay. Rupert said nothing. What could he say? Instinctively he laid his hand on her back. She sat up, leaned over toward him and rested her head on his shoulder. Her body softened, and soon he heard her whimpering. For the next few minutes, the two of them sat without talking. Rupert relaxed, sure he'd done the right thing.

Maggie was drained, her breathing strained. Any energy she had was gone. Finally, she spoke. "Boy, pain can make you do some terrible things. I think I could have jumped off any bridge to end the pain I just had. Thank goodness I was only here with you and not crossing any bridges."

"Yeah." Rupert wanted to tell her he'd gone through his own pain but quickly thought better of it. *I guess I'm learning a little*, he thought.

"I can see why people OD on painkillers if that's what they're going through. That was excruciating. I'll have to tell Lively about that, though I'm not sure what she can do. Controlling episodic pain like what just happened to me might be harder than controlling chronic pain. I guess you'll just have to keep me away from bridges and knives, Rupert."

"That's reassuring."

"Well, I don't want to die, but life under some circumstances is not worth living."

That caused Rupert to pull back a little.

"Now what did I say?"

He felt embarrassed that he'd betrayed himself by moving.

"Oh, nothing."

"Liar."

Rupert turned red. "Okay, what you said about life sometimes not worth living caused me to pause. I've had the message that life is sacred drilled into me since I left you and the family way back when. Why do you think Catholics are so opposed to abortion or assisted suicide?"

Maggie now sat up straight and looked at him. "Oh, I thought it was because those in the church valued babies' lives over the lives of their mothers." She turned away from him, but then thinking better of that move, she quickly turned back. "But that's not fair. You were talking about you and what had been drilled into you, not about the Catholic Church. Do you believe I shouldn't kill myself under any circumstances?"

"I really don't know, Maggie. My impulsive answer is still no, life is sacred. But I have a lot to think about before I'll really know what I think. My ideas, sympathies, opinions, judgments, and reactions disappeared long ago in the voices of those I identified as smarter, stronger, or wiser than me. I'd hoped those voices would become mine, fill up the emptiness I felt inside. I left our parents and you for the Church, and then I felt I was deserted by the Catholic Church. I felt I had nothing, and that's the way I lived for most of my life. There was no motivation to find anything else either, until your letter arrived. Somehow the affirmation that my sister was out there looking for me lit a spark, igniting desires long hidden and unacknowledged. I wanted new experiences. I became interested in books, learning how to think for myself, weighing options, and making decisions. And I risked changing. But I'm still stuck." Then he stopped. "That was a pretty long digression into *Rupert*. It just came out when you asked my opinion about committing suicide. After a lifetime of being told what to think and believe, I just don't know what *I* think about it."

"That's fair, Rupert. There's much I'd like to tell *you* someday about my relationship to suicide but not right now. I have a more important topic, something I'm dying, metaphorically, to share."

A smile crossed Rupert's face, making Maggie think for a moment about how much she liked it when he smiled or laughed. It somehow made him look human, not the priest she thought he'd wanted so much to become. She said nothing about this to him, though. "I meant to say 'share with my brother.'"

Rupert stood up and saluted. "Brother here, ready and waiting to listen."

She saluted back, and then they both laughed before she continued. "His name is Jake."

"Jake, hmm. Not to go too far out on a limb here, but I'm guessing there's a man in your life."

Maggie giggled. "Yes. You guessed it. I want to tell you the story of how we met and some about him. Since I only just met him, I really don't know much about him or his background, but I do know he's different from anyone I've ever met before. First, to set the scene: I, Maggie Callaway, in a bar—alone!"

"What?"

"Yes, and like in the movies, Jake came in and took the stool next to me. Now, as you can guess, my walls were up and in good repair until they crumbled when he began to talk. Just like I've seen it happen in the movies, I thought I was being seduced. And, though I can hardly believe this, I *wanted* to be seduced.

"At first, I was an unwilling participant, fighting, resisting, being defiant as I know how to do. But while doing that, I didn't get up and leave either. Why? you ask. Well, who knows for sure, but I can tell you he didn't do anything I expected him to do. He listened but was not passive. He did not, as I fully assumed from watching those movies I mentioned before, seem to be trying to get me into bed. He seemed genuinely interested in me. He acknowledged me even when I became directive. As I sat on that stool next to him, I felt myself surrendering, not so much to him as to myself, finally letting go of my fears. I can't tell you how liberating that felt. My need to take control come up, but I resisted.

"Really, I think my meeting him was serendipitous. The right person at the right time in the right place. But more than that, and similar to what you just said about yourself, hearing that you, my brother, might visit, also played a part in this. What for me had always felt impossible was about to happen, I hoped. Now Jake's in my life, and I want you to meet him sometime."

"That would be great."

"I feel so lucky, or blessed, as you might say, by what has happened to me since I left work. It's like I was putting in time there, doing something important for sure, demonstrating my skills and intelligence for the world, but somehow, I now know I had more to do and to learn. I guess a crisis can bring out both the worst and the best in us. Unfortunate for me that I had to wait for death to come as my crisis."

"Fascinating, Maggie. I would like to meet your Jake sometime, when you feel ready. And now I'm torn. Part of me wants to ask questions and hear more of your journey, and another part of me wants to commingle my story of awakening with yours."

"Oh, Rupert, commingle? That actually sounds a little sexy." She smiled, and Rupert thought she looked much more relaxed than before.

"Well, in a similar way, I have found, or actually, I think she found me, a woman named Sylvia to help me unplug, unseal, open my hardened soul. I even liberated the restrictions I held over my penis with her! Yeah, we've had sex several times now." Rupert smiled. "My first sexual experiences but I hope not my last. She offered herself to me and helped me open my mind and my heart. She teaches English literature. From our first meeting, she demonstrated a deep interest in me that I was, surprisingly, able to accept. When I finally emerge from the dark well I've been living in, I want to get to know more about her. Maybe I'll move down to Vancouver so we can spend more time together. I know I'm leaving the Church, which means I'll have to leave the house I'm in anyway. I'll need to go somewhere. When I left Canada to come here, though, I really didn't know where I'd go after you and I had reconnected. I feel so inspired by all the possibilities and don't want to commit to anything. Right now, I'm staying here with you, and we have many years of catch-up to do." Rupert saw Maggie's look of confusion. "I mean I want to use the time we have, Maggie, no matter how long we both shall last."

Maggie smiled. "Me too." To herself she thought, *Now I'm sure I did the right thing to change my will to include Rupert. He's going to need my financial help.* This brought tears to her eyes, thinking, *I won't be around long enough to do anything else for him.*

"I hesitate to ask what's wrong, but you're crying, Maggie."

She smiled. "Yes, a little. From happiness."

CHAPTER 52

"I'M HUNGRY," RUPERT SAID. "I know I had a big dinner earlier, but a roast beef sandwich suddenly sounds pretty good."

"Okay," Maggie replied. No one was going to cook, so Maggie ordered sandwiches from a food service. She knew she would eat very little, if anything, but still ordered enough for two. Then the doorbell rang.

Rupert looked surprised.

It was after midnight, but Maggie said, "Oh, I know who that is. Please let her in and then make yourself scarce will you. Remember I said I would need some alone time tonight to finish up some private business."

"I do. I'll open the door and then go unpack. If I finish too quickly, I'll go to the library, the room with all the books."

"Sure, that'll work. *Library* it is."

Rupert thought she might be being facetious but didn't respond. He let Sarah in and left.

"Thanks for coming Sarah," Maggie said. "Do you have the papers?"

"I do."

Maggie quickly scanned through them. She'd worked a long time with Sarah and so trusted it was all good. "Where do I sign?"

After she signed, Sarah stood to leave, "Well Maggie, I think that does it. Take care and call me if you need anything else."

"Thanks, Sarah. You've been a great help over the years. Goodbye."

"Goodbye, Maggie." Sarah turned and walked down the hall and out the door.

Rupert heard the door shut and came back to the living area. "That was quick. Never even made it to the *library*."

"Yeah. That was another one of my lawyers, and we didn't have much to talk about."

Five minutes later there was another knock on the door.

"That will be the food, right?"

"Right."

Rupert again answered the door.

Maggie yelled from the living room, "You have to have some money, Rupert."

He yelled back, "I assumed that, Maggie. I got this one."

Maggie said nothing but watched him pay for the sandwiches and bring in the food, thinking, *What good manners. Guess he got something from all those years in the Church.* "How does that saying go, 'mannerliness is close to godliness'?"

"No, Maggie, *mannerliness* isn't even a word. You mean 'cleanliness is next to godliness,' I think."

"Yeah, that's it. Thanks. You go ahead and eat. I'm not really hungry."

"You sure?"

"Yes. I'll jump in if I change my mind. Oh, and here's some money for all that." She took out her wallet and gave him fifty dollars.

Rupert reluctantly took it, more than the meals had cost. This was no time to fight over money, and besides, he knew he could pick up something for Maggie with the extra ten dollars later. He gathered his food and took his seat across from her.

Maggie watched him eat. That's really what she wanted, just to watch her brother eat—see how his mouth moved, see how he swallowed, and even see if he would do something like burp and how loudly if he did. Later she asked Rupert to get her a glass of orange juice and some ice cream. She ate the ice cream first. "I know Mom never told us this, but I've learned to always eat dessert first." She laughed.

Rupert smiled. "Mom had that frugality disease, common in the British Isles."

She laughed. "More like British restraint, wasn't it?"

"Whatever it was, she did have her rules for everything."

Maggie turned to her ice cream. She'd always liked vanilla, even though people laughed at her because they saw vanilla as so plain. For her, though, plain was better. *Maybe that's cultural too*, she thought.

When Rupert finished and saw Maggie was not going to eat any more, he started to clean up. Maggie reminded him about the cleaning lady coming, so he stopped.

Maggie didn't feel very good but wasn't particularly tired and didn't want to stop talking with Rupert. How much more time would she have to enjoy his company? She thought she probably should call Lively but didn't want to interrupt the time with just the two of them. Maggie no longer felt alone. If she died soon, she knew she wouldn't die alone. Not now, not anymore.

They talked a little longer.

Maggie continued to feel worse. Finally, she had to say something. "I don't feel so hot, Rupert. My pain has increased, and I feel a little nauseated."

"Do you want me to do anything? Get help?"

"No, but I think I need to go to bed. I hope we can continue talking in the morning."

"For sure, Maggie. I can't tell you how much this means to me. As I said before, I came here ready to stay until I knew it was time to move on to whatever comes next." He got up and helped her get ready for bed. She looked weak and suddenly frail. Maggie definitely needed his help.

"I'm going to need help with my pajamas too, Rupert."

He stared at her; his mouth opened but nothing came out.

"I know that might embarrass you, but remember, as I will, that we are brother and sister. Just not very practiced at it."

"Thanks for saying that, sis."

It all happened carefully and discreetly. Maggie loved it all. She experienced her brother reaching out to help her with a care and concern that touched her more deeply than any words. He was humble and full of brotherly affection. She stood next to him, absorbing every moment. Maggie thought nothing could have been more intimate for any family.

He's dressing me. "Thanks, Rupert. I'd like to give you a big hug, not big enough to fill all the years without any hugs between us but as big as I have left in my weak, failing body."

Rupert saw her looking at him with big wet eyes, and all words left him. He put his arms out, and together they hugged, firmly and lovingly. His body shook, but it felt good. Both cried but said nothing, silently talking to each.

They reached the end of their embrace at the same time. Rupert helped Maggie under the covers and was about to turn out the light and leave, but she grabbed his hand and looked up at him.

"Good night, Rupert, and thanks for coming. You've given me hope and a reason to live. I'll see you in the morning."

"Great, Maggie. I'll leave the door ajar, so if you need anything in the night, just call."

CHAPTER 53

RUPERT SLEPT WELL AND AWOKE AGAIN WITH THE SUN. He had not heard anything from Maggie all night. As usual, he craved his morning coffee, but then he realized he hadn't paid any attention to where Maggie kept things in the kitchen. Although he really didn't want to wake Maggie, his urge for coffee drove him to knock lightly on her door. She didn't answer immediately, so he stopped. *Oh well, she probably needs sleep more than I need coffee.*

While he waited for Maggie to get up, Rupert decided to look around. So far, he'd only seen a small part of Maggie's home. He found more bedrooms, all decorated differently with colorful wallpaper, plush spongy rugs, and art on the walls. He took his time examining the paintings. Though he knew relatively nothing about art, these pieces, to him, looked like originals. *I like your taste, Maggie,* he thought. Everything he saw was beautiful.

He found two small kitchens and several rooms that looked like studies. Each was large enough for a good-size meeting and was decoratively arranged with large desks and beautiful furniture. On all the walls, he saw books, shelves and shelves of them. As he scrutinized the titles, he wondered if she'd read them all. He picked up a couple to scan and chose one, *Winning* by Jack Welch. Rupert liked the title and thought it might have information he could use too. He read a little but soon dozed off, the result of missing his morning coffee.

Again, he went to see if Maggie was up. She wasn't, so he knocked louder. Still nothing. He opened the door a crack and called out her name. Still nothing, so he pushed the door open and entered. "Time to rise and shine; time for coffee." Rupert approached the bed and saw what looked like a slight smile on her face. "Maggie, wake up." He'd seen doctors feel the neck for a pulse, so he tried it. Nothing. "Maggie, Maggie, it's Rupert. Wake up, will you?"

She didn't. Maggie was dead.

Rupert remembered telling her he couldn't do the last-rites ritual, but now facing Maggie like this, he decided he wanted to do it. He didn't have anything special to wear so just sat down on the side of her bed, picked up her hand, and said: "Through this holy anointing may the Lord in his love and mercy help you with the grace of the Holy Spirit. May the Lord who frees you from sin save you and raise you up." It all flowed naturally, forcefully, and most importantly, meaningfully for Rupert. He gently gave Maggie a kiss on the cheek and said what he could not say to her while she was alive. "I love you."

And then he cried. It started like a trickle of water down his cheek but soon became a waterfall. Thoughts of Maggie filled his mind, her beautiful face, her free-flowing, auburn-colored hair, her petite size just like their mom. Apart from any increased weight she'd put on, she had always looked fragile, like their mom, compared to their father who had been big and brawny, good for working in the woods. Others might have seen Maggie not as fragile, probably only as tough and unbreakable. He knew, however, that, though she might have been guarded and calculating, she was also vulnerable, not weak but approachable.

The tears suddenly stopped, replaced with anger. His body became rigid, his face got red, and his fists clenched tightly at his sides. Rupert yelled, "Stupid, stupid people. You didn't know her, didn't want to get to know her." Then he fell over on the bed and cried as he thought about how he also did not know her and how people had not known him either. He knew he'd never shown all of himself, his strengths and his vulnerabilities; and she didn't either. They hid these, maybe even from themselves. "Oh God, I blew it; I missed my opportunity to have and to love my sister. Now she's gone forever."

Rupert continued to quietly sob for a while as he thought about Maggie and what he'd missed until he was jolted by a thought. *God, regardless of what I professed before, I don't believe we will meet again in heaven. Oh, what blasphemy, Rupert. What a rogue you are.* He hadn't thought this all through, the consequences and ramifications of what he was saying. The word *hell* popped into his head, and his fear turned into the pervasive dread he'd known so many times before. Rupert wished there was a place he could hide.

He looked at Maggie. She lay there with her eyes still closed as if asleep. "Wake up, Maggie. I need more time with you. Wake up, will you?"

Of course, she didn't, and tears again began to fall, though this time he wondered if they were for her or for him. Rupert began to feel sorry for himself and his loss of control, not just self-control but control over life. Uncertainty supplanted certainty, and certainty was what he had always wanted. He began to talk with Maggie as if she were there. "What's wrong with me, Maggie? You were always the smart one of the two of us. I thought I'd changed, given up my self-centered need to dominate everything, but no, it's still there, even now. I didn't want you to die because I wasn't ready for it."

Rupert stopped and looked down at her. "You look so peaceful. Are you at peace? Will my agony end with my death?"

Maggie said nothing.

"Silence, that's all you have?"

He fell silent too. To himself he thought, *Be quiet, Rupert. Too much thinking, too much talking. Grieve your loss. It's real.* He looked down again at Maggie. She looked dead now, not like she was sleeping. He let that sink in. "You are dead, Maggie."

Then he continued to say what had come to him. "You *are* gone, but I must go on." He paused a moment before continuing, "This time, though, I'm not leaving you behind. This time I carry you with me, inside and forever."

CHAPTER 54

RUPERT'S TIME TOGETHER WITH MAGGIE HAD ended. She had found him, he had had the courage to come to her, and they had met, talked, laughed, touched, and shared stories and food together.

"I hope, Maggie, that in these last few days you found what you had for so long wanted from me, amen," he prayed.

Rupert wailed. He sobbed uncontrollably, unable to maintain the stoic demeanor he'd always held to demonstrate his dominion over life's chaos and weakness. Seeing Maggie lying there brought out the sadness he'd held for years, sadness from all the profound losses he'd let happen, first the loss of his family and then of himself, his direction, his hopes, his beliefs.

Falling over on the bed next to Maggie, Rupert said, "We missed all those years we could have had together, and now you're gone. How could I have been so selfish? I was the big brother, the one who should have taken care of you and helped you in times of need."

When Rupert finally stopped crying, he rolled off the bed, stroked Maggie's hair, and kissed her cheek. He left the room, gently shutting the door, went to the living room, and sat in the chair across from where Maggie had sat, wondering at how things had changed for him, even in these last hours. The depth of his feelings of loss was so much more than he ever imagined it would be. Rupert sobbed tears he didn't know he had in him. Nothing had ever caused him to weep so deeply. His reservoir had broken, and the tears flowed freely, so freely he wondered if he might not be able to stop.

Exhaustion overwhelmed him. He couldn't move. Nor could he think. Rupert just sat there, staring at the chair where Maggie had sat and appeared so happy at the end. She was now all he could think about, still filling the room and filling him. He had only scratched the surface of getting to know her, but he now felt, weirdly, as if she had always been with him in his life, been part of him, even though they had separated so long ago. This seemed so strange.

His mind stayed blank, and yet his heart overflowed with feeling. He knew his life had changed. Rupert hoped that meant he wouldn't continue to analyze all his thoughts, though he suspected his struggles would continue. He felt strong, at least at this moment. It felt good even. He hoped he could continue to let life unfold without trying to control every outcome. *Knowing me, however, I'll waver and fall back into old ways but . . . that's me.* He smiled, like he was sharing a private joke with someone.

CHAPTER 55

Rupert sat there quietly, though his body trembled with the amount of sorrow he felt. He knew very little about his sister, but she now inhabited him. He was both sad and happy.

When the phone rang, he had a sudden reawakening to where he was and the possible predicament he could face. Here he sat alone in his sister's house with her lying dead in the bedroom. Who of Maggie's friends knew he was there? As far as he was aware, only Theresa, Maggie's lawyer, and Lively, the nurse, knew he'd come. He decided to answer the phone. After all, someone who knew Maggie had to be informed sometime of what had happened.

He felt relief when Theresa said, "Hello, Rupert. Is that you?"

"Yes, Theresa. Maggie passed away in the night. I just found her lying in bed."

Silence followed. Even though Theresa was a lawyer and as such should be ready to handle all emergencies with great aplomb, she, in the end, had come to see Maggie as a friend. "Oh . . . oh dear. I'm so sorry! Have you called 911?"

"No."

"Well, you do that, and I'll come right over."

"Okay."

Together there must have been ten policemen, firemen, and

ambulance attendants in the house when Theresa arrived. Rupert was in the living room with some of these emergency workers answering what questions he could. Everyone but Rupert, who still dabbed at tears, looked professional. He couldn't answer many of the questions they asked. How could he? He had just arrived, and everything was new and strange. Rupert did the best he could describing—in as much detail as he could—what had transpired. After she arrived, Theresa took over. She knew the answers, and even if in doubt, she spoke with authority.

Soon, their jobs done, everyone left, and Theresa and Rupert were alone.

Theresa knew where Maggie kept the coffee and a drip coffeemaker and brewed a pot. She poured two cups. Rupert drank his but not as eagerly as he thought he might. She sipped hers until it got too cold to drink.

"Thanks for coming over so fast, Theresa. I sure didn't feel like facing everything that just happened. We'd had such a good reconnection since I'd gotten here, and last night, after all our talking, we both—at least I think Maggie too—went to bed feeling happy and anticipating more time together. She hadn't felt well and considered calling Lively but decided against it. Now she's gone. We were just getting started. When I got here, we both exploded with feelings we'd held and hidden for many years. Even I, the reclusive, passive, and depressed priest, said my piece. And you know, Theresa, even though we ended up with just a short time together, somehow, I feel relieved of a burden of responsibility I've carried hidden from both myself and others. I sure hope Maggie felt some relief from that awful feeling of neglect that our parents and I forced on her. She didn't die with any apparent anger or hatred on her lips."

"I hope you're right, Rupert. If there really is such a thing as a lost soul, she was it. She was a disconnected, separated, and isolated CEO, wielding a big stick and generating fear and dread in everyone around her. Many times, I'm sure, her staff and others wished her dead or at least fired. No one above her would have fired her, though. She had to be the most successful leader this company has ever had, regardless of all her tirades and belligerent behavior.

"When she contracted cancer, she had to leave the job and face the reality of a life of radical aloneness. No one from the firm, which comprised her whole world at the time, made any contact with her again, except me. And at first, I was there only because it was part of my job as lead lawyer for the company. The other person she had in her life was Jake, a guy she met very recently while out walking. I never met him, did you?"

"No, I did not."

"From what Maggie told me he seems to have been the right guy at the right time in the right place. Of course, Maggie had changed a lot by that time. Facing death can change anyone, I suppose, and for Maggie, she became more available as the vulnerable, gentle person she was underneath the blunt, outspoken, and usually brusque CEO everyone knew before. Jake met a stranger, and he happened to be a different kind of man than you would expect she might meet in a bar. From what I heard, he wasn't sexually aggressive or threatening; he was kind.

"Then, of course, she had reached out to you. She really wanted to see you, but at first, I don't think she had much hope it would happen. Maggie didn't know where you lived or even if you were still alive. Her inner circle, before she met Jake, amounted only to me, the company lawyer, and the woman who cleaned her house. Her sickness changed her or, at least, helped to change her. Dying and no longer being the boss, she began to show the vulnerable person she may have really always been, a person in dire need of intimacy and affection. I think you, Rupert, were the one she most missed. When she heard you had left to come to San Francisco, she acted coolly, but behind that front, I saw excitement mixed with apprehension."

Rupert couldn't help but smile at this. "I guess hiding feelings ran in the family."

Theresa continued, "She seemed scared, much like a music prodigy about to give her first piano concert or the PhD student about to defend her thesis. Maybe, though, after your reunion happened, she felt complete, finished, and could die with a kind of peace she'd never known in her life. No more fear or defensiveness. I hope so."

Rupert choked up. Any words he might have wanted to say got stuck in his throat. Thoughts, however, still came to him. He began to berate himself for what he'd done to his family by leaving, never confronting any of them. He shook with the coldness that passed through his body. The coldhearted priest! Was that who he really was—a coldhearted cruel person? He became the priest who preached love, forgiveness, and reconciliation while living in isolation and separation from those closest to him, both his personal and church families. Had he even believed what he had preached? Now he could admit no, he hadn't.

Theresa had kept on talking about Maggie, even though Rupert had drifted off in his own thoughts. He had not really heard much of what she'd said and then tuned back in.

"Maggie was truly shaken and relieved when she heard you would come to San Francisco because she was not well enough to travel to see you. She even asked me, 'Do I really have a brother who loves me?' I think she really didn't know. Maybe she finally knew the answer before she passed."

"She did, Theresa. I'm sure of it."

Theresa just stared at him.

Rupert had joined the priesthood, not to give to others but to get for himself. He wanted what he thought priests had, tranquility, serenity, gratification, and happiness, things he'd longed for but never knew as a kid or as an adult. But then he wondered if others in the Church he'd met, studied with, even lived with ever love him. *Were they committed to me, did they even like me, or were they just committed to themselves? Can I answer that? Does it even matter now? I came here taking a risk without expectation or even hope. I just wanted to see my sister before she died. I didn't even know I came to make amends.* He said, "I came here at my own peril, Theresa. I exposed myself to an unknown, which sounds funny since Maggie's my sister, but so true in my case. I joined the priesthood to find something I wanted. Coming here, I had no idea what I wanted. I just came—and found love, family love."

Theresa began to cry. "I think I'll start to organize a few of Maggie's things. Do you mind?"

"Not at all. I think I'll just sit here for a while." Here Rupert was in his sister's home, talking with someone he'd only recently met. His shell, his wall, hardened over time, was cracking open after all those years of early training where the nuns had drilled into him rules for correct behavior, and the regulations for how to study, eat, and pray. He'd tried to do all they'd asked of him. He did it all but found no tranquility or connection. Rupert was depressed by it all. Now, on the verge of finding some connection with his family, this happens. What comes next? *Shit, what do I do?* He came to San Francisco to see his sister, and then she dies, leaving him to face a life that now feels totally out of order. *Can I handle what's ahead?* He felt lightheaded. Rupert thought of Sylvia, Father Brown, his neighbors back home, and even Theresa and her family. *Is this what happens when we face death?* He felt an intense urge to talk, engage, connect. Then, as if on cue, Theresa returned, and he asked, "How'd Alex do on his paper?"

Theresa jumped a little. "Where'd that come from?"

"Oh, sorry. I just remembered your son and how much he helped me find the courage to do what I'd come here to do. That boy didn't even know me, but he gave me, those two quotes from Churchill and Mandela. So how'd he do on the paper?"

"Got an A."

"Please give him my congratulations, and also please give him a hug to thank him for the gift."

"Okay, I will. Can I get you more coffee or something, Rupert?

"No, but I sure could use some food. Can I buy you lunch? You'll have to pick the place."

"Oh, you don't have to do that."

"I know, but I want to treat you. Just don't pick an expensive place, if something like that exists in San Francisco!"

"I think I know a place. Might be a little noisy but the food is good and cheap!"

"Sounds like my kind of place. Just let me make a quick phone call before we leave."

"Okay, I'll wait in the car. I'm parked right out front in the same car I had when we picked you up at the airport."

Rupert called Sylvia. He wanted to tell her what had happened to his sister. He knew she'd want to know. They talked for about ten minutes, and then he said he'd call back soon.

While he called Sylvia, Theresa contacted Guy to let him know she'd be gone a while longer and for him not to wait dinner if she did not return in time.

As they drove off, Maggie's phone rang. No one left a message.

Lively had heard through the hospital that Maggie had died but decided to drop by and offer her condolences. She let herself in, but no one was there. She decided to leave the key on the kitchen table. Then, as she was about to leave, the front door opened.

The cleaning person, Maria, came in singing and smiling. "Hello, Maggie. Sorry I'm late."

Lively introduced herself and told her the news. After exclamations of disbelief and some tears, Lively, suggested Maria leave for now and return sometime later to do the cleaning. She was sure someone would be in touch with her soon regarding her job. Then they both left.

CHAPTER 56

OVER LUNCH, RUPERT LEARNED A GREAT DEAL about Maggie's past in San Francisco, but Theresa spent substantially more time probing him for stories about his life.

"How did you expect to escape life and still not die? Sounds to me like you want freedom from *life*."

Without thinking, Rupert responded, "Maybe that's why I felt suicidal all the time, even if I never had the courage to kill myself. I wanted to die but without dying. I worked hard at my job, performing the sacraments for Catholics to help them find grace, forgiveness of sins, and the Holy Spirit. I made the Bible and Catholic doctrine the centers of my life, thinking that would save me, actually, *make* me. At that time, I saw myself only as a product of my limited childhood, not as someone who had any power over his life. I joined the Church as an *answer*, to free me from what I had seen only as the limitations of normal life, really to make me in God's image, like he promised. Rupert stopped a moment. "Maybe like Geppetto made Pinocchio." That made him smile but not for long because another thought had come. "I couldn't commit suicide since in some ways I saw myself as already dead, as *nothing*."

Theresa pressed on all this/

But Rupert had a hard time explaining. It all was just flowing out. What came to him, he said out loud. He thought, *It's so easy, no judgments, and yet I don't feel like I'm being ignorant, or rude. It's not bad, in fact it feels great.* "I know this must be hard to understand, but I hardly know what I'm saying, no less have a good grasp on it."

The lawyer sitting across from him just looked at him with tenderness and said, "Pinocchio lied."

"Yes. I hadn't thought of that when I made that analogy, but you just hit the bullseye. I set out to find something and ended up living a lie. You must understand, though, I was conscious of what I was doing. I started life as an innocent and lived innocently, naïvely. Pinocchio had his own kind of hell. I had mine. Pinocchio experienced a rebirth, a mystery of sorts, but he became real. As I recall, Pinocchio had to work for the life he was given."

"Go on."

"I can't. I don't understand what's happening to me or what I'm saying." Rupert stopped again.

"Go on."

"Something's changed for me too. I no longer feel like the innocent. It's mysterious, but as I lived this lie, certain circumstances and people have come into my life. Why now? Can't say, but the results are getting clearer. Things have changed for me, like the way I think or maybe don't think."

Theresa watched Rupert as he talked. He looked relaxed and energized at the same time. "This is all quite interesting, Rupert. You don't know this, but I was raised a Catholic. I left the Church a long time ago but have never talked to anyone behind the altar, on the inside like you. What was it like?"

"I was surrounded by other priests who, I thought, had found what I still longed for, a peacefulness, a real confidence. I performed my life. Who knows what was really true? Even when priests started to be accused of child abuse and sexual misconduct, we didn't discuss it or question the truth of the accusations. I even suspected a priest, Father Dominick, of getting too close to young boys in the choir but never confronted him or reported it to my superiors. I actually questioned its seriousness or importance. When it all came out, sure, we all felt ashamed, but that didn't really affect us either. We felt shame all the time. It was, after all, a motivator for us to work harder at finding God. Priests of old used to self-flagellate with a whip when accused of some wrong or they just perceived a wrong themselves. We punished ourselves with mental and emotional pummeling if something felt dishonorable, improper, or shameful. I would never question the behavior of others because I didn't want to be accused of not paying enough attention to my own business, my own sin."

"But you thought you were doing the right thing, didn't you?" Theresa asked. "You lived and acted with sincerity. You did it for a purpose, even if now you see it as a mistake. Like Pinocchio again, you had to suffer in your own hell before today could happen."

"Okay, but let me continue. Being a priest did not direct me back to my family. It did not encourage me to search out my sister. That happened only when that letter of Maggie's triggered something in me. How, I have no idea, but it prompted me, or probably more accurately provoked me, to break long-held behaviors. Something broke loose inside me. I was hit with the most sickening despair I've ever felt, but later that transformed into something different.

"And, as of now, I've mostly stopped trying to define things. Things, weird things to me, just keep happening, and I'm trying—and that's the key word here—to act on them. Maggie's dying was a punch in the gut, but I'm not dying myself. I must carry on for her but also for me, for the Callaway family." Rupert stopped.

Theresa sat staring, a little overwhelmed by what she'd been seeing and been part of over this last hour or so.

The waitress came by to fill their water glasses and asked if they were ready for the check.

Theresa looked at her watch. "Oh my, I have to get back. Are you ready, Rupert?"

"I think so."

When they got back to the condo, Theresa said she wanted to head home, so they decided he'd just stay at Maggie's and they could talk tomorrow regarding what came next.

"Staying here works for me," he told her.

"Okay, I'll head home for a while. While there, I'll call Maggie's personal lawyer to verify that arrangements for disposition of Maggie's remains are complete. I'll also make sure Maggie's body is taken to Serenity Funeral Home. They are close by and can handle the cremation. And, don't worry; I'll take care of planning a memorial celebration."

"Thanks. Glad you remembered the business details. I sure hadn't."

Rupert wrote down his phone number, and Theresa wrote down hers on a pad in the kitchen. She thanked him for the lovely lunch and left.

He walked into Maggie's room, sat down on the edge of the still unmade bed, and started to laugh, not because he thought anything was funny. No, this was relief. Maggie was gone, but she'd left him a gift of recognition. She had helped him see what he now believed had been there all the time, and he couldn't help but laugh. How could he have spent all those years trying to make himself feel worthwhile and fail to see his true value?

Joining the priesthood had just been a job. He'd worked hard but always felt inadequate, like it was all his fault and, if he just worked harder, he'd finally feel at peace. He had the wrong goal. Childhood suffering made him imagine an escape, a way out of this and all suffering. The two priests had shared their experiences, and he saw that as his *answer*. He jumped in full of hope but without question or reflection.

"Maggie, you exuded confidence, real or imagined. Well, spending time with you has left me feeling the confidence that has always escaped me. Thank you."

CHAPTER 57

THE PHONE RANG, CAUSING RUPERT TO JUMP. "Better get yourself together, Rupert. If you're going to now be Maggie's secretary, you'd better get serious and fast." The nearest phone was in the kitchen so he quickly went there. "Hello, Maggie Callaway's residence."

"Hi. You must be Rupert. This is Jake, a friend of Maggie's. She told me about your coming to San Francisco. I'm calling to talk to her if I could. I won't take long."

Rupert suddenly found himself at a loss for words.

"Hello? Can I talk to her, Rupert?"

"Well, Jake, I'm sorry to be the one to tell you, but Maggie passed away last night."

"How can that be? I know she was quite ill, but she didn't sound close to death when we last talked. What happened?"

"You know, Jake, I'm here alone and wouldn't mind some company, so if you'd like to stop by, we can talk."

"I'd like that, Rupert. I'll be there in about half an hour."

"I'll listen for the bell."

Rupert leaned back thinking now about how bizarre this had all become. He'd gone from barely remembering he had a sister to now sharing the story of her death with a man who, from all he'd heard so far, may have been her only close, maybe even intimate, friend. Why didn't he tell him over the phone what little he knew and then go on with his evening alone? Rupert knew why—Maggie would want her brother to do this, and he was, after all, her brother. He knew this, felt this, and was working hard to adjust to the idea himself.

He was not meeting with Jake as a priest. That moniker no longer fit, and he felt he would use it less and less in coming years. Overall, he felt pleased, but also sad. Maggie was gone. She would not have the opportunity to have the sister/brother relationship she had so badly wanted or whatever life she might have wanted with this guy.

Rupert went to the living room and switched on the radio. Maggie had it tuned to a classical music station. *Perfect*, he thought. *And different for me.* He remembered how he had always liked his house quiet and dark. He chuckled a little at the thought.

The doorbell rang. Rupert walked down the hall and opened the door. "Hello, you must be Jake."

A distinguished looking gentleman, showing some grey in his hair and a few wrinkles around his mouth, stood looking at him. He had very welcoming eyes and a protruding nose. Rupert wouldn't have called him particularly handsome but personable and, in his horn-rim glasses, smart for sure.

"Yes, hello, Rupert. Thanks for inviting me over."

They shook hands, and Rupert led the way back to the living room. Jake started asking questions, some of which Rupert couldn't answer. He could talk about the lead up to Maggie's death but couldn't say anything about what would happen now.

Jake told Rupert about how close he'd felt to Maggie in such a short time of knowing her, how he had looked forward to spending more time with her, and how she appeared to want that with him.

"Maybe she found her capacity to care, and it was compelling, Jake."

Jake started to ask Rupert about his life. Rupert felt at first as if he were with a lawyer again, but this was different. Jake was curious. His questions seemed to come from some engaging interest in him. Rupert told the story once again about how he'd left Maggie and the family to follow a path to becoming a priest. "But I've just recently decided to leave the priesthood." Now, this was not exactly the truth since he had only thought about leaving, but saying it out loud opened the door for him to say more.

"This path I took to the priesthood without design, but now it has led me back to my family and, through my sister, not church doctrine, maybe to a better understanding of myself. I believe I've lived mostly as a coward, afraid I couldn't live life with all its pain and sorrow, so I thought I'd found an escape, someplace where I would know only peace, happiness, and well-being. It didn't happen, Jake. Though people may see priests as somehow different, even special, priests are just like everybody else. We laugh and cry, argue and resolve, negotiate and maneuver, collaborate and plot. We preach and offer the sacraments, but it's also a job. A parishioner once shared with me a story she'd read, I think in a Philip Roth book, about a devout Catholic boy who happened to see some priests in a restroom after a sporting event. That was the first time he knew priests had penises! The myths about us continue, but the reality is quite different.

"Without knowing it, Maggie provided the trigger I needed to wake up, realize I wasn't happy, and start making different decisions. So far, the results have been fulfilling but are unfinished. I know that to finish my journey, I must take the biggest risk of my life and leave the security of the Church—and do it not alone, as I have done before, but with others. I've already met several people I want to stay connected to in Canada and even here in San Francisco." A broad smile came unbidden. Rupert felt good, worthy, grateful. Here he was telling his story to a stranger, no less. *Wow, something is changing.*

"A moving story, Rupert."

Thoughts and reflections had been readily flowing through Jake since the surprise news of Maggie's death. He recalled how quickly she'd drawn his attention. She'd looked alluring, even sitting at the bar with her back to him. Her hair had hung loosely to her shoulders, giving the impression she was younger than he thought she really was. Her clothing had not been fancy, but definitely had accentuated her figure. When they had started to talk, he could tell she was bright but also shrewd. What had surprised him the most, however, was that he had not felt any of the usual sexual attraction he had always felt before when he met women in bars or cabarets.

Jake noticed Rupert staring at him, probably wondering what he was thinking. "When Maggie and I first met, Rupert, she made it abundantly clear I would not get very far with her if I tried. Paradoxically, though, I knew she wanted me to try. And I wanted to. I was immediately drawn in, not because I found her sexy in the usual way. She seemed so vulnerable, so fragile behind that emotional wall or front she put up. I don't mean she was fake or playing a game with me. She was letting me know she needed someone or something. I think I was facing a woman whose emotional wall was already beginning to crumble and she knew she was near death. Maggie came across as both available and inaccessible. She was a wounded woman, bleeding but trying hard to not let me see. That changed as we talked, walked, and shared meals together. Her story flowed out and, frankly, drew me in ever deeper. You were the only family she mentioned with any feeling.

"Our last conversation took place during her last hospital stay. She'd called to ask me to visit. We had a touching, moving talk during which she asked if I'd move in with her. I said no, and it was the right thing to do at the time, but now I feel some regret. Of course, since she passed away quite quickly after that, it never would have happened anyway, but I sure know she'll continue to live with me in my heart and mind for the rest of my life."

Rupert felt tired, exhausted. He really liked Jake and could see how his sister had taken to him, but he needed to stop. "Thanks for everything, Jake. I'm sure we could both go on and on, but for now, I've reached my limit. Can we get together tomorrow or sometime soon and talk more? I know you'll want to know about any plans for a memorial and/or funeral."

"Sure, Rupert. Thanks, for seeing me and for your sharing. I feel honored to have shared time with your sister, indeed a very special woman."

Rupert walked Jake to the door and then, surprising himself and Jake, reached out and gave him a goodbye hug. "Thanks for coming over, Jake. I can see why Maggie liked you."

"Thanks, Rupert. I'll see you tomorrow. Have a time in mind?"

Rupert said, "Let's say around noon."

"Sure, that will work," Jake said and walked out the door.

Immediately after Jake left, Rupert went to the bedroom, fell on the bed, and dropped into a restless sleep.

CHAPTER 58

Rupert woke with the sun. He got up, showered, shaved off his growing beard, and dressed in comfortable slacks and a shirt. His clerical collar lay in the suitcase, but felt he absolutely no desire to wear it. Now he needed coffee, at least a cup, maybe two. But where? Maggie's neighborhood didn't look promising, but he set out anyway. It was a nice morning, and maybe he'd see someone who could direct him to a place, maybe a Starbucks. They were ubiquitous after all.

After walking for about a half-hour, Rupert began to lose hope and then turned a corner and found a cafe with coffee and more, but all expensive fare. *It figures in this location*, he thought. Hungry and in need of caffeine, he sat down at the counter, picked up a menu, and after perusing the options, decided he'd better check to make sure he had enough money. He did, but with little left to spare, so decided to go with only a side of egg and toast with a large coffee. Even that would stretch him. *If I end up staying in San Francisco*, he thought, *I'd better get a job!*

Rupert finished his meal and sat for a while, enjoying the view, so different from the one he had in Canada. The person next to him was reading the *Chronicle*, San Francisco's morning paper, which he glanced at, trying not to be noticed. He saw the headlines, "Robin Williams Takes His Own Life," before the person reading said, "You're welcome to have this section when I finish."

"Oh, thanks. I'm Canadian, and like to keep up on world events."

"Here, you take this section. I can finish it later."

Rupert took the paper and started to read. He was smiling, not because there was anything funny in the article but because he felt so pleased, prideful, in fact, with his newfound boldness."

Ready to leave, Rupert paid his bill and headed out. After walking a few blocks, he realized he was lost. He had not paid enough attention to how he'd come, but he did not panic. It was still early, and he was pretty sure he'd started off in the right direction. It was cool but he'd worn a sweater and was not uncomfortable.

His walk took him past many fine-looking buildings with well-maintained gardens. Maggie's place was nestled among many buildings obviously filled with the rich and probably many who considered themselves mighty. It was pretty, for sure, but it made him think about his place in Powell River. Although it too had plenty of beauty and charm, it was not home to him any more than this was. Rupert lived his life as a nomad, traveling through places, milking them for what he could get and moving on to wherever he was sent next. He was part of the Catholic tribe, taking for himself and giving what? He stopped himself but then continued his thought, *Giving nothing.* Then, like he was awakening from a dream, he shouted, "No, no more. No more Church for me."

Shouting like that embarrassed Rupert. He was, after all, walking someplace in Maggie's neighborhood. But he kept walking and soon any shame he'd felt passed. It changed to a sense of purpose. He had a reason for being here, as meaningful as anything he'd ever done. Powell River felt far away. Certainly, he no longer could call that his home. Rupert truly now had no home. But rather than fear, he now felt excited, energized. His pace quickened, not because he knew where he was headed but because he knew better who he was.

CHAPTER 59

RUPERT DIDN'T GET BACK TO MAGGIE'S UNTIL AFTER TEN, and when he entered, he met Maria, the housekeeper. She told him how she had come yesterday and learned about Maggie's death, but she wanted to keep to her regular schedule for now. She also said Theresa had called and asked him to call when he returned. He thanked her and walked quickly to the phone, eager to hear what Theresa had planned. Rupert totally missed seeing the tears that glistened in Maria's eyes.

Theresa answered on the first ring. She was at the office, not home, and word of Maggie's passing was spreading fast. Top brass had called a board meeting to begin the process of hiring a new CEO, so it looked like Theresa would be tied up there for most of the day. "They're moving on fast, Rupert. Maggie's not even cold, and they're taking no time to remember her or her contributions. What a place!"

Rupert wondered what Theresa thought they should do. Isn't that just business as usual? But he didn't really know much about the business world. "Okay, thanks. I'll see you later,"

He decided to call Sylvia but then remembered she'd probably be at work. He tried anyway. She answered because she knew it was Rupert. He filled her in on what was happening and then asked her what she'd been doing.

"Not much. It's exam time, so I'm administering tests and grading papers. I have to have this all completed within a short time. Students want their grades. I do it all online, so really, I've been sitting in front of a computer, drinking tea, and eating frozen dinners. When I finish, I've planned for a sabbatical to work on my book, a biography of Margaret Atwood. If I get it, I'll have more free time."

Though she didn't elaborate on what this meant, Rupert hoped she was implying she'd have more time to see him. "Great. Guess I'll have to read up on this Margaret Atwood. I know nothing about her, but if I'm to impress you, I'll need to know something."

"Frankly, I have no interest in becoming your teacher, Rupert. Unless we teach each other different sex moves! Our project could become Sex in the Mature Years!"

"Great idea. I can already feel my interest in Margaret Atwood fading."

They both laughed.

Rupert hadn't thought much about Sylvia since arriving in San Francisco, but talking with her now reminded him how important she'd become to him. His strong feelings rushed back. "I miss you, Sylvia. I wanted you to know about Maggie because you'd asked me to keep you informed, but as we talked, I realized how much I just wanted to hear your voice. Guess you're important to me."

"*Moi aussi.*"

"I know that's French. I live in Canada, after all. But I have no idea what you said. I'll assume it was good—*n'est pas*? Impressed yet?"

"Oh, Rupert!"

"Last night I hoped to have some time alone, but Maggie's friend, Jake, called, and so I invited him to come over. Quite good-looking dude and a little weird, not in a bad way but just different. Just a little full of himself. He seemed to have an interest in Maggie and to honor her for her past and what she was trying to do now at the end of her life. He came out of nowhere into Maggie's life and made a difference, an accidental stranger in the night it would seem. Come to think of it, that's how I met you!"

Sylvia listened carefully and fully. Her attraction to Rupert had begun because she had the impression he was trying to start a new life, innocently launching himself into something without knowing where he'd end up, much like a teenager moving through the years to adulthood. Rupert probably had never experienced that kind of teenage excitement as a student. She found the innocence, the naïveté, the decency, and the courage attractive. And now her eagerness to be with him was even stronger. "Sounds like you're continuing to live the risky life, Rupert."

"Yeah, that's the word, *risky*. Risk versus caution. I need to find the balance, don't I?"

Instead of answering, Sylvia asked, "What do you plan to do today?"

"Not sure yet. Maybe I'll check out San Francisco, eat a good meal, and then maybe later tonight or tomorrow, I'll get together with the lawyer to plan a memorial service. In fact, I'd better get going." Rupert really didn't want to stop talking with Sylvia but didn't know exactly what to say next. "I'll call back tomorrow and keep you posted on happenings and—on the state of my ongoing desires."

"Turn me on, Rupert. I never knew old guys had so much fun!"

"Good luck reading those papers and grading."

"Thanks. Bye." Then she dropped the phone on the table.

Rupert heard the phone fall and, at first, wondered if he'd said something at the end that angered Sylvia. Then he knew that didn't happen. She just dropped the phone. *How quickly my mind turns good to bad*, he thought.

He'd never allowed himself to imagine being close to a woman, much less sleeping with one, and then Sylvia came into his life. "I like her, she makes me feel good, and I desire her. I want her body, and I want her mind. She just turned me on to Margaret Atwood." Rupert really liked the idea now of reading. Since his little foray into the libraries at Father Brown's and Maggie's, he had begun to see what he'd missed by limiting his reading pretty much to only Catholic literature.

Crash!

The noise seemed to come from the kitchen, so Rupert got up to look, but before he was out of his chair, Maria flew in from the kitchen in tears.

"I can't hang on to anything today. I just dropped one of Maggie's favorite casserole dishes. It's busted, all over the floor. I can't remember ever doing something like this before. She'll have a fit, Mr. Rupert. I just can't work today. Before dropping the dish, I knocked over pictures while dusting, and maybe worst of all, I started the laundry without separating the white and dark clothes. My day so far, *Madre mia, esto es un infierno!*" Her hands flew up in the air, and she walked back to the kitchen.

Rupert followed but slowly. He could see Maria was deeply upset and knew it had to be over Maggie's death, but her anger scared him a little too. When he entered the kitchen, he could see the ceramic all over the floor. *Boy, that must have been one big casserole dish,* he thought, but he said nothing. Instead, he started picking up the bigger pieces. Maria was still mumbling in Spanish, but he could see tears streaming down her face. As she looked over at him, he saw her face turn red. She immediately popped up and flew out of the room.

He stayed there, picking up pieces of glass. Then he found a broom and dustpan. He swept it all clean, and then went out to see where she'd gone. He found Maria sitting in the closet off Maggie's bedroom. She was sobbing into her apron. Rupert said nothing. He had an urge to put his hand on her shoulder, but still unsure about all the rules of male/female contact, he didn't. Instead, he quietly backed out and waited in the hallway just outside Maggie's room.

When Maria did stop crying, she appeared in the hallway next to him.

He jumped in surprise.

"Aren't you a priest?"

"Yes. No. I mean I used to be a priest, and technically still am. But I've decided to leave the priesthood."

"Oh, you can do that?"

Rupert smiled. *This woman's opening a door for me, I think. Thank you, Lord.* "Yes, they can. Priestly ordination supposedly is permanent, but a priest can be released from the clerical state simply by walking away. After a while, usually some action is taken by his religious order to remove him. I can also petition the Holy See for a more immediate separation." *There, I think that sounded pretty good, if I do say so myself.* Nonetheless, looking at Maria, Rupert could see she was not impressed.

"Well, I feel terrible, and I thought you could at least say a prayer for me."

Rupert didn't know what to do. His first impulse was to say he didn't pray anymore, but he wondered if that was even true. He was still just trying on his new situation. There was much he had yet to figure out. "You know, I hardly knew Maggie. No, I didn't really know her at all. But when I found her dead, I broke down, much like you just did. And I'm still grieving. After a loss of a loved one, you are supposed to sob, break things, even stop routines for a while. You came to work, and maybe you actually were in a state of grief and not ready to be here."

Maria just stared up at Rupert. Her eyes were so brown, so big, so moist.

Neither spoke, but Rupert began to feel some discomfort as he faced her steady, searching stare. He had to look away.

"I've worked for your sister for over twelve years. I think that's the longest any housekeeper has held the position. She was a bitch, to tell you the truth. She often ignored me entirely, and when she paid attention to me it was often to complain. So, why did I stick around? Why didn't I leave like all those before me? She paid well, and the hours were flexible. But your sister also trusted me. She demonstrated it by, first, giving me a key to this beautiful place after I'd worked here for only a week, and second, sharing her feelings with me. Some days I'd come here, and she'd follow me around, talking about this, that, and the other with her work and always saying it with full-throated feeling, mostly anger and irritation, exasperation, full of passion. It wasn't personal. I think I became like her confessor, Father. I mean Rupert. She trusted me with all that passion, and I began to see her as a woman, yes, with a ton of money. but in deep distress, pain, and sorrow. I started to really care about her. And I never said a word to her about any of this. And now she's gone."

Rupert told Maria he understood.

"I feel better, Mr. Rupert. Almost slipped again and called you Father."

He smiled.

She blushed with embarrassment and turned away, while holding a little smile herself.

"It felt good to talk with you," Rupert said. "You know I don't even know your name."

"Maria De La Vega. Everyone just calls me Maria."

"Well, Maria, nice to meet you. Would you like to call it quits for today? Of course, I have no idea what hours you work, but given what just happened here, you might just want to go home for today."

She agreed.

"Goodbye, Maria. Maybe I'll see you on my next visit, if there is one."

"Thanks, Rupert. You know, when you're Catholic, your family's Catholic, and almost everyone you know is Catholic. It's difficult to address a priest, former or current, other than as Father."

Rupert told her not to worry about it.

Maria left. She not only had stopped crying, but she also seemed to have a smile on her face.

Could that have been a smirk? Rupert asked himself. *No, trust what you see and experience.* He heard this as an assignment, not a command. Rupert had lived so long as a follower of others, he wondered if he could change. Could he trust his experience as the primary guide for his life? He really wanted to say yes.

CHAPTER 60

THE DOORBELL RANG, IMMEDIATELY REMINDING RUPERT that he'd invited Jake to come over.

"Sorry I'm a little late, Rupert. My youngest daughter, who just went to college, called and said she was having money problems and needed cash. Since I don't really have any extra to send her, my answer was a simple no. Quick and easy. So I made it."

"Well, I'm glad you did. Would you have any interest in going out for a bite? I'm getting hungry."

Jake smiled. "I think I can find some cash for that."

"Thank goodness you didn't give it all away to your daughter."

"Yeah."

"Any ideas on where to go?"

"Well, not close by, but there is a place I've gone to that's within walking distance."

"Great. Let's go." Rupert grabbed his sweater, and they left.

They arrived about twenty minutes later and found a quiet table in the back.

A waitress came to their table. "Hi, I'm Debbie, and I'll be your server this afternoon."

"Hello, Debbie," Jake said. "We haven't looked at the menu yet."

"That's okay. I'll come back in a minute."

When she did, they ordered, and she hurried off.

"They generally move fast during lunch. I guess they think that most of those who are out for lunch need to get back to work."

"I never had that problem as a priest. Never went out to lunch much."

"Oh, how come?"

Rupert thought about how few friends he'd ever had and how seldom he was ever asked to lunch. The feelings he'd had of rejection still hurt, so he just said, "Oh I'd rather not spend time talking about that now. Let's save that for another day."

"Okay, sure."

"Nice day, isn't it?"

"Yeah, this is generally the way it is around here this time of year, sunshine with breezes off the bay. It fogs or clouds up fairly often too, and then it becomes cooler. Our nights are generally cool, good for sleeping."

"Up where I'm from, the nights are also quite cool. Of course, our days can be that way too and wet. A good deal of rain falls along the northwest coast. We're known for it like you're known for your fog."

Debbie returned with the food.

"Wow, that looks good." Rupert took a big bite from his tuna sandwich. "This is great. I love dill pickles mixed in like that."

"Yeah, this place has a good reputation." Jake waited for Rupert to say something more but wasn't surprised by his silence. Finally, Jake started the conversation with some questions about Rupert's life.

Rupert never liked being the center of attention, but now, as Jake asked him questions, he was surprised by how he was okay with it. Jake seemed genuinely interested in him, and it felt good. They talked on until Rupert's stomach growled. "You're going to have to give me time to eat, Jake."

"Sorry, Rupert. Guess I got carried away and didn't notice I wasn't leaving time for you to eat."

They then finished their meals before continuing.

Rupert noticed some anger bleeding into Jake's questions.

Jake was angry and had been ever since Maggie had shared stories about her brother going away and leaving her at home alone. He'd hoped to conceal these feelings, however, in an effort not to upset Rupert. Jake

decided to ask how Rupert could live all these years, as a brother and as
a priest, without knowing if his sister was alive or dead. How could he be
so uncaring, so detached? It seemed cold and callous to him.

Rupert put down his fork. His appetite had suddenly disappeared.
He realized Jake was mad.

"What did you tell the faithful when they asked about your family
background?"

Rupert felt like he was being questioned by the police. He put his
head down and endured the onslaught. He knew he would have to
address Jake's feelings, but he had no idea how to begin.

"What's wrong with you, Rupert? Are you just numb to feelings?"

Well, that sure wasn't true in this moment. He was feeling every
word thrown at him, but surprisingly, even to him, he didn't feel angry
or defensive. "Guilty as charged, Jake. I have nothing to defend myself
with. I have lived a life without honor, without self-respect, and without
deference to others, yes, even my family. You have seen me for who I've
been, and you know, oddly, I feel relieved."

Jake did not want to let him off the hook just yet. Rupert's response
made him more frustrated. "I don't understand, Rupert. You forget about
her and then come down here when she's dying, and you suddenly care?
Help me make sense of that."

Rupert still didn't know what to say or do. It's true, Maggie's letter
notifying him of her condition had deeply affected him, even maybe
stimulated his transformation. How could that happen? "How does
one make sense out of the nonsensical, Jake, except to say just that?
The absurdity of all that has happened over the last month has deeply
affected me, changed me. Maybe that's what led me to being here with
you now. "I lived my life, Jake, trying to first discover my goodness, my
worth, if I had any. I wanted some relief from the torture I felt as a kid
from bullying and family neglect. I didn't find it. But now, after hearing
from Maggie, I seem to have found the courage to be more honest about
my feelings."

Jake stood up to go. "Too abstract, Rupert. You know what I think?
I think you got this letter from Maggie, the sister you'd totally forgotten
about, and you felt deeply guilty. That's what sent you into a tailspin. You

need to take responsibility for your part." He started to walk out, but Rupert pleaded with him to stay. Jake suddenly questioned what he'd been doing. He realized he had turned his anger over his loss of Maggie into an attack on Rupert. *Who made me judge, jury, and executioner here?* he asked himself and then sat back down.

"I left home, Jake, because I was suffering. I was unhappy, miserable, bullied, and neglected. Maggie was my younger sister, too young for me to turn to for any understanding or connection. I didn't know where to turn. The priests at our local parish made me feel wanted. They showed me compassion and could explain suffering in a way that comforted me. They offered me a chance for fast change, from disquiet to peace.

"When I read Maggie's letter years later, I had begun to question what I'd done, to regret leaving, and to feel the dread of having made a terrible mistake. That letter stirred something primitive in me. Maggie didn't offer me an answer to my melancholia or shame. She roused me to what I had left, my only family, and that was her. It all became real. Maggie gave me a gift that I intend to take with me, even though I've lost the chance to have her in my life."

Jake got up to go again. This was a family affair, and he was not a member of that family. He had been a friend, an admirer, but not family. He had feelings to share, but he did not need to condemn. "Look, I cared about Maggie. Your family separation upset her, and now she's dead, so now I'm upset. It's not my place to tell you how to feel or act, and I'm glad you two were finally able to connect, but I feel like she deserved better. Maybe both of you did."

He left, and Rupert noticed other diners watching him. People obviously had overheard parts of their conversation. He smiled at them, and everyone quickly looked away.

Rupert paid the bill, using money Jake had left to cover his share, and left the restaurant. Out on the sidewalk, he looked around but didn't recognize a thing. He turned left and walked to the corner. Nothing looked familiar, so he went to the opposite corner. He decided he better return to the restaurant.

The maître d' could see Rupert was in some distress. "I'll be right back after I seat these people."

Rupert sat down and tried to think of ways to calm himself. He could feel himself sweating.

The maître d' finally returned and asked Rupert if he could help.

"I can't remember how to get back to where I'm staying."

"Do you have an address?"

Suddenly, Rupert felt challenged, and old feelings of inadequacy came back.

"I only thought that with the address I could call a taxi for you. But if you don't have that, what do you remember?"

That made Rupert angry. "Of course, I know the address. Do you think I'm an idiot or something? Jeez . . ."

"Okay, what is it? I'll call a taxi."

Rupert took a deep breath and gave him the address. The taxi was called, and soon Rupert was back at Maggie's place.

He could feel himself teetering on the edge of something, an abyss, a wall, some dark tunnel? What? The comfort he had begun to feel before was gone. *I should get out of here. This is not my home, not my place. I want my own space. This is Maggie's place, her things in her order, designed by her and holding her essence, her spirit, her ghost.*

When Rupert's phone rang, he bounced straight up, frightened by the sudden intrusion. "Now where's my phone?"

It rang and rang.

"Don't hang up. I'm here." He finally located it on the dining room table and answered, Hello."

Theresa told him she'd have to stay at the office until evening, but she'd stop by on her way home.

Rupert told her he had decided to move to a hotel for the rest of his visit. If needed, she could reach him on his cell phone.

"Okay, Rupert, if that's what you want." -

"I'll stay in San Francisco until after the memorial service, so please let me know when and where to come for that."

"Okay."

They hung up, and Rupert got up to pack. He called for a taxi and asked to be taken to the nearest La Quinta Inn and Suites. He knew these generally had less expensive rates, and at least in Canada, they had many locations. The one he was taken to was actually not too far away, so close, in fact, he thought he could walk back to Maggie's if he had to.

Rupert settled into his new place and turned on the TV to find only mindless fare, which soon put him to sleep. It was nearly seven at night when he awoke. He got some dinner in a nearby diner and went to bed early. No one called him.

Chapter 61

Sylvia had no teaching or meeting obligations on Friday, so she decided to call Rupert. When she did, his phone went to message. "It's me, Sylvia, just checking in. Call me when you have time." She figured he had a lot to do, probably planning a memorial service and maybe other things that had come up since Maggie died.

The truth was Rupert just didn't feel like answering his phone when she called. He didn't feel ready to talk with anyone right then. Out on a long walk, he was thinking a lot about things Jake had said. "Show some remorse," he'd said. Rupert knew he hadn't yet. He'd genuinely felt sad after Maggie died, but he had not felt any remorse, no deep sorrow or anguish about having left her so many years before. *Maybe that was wrong*, he thought, but she'd neglected him too right up until the end of her life. She did reach out, though, whereas he had done nothing.

If he hadn't received that letter, would he now be thinking about her? Probably not. So, he was culpable of continuous neglect and disregard, repeating an old family pattern. *I wiped Maggie from my history. What in heaven's name have I done?* A cold chill ran through him. He shivered, even as he walked in the warm sun. "How can I be cold? This is San Francisco, not northern Canada after all."

I didn't actually kill her by wiping her from my life, he thought. *She just died alone. And being alone was her choice.*

Sitting on a bench, Rupert found the thoughts and condemnations continued to plague his mind, especially the words *wiped her from your history*. Those really were the ones that weighed him down now. How could he, especially as a priest, have done that? But the Father Rupert part of his life was a fake, created to take him away from himself and his own life. He had only wanted something better, which he now knew he'd never found. In rewriting his life, he had written out Maggie. If he wasn't going to exist, neither could she.

Soon his head fell into his hands, and he began to sob.

An elderly man with white hair and a beard, came close enough to ask Rupert if he needed help. He got no response. Rupert didn't even hear him. So he moved on.

A bit later, a young woman came closer, leaned down and asked if he was all right.

This time, Rupert heard, and even though he didn't respond at first, he did sit up enough to see who was talking.

The woman saw this and again asked if he would like her to get help.

"No, but thanks anyway."

Rupert thought he did actually need help, but who or what could give him what he needed? Nothing came to him, but as he stood and prepared to go back to his hotel, he saw a steeple, a church phallus penetrating the sky. And it wasn't very far away. That's where he wanted to go. And not just to go to church; he wanted to go to confession as a penitent, as a repentant.

As Rupert went in search of the church under that steeple, he hoped someone was manning the confession booth. Addled and achy, he pressed on, but as he got closer, he began to wonder what he would say. Would he ask for forgiveness, or did he just want someone to absolve him for what he thought certainly must be a sin?

Finally, he arrived and began to climb the many stairs leading to the front door. Breathing got harder, his legs got heavier, and he felt dizzy. *Guess I should have spent more time in the church gym.* Rupert had to sit down. He wondered if he was going to faint as he'd done before. That made him imagine a headline in tomorrow's *Chronicle*: "Man Dies on Way into Church!" He had to smile at that but then thought, *How melodramatic, Rupert.*

He decided to sit there a little longer but must have dozed off. When he opened his eyes, he saw an elderly man staring down at him.

"I been watching you for a while, and you look to be a man in trouble, maybe with life. After all, you sat down while climbing the steps to heaven."

"Is that what you call this church behind me? I've spent some time in a place like that, and believe me, it ain't heaven. Not that I'm any expert, mind you, but when I went in a church, all I heard were promises, promises, promises, none of which went anywhere, for me."

"Bad experience, huh?"

"I have no idea who you are or why you're playing the Good Samaritan, but I doubt you want to hear my story, which, by the way, I've entitled 'How Rupert Annihilated a Family.' Everyone dies."

"Are you the Rupert in that story?"

"That's right."

"Well, correct me if I'm wrong, but you don't look dead to me."

"It's a metaphor."

"A what? Never heard of it. To me you're either dead or you're not."

Rupert laughed realizing he'd been exposed trying to hide in his words. He tried again. "How about if I said, I've given the world only a paper image of myself?"

"Like a paper tiger? Threatening to look at but really impotent."

"Well, you're close. No one would have seen me as threatening. Impotent, for sure. More paper than tiger."

"You've lost me."

Rupert suddenly felt hot, exposed, and rattled. This stranger had, with just a few words, revealed how he had buried himself in a way of thinking. No wonder he'd become such an awkward and lost participant in real life. He looked at this man and smiled. "What's your name? You know mine."

"Marvin. What did you hope to find in that church behind us?"

"Confession. I wanted to go to confession, to confess what I've done to myself and my family. But . . . confession is not what I really need." Rupert stood up, a look of anguish on his face.

"Hey, man, you look like you want to kill something or maybe be killed by someone."

"No, no, I don't. I can't kill what never was. I keep coming back to this place, a church, for something I always had. And my sister recognized that when she reached out to me. She was reaching out to her brother, not a piece of paper, not an impotent nobody. No, she wanted me, her older and dumber brother who felt bullied, neglected, and worthless. I thought those priests of my childhood could save me, make me into something worthy, and turns out I already was somebody worthwhile. Did they know that?" Rupert sat back down and sighed. "If I wanted to kill anyone, it'd be those guys." But he knew they weren't to blame.

"Just a reminder, those guys, your targets, are long gone. You look kind of ancient to me, and this all happened to you as a kid?"

"I don't know if they're dead or alive. I've been too busy chasing dreams."

"Well, I don't understand much of what you been through, man, but I got to go. Don't do anything weird."

"I won't. Trust me, I've already done the weird part."

Marvin walked away and turned a corner, out of Rupert's view.

Tears dripped down Rupert's cheeks. He felt he was finally breaking up, breaking the cement cage he'd constructed for himself. He stood up. Marvin was gone. As Rupert walked back down the steps, he wondered about the name, *Marvin*. Sounds a little like Merlin, and wasn't that the name of the enchanter in the stories of King Arthur? *Come on, Rupert, don't get carried away.* He reached the bottom of the steps, turned around, and took a long look at the church. "Goodbye." He wondered, but maybe he was finally done with the Church.

He still, however, had things to say to Maggie. "Oh, Maggie, can you hear me?" he said softly. "I hope so. First, I miss you, which might sound funny since I spent so many years away. What a fool I was, how selfish of me. I was so wrapped up in my own needs that I neglected all else, you, Mom, Dad, my family. It was you who first expressed the truth that we were a family. You reached out to me when you were most vulnerable. And I heard it. I came, and for that I am truly thankful. Why? I don't know that I can answer that yet without getting lost in my words, but I did show up, and that's what matters. In fact, figuring out why just seems irrelevant anyway. Maybe it always is. The why we do things only distracts from what we end up doing. Right?"

He waited for her to speak but there was only silence.

"Now you are gone, Mom and Dad are gone, and I am getting closer to my own end. My regrets are many, my loss is great, but you will remain with me for whatever number of days I have left. How this will all work out for me, I have no idea, but I know I am more ready for whatever comes. I'm truly sorry for all the years I stayed away but feel thankful for how I finally got in a visit." He stopped, not wanting to get too maudlin or too flamboyant. He'd said his piece.

Rupert looked around. Plenty of people were passing by, but none looked his way, which surprised and relieved him. He smiled and turned toward the church one more time. It was so big, so beautiful, so imposing, but now he could see it as something beautiful to look at, to visually enjoy, and to visit like any tourist.

It may take me some time to get used to my new way of thinking, Rupert mused, *but I will,* and he walked away toward his hotel.

CHAPTER 62

IT WAS AFTER FIVE O'CLOCK WHEN RUPERT GOT BACK TO HIS ROOM. He was exhausted and immediately fell asleep in a chair, waking only when his phone rang. It was Theresa.

She, together with Maggie's secretary from work, had planned a memorial service. They'd set it for the middle of next week, hoping he would stay in San Francisco long enough to attend. She also asked if he'd make a few comments.

"What kind of service or program have you planned?"

"A memorial service, not a funeral. We want to celebrate her life, for people to share how they knew her and anything about what she meant to them. You're her only living relative, so we all thought it would be great if you would say something. We will conclude things with an informal social and refreshments. It won't be a big crowd, so we decided to hold it in Maggie's living room. You've been there, so you know it's quite large with plenty of space for extra chairs."

"Okay, Theresa. Thanks for calling. Let me think about whether I want to say anything, and I'll get back to you later."

"The sooner, the better, Rupert."

"Okay."

After hanging up, he called Sylvia to tell her the plan.

She answered immediately. "Rupert, I hoped you'd call. I can't imagine what you must be going through down there. How are you holding up under all the stress?"

Rupert liked her using the word *stress*. He wouldn't have thought to use it himself. "It's been hard, but I'm getting through it all. The big decision I've made while here is that my life as a priest is over. I'm ready to stop using the Church for protection, a hideaway from the storm, the asylum I entered when I left home. Watch out!"

"What does that mean?"

"Oh, just one of my nightmares, that the monster that lurks within me is about to be unleashed."

"Monster? That's not what I saw when I met you in Powell River. To me you appeared as less the monster and more the unschooled, innocent cherub. It was your life story that turned me on, Rupert. I am a writer, you know!"

"Well, more yet to come, Sylvia. That's what excites me. You may have met only the cherub, but there's more that even I don't yet know fully, like maybe an erotic romantic is concealed somewhere in there."

"I think I can handle that. Remember, I'm younger than you."

"Well, we'll find out soon. But right now, I just called to update you. I plan to stay here, in a hotel by the way, through next Wednesday, the day Maggie's friends and associates have planned a memorial service. Sometime after that, I plan to return to Vancouver to see you. That's as far as my current plan goes. I don't have any reason to go back to Powell River since I will really have no place to live."

"What about your house there? You had such a pretty location."

"Well, that house belongs to the Catholic diocese, not to me. Since I'm leaving the priesthood, I won't be allowed to stay there, and besides, I want my own place."

"Oh, okay. Well, you're more than welcome to stay with me until you find a place. Or you could live here with me!"

"Thanks, Sylvia. I'll pay rent, unless you plan to charge city rates, which I probably can't afford."

"I hadn't thought that far ahead. Maybe you can sell me your story, and I'll write a book."

They both laughed.

"You probably were only joking, but in the face of so much that's new, I'm having difficulty sorting it all out. You were joking, weren't you?"

"Not really. But I know I shocked you, and believe it or not, I shocked myself. Usually I'm more discreet, filtering my comments to fit the situation. That one didn't really fit, but I can tell you the idea wouldn't be as bizarre as it sounds."

"Stop. I don't want to go there. You're right; it's not the right time or place for that talk."

"Sure, Rupert. You know what's best for you."

"Thanks. I think my self-confidence just jumped a few points!"

"Hopefully that'll help you navigate the memorial service, Rupert. I suspect your family ordeal will have a few more surprises and challenges before you're done."

"Thanks, Sylvia. But I better hang up for now. I feel pretty exhausted— maybe feeling my age. How much personal remodeling can an old man take? I'll call you again later. Bye."

"Bye, Rupert. I'll wait to hear from you."

"Hope I didn't give you too big of another shock, but I thought it was the right time to let you know how much I think of you. Maybe knowing that you have that effect on people will inspire you and help you as you face new challenges."

"Well . . . thanks. I think. Right now, the shock precludes any cogent thoughts. Bye, for now." Sylvia held the phone to her ear for a while after Rupert had gone. She wanted to hang up but couldn't. In letting him know how she felt about him, she just might have overwhelmed him. *Why do I wear my emotions on my sleeve like that?* she thought. *What makes my emotions jump out of control so quickly? I hope I haven't scared him away.* She put down the telephone.

CHAPTER 64

RUPERT SPENT THE WEEKEND EXPLORING San Francisco and Oakland. He rode the bus to a couple of places, but he mostly walked, a trekker without destination. On Sunday it was foggy, his first encounter with San Francisco fog since arriving. Even though he couldn't see much as he walked, it felt more like the Northwest. Droplets of water fell on him from tree limbs hanging over his route, and the familiar dampness left him feeling chilled.

Mostly he thought about Maggie. This was her town, and from all he'd heard, she'd made quite a name for herself here. If she felt lonely, no one knew about it. Maybe no one ever knew what she was really feeling. Maybe not even her. How much, he thought, sister and brother were alike.

He, however, would have more time to change, and he thought, *I'll just do the best I can.* Old illusions like the one that had given him hope from childhood that complete harmony and serenity were there for those who lived . . . Here he stopped, unable to remember the words he'd used to describe how he had to live. He assumed he'd heard them first from those two Catholic priests, but the specifics were already fading, being replaced by something he was still composing. Life is an endeavor to stay afloat that, as any swimmer knows, you must come to accept and possess, or you drown.

Rupert sighed, walked to a bench he saw nearby, and sitting down, said "More will be revealed!"

He had to smile as he thought how Sylvia would be curious about all this. He remembered her saying she'd been attracted to him for the way he seemed "unschooled and innocent," and she was right in her assessment, though he would have probably added the words *naïve, blind, and selfish. Little does she know how consumed I was by what I saw as personal injury, my trauma, my childhood wounds. Two priests gave me hope, introduced me to a dream. That shifted for me when I finally reached the point of no hope.*

Rupert's eyes closed, and a tear ran down his cheek, not from any sadness this time. It didn't make sense to him, but he was tearing up from excitement, a rising passion that made him have to get up and move. The fog had started to lift. He got up, stretched, and started to walk.

Passing a local library, he decided to enter. As far as he could recall, he'd only been in his school's library, never in a public library. What would he do when he got inside?

A librarian sat at the table near where he entered. She was busily talking to someone, so he decided he'd just look around. He saw lots of books, all classified with labels like mystery, science fiction, literature, and computer science. He decided to browse the literature section. Rupert saw interesting titles but didn't remove any books. One title, *The Handmaid's Tale*, tempted him because of the author, Margaret Atwood. But he left it in place.

After a while, a librarian approached and asked him what he might be looking for and if she could help.

Surprised, Rupert said, "Oh, nothing in particular. Just looking at your collection."

Okay, I'll be at the front desk if you need assistance."

Rupert smiled and thought, *I should leave,* but as he headed for the door, he had an idea. Maggie Callaway. Who was she? He went to the woman at the desk and asked if they had any books by or about a Maggie Callaway in San Francisco.

"I'll check."

After a moment at her computer she said, "Yes, several articles." She printed a list of magazine articles and showed him how to look them up on the computer.

The first was entitled, "Maggie Callaway—A leader of Woman in Business" in the *Economist*, and the second, "Woman Pushes City Council on Waterfront Development," an editorial in the *San Francisco Chronicle*. Finding the second, Rupert read:

> The mayor has appointed Maggie Callaway, CEO of International Asian Pacific Shipping Company, to advise officials on the new and costly renovations planned for the port area. Callaway will work for the next two months developing a plan for consideration by the counsel. Labor unions and environmentalists have reacted strongly against the appointment. According to John Peterman, president of the International Longshore and Warehouse Union, Local 10, "Ms. Callaway has a reputation for strong-arming the community and even her employees and will look at only business interests in her proposal."

Rupert checked the date of the paper, June 5, 2005, and wondered how this had ended. "I guess you left bodies all over the city, Maggie."

"Shh."

He'd had enough of the library so headed back to his hotel. The walking felt good. He thought maybe he'd walked four or five miles already. Rupert was now in a park he had no memory of passing before. Not real concerned but tired since he'd wandered randomly all day, he decided to ask for directions. There were runners and walkers everywhere. He stopped one as she passed. "Could you direct me to the La Quinta Inn?"

She gave him directions using lefts, rights, and straight-ahead suggestions.

Rupert thanked her but knew he'd never be able to follow her directions, or even remember them. He wondered what to do next. Given his limited knowledge of how to use Lyft or Uber, he hailed a taxi.

The ride lasted about ten minutes. It would have been a long walk.

As he exited the cab, he thanked the driver. "Regardless of what you read these days, you cabbies still perform an essential service."

The driver smiled. "Thanks. Tell your friends. Spread the good word."

By the time Rupert arrived back in his room, the exhaustion had caught up with him. He flopped onto the bed and within minutes fell into a deep sleep.

Rupert was awakened by a knock on the door. Getting up and opening the door, he saw a young man and woman.

The man held what looked like a TV camera. "Hi, I'm Alex, and this is Jen from KPIX 5 here in San Francisco. We're sorry to disturb you, but we've been interviewing people about the death of Maggie Callaway and heard you are her only surviving family member."

"Who told you about me?"

"Several people in the office at International Asian Pacific Shipping Company."

"Oh, I didn't know I was so popular."

"Can we come in for a minute?"

Rupert didn't know what to say. First of all, he'd just been awakened from a deep sleep, but more importantly, this was so far out of his experience he had no words . . . but one: "No."

"We'll only take a few minutes of your time, Reverend Callaway. Your sister's passing is big news. She was head of a company that employed hundreds of people in the San Francisco area, and she often made headlines as she did much to enlarge our port area and bring business here, especially from China. Your being family could add a lot to our story of her life."

Calling him *reverend* woke Rupert up. "Not only can't you come in, but stop calling me *reverend*."

"Sorry, my mistake, but if you want us to represent you fairly, let us do a short interview."

This last argument made sense to Rupert, but he still didn't want them staying long. "Okay, but make it quick. I haven't had anything to eat and I'm hungry."

After entering, Jen set up her camera while Alex stood by, holding the microphone.

Rupert thought he might throw up. His nervousness had never been so high. He realized he couldn't do this and didn't want to be any part of it. "Okay, wait a minute. I can't do this. You have to leave."

They stared at him and each other.

"You invited us into your room," Alex said.

"And now I'm disinviting you. Out." Rupert walked to the door and opened it.

As Jen walked by him at the door, she said, "You're a lot like your sister. Maybe we'll report that."

Rupert knew she was referring to Maggie's reputation as a merciless and demanding CEO. "Go ahead. It would make me proud to be like her." He smiled at them as they sheepishly walked out.

Now Rupert was wide awake, but he still felt exhausted. He picked up the only book he could find in his room, the Bible. He opened it to Genesis, an account of creation. Of course, he'd read it before and knew it included stories of condemnation and redemption, pride, ancestral history, and faith, among much else. It was, after all, the Judeo-Christian story of creation, and he knew it would help him get back to sleep. It soon did just that.

CHAPTER 65

THE NEXT DAY, AFTER RUPERT HAD DINNER IN A SMALL BISTRO, he walked back to the hotel. He could still feel his heart beating, probably faster than it should. *I hope I survive all this,* Rupert thought. *If I don't, okay, but if I do, I get to see what happens next. Some people have their kids to live for or maybe something still on their bucket list. I have only the mystery of an unknown future.* A little chill went up his spine. *I hope I'm up to this.*

Rupert sat down at the desk, thinking he might try to record some of his experiences. He'd never done that before, probably because nothing that happened before this enlivened or inspired him. This felt like his first big adventure. He pulled out the hotel pen from the desk drawer and put it to the paper. It didn't move. Thoughts passed through his mind so fast he couldn't capture them. He tried putting down words, *San Francisco, sex, family, Church, eating,* but one word just followed another until he wrote *death.* That stopped him long enough to write, "still scares the bejesus out of me."

He thought about all his years in the Church where the only comfort it could offer was that Jesus died for us and now we get to escape death and go to heaven. That didn't comfort him. He'd come to believe that escaping death was tantamount to escaping life, and he'd already spent too many years trying to do that.

Next he wrote "death = terror. Life = terror." He put the pen down, sat back in the chair, feeling its hard back and sharp edges, shut his eyes, and stopped trying to control his thoughts. With compassion for himself, he let it all flow through him. It wasn't easy. Different thoughts generated different feelings, and some of those feelings alarmed, troubled, and frightened him.

Rupert must have dozed off because the next thing he knew he awoke with chest pain. He wrapped both arms around himself and squeezed, which made him feel somewhat better. *Am I going to have a heart attack now and die right after Maggie?* Thinking that made him more afraid, and he began to sweat. *Shit, isn't sweating part of the heart-attack thing?* He wondered if he was dying. His body filled with fear. It grew stronger to a point where he thought he might explode. He didn't, and he didn't die either. His pain subsided slowly, leaving him sitting at his desk with sweat-soaked clothes and amazed he had not died.

Sitting up, Rupert looked at the bedstand clock. It was 9:36 a.m., Tuesday. All he could think about was how scared he'd been about dying. *That alone should have killed me,* he thought. *But it didn't. It didn't even leave me wounded, as far as I can tell.* He got up and checked himself all over. Nothing. He took off all his clothes, looked in a full-length mirror for something, any indication of what happened. Nothing. The dried sweat, however, made him look like someone had dumped him in a vat of salt. He just couldn't believe he hadn't died. Rupert laughed, thinking about how often he thought he would die after masturbation. That's what he'd been told would happen.

He started to shiver and felt cold, so he turned on the shower, setting it very hot. Then he turned on the radio, jumped in, and started to sing. He didn't really know any songs but recognized one they said was by Cat Stevens. *Wonder if that's a man or woman. Who cares?* he thought, and then did the best he could to sing along.

Morning has broken like the first morning
Blackbird has spoken like the first bird
Praise for the singing, praise for the morning
Praise for them springing fresh from the world

Rupert sang along, getting louder as the song went on. "Move over Cat Stevens. You ain't got nothin' on me!"

Opening his suitcase to dress, Rupert saw his few dark clothes. "Where's the color?" He'd change this as soon as he could. For now, he'd have to be satisfied with black pants and a white shirt. He checked the clock again and saw that it was now eleven thirty, still the day before he'd have his last chance to say goodbye to Maggie.

A loud knock on the door made him jump. He looked toward the door, but before opening it, he ran to the nearest mirror to make sure he'd finished dressing. Then he opened the door and saw a hotel maid who asked if she could clean his room. "Oh, sorry, I didn't realize it was so late. Wait there." He left the door ajar while he grabbed a sweater.

As he left, he said, "Off for a much-needed morning coffee. Thanks for all you do." Rupert had a spring in his step and a big smile on his face.

The maid shook her head and smiled back.

"Yes, I'm going mad," he said and danced on down the hall toward the elevator.

He went directly to the lounge and ordered coffee and a blueberry muffin. Not much but enough. The big TV was on, but he had no interest in any talk show or news. The place was mostly empty. *Guess most people in a city hotel like this eat at a more normal breakfast hour,* he thought. He ate slowly, and when done, he went back to his room to compose notes for what he might say tomorrow.

CHAPTER 66

BY THE TIME RUPERT GOT TO MAGGIE'S PLACE on Wednesday, there were already fourteen people in the living room. Theresa introduced him to some of those from work, including board members and Maggie's personal secretary. Each expressed his or her condolences, and the board members were effusive in their praise of Maggie's contribution to the company.

The secretary told him, "Maggie was sometimes the bane of my life, and yet, under her tutelage, I learned so much, and more importantly, I became a much stronger woman."

Rupert moved to the kitchen where he left his sweater on the pile already there. He didn't return to the living room right away. He was a little nervous about meeting all these people who knew Maggie and about giving a talk in front of them. The quiet of the kitchen comforted him. It didn't last long, however. Soon Maggie's housekeeper came in hoping to find a quiet place.

"Hello, Fa—I mean Rupert."

"Hello, Maria."

She started to cry and fled from the room.

Then Theresa came in. "Oh, Rupert, there you are. People are looking for you, one in particular."

"Who's that?"

"Come and see."

She led him out, and standing there was her son, Alex.

"Hi, Alex. Good to see you again."

"Hi. You nervous?"

"Alex, be polite."

"It's quite all right. I've come to appreciate Alex's candidness." Rupert smiled. "Yes, I am a little nervous. I want these people to like me, and I want to represent my true feelings about Maggie. But I think I'm ready for whatever comes."

"Great. Feeling courageous?"

"How do you young people say it? Right on?"

"That's kind of old school, Rupert. Really old school." Alex reached out and tapped Rupert on the shoulder. "But you're a little old, I guess."

They both laughed.

"Thanks, Alex."

Rupert moved through the growing crowd. All the chairs were taken now, and the room looked close to full.

"Hello, Rupert." Jake was standing on the edge of the crowd.

Rupert reached out to shake hands and Jake took it.

"Hi," Rupert said. "Guess no one expected this kind of turnout."

"No. I guess not, but given the effect Maggie had on me after just one meeting, I'm not really surprised."

"Well, I am. If I felt nervous before, now I'm trying not to lose it. Got to keep my stress level down. Last night I got so stressed I thought I was having a heart attack. False alarm but . . ."

"Wow! You look all right, but maybe you should get yourself checked over when you get home."

That thought had not occurred to Rupert. "That's probably a good idea. I think I just might do that. Thanks, Jake." He moved on to see if he could locate Theresa.

Maggie's ashes had been put in a beautiful hand-carved urn and placed on a table next to the lectern where, Rupert guessed, people would stand while they expressed their thoughts and gave testimonials. He wondered who else had been asked to speak. He certainly never expected to be asked, especially after Jake had taken him to task.

Rupert saw Theresa standing at the lectern looking at her watch, and he walked over.

"Guess we should begin," Theresa said. "It looks like we may not get everyone in anyway. Pleasant surprise, isn't it?"

"Whatever. You're in charge. Where should I sit?"

"Well, I'd say near here, but there are no chairs left, so I guess you'll have to stand nearby."

"Okay."

Theresa raised her voice to address the crowd. "Hello, everyone and welcome to Maggie Callaway's memorial. Sorry we don't have enough chairs. Maggie would be aghast. I can hear her now, 'What moron planned this event, anyway?' At the same time, I think Maggie would be pleasantly surprised that so many wanted to remember her. She deserved this, and I'm glad it happened. We have planned for some people to say a few words and then to open it up for everyone. I will start, as I guess I already have."

Everyone laughed.

"Next will be the board president and Maggie's brother." Theresa began her prepared remarks with how she'd met Maggie. "I walked into the conference hall on the second floor and saw this woman, young then, dressed in a longish skirt and a pure white blouse, scanning books in the bookcase. No one else was around, so I went over and introduced myself. She said hello, and then proceeded to ask me why we have books in our conference area. 'Isn't this a place for conferences and dialogue?' she asked. 'Yes,' I told her, 'but we thought it would look good to have books here for decoration.' She stared at me for a moment and said, 'Really!' No more was needed, and those bookshelves disappeared within a week."

People in the crowd snickered. They had all experienced Maggie's bluntness.

"Well, that was the beginning, and though her style was often hard to take, Maggie was right in almost everything she said and did here. I don't think she came here to be liked, but I, for one, grew to not only appreciate Maggie but also see her as a friend who cared about me and this company. I will miss her and will hold her in my memory for the rest of my life."

Michael Chen, the board president, stood next to speak. "I know people in my position are often accused of being long-winded and boring, but don't worry. I have only a few things to say about my time with Maggie, and I'll try to say them mostly as she would have liked. This first part would have embarrassed her, but Maggie was an accomplished operations manager, decision-maker, and communicator. She was an excellent CEO for our company. She led us through turbulent times, as well as smooth periods with her intelligence and her artistry. And for this, we all owe her our gratitude.

"Next, and perhaps more importantly, Maggie was a woman who led us well. She was a powerful woman, who led a company as well as any man, but because she was a woman, she was disliked, even hated for her strong leadership style. I saw this prejudice even in myself.

"Maggie dismissed being liked by coworkers as unimportant, and I didn't work to change the atmosphere. She was doing her job well, and the company was growing fast, so I guess I didn't think it was very important. Well, now she's gone—I'm too late—but I am glad so many came to honor her.

"I'm really not a religious man, but just in case, Maggie, you are able to look down and see us all here, I will end with a wave goodbye and thanks. Now everyone who would like, raise a hand and wave—your own goodbye and thanks."

The waves turned into an applause. Then Theresa stood to introduce Rupert but didn't see him. "Rupert? Rupert? Rupert are you still here?"

"Oh, yes, I am here, but I need a moment, please."

The room became very quiet. Children stopped coughing and talking; noise in the hallway quieted down.

Finally, Rupert walked to the podium and took the microphone. "Sorry, but I didn't really want to get up. No one here really knows me, not even those whom I've met since coming here. Hell—oops, excuse my language. That just slipped out, as is much in my life right now. Mr. Chen spoke about how he'd been helped and influenced by my sister, Maggie Callaway. What could I add to that? He, at least, had a life with her. I did not.

"Family? What's that? I was an older brother. What's that supposed to mean? That I loved and mentored my little sister, that I supported and admired her accomplishments? The rest is determined by context, and mine, and thereby Maggie's, was being born to Irish immigrants determined to survive. She and I were the baggage they dragged along with them. In their determination to survive, their children were not a priority. We were expected to take care of ourselves. We were emotionally wounded and starved for affection and care. I don't say that to blame. They did their best, but as with all of us, our best is not always the best. Circumstances and personality sometimes get in the way.

"Maggie used her natural intelligence to become successful, but I think she, like me, was always wanting something her intelligence and my piety would never provide. She was a successful woman in a man's world, but she was also my little sister who, in the end, taught me the importance of a sister to the life and happiness of the one born first.

"After decades of separation, she invited me to meet, and after much dithering and self-reflection, I came—luckily for me. In my short time here, I got to know her as the creative energy that made a company great while also damaging many people. I also got to know her as the tender, kind, and earnest woman she held hidden underneath her exterior bluster. It appears that most of you here also never experienced this sensitive, thoughtful Maggie until the end of her life. I guess we Callaways save the best of ourselves until the last act of the play!

"I've reflected on the parental neglect that marked Maggie and me and felt deep anger. Was it the mark of neglect that left both of us so insecure and wounded? Maybe. It was, however, not the neglect of the past I should have been so concerned with. I continued to neglect Maggie. But in the end, I found, and I hope Maggie did too, that we were healed from all that by its opposite—personal regard, respect, and the ability to see each other. I think Maggie lived her life as best she could, but she finished her life in full bloom and with flourish."

Rupert stopped but didn't sit down.

"I'll draw this to a close with a quote from Lao Tzu, you know, the great Catholic savant!" He stopped, looked at the crowd, and laughed. "Anyway, the quote goes, 'Being deeply loved by someone gives you strength, while loving someone deeply gives you courage.' That's for me to always remember. Goodbye, folks, and goodbye, Maggie. Rest in peace. God knows you deserve it."

Rupert walked into the crowd. A few people were crying softly. Rupert was one of them.

Theresa finally walked to the podium and carried on with the program. First, she asked if anyone wanted to say anything about their experiences with Maggie. Several hands went up. Most just wanted to thank Maggie for what she brought to the company and to them. Rupert had to smile when one person added, "First impressions aren't always the ones that will last."

When everyone had spoken, Theresa simply said goodbye and joked, "See you at the office. Now, for those who can stay, we have some snacks and wine, though I must say we never planned for so many of you to come, so sorry if we run out. But stick around, if you can, and enjoy each other's company and Maggie's memory."

Rupert had found a place to stand near the kitchen. Too anxious to eat and not wanting to drink anything after the distress he'd felt before, he decided to move to a chair out of the crowd and just listen to what people were saying. Maggie had been tough on most of these people at times, but some obviously felt moved by her, maybe by what she'd said to them at one time or by the model she set for how to do a good job. *Life is so strange, complex, and varied*, he thought. A few people passed by him and offered condolences and thanks. After a while, he was tired and got up to go.

As he headed for the door, Theresa came to him, shook his hand, and said, "Thanks for coming, Rupert. I know how important it was for Maggie. Are you staying in San Francisco after this?"

"My plans at this point remain liquid. Why?"

"Well, I hope you can come to the reading of Maggie's will on Friday. I'm sure she'll say what she wants done with her things and hopefully tell us what to do with her ashes. I have no idea. She had a private lawyer help her with this."

"I think I met her briefly here at the house," Rupert said. "She dropped by one evening to get a signature, probably on this will. I'll stay. Give me the address and time."

"Great." Theresa handed him a paper with the information he needed.

Rupert continued to head for the exit, but before he could get out, Jake approached him.

"I appreciated your words, Rupert. No preaching, just your honest thoughts and feelings. I especially liked how you equated the effect Maggie had had on you with her vulnerability. I felt that too and had a hard time putting that together with her strong penchant for controlling and alienating those she met, including me."

Rupert said nothing.

"Can I give you a ride?"

"No thanks, Jake. It's still quite pleasant outside, and I feel like a good walk."

Rupert left and got on an empty elevator. As he left the building, he turned to look at the door he'd first entered full of dread, not knowing what to expect from himself or Maggie. The thought he had next surprised him. He remembered the singer, Jimmy Durante, and how he ended his TV show with the words, "Good night, Mrs. Calabash, wherever you are." Rupert had no idea who it referred to but had always remembered it for the sadness that came up in him whenever he heard it.

"Good night, Maggie Callaway, wherever you are."

Then Rupert turned and left.

CHAPTER 67

IT WAS ALMOST FIVE O'CLOCK WHEN RUPERT WALKED through the front door of his hotel. He didn't feel like going to his room, so he went to the bar. Although neither hungry nor thirsty, he'd heard music and wanted to go listen. He sat at the bar, ordered a beer, and asked the bartender if he knew the band.

"No. I don't even know their name. On Wednesday nights, we give time to local bands to show off their repertoire. This one does oldies."

"My kind of music," Rupert said. "Oldies for oldies!"

The band played well, but Rupert had to admit most of their songs were unfamiliar to him. Then they played something he knew.

If you're going to San Francisco
Be sure to wear some flowers in your hair
If you're going to San Francisco
You're gonna meet some gentle people there

Rupert sang along, smiling, though he still held a pretty narrow perspective on the city. Would he now get more acquainted, learn why it seemed to generate such affection and pathos? No, he thought of it as Maggie's city. San Francisco was where his sister had made her life, forced her way into his consciousness, and drawn him out of his ghostly existence.

He ordered another beer, some guacamole and chips. While the music played in the background, he sat on his stool and thought about his experiences in his sister's city. After an hour, Rupert left for the elevator to his room, thinking it was time for him to go. It felt urgent. As sure as he'd felt about needing to come to San Francisco, he now felt as sure about leaving.

At the elevator, he joined the waiting crowd. When the elevator doors opened, no one moved. He was waiting for the women around him to get on first, something he'd done his whole life, while everyone else waited for him, their elder, to enter. Finally, he did and suddenly felt old. He had been spending so much time thinking about his life reborn; now he wondered how much time he had left. Rupert remembered he'd just had something like a heart attack and he'd nearly fainted at the airport after landing in San Francisco. *I can't die now*, he thought. *I finally have too much to live for.*

Back in his room, Rupert decided to call Father Brown just because he had to talk to someone. He knew it was late, but he called anyway.

"Hello, Father Brown speaking."

"Hello, it's Rupert."

"Rupert, you're the last person I expected to hear from tonight. What a welcome surprise. I've thought of you many times over the last week or so and wondered what happened when you visited your sister, or even if you did."

"I did indeed see her, just before she passed away."

"Oh dear, I'm so sorry. How are you? Are you coming back to Powell River?"

"I feel like I am recovering from my years of hiding in the Church behind the collar, and no, I have no plans to return to Powell River. The house there belongs to the Church, and when I leave the priesthood, I'm sure it'll want it back."

"Knowing the Church as I do, you're probably right. So why did you call, Rupert?"

"I just was riding in an elevator and feeling old, maybe like I might be done, like an overcooked roast. Just when I'd started to see a future, I was hit by how old I am and that I may not have much time left."

"I can't help you with your age, Rupert. You are old now, like many of us. We have to adjust, maybe try to get ready for what comes next for all of us."

Father Brown was talking about dying, but Rupert wasn't ready to talk about that. "Well, Father, I'm trying to make decisions about what I want to do while I still have life. What I know so far is that I promised Maggie's lawyer I'd meet her for the reading of Maggie's will. After that, I have nothing scheduled, a big empty space, lot of time to think."

"Big opening, heh? I'd certainly have some trepidation facing that myself if I were in your place. We Catholics try to make life a sure bet, but in reality, of course, it isn't. Big holes can become a big risk. Just remember you carry a lot more history and experience than you had as a twelve-year-old."

Rupert didn't know what to say. How could he go from a life where everything was programmed and known to one where he didn't even know what city he would end up in next?

"You still there, Rupert?"

"Yeah. Your words make sense, but words are just that, words. Meaningful but hollow, empty of experience."

"Remember when you told me about that letter your sister had sent and how violent—my word–it had felt to you? When violence happens, people die, get wounded, and fight desperately. Your struggles with your family and then the Church have left you wounded but not dead. You have, however, been left alone to carry on with whatever comes next. You don't know what it is, but since we're talking, you have started to try to figure it out. And, yes, it's dangerous, and death is an option, as it always is, but at your age, it becomes an even greater possibility. Keep struggling, Rupert, but remember that whatever strength or power you had that got you to leave Powell River and go to San Francisco is still with you. The only other big decision you made was to leave home and join the Church, though you did that only to escape your life. You left Powell River to find something you'd lost. Whatever is in you that helped you make that move is probably still in your back pocket, still with you."

"Thanks, Father. I'm glad I called, not so much for the advice but more because you confirmed something important for me as I now move on. I may be physically alone, but now there are others who will play a part in my journey."

"Call me again, Rupert, whenever, though earlier works better, especially if you want me at my finest. I'm not infirm yet but have noticed some limited thinking capacity after six p.m." He laughed.

After hanging up, Rupert felt satisfied, his mind at ease. Now he was hungry. He headed for the bistro, knowing the sandwich he'd stuffed in his pocket before leaving Maggie's wouldn't be enough. On the way back to the elevator, he chucked it in the trash.

Chapter 68

A T THE RESTAURANT, RUPERT SCANNED THE MENU. The prices startled him. He still had the Church credit card but wondered if he should stay. He did, but this incident served as a reminder that he'd soon not have the Church to support him.

The waiter approached his table. "Would you like something to drink, sir?"

"Yes, please bring me a glass of your house red." He stopped for a moment thinking, *This may be my last meal on the Church's dime,* and then added, "Wait. I've changed my mind. You can bring me one of the finer reds you're pouring by the glass."

"Okay, we have an Oregon Pinot Noir."

"That will work fine."

The waiter left and returned with his wine. Rupert lingered over it for a while and then ordered dinner. Too full for dessert, he just had coffee, sat back in his chair, and watched people sitting nearby. *This is the beginning of my new life,* he thought. *I can sit and observe life going on around me without drawing the attention I always did while wearing the priest's collar.* Anonymity, freedom and personal responsibility. Then he looked at his bill: eighty-eight dollars. "Yikes!" Rupert hadn't meant to say anything out loud and certainly not as loud as he just had. He'd drawn attention, even without his collar. Embarrassed, he quietly paid and slinked away. He'd not be able to afford a meal like that again soon, maybe ever again. Rupert would have to start living on the little savings he'd accumulated while serving the Church.

Back in his hotel room, Rupert dropped on the bed to watch the twirling fan over his head. Round and round, it went. He watched it but soon began to feel a little dizzy and got up.

He went back downstairs to where he'd seen a computer, sat down, and stared at the monitor. He had no idea how to even start the thing. *I have to try*, he thought. *Maybe the front-desk person can help.* He walked over. "Excuse me, but could you help me get started on the computer there?"

"No, I'm sorry. I'm the only one here tonight and have to stay at the desk. But I think you'll find some operating directions in the table drawer. That'll help you get started. It's really easy."

Rupert thought, *For you maybe*, but said, "Thanks."

He went back, sat down, and pulled out the directions he'd seen before but hadn't wanted to take the time to read. Then it struck him how insidious his life in the Church had been. He'd been trapped in ways he hadn't even realized, like this, expecting someone to tell him how, rather than discovering the solution for himself. In his experience, the Church feared self-determination. It could lead you down the wrong path, to sin and destruction. "Bullshit." Again, his talking to himself had drawn attention. This time it was just the night clerk, but still Rupert felt embarrassed. "Sorry, I won't do that again."

The clerk didn't respond.

Rupert quickly discovered how to turn the computer on but ended up struggling mightily to figure out how to find the internet. He kept being asked for a password, which he didn't have and still felt too chagrined to go over and ask the clerk. Finally, he found it in the directions but by then he was beginning to tire from all the effort. He'd have to look up jobs for older males some other time.

CHAPTER 69

THE NEXT DAY WAS THURSDAY, one day until the reading of the will. Rupert had said he'd stay and so he would, even though he felt more than ready to leave for somewhere.

He dragged himself out of bed around nine fifty, ten minutes before the hotel breakfast shut down. Dressing quickly, skipping any shower for now, he entered the breakfast room right at ten o'clock. Rupert got some fruit, an English muffin, scrambled eggs, and sausage plus coffee. Most of the other guests had already eaten and left, but a few remained, lingering over coffee or watching TV. He knew if he'd worn his collar, several of these folks would have said hello or "Good morning, Father," but now no one even looked his way.

After eating, Rupert headed back to his room to take a long shower. When he got there, though, he went directly to the phone and dialed Sylvia. "Hi, Sylvia. It's Rupert. I'd like to pop over and take you to bed. Interested?"

"Hello! Is this really Rupert? What happened to the depressed, lost little priest I used to know?"

"That's a mystery. But you haven't answered my question."

"Well, I don't know. Isn't a nice girl supposed to go slow, curb those wild hormones men can't control? And, besides, aren't you a thousand miles away? How could you just pop over anyway?"

"Sylvia, you still haven't answered my question."

"Okay, okay, okay. Yes."

"I have some business related to Maggie's death yet to handle here, but I should be ready to go north on Saturday."

"Great. I'm teaching a Saturday seminar that morning. If you get in early, I won't be able to jump in bed. Can you wait?"

"I'll do my best. But you know what those raging hormones do to a man."

"Well, guess we'll just have to wait and see what comes up—ha, ha—won't we? But right now, I have to run. Bye for now."

Rupert didn't hang up right away. He felt too good and didn't want to move, as though it would interrupt the moment. He smiled. *What a lascivious old letch I've become!*

He decided to take a walk and then do some reading in his room. Around four thirty, Rupert went out for a light dinner. When he returned, he turned on the TV but didn't find much of interest except the local PBS channel running an educational piece on wildlife of the Amazon. By nine thirty, he was in bed and asleep.

CHAPTER 70

SUN SHINING IN RUPERT'S ROOM WOKE HIM. He'd slept in, and there was nobody to criticize him anymore. He got up, took a shower, and made himself a cup of coffee. While it brewed, he called Theresa to find out where to go and when.

She told him and then added, "Remember, besides dealing with the will and all its intricacies, we also will address disposition of the ashes."

"Yes. I'll see you at eleven thirty."

While he waited to go to the lawyer's office, Rupert called the airline to book his flight to Vancouver. Would he stay there? Sylvia waited for him. *Do I want to live with anybody again?* He reflected on the retirement years he'd spent alone by the sea. Yes, walks to the water had really saved him, perhaps from killing himself. He could still smell and taste the salt, feel the cold water sloshing over his feet, as well as the urge he sometimes had to submerge himself in it. Then he remembered the dark house, how comforted he felt surrounded by the dark but also how lonely he'd felt there. *That was a different time, Rupert. Things have changed. You can't go back.* He knew he was right.

Theresa, Maria, and Jake had all been invited and were there when Rupert arrived. He sat down in the back.

The lawyer, Sarah Abernathy, introduced herself and opened with an introduction about what would happen. "Maggie called me last week wanting to revise her will. She said things had radically changed for her and wanted to recognize that now at the end of her days here on Earth. First, she wanted me to read you a statement.

Hello, everybody. I hope everyone could come to my final show. I want you to know you have each played a big part in my life, especially in these last few months while I waited to die. Yes, I suffered during those days but not nearly as much as I suffered throughout my life. All my days were long, and as the days never seemed to end, I thought too that my life would never end. And many days I wanted it to end.

However, that all changed after I accidentally and fortunately ran into you, Jake. After that, I started to want my life to last a long time. You awakened love inside me, Jake. You even awakened a sexual feeling that brought my body to life like never before. I now go out with a fire burning inside, not just cold dust.

Rupert, your coming down from Canada to spend time with me made my life feel complete, from whole family to no family to whole family again. I read one time that, for some people, co-workers become family. Not for me. To me, family was where I started and where I longed to be again, so much so that I sometimes had Sunday dinners at home where I'd set the table for four people and imagine everyone sitting with me talking about our work and play. Those dinners would last for hours with me talking and talking but never laughing, until you, Rupert, showed up at the end. The emotion I felt and saw in you restored me. I hope to die with you nearby.

Maria, we never said goodbye, at least not formally. But we never formally said hello when we first met either. You and I had one of my few, maybe my only, informal bonds. With you, I felt free to show my down and dirty side. And believe me, I wouldn't have survived the life I had without that. You accepted me just as a woman. You may not have even known my title, and believe it or not, that helped. I wish I could have been more in touch with myself as a woman. Mostly I lived life as a male—compet-itive, ambitious, aggressive. People around me became rivals or instruments to use, and I have left a trail of human debris in my wake because of this. Thank you for accepting me as I was.

I can't say enough positive things about you, Theresa. You helped me keep good boundaries, protected me from those who sought to hurt me or the company, and saved me when I failed to heed your advice. And in the last years when I became less of a machine, I think we became friends. In one of our last talks regarding Rupert's visit, you even called me *friend*. For me, that word had always been meaningless, way too touchy-feely, until I started to get sick. So, though I may not have used the word *friend* much, it was there—on the tip of my tongue!

Now I am gone, to where I have no idea, though I guess by now I have found out. And you are left with all I've left behind. I leave it to your care, whatever that means. I hope, in some small way, it can help you further realize your goals and ambitions. Thanks, and goodbye. Take it away, Sarah.

Sarah waited while people dried their tears and looked ready to con-tinue. "Okay, now I will read Maggie's wishes."

To Maria, I bequeath my furniture and all the contents of my kitchen to either sell or keep.

To Jake, I leave my library of books, TV, radio, and $100,000.

To Theresa, I leave all my papers and $800,000.

To Rupert, I leave $500,000, my primary computer (I think it's about time you learned how to use one, Rupert, and to take advantage of its resources), and my ashes. I want you to take them back to Canada and scatter them across a forest near wher-ever you end up living. Our dad made his living and supported us in the forests of Canada, and I want to help nurture the future growth of trees.

Sarah will sell my home and then distribute all the funds received, plus the rest of my financial estate, among several charities: Helen Keller International, National Women's Law Center, and A Woman's Place in San Francisco.

Goodbye, everyone.

No one moved. Maria was in tears; everyone else was caught between shock and surprise. None of them had had any idea what to expect.

Sarah came over to Rupert and set the urn with Maggie's ashes on the table in front of him. "Hope you have a little extra room in your suitcase, Rupert."

"Not really large enough for this, but I'll manage somehow. At least I know now I'll return to Hazelton sometime to take Maggie home."

"I already cut a check for you to take since I assumed you might not stick around San Francisco much longer. You can pick it up from my secretary at the front desk. Goodbye and good luck. Here is my card. Feel free to call if any questions about the will come up when you get back."

"Thanks."

They shook hands and Sarah walked away. Rupert sat in a nearby chair, not quite ready to leave. He saw everyone else talking and laughing, but he had no desire to join in that. No, it was his time to go back to Vancouver and to Sylvia. "I'm going to leave now," Rupert announced.

They all stopped talking and looked his way.

"I didn't want to leave without saying goodbye and telling you how glad I am to have met you. In some ways, it's been excruciating at times, getting to know you. I think I've mostly held it together, and I leave feeling tougher, more courageous and determined. I came here frightened of what I might face, and now I leave frightened by what I might face, but I do feel more prepared."

As Rupert headed for the door, Maria shook his hand.

Theresa gave him a friendly hug and said, "Please keep in touch, Rupert. Your coming down here helped Maggie with her ending, and it has helped me grow in my understanding and appreciation of family. When you have a new address, please let me know. I'll want to contact you. You know I have to travel for the company. Maybe I'll end up in Vancouver sometime."

Jake came over and shook his hand. "I guess I was the last to join this party, Rupert. If you come to San Francisco again, maybe we'll bump into each other. San Francisco is a small town in many ways."

"Thanks, Jake, and you too, Theresa." Rupert waved goodbye and, after picking up his check, walked out into the San Francisco sunshine.

CHAPTER 71

RUPERT ARRIVED BACK IN VANCOUVER around five in the afternoon the next day. He went right to Sylvia's place. All the thinking and worrying he'd done about where he'd go after San Francisco had ended. He wanted something new. Rupert did not want to return to Powell River and, since he was leaving the Church, really couldn't return there anyway. Although he had no place to live, the money he'd received from Maggie gave him plenty of cash to start in a new place.

He had met Sylvia, really by accident at the exact moment the totems of his sacred life were collapsing. Now he returned, a man in a new search for where he belonged. He really liked Sylvia. She was intelligent, attractive, and engaging, all making her a great place to start his new life, and maybe finish.

Rupert had already decided he'd scatter Maggie's ashes in the forest outside of Hazelton, British Columbia. Their father had made his living in those forests, and they'd all grown up nearby. But that would come later. Now it was five thirty on a Saturday afternoon, and he was in a cab headed for Sylvia's.

Sylvia came to the door wearing a blue summer dress and sandals. Her hair fell down on her shoulders, and to Rupert, she looked more attractive than he remembered.

He put out his hand as if he expected they'd shake.

Sylvia just smiled. "Really, Rupert, after our long separation and long talks, you want to shake hands?"

"No, not really."

He then opened his arms, and she jumped in, almost knocking him over. They hugged and laughed till Rupert had to put her down, too tired to continue. She took his hand and led him inside.

"I'd rather not start off telling you all that's happened, Sylvia."

"Okay with me."

"Well, Ms. Plath, thank you for that. Now we can attend to getting reacquainted."

"Why the formality, Mr. Callaway?"

He laughed, "Frankly I'm knackered from trying to heft you up but still feeling overwhelmingly pleased at this moment. I'm having a fantasy of picking you up again and carrying you off to my lair."

"Oh, how cheeky! Don't get your knickers in a twist, all right?" Sylvia laughed. "Playfulness does become you though."

"I think so too." Rupert followed through on his fantasy, picking her up again and continuing down the hall in front of him. "I hope it's not far."

"Wrong way," she said.

They laughed so hard he almost dropped her.

"Turn left."

He did and entered the bedroom. Using every ounce of energy he had left, he kicked the door closed and made it to the bed, where they fell over, him on top of her. Rupert lay there a minute catching his breath while Sylvia began removing his clothes. It did not take long before they both were naked and lost in a passionate embrace that, as far as they were concerned, could now go on forever.

ACKNOWLEDGMENTS

I WANT TO ACKNOWLEDGE GREG SLETTELAND AND the staff at Folio, who went out of their way to offer me insight into the art and mechanics of novel writing; Alex Smith, who provided valuable web advice and held my hand during times of stress; and my valuable readers: Judy Smith, Paul David, Jan Eisenhardt, and Julia Akoury, whose observations helped me with editing and ideas to improve the work. I want to offer these folks my deepest gratitude.

ABOUT THE AUTHOR

KENNETH SMITH retired from psychotherapy and teaching in higher education and now spends his time reflecting and writing on life and the vast human experience. He lives in Seattle with his wife, Judith Smith.

Made in United States
Orlando, FL
18 January 2022

13646989R10196